A London childh... ...by the mixed pleasure of having four elder brothers. Unused to the country, I declined to stay there more than a month or two as an evacuee, and returned in good time for the Blitz. Later schooldays were spent watching doodlebugs flying overhead or ducking those that failed to fly overhead.

Working life was, first, a long connection with the *Reader's Digest*. I worked for its chairman, travelled to other *Digest* companies in Europe and America, and learned from my boss anything I know about the writing of English.

Marriage eventually meant separation from London. My husband and I moved out of the shelter of a huge concern, to try running our own small one. We missed the boom, caught the backwash, and finally failed . . . back to being employed again. This time, to broaden our experience if not our minds, we entered the groves of Academe.

Then I entered a magazine story competition and, astonishingly, won it. Now, many stories later (published by *Woman's Weekly*, *Woman & Home*, Mills & Boon, Piatkus, and Corgi) I am an addict, and reach for my pen as an alcoholic reaches for his glass.

My husband's and my retirement from Oxford University brought us to the green hills of Somerset, and the pleasurable oddities of village life. We like to roam about Europe, or contentedly apply ourselves to the other good things of life – friends, food, wine, music, and our garden.

Also by Sally Stewart
ECHOES IN THE SQUARE
and published by Corgi Books

THE WOMEN
OF PROVIDENCE

Sally Stewart

CORGI BOOKS

THE WOMEN OF PROVIDENCE
A CORGI BOOK   0 552 13637 9

First publication in Great Britain

PRINTING HISTORY
Corgi edition published 1990

This book is set in 10/11 Sabon
by Kestrel Data, Exeter

Corgi Books are published by Transworld Publishers
Ltd., 61–63 Uxbridge Road, Ealing, London W5 5SA, in
Australia by Transworld Publishers (Australia) Pty. Ltd.,
15–23 Helles Avenue, Moorebank, NSW 2170, and in New
Zealand by Transworld Publishers (N.Z.) Ltd., Cnr. Moselle
and Waipareira Avenues, Henderson, Auckland.

Printed and bound in Great Britain by
Cox & Wyman Ltd., Reading, Berks.

1880

CHAPTER ONE

''Ere she comes . . . long-shanks Gertie. Reckon she's a witch with all that black 'air. Gertie Hoskins is a witch, a witch, a *witch*!'

Every morning they'd be waiting for her at the bend in the road, never tired of the game of chasing her the rest of the way to school. The taunts didn't vary much and always had to do with the things that marked her out from the rest of them – her long thin legs and long dark hair, or the clean white pinafore her mother always insisted on. But the 'game' had an edge to it. Mostly she could out-run them; if not, she took her place in front of Sarah Simpkin angry and dishevelled, with her hair pulled out of its plait and her pinafore streaked with dirt.

It didn't occur to her to tell anyone in authority about this daily torment. For one thing, 'tellin' tales' was a punishable sin; for another, it didn't surprise her to be singled out for different treatment. She knew she wasn't the same as the village children; why shouldn't they know it too? They'd all been born at Haywood's End and were mostly related to each other. The cottages where they lived were stuck huggermugger in the lanes and alleys leading to the village green – close enough together for their mothers to be able to 'have a tell' across the washing-lines and borrow small items from each other till payday came.

Gertrude and her parents lived half a mile away, in the pleasant stone house that went with the Home Farm. It had been split in half and they shared it with the Moffat family. 'Old' Sid Moffat ran the farm; his son 'young' Sid was her only friend, who *did* know about the daily chase to school. 'It's like this,' he'd say with the undisputed authority that came of being fifteen. 'I could wallop 'em for you, Gertrude, but it'ud do no good, see? You got to stand up and fight yourself; otherwise they'll taunt ye all the more.'

She could see that he was right, and fighting might be necessary, but it wasn't what Emma Hoskins expected of her daughter.

She knew that her father was something called land agent to the Squire at Providence and that he'd come from further to the south and west; his voice still kept a softness that was different from the Midland sounds of old Sid Moffat next door. Her mother had been the daughter of the curate in Warwick, seven miles away, and *she'd* come to the big house when she was eighteen, to be governess to Sir Edward Wyndham's children. That was as much Hoskins family history as Gertrude had managed to assemble by the time she was ten, and it didn't explain why they and Haywood's End didn't seem to accept each other. In the end she was driven to ask her mother, although plaguing a frail invalid with questions was one of the many things she was not supposed to do.

'Because the land agent on an estate is always hated, of course,' Emma Hoskins said wearily. 'The tenant farmers and the labourers blame *him* for everything. If the rents are more than they can pay, or their cottages leak, it's *his* fault.'

'Why don't they blame Squire Wyndham . . . it's *his* cottages they live in?'

'Blame the Squire indeed! I should think not. They'd do better to be thankful they have anywhere to live at all.'

As usual, Gertrude felt she was being given only half an answer; she could never get to the *bottom* of all the things that puzzled her.

'The men's wives don't seem to come to tea . . . do they blame *you*?'

Emma looked disdainful and pleased at the same time. 'They don't come because I don't invite them . . . the village women are coarse and common.'

It was hard to understand how she knew, seeing that she never went near them. Women like Queenie Briggs and

8

Maria James certainly shouted a lot to each other, and spent the days slaving to keep their miserable homes and families clean, but did that make them common? In order not to be coarse but delicate, did a woman have to do what *her* mother did, and lie on a couch all day? The word was often used in the Hoskins household. The best china teacups, only used when Lady Hester called, were delicate, and so was the behaviour Emma required of her daughter. There were agonizing times when the teacups and the behaviour had to go together, because the ladies from the big house must always be offered tea when they called.

Gertrude didn't mind Lady Hester's visits, but she could have done without being stared at by Louise Wyndham, who occasionally stopped her governess cart at the gate and delivered fruit from the Wyndham conservatory. For as long as she was prepared to sit in the parlour sipping tea and talking about the past, Emma was happy. Gertrude knew by now that William had been a biddable child, his younger brother James a tease, always thinking up devilments to disrupt schoolroom routine. It wasn't hard to believe. James had been the one to scoop her up on his horse when she was small, and canter along the drive with her; he was a laughing, bright-eyed young man now, and even the most cantankerous old women in the village smiled when he lifted his hat to them.

Gertrude saw the difference easily enough between Lady Hester and Queenie Briggs, but what about the women in between who *were* allowed into the parlour?

'Mrs Moffat comes to call,' she said tentatively, 'and Dr Markham's lady, and Miss Roberts from the rectory . . . I suppose they're all delicate enough?'

Emma sighed; this tiring persistence was one of the many faults she found in her daughter. 'Maud Roberts is a gentlewoman, Gertrude, like her ladyship . . . a little odd in matters of dress sometimes, but a well-born Christian lady. *Her* manners you needn't fear to copy. Mrs Moffat and Mrs Markham are good kind women, who come because they know that I am far from well. There is a small

9

important difference which you are too young to understand at the moment.'

It seemed to settle what Emma thought of the neighbourhood, but Gertrude kept to herself what Haywood's End thought of *her*. Half-understood scraps of conversation overheard on the village green were hoarded away and pondered over when she was cleaning and polishing for her mother.

'Poor thing, ain't she? If anyone but 'Oskins were 'er 'usband, you'd 'ave to pity 'im.'

'True! Mine 'ud not put up with sich airs and graces.'

'One child and she's bin lyin' down ever sin', readin' books. Better if she stirred 'erself, I reckon.'

Gertrude knew about the book-reading. Apart from visits from the Wyndham ladies, it was the only thing that made Emma's face flush with happiness. Before George Hoskins had had time to pull his boots off, she'd demand to see what new volumes he'd brought her back from Warwick. It was also true that she spent a lot of time lying down, but if the other women despised her for this, it was only because they didn't realize she was delicate. Gertrude felt it was time to make this clear to Mrs Briggs one morning, but her explanation made Queenie's normally good-natured face look put out for a moment.

'Long ears you got, Gertie! Your mam's delicate, is she? I didn't think o' that.'

The hated shortening of her name had to be accepted from the village women, but perhaps not from their children; the day came when Daisy James laid on her back the final straw that sent delicate behaviour to the four winds. She'd evaded the early-morning race for once, but they were waiting for her as soon as it was time to be turned out to play in the yard.

'Jest like yer mam, ain't ye, Gertie? Too set-up for the likes o' us, cos we be only village folk!'

She was only repeating what she heard her mother say, but Gertrude stared at her grinning face through a red mist of hatred that blotted out not only Emma's strictures but the promptings of fear as well. 'Stand and fight,' young Sid had said; the time had come to do so. She couldn't remember afterwards how Daisy came to be on the ground beneath her, but suddenly they were fighting like cats in the dust of the school yard.

'I won't have you call me Gertie . . . my name's *Gertrude*!' She screamed the words over and over again while the others stood in a circle, prepared to watch for as long as the battle seemed roughly equal. It was better any day than going back in to school. Daisy's fingernails tore a long scratch down her opponent's cheek, but Gertrude was too busy trying to bang her head against the ground to notice. She didn't even remember that she would normally have been set on by now, by Daisy's brother and sister. It was the month of June – haysel-time – and children big enough to walk behind the mowers and rake up the cut hay suddenly disappeared from the schoolroom. It was supposed to be frowned upon now that they were all meant to attend school, but the farmers were glad of help and parents thought more of the extra shilling or two earned than of a few lessons lost.

Miss Simpkin finally came out to see what kept her class bunched like sheep in the yard. With the unwilling help of Willy Briggs, she managed to drag the fighters apart.

'You're like animals!' she cried. 'Gertrude, *you* at least ought to know better.'

Smarting in several places, it seemed unfair that she should get all the blame as well, but it was something that even Governess insisted on separating her from the rest of the herd.

Miss Simpkin had more reason to be agitated than they knew: behind them a gig had drawn up at the gate, and a groom was about to hand down the Squire's lady. She came quite often to the school, but she'd chosen a morning to call when they were anything but ready for her. From sheer force of habit a straggling line of curtsies and ducked heads greeted Lady Hester and she nodded back pleasantly as usual, but Gertrude knew as well as Miss Simpkin that her ladyship would have had to be blind not to notice their bloody weals and filthy pinafores. The expression on her long gentle face said clearly what she thought – they *were* no better than animals, and she'd expected more of George Hoskins's daughter. Gertrude would have liked to shout that it was hard to be sure *what* was expected of her. She knew, because her father frequently said so, that people were born where God intended them to remain, but what if He didn't make matters clear? If she didn't belong in one village, where did she belong? She had a strong feeling, not even confided to Sid Moffat, that her own parents didn't much want her, either.

Lady Hester's cool voice announcing that she would postpone her inspection was followed by a screech from Sarah Simpkin.

'Gertrude . . . don't you see her ladyship is leaving, you ill-mannered child?'

She ducked her head roughly in the right direction, hating them all. Daisy and her cronies didn't dare snigger but they were bound to be enjoying themselves. Call-me-Gertrude Hoskins made to look a proper fool – they probably wouldn't mind now that she'd arrived knowing how to read on her very first morning at school, because Emma had made her learn when she was small. To those who could scarcely manage it yet the accomplishment had always seemed not only unfair but downright unnatural.

The gig was driven away, dirt washed off at the pump in the corner of the yard, and the morning lesson resumed. Apart from the fact that Miss Simpkin stayed unusually cross, the day seemed to revert to normal again, but it was the beginning of a change. From then on, as if they'd suddenly got bored with the game, the children left her alone. She could walk sedately to school and arrive home unmuddied, but she had no friends to giggle and talk with. Relief, even the pleasure of being different, didn't make up for the loneliness of being excluded from the others' games, but it became a matter of pride to pretend that she didn't mind.

She didn't understand why life was arranged differently

for different people, but it clearly was and that was that. A bored-looking Louise Wyndham had to drive out with her mother – 'making calls', Emma explained with pride – while Daisy and her friends tore round the green, and Gertrude Hoskins polished the furniture at home in case Lady Hester called. They shared a maid for the rough with Mrs Moffat next door, but there was plenty for the daughter of an invalid to do.

Usually Gertrude remembered that Emma had no interest in what went on at Haywood's End, but one afternoon she took home from school the news that Mrs James was expecting again.

'The only news worth the telling would be if Maria James *wasn't* expecting again,' Emma said sharply. 'Not that she's any worse than the rest of them.'

It was true that the village women took it in turns to disappear, and in next to no time their eldest daughters would be pushing a pram round the green again with the latest baby inside. Alone among the girls there Gertrude hadn't had to perform this duty for even one small brother or sister and, although she didn't particularly want to push a pram, she couldn't help feeling that she was missing something. In any case, she needed to know what was wrong with Mrs James adding to her family each year if she wanted to. She put the question to her father when they were safely away from the parlour, weeding vegetables in the garden.

'Why?' he asked frowning at her. 'Because rearing six children in an overcrowded cottage is worse than trying to rear five. Feeding six on a labourer's wage is harder than feeding five.'

Gertrude accepted that he was bound to know. In the course of his work he went into all the cottages on the Squire's land. Her own glimpses of them only came from outside when a door was open, but she knew well enough that none of them had more than two bedrooms shared between parents and however many children the family contained.

'We're not overcrowded,' she said after a moment's

thought. 'Is that why the village people don't seem to like *us*?'

'Life's easier for us all round. A pump in the kitchen is better than fetching water from a well, and we don't go hungry if a pig that's being fattened for the winter dies before its time.'

'Well, life's easier still for the Master up at the big house . . . why don't they seem to mind him?' She remembered asking this question of her mother and being fobbed off, and wasn't unduly surprised when her father did the same.

'You're talking nonsense, child. Sir Edward is the Squire. It's not for the village folk to mind or *not* mind him. All they have to do is pay their rents and be respectful to their betters.'

Being respectful was as important to him as being delicate was to her mother. She knew that respect was due to their Heavenly Father, Queen Victoria, and the Wyndham family, in that order. That was how things had always been, and there was no reason why they should ever change. But even in *their* valley, hidden in the depths of Warwickshire, there was talk of people with a different point of view. Sid often told her so. A man called Joseph Arch had started preaching to the men who worked the land. Joined together in something he called a union, they would be able to change things eventually . . . Gertrude couldn't remember how, but she thought being less respectful to the Squire came into it. The idea was interesting, but it seemed to be getting them away from the matter in hand.

'*We're* not overcrowded at all. Mrs Briggs says Mam would do better if she read less books, and I think I'd *like* some sisters.'

The sudden redness in her father's face warned her that she'd made him angry, but there was sadness and bitter regret as well, if she'd been old enough to notice. 'Don't tell me what Queenie Briggs says . . . she talks a sight too much!' he shouted. 'Your mother's different – book-learned, and frail, not like the village women throwing off children as easily as a cow calves. She nearly died when you were born

14

. . . should never have . . .' He stopped himself abruptly, but not before Gertrude finally understood. It was *her* fault that Emma scarcely moved from the couch in the parlour; there'd only been strength enough for one, and both her parents regretted that it had all been given to *her*. Her face went so white that George Hoskins, normally a quietly-spoken man, felt ashamed of his roughness. 'No need to fret yourself, child,' he said more gently. 'We have to take care of your mother, that's all. Instead of wishing for kin you haven't got, think yourself lucky you don't have to share a bed as well as a room, or take it in turns to go to school because there aren't enough shoes to go round.'

Gertrude nodded as if to accept what he said. It was true their life in the farmhouse contained none of the hardship the village people knew. There was always enough to eat, and they didn't live only off dried bacon, bread, potatoes and cabbage. There were floorboards to be polished, instead of beaten earth floors covered with bits of sacking. Still, she knew children like Daisy James had something she *didn't* have . . . homes where there was laughter as well as roughness, and the warmth of knowing that if troubles threatened they could always be shared. She knew that she and her parents somehow *didn't* make a family.

'Why don't we have cousins and things?' she asked suddenly. 'The lady in the bible in the parlour . . . Alice Hoskins . . . is *she* my grandmother?'

'Your grandparents are dead, and so is Alice. It was she I married first time round, you see. She died young, poor lady. Afterwards I came to Providence and met your dear mother – Miss Rastell, she was then, and governess to the Squire's children.'

The gentleness that always softened his voice when he referred to his wife sounded in it now. The village women might pity him because she was always ailing, but Gertrude knew how little he minded the job of looking after Emma; the more helpless she became, the more tenderly he took care of her and the more Gertrude felt the blame for a situation that Queenie Briggs maintained 'weren't natural'.

In what remained of her childhood at Haywood's End there wasn't a great deal to mark one year out from another. In cities like Birmingham to the north of them, getting bigger, noisier, and more prosperous every year, the talk was all of mining coal, and making things, and sending them out to the four corners of a globe that mostly seemed to belong to Queen Victoria. In the village they didn't know about such things, or greatly care about colonies and world trade. What mattered was being able to get the ploughing done by the end of January, and being blessed with fine weather for as long as it took to bring the harvest in. The railway that now carried passengers from Birmingham to London in not much more time that it took the carrier and his horse to trot from Warwick made no difference to people who never went outside the village where they'd been born.

There were places where new-fangled machines were beginning to take the place of men, and George Hoskins felt obliged to try to persuade Edward Wyndham to invest in them.

'They'll be cheaper in the long run, do you see, sir. With wheat prices falling all the time, we should do everything we can to cut the costs of farming; otherwise the tenants will never be able to meet the rents, however much we lower them.'

'If they work hard and still can't pay, the rents must be reduced till times get better,' said the Squire. 'Prices can't go on falling for ever. Meantime we must all hang on . . . ride over the rough ground together.'

Hanging on for Sir Edward meant, perhaps, foregoing one new hunter that he'd have liked to tell Hodges to add to his string, or postponing yet again the idea of installing in his home the sort of conveniences that his neighbours were acquiring. Providence had always been lit by candles and lamps, and warmed by open fires . . . he saw nothing wrong with it as it was. His wife didn't go short of servants, so what did conveniences matter? The gas-lighting could wait another year. It was left to his land agent to frown over cottages that needed repair, uncleared ditches and rutted lanes, while the Squire cantered happily off with his younger son and daughter to wherever the hunt was meeting next.

Both William and James, home from Rugby for good, were now young country gentlemen, doing the things that were expected of them, but only James did them with gusto. The Squire's heir was rumoured to be bookish, if not downright weak in the head, and it was well-known that if he attended a meet, he never stayed long enough to see the fox killed. The village despised him for this as much as the neighbouring gentry did. Even Louise, disliked by the servants who had to put up with her, was reckoned to be a proper chip off the old block, not like her soft elder brother at all.

'She'll make a fine marriage one of these days,' Emma would say proudly, after Louise had visited the farmhouse; 'the only pity of it is that then she'll go away from Providence.'

For once Gertrude spoke without thinking. 'I hope she *does* go away. Whenever she looks down her long thin nose at me from that great horse of hers, I know she's laughing at my boots.' The thick ugly boots she wore outdoors rankled more than any other injustice in life. Louise wore beautiful soft shining boots, and Lady Hester stepped out of her carriage in delicate leather shoes. Gertrude coveted them with all her soul.

Emma ignored the boots but not the slur cast on someone she thought perfect. 'You're being impertinent, miss,' she said sharply. 'Louise has the Wyndham nose, and very distinguished it is.'

'But still long and thin,' Gertrude insisted to herself. It was a small blemish, though, to set beside the rest. In the black riding habit that looked as if it had been poured over her, and the veil that hid her nose, there wasn't any doubt that Louise was very distinguished indeed. She went hunting with her father four days out of seven and, like him, was rarely seen separated from a horse. As a small child Gertrude had imagined him to be part and parcel of the animal because she never met him out walking on his own two legs. Viewed from the height she then reached, all she saw of the top of him was a hat-brim, nose, and greyish-gold fuzz of beard, like the pussy willows in spring with the sun on them. He always smiled when she curtsied to him, and asked in a loud voice how she did. Did what? She didn't know, and simply stared at him till he rode on. Only gradually did she decide that he found it as hard to know what to say during these encounters as she did.

William, met occasionally along the road or in the park of the big house, didn't have much to say either and smiled vaguely as if not sure who she was, but the other young men at Haywood's End had no difficulty in remembering her. She was thin and leggy still, but James hadn't forgotten the sight of her one day running across the park, as graceful as a wild thing, the hated boots held in her hand. Growing to be a woman was a messy business, reluctantly explained to her by Emma, but there were compensations – especially when the Squire's younger son tipped his hat to her, and his bright blue eyes said that he enjoyed looking at her. Young Sid stared at her as well, but the way *he* looked only made her angry; she wanted him to stay her *friend*. Albert Wilkes, the carrier who visited them once a week, frightened her. His pudgy hands covered with tufts of ginger hairs always seemed to be reaching out with some disgusting idea of touching her.

She did her best to avoid him, but he caught up with her one afternoon just as she set out to walk back from the village.

'A ride now, Trudie girl . . . hop up here beside me and I'll have you home in no time – well, maybe no promises about that!' His red face leered down at her but she did her best to remember that she must never be rude.

'Thank you, Mr Wilkes, but I think I'd rather walk.'

She slowed down, pretending to stare at a wild flower in the hedge; Wilkes slowed his horse too. She began to run, because the road seemed lonely and deserted, but the horse

18

kept pace with her and all the time the carrier wheedled and laughed because her face was growing palé. It was ridiculous as well as frightening and she was near to tears when the clip-clop of horse's hooves sounded behind them. A moment later James, haloed in a saviour's light, had swung himself down beside her.

'Afternoon, Wilkes,' he said with his usual pleasantness. 'I dare say you're wanting to get on your way home. Don't let us keep you.'

'That's right, sir,' the carrier agreed heartily. 'No sense in dawdlin' here.' He touched his whip to his cap, and then laid it across the back of the horse. 'Home, Nelly girl.'

When he'd driven away James glanced at the white face of the girl beside him. 'No harm in Wilkes . . . sometimes a bit too friendly, that's all,' he murmured after a moment.

'Albert Wilkes is a fat, oily, red-faced slug,' Gertrude said distinctly, and felt hurt to see James laugh, even though she was passionately grateful to him. It relegated her to being a child again, not to be taken seriously.

'Sorry, young Gertrude . . . I'm only laughing because you reminded me of your mother just then – it's exactly how she used to correct me when I insisted that Paris was on the Loire instead of the river Seine! However, to get back to Wilkes, if he bothers you again, there's no need to fight battles on your own; tell Mr Hoskins, or my father.'

She thought Sid Moffat had given her better advice, but didn't say so; something else he'd said was more interesting.

'My mother doesn't tell *me* about the times when she was a governess, although she loves talking to Miss Louise. Was she strict with you?'

'She tried to be, dear Emma, because she was very industrious, but more often than not we'd finish up laughing over something or other, and then go outside and play games!'

Gertrude digested this in silence, wondering what her mother had looked like when she was laughing. Then James went on, 'We'd dress up and play charades, too. My Uncle Henry wasn't much good, but when he visited us once from

America, he brought a friend with him, an Irishman called Maguire, and *he* was the best of all. Your mother was happy then, I think.' He didn't say that she'd never been happy since, but Gertrude felt sure that it was true.

'I'm going to join Uncle Henry and Daniel Maguire,' she heard James say suddenly. 'They're involved in the railways that are being built right across America. I've got to do *something*, and that sounds like more of an adventure than going into the Army in peacetime.'

She felt cold and sad, but unsurprised . . . of course James Wyndham would go where the call of adventure was most plainly to be heard. It was a piece of news to take home that her mother *would* be interested in, but she found her parents already knew. Emma was looking flushed and upset.

'Such a long way away, America . . .' she murmured. 'Her ladyship will be sad.'

'James should have been the one to stay and inherit,' George Hoskins said guffly. 'Squire's too old and set in his ways, but James understands what needs to be done. William's nice enough, but he won't be any use when it comes to saving Providence.'

In the novelty of this idea Gertrude forgot for a moment that her heart was almost broken at the thought of James going away. 'Who does Providence have to be saved from . . . people like Albert Simpkin? Miss Simpkin says it's been here for four hundred years and will last another four hundred, but her brother works in a manufactory in Birmingham and thinks she's got a feudal mentality. He says places like Providence have got to be swept away.'

If Emma had been strangely upset before, she was now furiously angry. 'We're not interested in creatures like Albert Simpkin, or his revolutionary ideas, thank you, miss. Providence will still be here when *his* ramshackle manufactory has fallen into dust.'

Gertrude opened her mouth to argue and closed it again. Upsetting her mother was the thing above all others that she wasn't allowed to do, and it didn't require the frown on her father's face to tell her so.

*

The morning of James's departure arrived all too soon. He was to go to Bristol, and board a steamship there for New York. All the workers connected with the estate gathered round the archway to the stable-yard to see him driven away, and Gertrude invited herself to stand there also with her father. It was a morning of spring . . . green and gold and full of promise . . . but she had the feeling that even daft Artie who helped Hodges with the horses knew some gladness was going away from Providence. James found something pleasant to say to everyone in turn, then stood talking for a moment or two with Gertrude's father. There was time to stare at him and try to fix in her memory a smile that was quite different from Sid Moffat's way of smiling.

When James stood in front of *her*, she was still staring at him. He was full of his own mixed regret and excitement at leaving home, but he found himself wondering what would become of George Hoskins's tall, thin daughter, whose grey eyes under black, strongly marked eyebrows were fixed on him solemnly; he hadn't properly noticed it before but she was growing beautiful. The moment suddenly seemed important, but he had no idea what to say. The words that came in the end were picked at random.

'Goodbye, Gertrude . . . take care of Providence for me.' He bent towards her on an impulse, and she felt his mouth soft on her cheek.

She wasn't aware of the moment when his carriage turned through the gateway out into the drive. For the first time ever, he hadn't called her 'young' Gertrude, and he'd kissed her, but even that seemed to matter less than what he'd said to her. The others drifted back to their work, but she still stood there, staring at the house James had put into her care. She'd never really thought about Providence itself before . . . only of the people who lived there. Now, she saw it as it was – a huddle of stone walls, timbered gables, and red-brick chimneys twisted like the barley-sugar sticks Mattie Lucas sold in the village shop. The house was three-sided, because the fourth side her mother had told her about had fallen down long ago, and no Wyndham since had been rich enough to build it up again. Emma had sounded regretful about it, but Gertrude decided that she liked it as it was. Nowadays a garden filled in the space between the three wings and Biddle kept it planted with white, gold and blue flowers – the colours in the Wyndham coat of arms. Providence was beautiful now that she looked at it properly – doubly beautiful, in fact, because it peered at itself in the quiet waters of a moat that encircled it like a sash of grey silk.

Her father had seemed to think it needed saving, and James had given the job to her. She didn't know how it was to be done, but if the Squire and William Wyndham between them couldn't keep Providence safe from people like Albert Simpkin, then Gertrude Hoskins would have to do her best.

CHAPTER TWO

George Hoskins cherished Providence in his heart, but there were times when he wished it had been planned more conveniently for the man whose job it was to look after it. The truth was, of course, that it hadn't been planned at all; it had just grown, with the whims and fluctuating fortunes of generations of Wyndhams. The estate office lay at the end of the west range of the house, which meant a walk every time he needed to go to and from the stables – either through a maze of corridors to the courtyard garden and the main bridge to the outer world, or across the servants' bridge at the back of the house and past the south wing that faced the gardens and the orchards. The moat made an island of Providence, and he occasionally found himself wishing that some long-ago Wyndham had taken it into his head to fill it in. On the other hand, where else could he lean out of his window and watch a family of ducklings skimming the surface of the water with the same mindless velocity as birds in flight? Across the park, the horizon was bounded by Hay Wood, last remnant of the great Forest of Arden that had once almost covered Warwickshire. At this season of the year it was turning bronze-green again, and the lake on the north side of the house was a mere gleam of water seen through a mauve and crimson screen of rhododendrons.

He stared at the view for a moment or two, thinking that young James must have hated leaving Providence in the spring, for all he'd managed to look so bravely cheerful. By the time they saw him again William might, God willing, have found himself a rich wife, or the Squire might have been made to understand that he couldn't go on living in the style of twenty years ago when his income had been far different from what it was now. George gave a little sigh, and turned his attention to the estate papers that kept him indoors on a fine spring morning when he might otherwise have been outside.

An hour later he was still immersed in them when the sight of Lady Hester in the doorway brought him quickly to his feet. The shy smile that only she could draw from him lightened his mournful-looking face, jowled and wrinkled in a way that put her in mind of a loved bloodhound of her youth.

'Milady . . . you should have sent a servant. What can I do for you?'

'I wanted to talk to you, Mr Hoskins . . . Smithers said you were here.'

They always treated each other with formality, but beneath it lay true friendship and a trust that warmed the relationship for both of them. She sat down in the chair he set for her and folded long, thin hands in her lap. He watched her with pleasure, thinking that she was the most restful woman he knew. Her life as lady of the manor hadn't been easy, but in her case duty had been done with grace as well as thoroughness. A ray of sunlight fell across her hair and he noticed that its darkness was beginning to be meshed with silver. She was five years older than himself – not old at fifty, but getting a little tired perhaps, and certain to be sad at losing James.

'I called on Emma yesterday,' she said in her quiet voice. 'Dr Markham has seen her recently, but I still felt worried about her – so pale and languid when I arrived, and then so feverishly bright for as long as I was there. I know the care you take of her, but is there anything *we* can do?'

'I fear not, milady, though you're very kind to ask. Markham has nothing more to suggest. Peace and quiet and loving care . . . he says it's all we can offer her. Reading is a great solace, but she can't read all day long; then she gets depressed.' He looked up from the sheet of paper he'd been carefully folding into smaller and smaller shapes, and found her ladyship watching him. 'Master James's going to America upset her . . . brought back the past. It isn't only weakness that ails her . . . my poor Emma has unhappiness to contend with as well.'

It was a long speech for him to make, and wouldn't have been made to anyone but the woman in front of him. Lady Hester nodded, but her expression remained firm. 'You know how fond I am of her, so I need not hesitate to say that I'd hoped she would make a little more effort. In my opinion, she has more to be grateful for than she seems to realize.'

George's face flushed because he detected a hint of praise, but his hands sketched a little gesture of defeat. 'Whatever we do, Gertrude and I, it isn't enough to make her happy. Her life isn't what she hoped it would be.'

'And *that* is a conclusion a great many other women have had to come to,' said her ladyship with unusual dryness. Her voice laid no stress on the statement, but he wondered whether *her* partner had been what she would have chosen. Husbands had been found for young women like the Lady Hester Goring, younger daughter of an earl with a long lineage and very little else. She could have done a great deal worse, because her husband was a kindly man and the home he'd brought her to was beautiful; but what could a cultured, artistic girl have had in common with bluff, horse-mad Edward Wyndham?

She gave a little sigh and abandoned the subject of George's sad wife. 'There is another matter. Emma seemed reluctant to discuss Gertrude's future, but the child must have one, you know. She's a lonely, self-contained creature, and the village children have been no friends to her . . . we should have guessed, perhaps . . . tried to . . .' her voice petered out, admitting the truth that there had been nothing else to do with little Gertrude Hoskins.

'Emma wasn't well enough to go on teaching her,' George said quickly. 'It had to be the village school. As to her future, she's needed at home, milady.' He had his own idea of what should happen to Gertrude: in the fullness of time she would simply move to the other end of the farmhouse as the wife of young Sid Moffat. He didn't say so, having an idea that Lady Hester might not approve, but something in her expression told him she knew what was in his mind. 'Do you think we're unfair to the child?' he asked bluntly. 'Maud Roberts does . . . she says Gertrude's clever – ought to be allowed to study. But then Miss Roberts is something of a bluestocking herself, and very keen on these new colleges for ladies at Oxford!'

Lady Hester smiled in spite of herself at the note of deep disapproval in his voice. The land agent was a conventional Englishman with the simple view that a woman's place was in the home of some man – her father's giving place to a husband's when the time came.

'I think *life* has been unfair to Gertrude,' she said gently. 'We can't change that, but we must do what we can. Maud Roberts is probably right, but we must be practical. Gertrude is needed to help look after her mother, but she must have something else to do that takes her out of the house. All I can suggest is that she becomes a pupil-teacher at the school. Poor Miss Simpkin is barely in control of all the children she has to deal with, and she admits that Gertrude can read and write quite as well as she can herself. If your daughter can keep order a little better than she can, Haywood's End school will benefit! There are certificates that pupil-teachers can obtain. Eventually Gertrude would be able to improve her position . . . perhaps even get a school of her own.'

George agreed to the idea, while reserving to himself the thought that it would keep Gertrude occupied but still under young Sid's eye. Lady Hester undertook to discuss the suggestion with Miss Simpkin, and then got up to go.

'Now for my daily interview with Mrs Smithers! I find myself putting it off for as long as possible. In the course of settling the menu for dinner she will complain obliquely about the old-fashioned range in the kitchen, and hint that if working conditions aren't made easier we shall soon have no maids left who are willing to stay at Providence. Life is full of problems, is it not?' She smiled as she said it, to let her friend know that he need not add her worries to his own, but much as he disliked both Mrs Smithers and her ponderous husband, he knew that the servants *did* complain.

He saw Lady Hester to the door and sat down at his desk again. Anxieties seemed to be piling up like storm clouds in a summer sky, but his mind refused to grapple with them; Gertrude's future, overdue cottage repairs, a much-needed lighting system for Providence . . . these should have been the things he was thinking about, but his thoughts lingered sadly on a woman who yearned for a happiness he would never be able to give her.

By the time school ended for the summer holiday the matter had been arranged with Miss Simpkin – she would acquire the services of a pupil-assistant at the start of the Michael-mas term. The prospect didn't fill Gertrude with joy, but it was no worse than being apprenticed to a milliner in Warwick like Ethel Lucas, and better than Daisy's fate of becoming a junior housemaid at Barham Manor ten miles away – both arrangements also neatly contrived by Lady Hester, who was relied upon by Haywood's End to find its daughters respectable and safe employment.

The August days were unusually hot and fine, adding to Gertrude's memory afterwards of a time that seemed im-portant because she was poised between childhood and whatever was to come after it. She nursed the invalid at home as usual, cleaned and polished in case the Wyndham ladies should come to call, and then wandered about the park of the big house, filled with a mixture of emotions she could scarcely recognize. There was satisfaction at the idea of growing up, but regret came into it too, for a time that had presaged nothing worse than the struggle to hold her own with the village children. At nearly fifteen, the future seemed likely to contain more complicated problems, and the one that loomed nearest and largest was Mr Moffat's son next door.

Sid was now a broad, sandy-haired giant of nineteen. She

knew, because he often told her so, that he was going to become an even better farmer than his father. That she didn't mind – her father had taught her that the land had to be well taken care of – but she had the worrying feeling that Sid was set on another idea as well, and waiting with the patience of a countryman for the time when she was old enough to be hauled off to the parish church. He was her true and valued friend, but she was quite sure that she would never want to marry him. She'd tested him one day by sharing her favourite poem with him. Sid had simply scratched his head and said it sounded daft to him.

Gertrude eventually took the problem to a new-found friend, Mr Roberts's sister at the rectory.

'Miss Roberts . . . you've managed not to get married to anybody. Is it very difficult?'

If the question took Maud Roberts by surprise, she wasn't offended by it. 'If no-one asks you, it isn't difficult at all,' she said candidly. 'I was a very plain girl, you see. Try as she would, my dear mother couldn't teach me to simper and look sweetly virginal. *That* I was, of course, but the outward effect left something to be desired, apparently!'

A smile lit her long bony face at the memory of it, making Gertrude wonder that no-one had realized how pleasant it then became. It was true that a high forehead and masterful chin perhaps didn't lend themselves to simpering, but she suspected that Maud could have found someone sensible enough to marry her if she'd wanted to. For herself, Gertrude was delighted with Miss Roberts's single state . . . married, she wouldn't have been at Haywood's End rectory. Their friendship had come about recently because Maud had tackled Emma Hoskins with her usual bluntness. 'Send the child to me once a week – she's intelligent; needs something to get her teeth into.'

What Gertrude was offered was a feast of learning: no less than the French and Italian languages in which Miss Roberts was fluent. The lessons opened fascinating new doors but gave her something just as precious as well – a kindred spirit to laugh with. The rector's sister relished Haywood's End's opinion of her – 'a good woman, mind, even if she be peculiar' – and didn't care at all that she scandalized the neighbouring gentry. She not only worked in the garden herself, but did it wearing her brother's old panama hat and a pair of breeches she'd commissioned from the astonished seamstress in the village.

'They don't get in the way like wretched skirts and petticoats,' she explained to Gertrude. 'I told the duchess about them and she said demme if she wouldn't have some made herself. It's something for *me* to be setting a fashion!'

The anxious question about matrimony still waited to be answered and Maud thought about it while she looked at the thin, vivid face of the girl in front of her. Gertrude's problems in avoiding marriage were likely to be more troublesome than her own had been.

'There's nothing *wrong* with marrying,' she said finally. 'Quite a lot of women seem contented with it.' She acknowledged to herself that it begged the question of the sort of husband Gertrude Hoskins could expect to get in Victoria's England. The social system worked after its fashion, but it was cruelly rigid for a girl like this one, born out of place and not fitting into either high society or low. Life would have been easier for her if she'd been less intelligent, or less curious about a world that didn't seem to want to accept her.

'A lot of women have no choice but to seem contented,' Gertrude pointed out. 'I don't want to be like my mother, unhappy, and tied to a couch all day, nor like poor Queenie Briggs, hung about with children who *always* need feeding. It's a pity I haven't got a brother to take care of, like you.' She debated suggesting that if Miss Roberts got too old for her present job of housekeeper to the rector, she might care to pass it on. But Emma always insisted that ladies preferred one not to dwell on their age, and she liked Maud too much to want to hurt her feelings. She heaved a sigh instead, and then smiled cheerfully. 'I expect I'll just say no, if it comes to it.'

Miss Roberts agreed that this would be a very sensible thing to do, and they abandoned the subject of matrimony for the more interesting one of French irregular verbs.

The harvest was a fine one that year as a result of the glorious weather, and even if the price of wheat went on falling, it was still the crowning achievement of the year to bring in a crop of good ripe corn. The special harvest rate of pay was duly bargained for and agreed, the men took their scythes to Matthew Harris at the forge to get them properly hung, and the work began. Safe in the knowledge that Sid Moffat would be too busy to notice her, Gertrude escaped from the house to station herself at a vantage point overlooking Mr Moffat's ten-acre field. She sat entranced, caught up in the rhythm of the men working their way across the field in a staggered line, taking their time from the leading man, or 'lord', as he was called. The swish of the scythes was a kind of music of its own, but often the men took up snatches of song themselves.

'Watch it and remember,' said a voice suddenly beside her. She turned to see William Wyndham staring at the scene in front of them. 'It's the grandest country sight of all, and before we're much older we shall have seen it for the last time. Even my father's land agent wants to bring in machinery to reap the corn.'

'The Squire's land agent happens to be *my* father,' she pointed out sharply, 'and he wants what's best for Providence. If *he* thinks machinery's needed, then it is.'

She had deflected William's attention from the field and he turned to stare at her. 'Bless my soul . . . it's young Gertrude. Have you grown since I last saw you . . . I think you must have done.' Having apparently made up his mind about this point, he waved at the field in front of them. 'That's perfect as it is, *without* machinery.'

She did her best to remember that he was the Squire's son, and couldn't help it, poor creature, if he was soft in the head; even so, indignation got the better of her.

'It's perfect if your back doesn't break after spending ten

hours bent over a scythe and the farmer can afford to pay you enough to feed your family.'

Unexpectedly, William smiled at her and she saw in his face a resemblance to Lady Hester.

'Ha . . . a firebrand . . . even something of a revolutionary! Very well, Gertrude. I take the point that I've never tried cutting a field of corn myself, but there *is* something to be said for the old ways. I don't want to see Providence change as everywhere else seems to be changing.'

'Perhaps it can't last without changing,' Gertrude pointed out soberly, 'and it's *got* to last – for ever.'

Her intense face interested him because it didn't seem to belong to the child he still vaguely imagined her to be. The long dark plait hanging down her back confirmed the schoolgirl, but she hadn't spoken like a child, and her eyes under their strongly-marked black brows seemed to insist that she was an equal. Somewhere in their grey depths he fancied he saw that she was disappointed in him.

Then she suddenly reverted to the primness that Emma no doubt had taught her. 'I hope you have good news of Master James?'

'My brother is enjoying himself too much to acquaint us with his news very often, but I suppose we may take *that* as a good sign! And your news, Gertrude . . . what about that? I suppose you are on holiday from school at the moment?'

'I'm not a pupil any more. Come Michaelmas, I shall be Miss Simpkin's assistant.'

She was pleased to see that William looked impressed, but he said nothing more – only gave her a little bow that made her feel grown-up, and wandered on his way.

With the cornfields bare again except for women gleaning what the men had left, it was time for Haywood's End to settle rents and debts, and to buy items like shoes that had to await harvest payday. Labourers without tied cottages went to Warwick Fair to find a change of work, and George Hoskins frowned over the numbers who drifted away from the land altogether to find a worse drudgery in the factories in Birmingham. Gertrude couldn't fail to notice that he looked tired and abstracted at home, but there was her own first job to think about, and the prospect of receiving payment for it – the richness of £12 a year!

Apart from abandoning her pinafore and coiling her plait in an awkward knob that she could feel every time she moved her head, it seemed not much different from being one of Miss Simpkin's monitors again. She was given the youngest children to look after, and once nervousness had disappeared, impatience with them soon set in. They had no interest in the alphabet letters she was trying to teach them; the fine weather still held, and they'd much rather have been outside, hunting the hedgerows for berries and running wild across the green. Gertrude struggled to keep their wandering attention fixed on the blackboard, but she couldn't blame them for looking bored . . . she was bored herself. The humiliating fact was that Daisy James would have known how to cope with them; she'd have boxed their ears without a second thought, and then laughed them into listening to her.

Emma took no notice of her daughter's classroom trials and complained fretfully that it was rare nowadays for dear Louise to pay her a visit. Eventually, in the early spring of the following year, the reason for Louise's frequent absences from Providence became clear – her betrothal was announced to Captain the Honourable Alec Trentham, of Her Majesty's Hussars. The news caused a flurry of excitement at Haywood's End and lifted even Emma out of the state of apathy into which she'd sunk. It seemed to Gertrude that *she* was more excited about the marriage than the bride-to-be.

'Dearest, tell me all about it, please,' Emma pleaded when Miss Wyndham next sat drinking tea with her in the parlour. 'Tell me about Captain Trentham . . . you've been very secretive, you know.'

Louise gave a little shrug. 'Until last weekend's house party at Warwick Castle, there'd have been nothing to tell, except that I'd shared half a dozen dinner parties, three balls, and a couple of days' hunting with him. In the course of them we discovered that we could talk, dance, and ride together quite enjoyably!'

'You're teasing me,' Emma insisted. 'You *can't* be as matter-of-fact about it as that; he's swept you off your feet, but you don't like to say so.'

A little smile touched Louise's mouth. 'I was twelve when a man had that effect on me! Sam Harris, the blacksmith's son, used to smile at me when he was shoeing my first pony. It only happens to us once, I think, that we get swept off our feet.'

The brightness died out of Emma's face, leaving it white and bleak. 'Yes . . . only once,' she whispered.

For once Miss Wyndham spoke with a gentleness that took Gertrude by surprise. 'Don't look so disappointed, Emma dear. You'll approve of Alec Trentham, and we shall get on well together even though I *don't* go into raptures about him. Anyway, Mama thinks it's time I settled down, and I'm sure Haywood's End does too.'

Emma roused herself to ask a question. 'A summer wedding, I expect . . . we must pray for fine weather.'

'No need to bother – I've no doubt I shall soon be sick of sunshine. The wedding has to be hurried forward because we sail for India at the beginning of May. Alec's regiment is being sent to some place like the Khyber Pass! He wanted the wedding to wait until his first home leave, but other wives are going and I refuse to be left behind.'

She went on talking, trying to ignore the desolation in Emma's face, but the tears beginning to flow down it defeated her.

'Please don't weep . . . we shall come home from time to time. But I *must* get out of Haywood's End or die of boredom. Riding horses and visiting the sick aren't occupations for a lifetime.' Emma's face told her that she'd been unintentionally cruel. 'I didn't mean *you*, my dear Emma. I shall come home and visit *you*.'

Emma nodded but continued to weep and in the end there was nothing for Louise to do but kiss her and go away.

The wedding a month later was reckoned to be a fine affair, with the calm-faced bride splendidly gowned in white satin trimmed with orange-blossom and knots of ribbon, and a train that cascaded behind her like a waterfall on the blue carpet of the chancel floor. The captain and his fellow-officers looked suitably dashing in their regimentals, but Gertrude thought wistfully of James Wyndham . . . he would have looked even better in them than Captain Trentham who wasn't particularly handsome. Emma left the house for the first time in several years because, although the sadness of the occasion and the exertion were almost too much for her, it was unthinkable that she should not attend Louise's wedding. Sir Edward was in his element, and the hospitality of Providence was offered to all. The village reckoned the thing had been done 'seemly', and agreed that it was best to make the most of it, because there was no telling about the future with Master William.

Once the excitement was over Emma drooped back into lethargy again, abandoning any pretence of being in charge of the household. It was left to Gertrude to worry about the fact that her father nowadays came in almost too tired to eat. One evening she watched him toy with the rabbit stew and dumplings she'd put in front of him, until anger got the better of her.

'Why don't the Wyndhams do something to help you?' She shouted the words at him because the alternative seemed to be to burst into tears.

He looked surprised by her fierceness, but answered in his usual slow, deliberate way. 'The Squire pays *me* to do the work for him. He does what *he* has to do.'

'Yes, sits in the Wyndham pew on Sundays! Well, if *he* can't spare time from hunting, it wouldn't hurt his son to help you.'

'William's not a farmer, maid. He spends his time reading and doing clever bits of colouring, I understand.' George Hoskins spoke without irony. It didn't seem strange to him that men weren't all the same; no two pigs or

34

sheep were identical, so why should humans be?

'Bits of colouring aren't going to save Providence,' Gertrude flared. 'Can't *he* see that, instead of wringing his hands over the fact that you want to instal machines?' She saw her father's eyebrows lift and hastened to explain. 'He was watching the reapers with me one day . . . thought they looked grand!'

In spite of himself her father smiled at the scorn in her voice. 'They *do* look grand,' he insisted. The passionate concern in her face led him to go on talking for once. 'It's like this, maid. I'm for the old ways too, but we have to reduce the cost of growing food, which means employing fewer men. For centuries past England's been a farming country. Now, all people can think of are coal mines and factories. Nobody cares that times are hard for farmers – least of all the Government, seemingly. Instead of supporting English wheat, they let in more and more American grain free of tax, and there's even refrigerated meat being brought from Australia and South America. Home prices are falling so low that farmers can't afford to pay their rents, and landlords can't evict them if they wanted to, because no-one else would be fool enough to want to take up the tenancies.'

Gertrude looked at his troubled face and thought of the Squire, cheerfully riding along the lane with nothing on his mind except the day's hunting. 'It's not *your* fault . . . it's not even your land . . . let the people who own it worry about it,' she said fiercely.

He gave a little sigh that said she was a child still who didn't understand. 'It isn't the owning of the land that matters . . . it's what becomes of it that counts.'

She inspected the Wyndhams carefully after that, expecting them to look changed because of what she now knew about *them*, and American wheat, and the falling rents from land. But the Squire still jogged happily along the lane, William wandered about the park as usual, and Lady Hester was driven out alone now on her never-ending round of neighbourhood calls. If ruin lay ahead, none of *them* seemed to know about it, and if things were changing elsewhere, curtsies were still bobbed and caps lifted when the Master rode by. Albert Simpkin's message hadn't yet reached Haywood's End.

CHAPTER THREE

Emma died on a cold brooding afternoon in January of the following year. It was 1887, and Gertrude was nearly seventeen. Looking from *her* sheet-white face to her mother's dead one, it seemed to Maud Roberts that Emma looked satisfied at last. She had finally proved to them that nothing they could do made life bearable for her.

'No pain, my dear,' Maud murmured, 'and no fear, either. I don't think your poor mother minded dying.'

'She didn't die . . . she just gave up; there's a difference,' Gertrude said slowly. It was the last thing to mark her out from the women she'd kept aloof from. Haywood's End held it as a creed: for high or low, giving up wasn't allowed. Louise Wyndham had never hesitated in front of the worst fence in the hunting field, Queenie Briggs and the others went through each hard confinement without complaint. Not to flinch was what gave a woman self-respect.

But whatever they had thought of Emma Hoskins, the whole village turned out for the funeral, and offered her daughter the rough, warm kindness they would have given each other. It was well-meant, but embarrassed Gertrude because it made her feel a fraud.

'They're expecting me to grieve because they think "grievin's seemly",' she said to Mrs Moffat. 'They didn't like my mother, but they'd be shocked if I said her dying made no difference to me. It's hard to love someone who doesn't love you. I don't know *why* she didn't love me, just a little bit at least.'

Mrs Moffat didn't know either. She was distressed, but also slightly shocked herself at such plain speaking. 'Don't let anyone else hear you say such things, my dear. Just remember Emma was too poorly to be a real mother; things would've been different otherwise.'

The morning of the funeral was still very cold, but also cruelly beautiful for burying someone in the ground and throwing earth over her. Gertrude struggled to make sense of what the rector's deep voice was saying, but failed. ' "My Father's house hath many mansions . . ." ' perhaps, but surely this dark gaping hole in the ground couldn't be one of them? ' "Death is swallowed up in victory",' Mr Roberts said confidently. ' "O death, where is thy sting? O grave, where is thy victory?" ' She knew he was trying to give comfort but in her mother's death she could see only defeat, not victory.

Afterwards, as the harsh winter slowly released its grip and grudgingly offered them spring instead, she felt ashamed to admit even to Maud Roberts that it was a relief to walk home from school and find no thin, complaining figure lying on the couch waiting for her. It made her feel an unnatural creature who'd have been less deceitful if she'd abandoned the mourning clothes that convention obliged her to wear.

Unnatural was the word Sid Moffat flung at her one morning, but for a different reason. He caught up with her because she'd stopped to watch the new lambs taking it in turns to climb a little hillock in the meadow behind the stack-yard. Each one got to the top, only to be nudged off it by the one behind. Gertrude's hair was released from its severe braids for once, and the antics of the lambs were making her laugh. He didn't waste time thinking that she was lovely standing there; his mind just said that he'd been patient long enough – she was getting old enough to belong to *him*.

His arms made a grab at her before she could move away, and his mouth pushed aside her hair so that he could find the nape of her white neck. She struggled to get free, half-laughing and half-angry, but it made his grip tighten as he pulled her round, so that he could kiss her mouth instead.

It didn't occur to her to be alarmed; she'd known him since she could remember anyone, and couldn't be frightened of him. But when lack of breath caused him to lift his head, she was purely angry and not laughing at all. 'Let go of me, Sid Moffat . . . this minute! *I* won't be mauled about, even if the village girls like it.'

'I don't know what *they* like – I was only trying to kiss *you*. In any case, 'tisn't natural not to want to be kissed. What's *wrong* with it, Gertrude?' His voice rose steadily and ended in an infuriated roar that had the opposite effect of making her begin to laugh, but it goaded him into kissing her again, more roughly this time. When he finally had to let go of her, they were both breathless and uneasily aware that an old friendship might not survive the onslaught of this new passion.

'I know you're over-young still, maid, but I want to *marry* you,' Sid muttered.

It would have been easier just to agree and hide behind an argument he would accept – that seventeen *was* too young to plunge into marriage – but she preferred to make things clear.

'I'm not going to marry anyone, Sid.' It sounded bald, and she tried to soften it with some helpful advice. 'You must pick someone else . . . Maggie Lucas, maybe, or Matthew's daughter at the forge . . .'

'Sweet Jesus . . . *listen* to me, girl. I don't need to be told who to marry. I haven't looked at another maid but you; you know that, and so does your father. He'd say you're too young still, but I know how to wait for what I want.'

He did, too; unless she could persuade him otherwise, he'd wait till kingdom come.

'Sid, *you* listen, please. I'm going to be like Miss Roberts and Sarah Simpkin – a single lady; I've made up my mind to it.'

He stared at her thin face, not believing her but faintly alarmed by the stubbornness he knew lay like a rock beneath the sweetness of her nature.

'You want to go on playing schoolma'am for a bit . . . is that it? Well, there's time enough if you're happy doing that.'

'Happy? I *hate* it,' she said fiercely. 'I don't know yet what I'll do, but I'm not going to grow old like Sarah, forever wringing her hands and apologizing to Mr Roberts because the children *still* don't know their catechism.'

Sid pushed huge hands through his mop of hair. Women were the devil to understand; his father had warned him of it. 'You have to humour them, boy . . . they're like mares always wanting to kick up their heels and play friskmahoy just when *you* want them to go quietly to their stable. Gentle them and they come round to your way of thinking in the end.' He hadn't done much gentling this morning; made a proper botch of it, in fact, and there was Gertrude's black dress to remind him that Emma Hoskins was only recently dead.

'Sorry, girl . . . I was over-hasty just then.' He gave her a sweet shy smile. ''Spect it's the spring making me as daft as those lambs over there!'

She laughed and agreed, and they parted friends, but on her way home she realized it was time to do some serious thinking. The only way to persuade Sid to turn his attention to some other girl would be to leave Haywood's End altogether. Her father could probably manage without her, and so could the school, but the morning had stirred up a memory that had been tucked away at the back of her mind for safe-keeping. On another spring day James Wyndham's mouth had touched her cheek and he'd seemed to put Providence into her care. She had common sense enough to realize that he'd never intended her to take him seriously; all the same there seemed something wrong with the idea of turning her back on Haywood's End.

The following Saturday morning there came an unusual break in the domestic routine. Instead of setting off for his office immediately after breakfast, her father stood fingering the bowler hat that set him apart from the cloth caps the other men wore.

'Don't start polishing, Gertrude . . . her ladyship wants to see you up at the house.'

'Up at the house? Whatever for?' she asked in astonishment. 'It's bound to be something about the school, and she was only there yesterday.'

"'Tisn't a school matter. She'd talk to Miss Simpkin about that. Better put your Sunday clothes on, maid.'

'It's not a social call; I'm being sent for.' Then she smiled at him with sudden sweetness. 'I'll take my apron off – will that do?'

He only nodded but she saw his mouth twitch with amusement. They were beginning to understand one another, and she thought the fact secretly pleased him as much as it pleased her.

The back entrance to Providence was familiar ground to her because Emma had sometimes sent her with messages to the estate office. This morning she was surprised to be taken towards the bridge that led to the great front door. Across the moat the house waited for them, grandly battle-mented and yet homely, all at the same time. For a moment she regretted her working clothes. The visit suddenly began to seem important and, although her cupboard didn't contain many clothes, she could have done better than a darned skirt and shawl. Nervousness suddenly took hold of her, making her linger in the courtyard garden that Biddle had planted with white and gold narcissus and heavenly hyacinths, but her father wasn't minded to let her dawdle.

'Come along, maid. We shall keep her ladyship wait-ing. You can sniff flowers on the way out if you feel inclined.'

He led her into a part of the house she'd never seen before. It seemed dark after the blaze of light and colour outside and she shivered in the cool dimness of a hall that the sun probably never reached. Then he tapped on an oak door so immense and old-looking that her imagination ran riot, expecting it to open and reveal a stairway leading down to a horrific dungeon, at the very least. The reality was so different that she gave a gasp of astonishment. Sunlight poured into the room in front of her, through windows full of painted glass that threw down shafts of coloured light. There was time to see soft rugs strewn on the stone floor,

41

and bowls of narcissus reflecting themselves in the polished surfaces of old chests and tables.

'Gertrude, my lady.' The note in her father's voice reminded her of the way he spoke in church.

'Thank you, Mr Hoskins.' He and Lady Hester smiled at each other, and Gertrude was aware of several things at once. The two of them were friends, and she was there because something had already been discussed and settled between them. He gave the woman seated in an armchair by the fire a little bow and then dismayed his daughter by abandoning her.

'Come and sit down, child. I want to talk to you.'

Gertrude picked her way warily to the nearest chair, conscious that her boots made too much noise on the stone flags but afraid to walk with them on something as fragile-looking as the rugs. Then, sitting bolt upright, she waited for whatever instruction might come next. Her ladyship seemed in no hurry to say anything else, and Gertrude had time to stare at *her*. Lady Hester's hair was parted in the middle and drawn back into a knot. The dark green stuff of her dress spread round her on the floor, and a little ruff of white lace encircled her throat. Gertrude had never seen her like this before, inside Providence – she suited the house she lived in.

'I saw you at the school yesterday,' Lady Hester said at last. 'The children didn't seem very interested in what you were reading to them so beautifully.'

It was her way of saying that they hadn't listened at all to the story of Moses being hauled out of the bulrushes. The same thing would happen when the inspector came round, so if her ladyship wasn't about to suggest that the school could manage without Gertrude Hoskins, *he* certainly would. Her mouth had gone dry and her heart seemed to want to jump into her throat.

'I'm not very good with the younger children,' she agreed hoarsely. What was the use of saying that her parents hadn't helped by omitting to supply her with even one brother or sister to practise on?

'You're not very happy either, I think,' Lady Hester said gently. 'Your father agrees with me that you should give up school work, Gertrude.'

She felt herself go cold despite the warmth of the room, had to struggle not to weep for the pain of knowing that she didn't even belong at Haywood's End school. She had hated it from childhood up, but she wanted to cling to it now that it was being taken away from her.

'Then . . . then what shall I do instead?' She'd forgotten to say 'milady', but it was too late to tack it on now.

'I wondered if you would like to come here.' The calm suggestion fell into a pool of silence in the room, broken only by the sigh of a log settling on the hearth.

'What . . . what to do?' Gertrude muttered at last.

'Would it sound very dull if I said as a sort of companion-help to me?' She smiled at the expression on Gertrude's face, but began to explain.

'I miss my daughter . . . she used to help me write letters, keep track of names, and calls to be made . . . all that sort of thing. I find I get into muddles without her. That is one thing. Another is that you could learn the running of a house like this. With training and experience you could strike out in the world; you don't have to stay at Providence for ever.' She hesitated a moment, looking at the face of the girl who watched her intently. 'Shall we be frank with each other, Gertrude? I know your father has young Mr Moffat in mind as a husband for you. If you like the idea, all well and good; if not, there is very little choice at Haywood's End.'

'I don't see any choice at all,' Gertrude said bluntly; 'Sid is a friend . . . at least he is when he's being sensible . . . but I'm not going to marry him. I'm not going to marry anyone.'

Lady Hester accepted this firm statement with a grave nod of the head. 'In that case I think you would certainly do well to come here.' She made it sound, Gertrude thought gratefully, as if a dozen other possibilities were open to her. The idea was beginning to look enticing but there was a difficulty she felt obliged to mention. The problem was how to do it tactfully to someone who was Squire Wyndham's wife.

'There's my father to think of,' she finally pointed out. 'Without me to badger him, he might not eat at all. He works too hard . . . I mean, he gets tired and forgetful about things like dinnertime.'

Lady Hester received the message that she realized was intended for her husband. 'Mr Hoskins certainly mustn't be neglected, but if something could be arranged with kind Mrs Moffat, would that solve the problem?'

Gertrude sat deep in thought, concerned not so much with meals and Mrs Moffat as with the fact that she'd been right to feel something important hung in the balance when she walked across the bridge to Providence. Now that she'd had time to get used to the idea, there was nothing strange in it. It was simply another part of the pattern life had already drawn for her. She took a deep breath and smiled at the woman watching her.

'Yes, ma'am . . . I think in that case I'd like to come to Providence.'

She went with Miss Simpkin's doleful good wishes and a blessing from her father that sounded unexpectedly sad. His face reproached her for forgetting how much he missed having Emma to take care of. Whenever he came in his eyes still went automatically to the couch as if he hoped to find her there.

'Do you mind, after all?' Gertrude asked suddenly. 'I don't have to go . . . but I thought you wanted me to, and everything was arranged.'

'Everything *is* arranged. Moffat will offer to play chess with me every evening, and I shall be stuffed with food, just like one of his wife's prize geese!'

'But something's wrong all the same.'

He took longer than usual over the business of stuffing tobacco into the bowl of his old pipe. 'Not wrong exactly, maid, I'm just not sure it's the best thing.' A smile flickered across his face, warming it with an affection that made her feel both glad and sad. 'Companion to her ladyship sounds grand, but remember you're a servant, like the rest of us. Don't go getting ideas above your station!'

'Or "too set-up, Gertie" . . . that's what the village children used to shout at me!' she confessed ruefully. 'Well, I'm to be the companion-*help*, in any case – there's nothing very grand about that.'

'Nothing at all,' he agreed, and astonished her by kissing her cheek.

Her first day at Providence certainly wasn't calculated to make her feel important. The Wyndhams were away from home, attending a function at Barham Manor, and she was left to the mercies of the housekeeper, Mrs Smithers. She was given a little room in the servants' wing and told to eat with the rest of them. But the other girls stared at her without saying anything, the elderly woman who was Lady Hester's personal maid said jealously that *she* looked after her ladyship, and Mrs Smithers's only attempt at conversation was a frigid reminder not to make her own bed because *that* was the job of the chambermaid. At the end of the day she went thankfully to bed, wondering what she was doing there.

The following morning things looked less hopeless because she was set to work, penning notes in Lady Hester's boudoir. The first one had to be done three times because anxiety made her hand tremble and she was determined to inscribe it perfectly, but at least she could now see that there was work to be done.

In the course of time she began to realize how much; Wyndham charitable interests extended well outside Haywood's End, and their social connections far beyond that. When there was no correspondence to be done, there were domestic affairs to be learned. Lady Hester taught her how to darn the fragile old fabrics of which the curtains and chair coverings were made, how to handle precious pieces of china and glass, and how to run the still-room of a country house. Gertrude and Sir Edward even grew accustomed to each other. After a day when he'd ridden out to inspect a horse instead of attending a meeting of the Justices in Warwick, Gertrude had taken to keeping a diary which she now consulted very diligently, and the Squire got into the habit of calling on her in his wife's boudoir each morning.

'What have I forgotten today, Gertrude? You'd better look in your book for me!'

'Nothing today, sir, except the rector's usual call to settle the lessons on Sunday.'

'Ah, now I shall remember . . . thank you.' She suspected him of laughing at her in the depths of his beard, but not unkindly, and went on reminding him of appointments he would much sooner have forgotten. 'Can't *not* go,' he explained to his wife. 'She'd be disappointed.'

Gertrude soon felt so at ease that it was hard to remember the purgatorial days spent with Moses and the children at school. Only William Wyndham seemed to ignore her, but his life seemed to be mainly lived in the room they called the Great Parlour, where his painting easel was set up.

'We never see you except at meal times,' his mother complained gently one day. 'I don't think you've said one word to Gertrude ever since she arrived.'

'I bolt in here to avoid her,' William confessed. 'She frightens me . . . stares at me with those extraordinary eyes of hers which say very clearly what she *doesn't* say – that I'm a disgrace to fifteen generations of Wyndhams, and ought to do something more than daub paint on canvas all day!'

It was exactly what Gertrude did think. Painting seemed scarcely a manly or a fulltime occupation for someone who would be the owner of Providence one day. She never had occasion to go to the Great Parlour but Annie, whose job it was to polish the floor, often amused the other servants by describing the pictures she saw there – 'nothing but two twigs stuck in a jar, along o' a rotten apple and a handful of dried-up nuts! . . . what are ye supposed to make o' that?' she'd ask, slapping herself with glee. 'Master William caught

46

me lookin' this morning . . . still life, he said it was; still death, if ye ask me!'

Gertrude felt disloyal to Lady Hester in laughing with the rest of them, but it was hard not to agree with the general view that the Squire's heir was a poor thing. Mrs Smithers, whose majestic bosom encased in black bombazine hid what the companion-help thought of as a distinctly indelicate streak, was heard to say bluntly that he wouldn't know what to do with a woman even if her ladyship managed to find him one. Certain it was that he wouldn't go looking for himself.

Knowing what was said about him, Gertrude was relieved that their paths didn't cross, but one morning she bumped into him in the library. He wore the old velvet jacket that seemed to be the only coat he possessed; his fair hair straggled over its collar, and his shaggy moustache drooped as well. But his voice was pleasant when he spoke to her.

'Good morning, Gertrude . . . you're not afraid to be alone in here? The rest of the staff are, I'm told.'

The story he referred to was squealed over by the maids every time it was mentioned downstairs. A long-ago master of the house had slain his wife because she was said to have been unfaithful. The rumour had been false, started by her husband's sworn enemy, and she was supposed to have haunted the library ever since.

'Her ghost has more right than I have,' Gertrude replied, made brave by morning sunlight. It might be a different matter on a candle-lit winter afternoon, but he hadn't asked her then. 'I feel sorry for the poor lady.'

'Pity Ralph Wyndham too,' William suggested. 'He spent a fortune improving the parish church in the vain hope of being forgiven for the crime! It's a very small part of the story of this house. If you're interested in the rest of it, there's this collection of papers that you might like to take away and look at.' He held out a leather-bound volume. 'Here you are . . . the history of Providence.'

Her face flushed with pleasure at being trusted with

47

something so precious. 'I'll take great care of it,' she promised with an earnestness that made him smile. The thought of poring over the stiff yellowing pages in the privacy of her room instead of trying to read or sew in the servants' hall was a pleasure in itself, apart from learning about Providence.

It was perfectly clear to her by now that, however hard she tried, she couldn't make the other servants accept her. She thought they might have done if Mrs Smithers hadn't made it clear that she resented having her there. The housekeeper was obliged to carry out Lady Hester's instructions and explain the mysteries of her domain, but she did it as sketchily as possible and ignored the questions Gertrude asked about the store-rooms and the account books that were supposed to be kept. In front of her mistress she was careful to be civil, otherwise it amused her to refer to 'Miss *Hoskins*' with an emphasis that made the other servants snigger.

'If my name sounds funny to you, I wish you'd just call me Gertrude,' she said bluntly one day when she was alone with the housekeeper, and had just pointed out that only two of the dozen hams listed in the store-book were actually hanging up. Mrs Smithers had found an explanation, but having to do so had inflamed her uncertain temper.

'Bless me, no . . . her ladyship insisted it was to be "Miss Hoskins". Well, she would, of course.'

'Why not? It's my name.' It occurred to her that she'd been insisting on it – Gertrude Hoskins – for years in one way and another, probably because she was reminded suddenly of Daisy James by the smile on the housekeeper's face. There was no humour in it, and her eyes, as shiny and hard as jet buttons, gleamed with malice.

'Call yourself what you like . . . her ladyship should never have been saddled with you, and nor should we.'

'Why not tell me what you're really trying to say?' Gertrude suggested quietly.

Mrs Smithers's flushed face looked frightened for an

instant, but she couldn't stop now, and in any case the Wyndhams could do without this girl easily enough but they couldn't do without her and Smithers.

'I should've thought it was plain enough . . . you're no more George Hoskins's daughter than I am. Why d'you think a soft job's been found for you here? Everybody knows Emma Rastell had to be married off in a hurry, and you're just like her . . . same nasty, sly ways.'

'Whose daughter *am* I supposed to be?'

'You're the Squire's bastard, of course.'

Gertrude stared at her, tempted almost beyond what self-control would stand to pound her fists against the woman's sneering face. Instead, she flung words at her. 'You're an evil old *cow*, and if you say that to anyone else I'll kill you.'

Mrs Smithers smiled in triumph. 'No need to . . . they all know!'

Gertrude ran out of the room, hurled herself up the back stairs, and round to the corridor in the other wing. A line of portraits hung there, Wyndham after Wyndham, all with the same fair colouring, pale eyes, and long thin nose. Back in her bedroom the little hand-mirror confirmed that her own hair was dark as a blackbird's wing, her nose broad and snub. She looked nothing like a Wyndham. It was enough to calm the frantic thudding of her heart until another thought occurred to her. She was nothing like George Hoskins either, and there had always been the feeling, hidden but strong, that her parents hadn't wanted her.

She found her father outside, deep in conversation with Biddle in the kitchen garden. Her pallid face and desperate eyes spoke of some distress that she could scarcely contain, and he walked quickly towards her.

'Something wrong, maid?'

She nodded, but only managed to stammer, 'I c . . . can't say it . . . Mrs Smithers . . .'

'Has been raking up the past, I dare say. Wicked woman *she* is, and her husband's nothing but a scripture-spouting

49

humbug.' It was strong language for George Hoskins, but it didn't make Gertrude's strained face relax.

'She said I was the Squire's b . . . bastard. I called *her* an evil old cow.'

He didn't look shocked, only grave; it was enough to tell her there was something she didn't know. 'It's time to give you the truth, maid . . . we can't hurt Emma now. Some of it you know already. I came to Providence after my first wife, Alice, died in childbirth. Emma – Rastell, she was then – was nineteen, and so pretty and spirited you'd not believe, knowing her only as an invalid. She loved the Wyndham children and the Squire and Lady Hester treated her with great kindness . . . like one of the family, almost. Then Sir Edward's brother Henry came back from America and brought his partner with him, an Irishman called Daniel Maguire; a smoother-spoken fellow you wouldn't meet in a month of Sundays, with eyes that always seemed to be laughing. He seduced Emma, then went on his way, leaving her with child. She tried to drown herself when she found he had a wife and daughter in New York. I found her in time, and with the Squire and Lady Hester's help married her. We sent her to the Wyndhams' old nurse until you were born, but she never recovered her health or her happiness. That is the truth; Mrs Smithers's version is not. Nobody knows except Squire, Lady Hester, and the Roberts.'

Gertrude had a vivid recollection of James telling her that a man called Maguire had been the best of them at playing charades. He had indeed. 'Did the Irishman know about me?' she asked after a moment.

'No, Emma wouldn't have him told. In any case, there was no point. The man had disappeared from our life . . . it was better to let him go.'

He saw a strange smile touch Gertrude's mouth, heard her suddenly begin to laugh – great shuddering bursts of laughter that he found terrible and distressing. 'Disappeared? Oh no . . .' She managed to gasp, 'Lady Hester heard from James this morning. He's planning to visit Providence . . . proposes to bring the lady he's just married.

She's the daughter of Henry Wyndham's partner, and her name's Kitty Maguire!'

Gertrude suddenly crumpled into tears as convulsive as her laughter had been, and George Hoskins held her cradled against him while she wept. When she was finally calm again, she stared at him out of tear-drenched eyes.

'I always used to be aware you didn't want me . . . I'm very sorry about that; I'd have *liked* you to be my father.'

His face was a mask of sadness. 'Emma got upset if she thought I was growing fond of you. But in law I'm still your father, and in affection I am too. Never forget it, maid.'

'I won't . . . every time I have to look at my half-sister it will be a comfort to me.'

CHAPTER FOUR

The news was all round the village that James Wyndham
would be home in time for the garden party the Squire was
holding to mark the old Queen's Jubilee. It set the seal on
a day that was eagerly anticipated in any case, even though
not much of the prosperity of her long reign had brushed
off on Haywood's End. A holiday in itself was a rare enough
event to be enjoyed; now there was not only the added
excitement of seeing what America had done to young
James, but the prospect of looking his wife over as well.
The men's opinion, aired only in the alehouse, was that
she'd be good-looking if she'd managed to catch James's
eye; the women told each other on the village green that
she'd be rich and grandly dressed – all the more reason,
then, to hunt out their own bits of finery and pick a flower
or two to tuck in the band of their old straw hats.

The afternoon was fine and hot – 'Queen's weather',
everyone said, and 'no more than the old lady deserved'.
After grumbling for twenty years that she'd hidden herself
away grieving for dead Albert, it suddenly seemed that
England hadn't seen such a monarch since the days of great
Queen Bess. It was high noon for Victoria and her Empire,
so what should the sun do but blaze down out of a cloudless
sky?

The Squire's entertainment, which Gertrude had helped
to organize, was reckoned to do Haywood's End proud.
The neighbouring gentry sipped tea indoors, but out in the
grounds was where the fun was to be had – booths and
side shows, music provided by the Warwickshire Militia
band, and tea in a huge marquee brought all the way
from Birmingham. There was also the traditional cricket

match fought with the neighbouring village of Hockley, in which daft Artie distinguished himself by running out the captain of his own side. Artie was a demon hitter when the fit took him, but there were known to be risks in including him in the team. At a crucial point in the game he cantered down the pitch, ignoring Matthew's roar from the other end to 'go back, you great ninny'. With both batsmen now at the same end, there was nothing for Matthew to do but retire to a chorus of insults from the Hockley fielders.

The day culminated in fireworks when it grew dark, and the lighting of a bonfire linking them in a chain that blazed from Land's End to the Shetland Islands. The only disappointment was that Mr and Mrs James Wyndham failed to appear.

'What's happened to James?' Maud Roberts asked Gertrude during the course of the afternoon. 'Did my best in honour of the bride . . . even found a hat to wear, and some gloves.' The gloves were odd ones but, eyes brimming with laughter, Gertrude decided not to point this out. Miss Roberts had indeed done her best.

'I'm not exactly *dernier cri*, of course, like all these grand ladies with their bustles and leg-of-mutton sleeves,' she admitted, 'and nor are *you*, but it seems to me that you look more elegant than they do.'

Gertrude flushed with pleasure at the compliment, even if Maud's judgement might be considered suspect. She'd taken great pains with the grey skirt and muslin blouse she'd stitched for the occasion, and daringly tucked a spray of white daisies into the knot of her dark hair.

'A Puritan maid,' William murmured to his parents, catching sight of her.

'A *charming* little maid,' the Squire said appreciatively. 'No wonder young Moffat is keeping close behind her, like a beagle with his eye on a hare!'

Gertrude was well aware of Sid, and prudently stayed beside the man she still thought of as her father. He looked hot and uncomfortable in a thick dark suit, but it wouldn't have occurred to him to wear anything less in honour of the Queen.

'I'm sure Biddle's hating this,' she said, sweeping an arm round the scene in front of them. 'The two of us have a secret understanding – Providence doesn't belong to Sir Edward at all; it belongs to Biddle and me! He won't be happy till all these people have gone home and left us in peace again.'

George Hoskins glanced down at her. A month or two with Lady Hester had changed her already, in ways he couldn't quite put his finger on. He doubted that she'd had an easy time at Providence, with Mrs Smithers and the other servants so hostile, but she was more sure of herself now and he was beginning to fear that poor Sid was being left behind.

'What happened to young James?' he asked, repeating Maud's question.

'Lady Hester got a telegram . . . they stayed in London for a night because Mrs Wyndham wanted to see the celebrations *there*.'

He smiled in spite of himself at the scorn in her voice, but felt obliged to be fair.

'Don't make up your mind you're going to hate her before she arrives, maid; likewise, it's no use blaming *her* for anything.'

Gertrude looked thoughtful for a moment. 'I hadn't allowed for that,' she agreed slowly. 'Now, we'll go and find a cup of tea . . . you're looking thirsty.'

It wasn't until the following afternoon when the crowds had gone and Biddle was looking cheerful again that the rattle of hooves on the gravel of the forecourt signalled the return of the carriage that had been sent to the railway station. When Sir Edward and his wife went outside, James was helping his wife to alight and there was time for them to make a quick inspection.

'A pocket Venus, by Jove . . . well done, James!' murmured the Squire.

Lady Hester's anxious appraisal had a different object.

54

Kitty Wyndham was dark-haired, but otherwise she could see no resemblance at all to Gertrude. *This* girl was small and richly curved, with large blue eyes, rounded cheeks and chin, and a prettily pouting mouth. No, thank God, not a bit like Gertrude. A toque entirely covered in flowers sat like a garland on her black hair, and her travelling dress of pale blue silk would have graced the previous day's garden party. She looked expensive, exquisite, and faintly silly . . . just the sort of daughter-in-law the Squire would love, Lady Hester reflected with relief; for herself, the joy was to see James again.

'Dearest Mama, you've shrunk,' he said, enfolding her in his arms. 'You weren't supposed to have changed at all.'

She apologized humbly, trapped between laughter and tears, and then it was time to welcome his wife. William delayed matters by sauntering out to join in the greetings, but eventually Hodges and Artie were able to lead the steaming horses to the stable-yard, Smithers dealt self-importantly with a mountain of luggage, and Kitty was ushered into the house.

Gertrude looked out of the boudoir window at the end of the fifteen minutes she'd vowed herself to, and found the forecourt empty. She'd have liked a glimpse of James, and both wanted and feared to see Kitty, but she saw neither of them that day; only the servants' excited chatter at supper told her that Master James was 'more handsome nor ever', and 'Mrs Kitty with a wardrobe that would put the ladies at Barham Manor properly in the shade'. There was time to talk herself into calmness. If she thought of Kitty Wyndham as simply the daughter of a man she didn't know, she'd be able to wish her an occasional good-morning easily enough and think no more about her than she'd think of any other visitor to the house.

She went outside early next morning as usual, to pick a posy of flowers for the desk in Lady Hester's room. The courtyard garden inside the three wings of the house was a warm, sheltered place of grass and flowers, divided by paths and the dark green spires of clipped yew trees.

Bees and butterflies seemed to love it as much as Gertrude did.

'I hope Biddle knows you're raiding his precious flowers,' said a voice behind her.

She spun round to find James watching her; he'd arrived so quietly from the bridge outside that she didn't know how long he'd been standing there. For a moment or two longer they stared at each other, caught in a trance of stillness . . . a tall, slender girl in a long black skirt and white muslin blouse, and a man with a smile in his eyes and a beard that looked the colour of red gold in the sunlight.

At last she remembered what he'd said. 'The flowers are for Lady Hester . . . Biddle allows that.' Then she smiled for the pleasure of seeing him and he observed that a dimple sprang into the thin cheek.

'He's probably putty in your hands, like my father. According to Mama, you rule *him* with a rod of very gentle iron!'

The smile lit her face again, but she shook her head. 'He's kind enough to let me organize him a little, that's all.'

James still watched her, trying to recognize in this friendly, self-possessed young woman the adolescent he had left behind.

'I'm very sorry about your mother, Gertrude, but I'm glad you're here. Time's gone too fast for me . . . when I went away you still wore a pigtail and pinafore, and those dreadful black boots!'

'Your sister used to stare at them – I hated her and them. Now I'm at Providence, and poor Mrs Trentham has to make do with India. Life's very unexpected,' she said solemnly.

'Yes, but that's part of its charm! America is unexpected – that's why I enjoy it so much.'

She could see that he did; satisfaction with life shone in his eyes and smile, and even seemed to put a glow on the weatherbeaten skin that made his pale eyes look blue. Lucky Kitty Wyndham to be the sharer, perhaps the cause, of such contentment.

'I hope your wife will enjoy England as much as you like *her* country,' she said with an effort at politeness. 'She can't help but love Providence, of course.'

'She's impressed, but missing certain things that we now take for granted – like taps that yield hot water and light that doesn't go out in a draught and plunge us in darkness!'

'New-fangled things, my father calls them. We don't set much store by them at Providence.'

'No, but perhaps you should. By the look of what I've seen this morning, there are other things Providence doesn't set much store by – land lying uncultivated, and buildings in need of repair.'

She was glad to have a reason to be angry with him, because anger might drown the sadness that was growing heavy inside her. 'Times are hard here for farmers,' she said indignantly. 'Ask my father if you like, but don't *dare* blame him. He does the work of two men and gets no help.' She wasn't aware that she spoke to the Master's son as if she were his equal, nor that the sudden flush of colour staining her cheeks made her beautiful. James was aware of both things, and of an electric tension sparking across the gap between them.

It was interrupted by the arrival of his wife. Kitty's silk skirts rustled on the flagstones with an irritable little noise that echoed the fretfulness in her voice.

'James . . . we are all waiting for you in the dining-room, and no doubt this girl has work to do.'

'She's an old friend, Kitty,' he explained easily. 'This is Gertrude Hoskins, who now helps my mother.'

Kitty stiffly inclined her head to Gertrude's murmured 'good morning, Mrs Wyndham', but spoke only to her husband.

'It's time we went in to breakfast.'

He immediately offered her his arm and they were almost at the door when he stopped and turned round again. There was something still to be said to the girl who stood there alone in the sunlight, watching them.

'Gertrude . . . I wasn't blaming your father. God knows Providence would be lost without him.'

She nodded without saying anything and the next moment they were swallowed up in the dimness of the hall. The scent of the flowers in her hand finally reminded her of why she was there. She looked down at them and saw that her fingers were trembling. The first, worst glimpse of her half-sister was over. No subconscious bond of blood and kinship had produced the smallest hint of friendship; quite the reverse, because she had the impression that Kitty had taken a dislike to her. Now she could get quietly on with her work, and wait for James to take his wife away from Providence.

During the month they stayed there the house was full of the noise and bustle of entertainment. Lady Hester amused her daughter-in-law with a round of neighbourhood calls, while the Squire took his son riding about the estate, and there were evening parties with elaborate dinner menus that threw Mrs Smithers into a state of irritable agitation. Her husband enjoyed himself more than she did, because formal entertainment meant that he could stalk in and out of the dining-room looking important. There was a smell of cigars hanging in the still air of the courtyard garden, and the sound of laughter and the pianoforte in the drawing-room being played by William. It was impossible for Gertrude to pretend any longer that Providence belonged to her; she had to accept the bitter truth, that she was as invisible to the people who did own it as the ghost of the poor lady in the library.

James saw no point in worrying his father with his views about a neglected estate, but he was outspoken with William when they were alone at the breakfast table one morning.

'I know Providence is buried in the country, but so are Barham and Endlicott and they've both got electricity; even Shillington Hall has gas-lighting. Only *we* still grope about with candles at night and wait for some wretched skivvy to climb the stairs with cans of hot water. Why?'

William's smile was faintly mocking. 'I suppose because we like Providence the way it is . . . picturesquely medieval!'

'Do the servants like it like that?'

'I don't know – I haven't asked them.'

James tried again. 'It isn't only the house. There's arable land lying idle, and cottages that look as if a puff of wind would blow them down. It's no way to run an estate, but I have it on good authority that George Hoskins can't work miracles.'

His brother's smile was suddenly pleasant. 'At a guess, you've been talking to Gertrude! She's right, of course; the neglect is certainly not her father's fault. The simple answer is that we lack money. I'm not encouraged to know what's going on, but Hoskins lets fall things now and then. Farm prices have been dropping for years, and the Wyndhams' income with them, like every other landowner's. There are things that would help – more machinery, fewer men; less hunting, fewer expenses – but they don't commend themselves to my father.'

'At this rate you'll have nothing to inherit but sour land and a dilapidated house.'

'That's how it often seems to me,' William agreed.

'Good God . . . don't sound so calm about it. *Do* something . . . find yourself a rich wife and save Providence that way.'

'I shall probably have to try . . . I have the feeling that Gertrude expects it of me!'

James smiled, but only briefly, and then his expression was unexpectedly sombre. 'Fortune *and* beauty if you're lucky, like me; but don't expect intelligence and humour as well; that is too much to ask!'

William stared at his face, uncomfortably aware that his brother's mask of smiling contentment had slipped for a moment.

If the domestic shortcomings didn't trouble *him*, they certainly irritated his sister-in-law. Kitty would have sacrificed linenfold panelling any day to the pipes needed for running hot water, and had much to say to her husband on the subject of the plumbing arrangements at Providence. Lack of the comfort she was used to made her short-tempered with whoever had the job of waiting on her, and within a week two girls hired to look after her had returned to Warwick. On the morning of a grand ball at Warwick Castle she was without a personal maid again. Old Rose grumbled in the servants' room at the prospect of waiting on *her* as well as her own mistress, and it was probably agitation that caused her to cut her hand so badly at the lunchtime meal that Hodges had to drive her to see Dr Markham in the village. She returned white and shaken, with her hand stitched up, and fit for nothing but to be allowed to go to bed. Lady Hester looked so worried that Gertrude diffidently offered her own services.

'My dear . . . do you think you could help Mrs James?' her ladyship asked. 'I suspect that her toilette will be more complicated than mine.'

Gertrude thought she could, and found herself faced with a situation that either had to be laughed at or wept over. It turned out to be more difficult than she'd anticipated to wait on this spoiled girl not much older than herself. It was hard not to covet underclothes of silk and delicate lace, harder still not to feel resentful of the way life handed out its pleasures. Her half-sister's share was to dance the night through with James; Gertrude Hoskins's was to listen to Annie and Ethel reading fortunes in their teacups after supper, or sit alone reading in her own room. Envy rose like sickness in her throat, bitter as gall and more humiliating. She was saved by the knowledge that Kitty was staring at her in the mirror . . . stupid, but not so stupid that she wasn't aware of Gertrude's envy. She appeared to enjoy the situation. This enabled Gertrude to make the effort of smiling at her as she asked which of two dresses spread out on the bed was to be worn.

'The white satin?'

'No, I'll have the lilac silk.' The dress was beautiful, but it had been made for her wedding trousseau some months before, when she was less amply curved than she was now. Gertrude struggled with the line of tiny silk-covered buttons at the back, and was defeated by them.

'You haven't laced me tight enough,' Kitty said furiously. 'Do it again, for goodness sake.'

Tighter lacing helped a little, but not enough; button and buttonhole simply wouldn't meet. The situation was so close to farce that Gertrude was perilously tempted to laugh – even tempted for a moment of time to think that she could tell Kitty the truth about their relationship. They might then be able to laugh together about the dress, and some of her mother's unhappiness might have been redeemed in friendliness and understanding. The expression on Kitty's face stopped her: it was devoid of anything but the flush of rage because an insolent servant was deliberately trying to make her look ridiculous.

'It's *your* fault,' she hissed. 'You're good at making sheep's eyes at my husband, but a child of ten would make a better lady's maid.'

'I'm *not* a lady's maid,' Gertrude pointed out quietly. 'But even I could do up your dress if it would fit. The truth is that it's too small. Why not try the white one?'

'I shall wear *this* dress,' stormed Kitty. 'Leave it alone . . . you'll only tear it. Send Rose here, and go back to your sweeping, or whatever it is you *can* do.'

Gertrude stood for a moment beside her so that they were reflected in the mirror together – one of them a tall slender figure in severe black and white, the other half-swathed in rich lilac silk, but definitely squat by comparison.

'Rose cut herself this morning. Her hand is bandaged, and she's lying down.'

Kitty hesitated and saw just in time the futility of cutting off her nose to spite her face.

'In that case I shall wear the white dress,' she said coldly. 'It's less complicated than this one, so perhaps it won't be more than you can manage.'

The dress was fastened without much difficulty, Mrs Wyndham's shining mane of black curls readjusted, and she was able to make a grand exit, ready for the ball. She left behind her a girl shivering with reaction from the scene, and desperately trying to dislodge from her mind the barb that

Kitty had planted there. It wasn't often that she caught sight of James, but she knew that she *did* look at him then . . . everybody did, because of some magnetism about him. She remembered what her father said of the man called Maguire: he couldn't help but charm people; it was just as true of James. But if Kitty had noticed that she looked at him, perhaps everyone else had too. The thought made her feel so sick with humiliation that there was no room left in her mind to picture a crowded ballroom, with Kitty in the middle of it dancing with James.

The following afternoon – a Sunday when she was free – she walked across the park to visit her father. One glance at her face told him that need had brought her there.

'We should've told her ladyship that you knew about Maguire,' he said quietly. 'It's troubling you too much, having to keep to yourself what you know about him, with Kitty Wyndham there.'

Gertrude's thin hands sketched a little gesture of despair. 'I did try not to hate her, but the effort was wasted anyway because she hates *me*. I wish they'd *both* go away . . . I wish they'd never come.' The words were torn out of her, revealing much more than she'd meant to say, and shattering what was left of self-control; she nonplussed her father by suddenly bursting into sobs that racked her body. She wasn't aware that he'd left the room until he returned with a cup of tea that he put in front of her.

'A sip of that will calm you,' he said hopefully. 'Haven't known you weep since you were nothing but a tiny maid. Women are supposed to need a tear now and then . . . men take their troubles to the alehouse.'

She wrapped her hands round the cup, comforted by its warmth, and stared at him over the top of it.

'I think it's time I left Providence. You warned me not to get ideas above my station – well, I gave that a try too, but for all the good it's done, I might not have bothered. I'm betwixt and between . . . don't belong anywhere, not even with the rest of the staff. I never shall, so I'd better go before I love Providence so much that leaving it breaks my heart.'

'There's still a house waiting for you here, and . . .'

'Poor waiting Sid, as well! I know. But I think I need to go farther away from Haywood's End than that.'

He nodded, and decided that it was time to change the subject. 'Been talking to James now and then; he still notices more than his father and brother put together.'

'Notices, but doesn't understand,' Gertrude said angrily. She wasn't allowed to love him, so she would try to hate him instead. 'I expect he rides around with the Squire pointing out all the things he thinks *you* aren't doing. It doesn't matter that you nearly kill yourself working for the Wyndhams.'

He blinked at this fierceness, and felt a twinge of pain because it reminded him of Emma. Gertrude was more like her mother than she realized . . . angry because life didn't arrange itself as required, expecting more than it was likely to deliver.

'The things that are wrong don't need pointing out,' he said after a moment. 'Squire can see them for himself, and he knows there's very little we can do about them. It's hard to make farmers change their habits, however many times you tell them there's more profit now in dairying than in the wheat they've been used to. You can't hurry them; they have to come to things in their own good time.'

'Well, I still hope James goes away soon, and takes his wife with him.'

'Happen you wouldn't like Mr William's wife either, if he took one.'

'The servants don't reckon he ever will.' She hesitated about repeating some of the wilder flights of fancy that were aired in the hall. Since no-one liked Kitty Wyndham or set much store by the Squire's elder son, the theories ranged from *her* pushing him into the lake so that James could inherit, to *him* falling in absent-mindedly and drowning himself. No-one ever suggested that he was capable of doing what Providence needed – finding himself a rich wife and begetting an heir. 'Even Mrs Smithers thinks he's a born bachelor,' Gertrude said at last.

'Well, she needn't worry herself yet. Squire's only fifty-seven, and still fit enough to spend all day in the saddle. Think of your own life, maid, but don't tease yourself about what happens to Providence. And no need to fash yourself over Kitty, either . . . she'll be gone soon.'

He was right. A week later the carriage took James and his wife to the railway station, on their way to Paris. From there they were to travel to Le Havre and catch the steamship that would take them back to New York. When it was time for them to drive away, Gertrude hid in her room so as not to have to stand in a line and shake hands with James. Kitty's presents to the staff, graciously handed out as she walked along saying goodbye, included one for Gertrude which Annie delivered to her – a small volume entitled *The Proper Duties and Attainments of a Lady's Maid*! It seemed to give her half-sister the last word.

CHAPTER FIVE

After James and Kitty had departed Providence seemed to sink back into tranquillity again with a sigh of relief, as if to say that bustle and excitement were all right for younger things. Sir Edward missed his son, and a charming daughter-in-law who hung on his arm as they inspected the portraits upstairs and assured him that she was 'just left speechless by it all'. All the same, it occurred to him that his wife wasn't entirely sorry to see her visitors depart.

'You're looking tired, Hester . . . was all that racketing about too much for you?'

'Not seeing dear James, of course not; but having both Daniel Maguire's daughters under our roof at the same time *was* something of a strain. I had hard work not to let my opinion of *him* colour my attitude towards poor Kitty, and it was even harder not to treat Gertrude differently from normal. It's strange, given the unfair gap in their circumstances, that I never think of Emma's daughter as "poor" Gertrude!'

Sir Edward nodded but decided to change the subject. 'James looked very successful and prosperous, but I don't think he thought the same about us.'

'Well, we're *not* very prosperous,' she agreed calmly, 'but fortunately nobody expects us to be nowadays.'

'No, still, things get more difficult all the time. I can see that I shall have to do what Hoskins wants, even though he can't quite bring himself to suggest it. I *know* that running the hunt myself is an expense we can't afford; we shall have to share the cost, but it means letting in the damned get-rich-quick johnnies from Birmingham. They'll cram their horses and generally make a disgusting mess of things.'

'They'll soon learn,' was all the comfort she could offer him.

With James and Kitty gone, Gertrude's mood of desperation disappeared as well. She couldn't remember why she'd wanted to leave Providence when she could feel part of the house again, and genuinely useful to the people who lived there. They now identified themselves in her imagination with certain rooms: Sir Edward was the spirit of hospitality in the dining-room, aglow with the rich dark gleam of candlelight on wine decanters, and smelling of cigars; William was the airy lightness of the Great Parlour where he stood at his easel painting all day; Lady Hester belonged to the firelit serenity of the room in which she received her guests, and also to the chapel room which no-one else seemed to use. It was her habit to sit there talking to Hubert Roberts after the luncheon they shared every Friday.

She kept flowers beside a statue of the Virgin Mary on the table that served as an altar, and these Lady Hester insisted on gathering herself. One morning, glancing out of the lower corridor windows, Gertrude saw Biddle run across the grass in the courtyard garden. The anxiety in his face sent her outside as well, and she arrived in time to see him helping Lady Hester to her feet.

'Nothing to worry about,' she said, trying to smile at their worried faces. 'Stupid of me to have tripped over a flag-stone.'

Biddle glared at the offending stone, but it stared blankly back, defying the possibility that its smoothness could have been to blame. Gertrude held out an arm to her mistress.

'Let me take you indoors, milady . . . I think you should lie down.'

'Perhaps I will . . . oh, I was forgetting my poor flowers . . .' but Biddle was already gathering them lovingly together in a hand as hard and brown as a bit of old leather.

'No harm done, milady . . . you might say they jest floated down!'

She thanked him and allowed herself to be taken indoors,

but insisted on going to the chapel room. Gertrude brought fresh water for the vase and was almost out of the room when a cry of distress sent her running back again. The vase was lying on its side, and water trickled over the delicate lace of the altar cloth on to the floor. Lady Hester's face was as white as the cloth, and her hands were trembling.

'You *were* shaken by that fall, milady,' Gertrude said quickly. 'You must let me see to this while you go and rest.'

The strained face opposite her broke into the travesty of a smile. 'The fall is part of it, but it's time to tell you the truth, my dear . . . I think I'm going blind.'

Gertrude wasn't aware of moving, but she found that she was holding her mistress. She wanted to defy God or Fate to deal with her in this terrible way, but there had been times recently when she'd seen her mistress fumble for things, seem uncertain of her step.

'It's the dim light in here . . . perhaps the Master *should* install this gas-lighting everyone talks about.'

'I don't think it has anything to do with candle-power. Dr Markham is arranging for me to see a specialist soon, in London; then we shall know.'

Between them, they restored the flowers to the vase and mopped up the water; then Lady Hester spoke again.

'Gertrude . . . perhaps I've imagined it, but it has seemed to me that you were becoming unhappy here. What I've just told you must make no difference to *you*; you need never feel obliged to stay here, and the world contains more beauty and interest than Providence can provide.'

Gertrude had been schooled from childhood to think before she spoke, and, whenever possible, to think twice before she acted; now, without any thought at all, she leaned forward and kissed Lady Hester's cheek. 'I'd like to stay for as long as you'll let me . . . there's as much of everything at Providence as I can cope with.'

'Then use this room as a refuge when you're troubled; it's what I do,' her ladyship said, smiling at her.

Gertrude thought that if the chapel offered a refuge, it also seemed to demand honesty. 'I'm not much for praying, milady,' she confessed awkwardly. 'When we go to church and listen to the rector and sing the hymns, it doesn't mean as much as it should.'

'Praying is up to you . . . just come and sit here when you want to.'

Lady Hester walked across the uneven wooden floor to a corner of the room. 'Let me show you something.' She gave a little tug and the panelling of the wall slid open enough to reveal a space for a man to walk through. 'It leads down to a hiding place in the tunnel that runs just above the level of the moat, which was our drainage system once upon a time! Providence was known as a safe house for Catholic priests who were being persecuted in the reign of Queen Elizabeth. A number of them were saved, and the hiding place was never found. Much later, when people were free to worship as they pleased, this room was turned into a chapel in memory of those terrible days.'

Gertrude had read about this in the Providence papers William had lent her, but its reality only came alive now as she stared into the cold darkness in front of her. Imagination painted a picture in her mind of holy men harried into the safety of a foul drain while soldiers hunted them like animals up above.

'That's why Providence feels as if it's holding out its arms to you when you walk across the bridge . . . you feel safe here.' She explained it slowly because, although the feeling was strong, she hadn't tried to put it into words before.

Lady Hester nodded, pleased that she had understood. 'The Wyndhams were suspected, of course, and punished by being refused the State appointments that made other families rich. But even that had its advantages – they couldn't afford to keep tearing the house down and re-building it . . . it had to remain just as it was.'

Gertrude recognized one other person, at least, who didn't want gas lights and hot-water pipes. It did not alter the difference in their station, but gave them something to share. Before she left the chapel she reverted to what was weighing most heavily on her mind. 'About your eyes, milady . . . don't think I shan't be able to manage a prayer for them.'

The visit to the London specialist took place a few weeks later, and the Squire unexpectedly insisted that Gertrude should be the one to travel with them. Rose resented the decision, but hesitated to say so because she was also relieved not to have to go to a place that frightened her. While Lady Hester was with the specialist in his consulting room, Gertrude and Sir Edward waited outside, silent and miserable in a room heavy with mahogany furniture and mournful-looking pictures in heavy gilt frames. Staring at one of them, a fox being torn to pieces by a pack of hounds, Gertrude began to think quite kindly of William's bits of colouring – at least they were full of light and a delicate kind of beauty she would view differently from now on. The Squire only stared at the hat in his hands, but she saw that his fingers were trembling.

'Glad you're here, my dear,' he said suddenly. 'Don't like this sort of place . . . frightens me. But I wish I was in there, instead of her ladyship.'

The only comfort she could give came unthinkingly in the terms of Haywood's End. 'Whatever happens, sir, Lady Hester won't flinch.'

'No, women don't as a rule. The truth is they're braver than we are because they have to be . . . life is often cruel to them.'

She didn't know whether he was thinking of his wife, or of the women in the village, struggling to keep their families clothed and fed, and their miserable cottages as clean as constant work could make them. Then the door opened and Lady Hester was ushered out. Gertrude knew at once by the way she smiled that her visit to London hadn't provided her with a cure, even if it had reassured her in some way.

'Good news,' she said calmly. 'My eyes are not going to get any worse than they are now.'

'No better either?' Sir Edward asked in the whisper that

seemed suitable to their surroundings. 'My dear . . . is there *nothing* he can do?'

'My learned friend says not. It's a relief to know. Now I can go home in peace, and thank God that I'm so beautifully taken care of.'

She insisted that they spent another night in London, so that Gertrude could be shown Westminster Abbey and St Paul's, and the extraordinary memorial to the late Prince Albert that had recently been completed on the fringe of Hyde Park. It was impossible not to be interested, of course, but the truth was that the huge city overwhelmed *her* almost as much as it did poor Rose. She hated its noise and dirt; parks and grand buildings couldn't make up for the sheer weight of human life and misery that was crammed into its streets. At the end of their journey home, Providence seemed more than ever to be holding out its arms, offering tranquil beauty and something that the Rector always insisted belonged only to the Lord: the peace that passed all understanding.

The visit to London marked a change in Gertrude's life at Providence. As the days unrolled in a slow, seamless procession of seasons and the varying village affairs that depended on them, she became more companion than help. She was always at hand to guide her mistress along the uneven stairs and passages of the house, or to drive out with her if someone at Haywood's End needed visiting. There were few visitors during the winter months, but when they came it was now taken for granted that Gertrude helped to entertain them.

On afternoons when they were left alone, Lady Hester would listen while Gertrude read to her, or they would wrangle happily over the merits of their favourite poets. They always sat in the Great Hall – it was stone-flagged, and no doubt draughty by the standards of someone like Kitty Wyndham, but when logs burned in the huge fireplace and the candles were lit, it seemed to be the very heart of the house. Sometimes, instead of being read to, Lady Hester would choose to talk about the past, and her childhood in a castle further west that sounded bleaker by far than Providence. Once, she talked about her son.

'I worry about William, Gertrude . . . and about the future here. I should die content if I knew that he and the house were taken care of.'

'*He* seems happy, milady.' She said it without being sure that it was true. For all his odd and solitary ways, he was a clever man, and too sensitive a one not to know that his mother was anxious about him. He'd formed the habit of looking in on them from time to time; seeing that they were content together, he would smile and go away again.

'He needs a wife,' Lady Hester said. 'I shall have to bestir myself and find someone . . . I'm much afraid I can't leave the matter to him!'

She did her best as the months passed, and regularly cajoled him into attending local functions that he would much sooner have ignored. He was a courteous escort when driven to the task, but his mother gradually despaired of a man who only rode a horse when the distance was too great for him to walk, who shied away from ballrooms, and who seemed struck dumb before powerful matrons whose daughters required eligible husbands. What suited William best was to be left to wander about the park or woods until his eyes spotted some curiously-shaped twig or plant that appealed to him. Gertrude met him occasionally bringing home his spoils, and he would stop and explain to her what it was about them that he found paintable.

November of the following year confirmed a hope that had been disappointed in the past. This time Louise Trentham really was coming home for a long overdue visit and could safely be expected in time for Christmas. Her husband had to remain in Delhi, where he was now an ADC, but Louise was setting off on the long journey to the coast with her small son Harry, and his native ayah. Unable to wait for them to arrive at Providence, Sir Edward went to meet them off the ship at Tilbury, and brought them home the day before Christmas Eve. He was still getting accustomed to the joy of seeing his daughter again, and his eyes filled with tears at the sight of Louise and her mother embracing.

'Dearest child . . . you're a *wraith*,' Lady Hester murmured brokenly, when they could stand and gaze at each other. 'It's that damnable climate, I suppose.'

'It's the damnable clothes we insist on wearing! If only we had the sense to adopt the beautiful cool saris the native women wear!' The climate had aged her daughter as well as made her gauntly thin; her skin seemed almost transparent now, stretched tightly over the sharpened bones of her face, and the Indian sun had bleached the colour from her beautiful hair. She looked competent, self-possessed, and immensely elegant, even after a long and taxing journey, but worn. Lady Hester secretly mourned the changes, while her heart nearly broke with pride. Daughters such as hers served Victoria's Empire as surely as regiments of soldiers did.

A tired and puzzled small boy was put to bed, and his tired and frightened servant was allowed to sleep alongside him. The following day she still looked nervous but he, at least, had recovered completely. By the time the rest of the family sat down to breakfast Harry was already outside, being lifted on to a pony by a besotted grandfather, and Artie had become Harry's slave.

Louise turned away from the window and sat down at the table. 'I'd forgotten how green England is, even in winter . . . what a fortunate thing I didn't promise Harry snow! He holds very literally to anything that's said to him.' She poured coffee for herself, then looked across at her mother. 'I saw Gertrude Hoskins on my way downstairs – quite a change there! I didn't expect her to curtsey, as in days of yore, but she seemed remarkably self-assured.'

'You sound disapproving, dearest,' Lady Hester suggested.

'Well, surprised, let's say. I can't help wondering whether it's a good thing for the daughter of Papa's land agent to be quite so at home here – for her, I mean.'

Lady Hester looked from her daughter to William,

watching them across the table, and made up her mind to speak frankly.

'Would you object to the daughter of Daniel Maguire being here?'

'James's wife Kitty? Mama, of course not.'

'Not Kitty . . . Gertrude! She doesn't have the faintest idea of it, but Maguire was *her* father, too, not George Hoskins.'

There was complete silence in the room for a moment or two. 'That explains a lot of things,' Louise said eventually. 'Poor little Emma!'

'Why not poor Gertrude?' William put in quietly, 'although from what we now know of Maguire, she was infinitely better off with the gentleman whose name she bears.'

'I think so, too,' his mother agreed. 'The truth can't hurt Emma now, and it's time you knew, but no-one else is to be told.'

'All right . . . but what is going to become of *her*?' Louise asked.

'Mr Hoskins hopes she might still marry young Moffat at the farm, but I don't think she will. For the moment she seems content to arrange your father's life beautifully and take care of me. If some great opportunity away from here was to arise, we should have to find a way of making her accept it, but she's very staunch, and devoted to Providence.'

With the arrival of Louise and Harry, Gertrude retreated into the background; Lady Hester no longer needed her, and Louise's cool greeting had made it clear that she hoped to see as little of the companion-help as possible.

Christmas morning dawned with a cold clear brilliance that sent Gertrude out very early to lay a sprig of berries on her mother's grave in the churchyard. She stooped there, absently rubbing hoarfrost off the headstone, lost in emotions she didn't bother to analyse – sadness came into them, but so did joy at the sheer beauty of the morning. A graveyard was the best place she knew for feeling that it

73

was a privilege just to be alive. Footsteps crunched on the gravel behind her and she turned to find Louise Trentham there, wrapped in her mother's old furs but shivering in spite of them in a temperature she wasn't used to.

'Like minds! I wanted to visit Emma too, before Harry took over the day completely.' For once a smile warmed her eyes, and Gertrude felt that she had been given an unexpected gift. 'I'm sorry about your mother,' Louise added gently.

'Captain Trentham must be wishing he was here,' Gertrude murmured, 'and so must you.'

'Yes, poor man. He adores his son more than is good for him, and if we stay here very long, *my* father will complete his ruin!'

They turned back together in the direction of Providence, suddenly at ease with one another for the first time in their lives.

'England's a hundred shades of green, with bits of grey and russet here and there,' Gertrude remarked after a moment, 'but I have a picture of India in my mind that is all brown and white – baked brown land and brown-skinned people, and everything else bleached white by a cruel sun. Is that anything like it is – splendid and terrible, all at the same time?'

Louise nodded. 'That's roughly it, although there *is* colour. The Indians produce the sort of scarlet and jade and gold that defies even their sunlight. The splendour is there, but we live in a strange mixture of luxury and discomfort. What makes it terrible is the sharpness of the contrasts – such light and darkness, and such immense wealth and indescribable poverty; above all, such ease for the few people who have a place in their society, measured against the misery of millions of Indians who belong nowhere. It's a brutal, beautiful place; you either have to love it, or get out.'

'Which is it for you?'

'I've learned to love it, and my husband has, too.' She turned to glance at the girl walking beside her. 'My impression is that *you* love Providence.'

'Yes,' Gertrude said simply.

Louise stood still, giving her companion no choice but to stop as well. 'My friends and certainly my servants in India would tell you that I'm much given to advising them how to run their lives! You probably don't need my advice any more than they do, but I shall offer it all the same. *Don't* feel obliged to give your life to the Wyndhams and Providence. My mother needs help, but it doesn't have to be yours.'

Gertrude stared at her gaunt face and could see in it only understanding and an unexpected kindness. 'I think that what you're really saying is: don't get too attached to a house and family that aren't mine.'

'It's what Emma did,' Louise pointed out gently. 'Don't make the same mistake, Gertrude. She couldn't be happy away from Providence, but you must know that better than I do.'

'Yes, I know it, and I understand what you're saying. But I must stay for as long as Lady Hester needs me. Providence itself I may have to trust to your brother, and his wife when he takes one.'

She spoke so seriously that Louise couldn't smile at the idea. Instead, she nodded and then changed the subject by pointing at Gertrude's feet as they walked on together. 'I envy your dear little buttoned boots!'

They looked at each other and grinned; the black boots of childhood were dead and buried at last.

'Mr Lucas in the village made them for me. Three months' wages, but worth every penny,' Gertrude confessed.

They parted company across the moat, but she had the extraordinary idea that they parted friends.

That Christmas was memorable, and after it the rest of the visit flew. When the time came for departure the whole household seemed to be plunged in grief, and Harry disgraced very small manhood by weeping bitterly. The day was saved by Artie, who thrust into his hands at the crucial moment a carved wooden figure of Hercules, Harry's favourite pony. It could only be recognized as such with the eye of love because Artie was no great craftsman, but Harry's heart told him the value of the gift. The Squire was quiet when he returned alone from Tilbury, and even hunting couldn't comfort him.

There was only the coming of spring to look forward to. One day on a walk to the school-house to visit Sarah Simpkin who was ill, Gertrude passed William leaning over a stile, watching Mr Moffat's ploughmen at work. The leader and the most experienced horses would 'cut out' each field in turn, leaving the other teams to plough the straightforward ground in between. The ribs of turned brown earth ran uphill to meet a pale blue winter sky, and the only sounds were the jingle of the harness, the loud noise the horses made blowing through their noses, and the shrill cries of the starlings that flocked behind the plough. William seemed absorbed in the scene, and Gertrude intended to leave him undisturbed, but he turned to smile at her and lift his old tweed hat.

'Come and watch, Gertrude. I know we shall have to put up with steam-ploughing before long, but I hope the old ways die *last* at Haywood's End.'

She watched as she'd been told, but felt obliged to argue with him as she had once before.

'Haywood's End's no different from anywhere else. My father says more and more men are leaving the land. None of the young ones want to learn the secrets that Jem Martin over there knows.'

'Yes, and what are they leaving for? A worse drudgery by far in some noisome stinking factory than their fathers ever knew here.'

'Perhaps, but the drudgery pays better and they can learn things in towns – there are classes for them to attend, and reading rooms. What is there for them here, except an evening in the alehouse instead of in their own overcrowded cottages?'

He couldn't deny the truth of it, but still looked regretful. 'I know that some changes are long overdue, and that they'll come whether I like them or not. Others not so necessary

76

are on the way as well. Not only steam ploughs but motor-cars are about to confront us. *They* horrify my father, because they frighten the horses. Fortunately he's managed to convince himself they're a rich man's craze that we needn't take seriously.'

Gertrude smiled, then lifted her hand in a little gesture of farewell, and went on her way to Sarah. She hoped the Squire was right about motor-cars – they covered the hedges with white dust and tainted the air.

As things worked out, he was proved wrong, but in the way that life has of arranging itself, he didn't live long enough to know it. He came home from a week's visit to Leicestershire complaining of a heavy cold. It hadn't stopped him riding for hours in the sleety rain of a cold March day, but it was severe enough to turn into pneumonia. Before March was out he was dead, and William had become the new master of Providence.

CHAPTER SIX

The recently invented international telegraph allowed James and Louise to be told quickly of their father's death, but there was no chance of either of them being able to return in time for his funeral. The estate workers carried his coffin to the churchyard, and Gertrude walked with George Hoskins in the procession of servants that followed his widow and his heir. Lady Hester was veiled and hidden from the kind, curious eyes of the village people, but William – a white-faced stranger to Gertrude in the formality of a black frock-coat – had to endure the ordeal of being watched and measured. Countrymen like Matthew Harris and John Biddle accepted the Squire's death with a kind of biblical simplicity . . . 'his time had come . . . his thread was broken' . . . but the tenant farmers, labourers, and their wives, having paid their respects to a man they'd reckoned a proper Squire, couldn't help but think about the future. The old order had passed away with Sir Edward, and they hadn't much faith in William.

They were wrong; he did more than even his mother expected – took his place uncomplainingly on the school board, sat on the Poor Law Committee, and forced himself to canvass for a seat on the newly-formed county council. Not so long since, like every other landowner, as a Justice of the Peace he would have attended the Quarter Sessions in Warwick and helped to run the administrative and judicial affairs of the neighbourhood. He would have had much to say in the selection of the local parliamentary candidate, even if he didn't choose to go to Westminster himself, voted there by his tenants. Now, things were different: there were special committees to select candidates for the House of

Commons, and the landowners had to offer themselves for election to the county council if they wanted a hand in running local affairs. Some of William's neighbours refused to canvass for rights and responsibilities that had once been theirs automatically. Lady Hester was surprised into asking him if he relished speaking at meetings and persuading people to vote for him.

'Relish it? I hate the whole boring ridiculous business. But *someone* must speak for the countryman. England is being run now by and for the industrialists; if *they* listen to anyone, it's to the great urban masses who toil for them. The only cries we hear are for the sanctity of Free Trade and the necessity of cheap imported food. The men who work the land don't matter.'

She nodded, remembering more clearly than he did a past when things had been organized differently. 'Before you were even born Lord Beaconsfield – Mr Disraeli he was then, of course – spoke of two nations: the rich and the poor. Perhaps he might as easily have been talking of the towns and the countryside.'

William smiled at her. 'I met one of the new breed of industrialists the other day, a man called Arthur Thornley – short and broad, with eyes like black shoe-buttons and a truly excruciating taste in clothes: the very portrait of a selfmade man! But according to George Hoskins, he's not to be despised. In the space of twenty years he's made himself the biggest manufacturer of agricultural machinery in Birmingham, or anywhere else for all I know.'

'How does Mr Hoskins come to know such a man?'

'We need to buy his machinery, apparently, because another farm has just had to be taken in hand. Jim Willis has finally admitted defeat and decided to join his son in Australia. Moffat says he can run it himself, but only if he gets a mechanical driller and one of Thornley's combined reaping and binding machines.'

'Well, at least he sounds too busy to be the sort of townsman your father disliked so much. Industrialists were tolerable as long as they stayed where they belonged – in their own towns!'

William thought those words summed up his father's simple philosophy, that everyone should keep to their proper station. The philosophy was an agreeable one if you happened to have been born Sir Edward Wyndham; less so if you were Jim Willis trying to make a living out of a hundred acres, or Arthur Thornley with only native wit to earn yourself a place in the world.

'I don't think Thornley would bother about setting himself up as a country gentleman; he's too proud of Birmingham. Without intending to, I said something about it he considered disparaging and got trounced by a man who knows its history backwards – Matthew Boulton, James Watt, the Lunar Club and all!'

'The *what* club?'

'Lunar. I don't think it exists now, but in Boulton's time it was in its heyday – a society of very accomplished men who met only on nights of the full moon, so that they could see to drive home afterwards.'

William discovered that he'd been wrong in thinking that Arthur Thornley had no interest in the countryside except as a market for his machines. One morning, returning from the village through the home farm stack-yard, he met Thornley again, deep in conversation with his agent and old Sid Moffat. The two of them naturally touched their hats, but the visitor from Birmingham swept off his bowler in an exaggerated gesture that managed to be obsequious and mocking at the same time.

'You met Mr Thornley in Birmingham, sir,' George Hoskins put in quickly.

'So I did. What brings you here, Mr Thornley?'

'Curiosity, you might say, Sir William. What Arthur Thornley doesn't know about, interests him; I know all about the running of factories in towns, but I need to know how the countryside gets run. And I wouldn't mind taking a look at that mansion of yours – Mr Hoskins tells me it's been standing for a goodish while.'

'Four hundred years or so. We think of it as a manor house, by the way, not a mansion.'

'Well, there you are, you see . . . that's the sort of fine distinction a man like me doesn't know about.'

George Hoskins was of the opinion that his employer didn't like Mr Thornley. William reckoned that he was overdoing the role of ignorant townee; he also felt strangely reluctant to introduce *this* visitor to Providence. Thornley would see it either as a relic that was antiquated and shabby, or as a symbol of a past that wasn't dying fast enough.

'Come and look at Providence, by all means,' he agreed, having failed to find a courteous way of refusing an invitation. Mr Thornley bowed again, and the two of them set off for the house, William considerately adjusting his stride to the short, piston legs of his visitor.

'Business is good, I trust,' he said politely.

'Booming . . . can't keep pace with it; fast as we expand, we run out of space again.'

'Well, you seem to be in an enviably strong position – the more of our men your factories suck into the towns, the more we must fall back on your machines to farm the land they leave behind.'

'That's right, sir – it's called the industrial age! That's to say progress, and betterment for the people at the bottom end of the scale, who haven't had much of a look-in up till now.'

William had the feeling that he could easily dislike Arthur Thornley very much; people who dealt plausibly in half-truths were dangerous, and never more so than when they believed their own distortions. *This* man was too intelligent to deceive himself, which made it all the easier for him to deceive other people. 'You take a simplistic view of progress,' William said. 'I'll make you argue it one day. Meanwhile, here's the back entrance to the stable-yard.'

His guest showed no interest in the horses that Hodges and Artie were bringing back from exercise; indeed, he looked wary of them and seemed relieved to be out of the yard and walking across the gravel to the bridge.

'Welcome to Providence,' William said with cool formality.

The man beside him didn't reply, because his attention was riveted on the house that lay sleeping in the morning sun. The light of high summer turned the stone walls to pale gold above the blue water of the moat; its twisted chimneys glowed rose-red, and its battlements fretted the sky. Thornley's face, square and pudgy and powerful under a thatch of grizzled hair, gave nothing away. One of the things he prided himself on was that the world was never made a present of his thoughts.

'I see what you mean now,' he muttered eventually. 'It's not a mansion, but I dare say you're proud of it all the same.'

'Yes, I'm proud,' William agreed. 'Won't you come inside?'

In the Great Hall he found his mother talking to the rector's sister. 'Mama, Maud . . . may I present Mr Thornley from Birmingham?' He turned to his guest. 'The Lady Hester Wyndham and Miss Roberts.'

This time there was no mockery in Mr Thornley's bow. His gaze passed over an odd-looking woman in a gown that was ten years out of date, and fixed itself on the older lady. She was dressed in black, with white lace at her throat. He had the feeling – as Gertrude had long before him – that she suited what lay all around her. She made him feel that *he* didn't suit it at all, although he didn't suspect her of trying to make him feel all feet and hands.

'Not intruding, ma'am, I hope,' he said with a diffidence that would have astonished his workmen. 'Sir William suggested taking a look, seeing that I was interested.'

'Not intruding at all,' she agreed smilingly. He saw the humour in her face, but didn't know that Lady Hester was wondering what Mr Thornley's check suit looked like to someone who didn't have the advantage of being half-blind!

He was at a loss what to say next – so rare a situation to find himself in that he spoke almost at random, sounding critical when he didn't intend to.

'All right in here *now*, but cold in the winter, I dare say
. . . dark, too.'

Maud Roberts thought she heard a challenge which she
resented on behalf of her hostess.

'Do the citizens of Birmingham all live in houses that are
not only beautiful but warm and well-lit as well, Mr
Thornley? We had supposed *not*, from what we hear.'

'No doubt you hear they live like animals in hovels. I
can't speak for other employers, but *my* workpeople are
paid wages that enable them to live decently. What's more,
thanks to a man called Joseph Chamberlain, they've got the
grandest town hall in all England, not to mention a museum
and art gallery, paved roads, street lighting, and proper
sanitation.'

Lady Hester saw the joyous light of battle in Maud's eye
and judged it prudent to intervene. 'My son told me you
were proud of Birmingham,' she said gently.

'That's right, ma'am, I am; come and take a look for
yourselves, just as I'm taking a look at what *you've* got.'

William offered to continue the inspection, and ushered
his guest to the door. Maud grinned at her friend. 'I have
the feeling that I've just been flattened by one of Mr
Thornley's reapers! I shall go and call on him in beautiful
Birmingham one day and make him introduce me to his
happy workpeople!'

The machines that George Hoskins and Sid Moffat wanted
were bought, and men accustomed to simpler tools were
taught to use them. They enabled the land to be worked
with fewer labourers, but couldn't reverse the slow per-
sistent decline in income from the estate. When Michaelmas
quarter day came and the reckoning that marked the end of
the farmer's year, William examined the depressing figures
and listened to his agent trying to explain why the revenues
were even lower than he'd expected.

'It's like this, sir . . . two thousand acres of good
land ought to mean an income of something like £2,000 a
year – enough and more to keep Providence going; but

we're nowhere near that figure. Three of the farms haven't even managed to pay their way this year. If we insist on taking the full rents, the men's families will go hungry.'

'Then of course we lower the rents,' William said sharply. 'No-one can be allowed to starve at Haywood's End.'

George Hoskins sighed over the figures in front of him. 'Yes, but it's not as easy as that . . . things want doing, you see. Half a dozen cottages need repair, there's any amount of hedging and ditching that's been neglected for years, and even this house needs re-tiling – and that doesn't take account of the fact that the servants complain it's old-fashioned and hard work to run.'

'The house is as it's *always* been,' William pointed out. 'Why should they complain now?' He looked genuinely puzzled, and irritated by an extra complication that seemed unreasonable. He was just like the old Squire at times, Mr Hoskins reflected.

'I can only tell you what the Smithers tell *me*, and what Gertrude hears in the servants' room. They can find work in houses that *aren't* old-fashioned – places with gas or even electric light, modern ovens, and contraptions for heating water so that maids don't have to carry heavy cans up flight after flight of stairs.' His employer's face looked so miserable that it was a temptation to let him off the rest, but he told himself that they were there to confront their problems. 'Servants elsewhere don't just have an easier life – they get paid more as well, so that they won't want to go and work in factories.'

'These other employers . . . how do they manage so much better than we do? Why aren't *their* houses falling down, and their servants rebellious?'

'They're mostly men who own big manufactories and look around for an estate to spend their money on. Old-time landowners are in the same boat as you, sir, unless their estates are being worked for coal or iron . . . that's what keeps *them* rich, not farming.'

William smiled suddenly, with a sweetness that was more

reminiscent of his mother than Edward Wyndham. 'Don't let's repine because we have no coal . . . we want to preserve Providence not disembowel it! Is the situation gloomy or hopeless? Is there *anything* we can do?'

There were two possible suggestions to be made, but George Hoskins balked at one of them – it wasn't for him to tell the Squire to find himself a rich wife. 'The only thing as I see it is to do what others have done: ask the bank for a mortgage on the land till things get better.'

William was silent for a while. At last he gave a little nod. 'It's unpleasant, but better than having to sell, which I gather from *The Times* is not uncommon these days. Let us try the bank, by all means, Mr Hoskins.'

A reminiscent smile lit the land agent's face for a moment. 'It's called getting over rough ground – that's what your father would have said!'

If the same thought occurred to both of them, that Sir Edward's years of extravagance had helped to bring them to the present situation, neither of them would have dreamed of saying so.

While William grappled with the problems of his inheritance, Gertrude noticed with anxiety that Lady Hester seemed to be growing increasingly frail. Her husband's death on top of the absence of two of her children had left her disinclined for the old social life of the neighbourhood. She was a widow and ought by now to have been a dowager, she said wistfully; it was time to follow her inclination and live quietly at Providence. She still interested herself in the affairs of Haywood's End, but at a distance. More and more often, Gertrude took her place when it came to visiting the sick, or presenting a needed gift of blankets or clothes for some small new arrival in the community. She became familiar with the inside of the cottages at last, and was gradually accepted by women who had been on the watch for the smallest sign of triumph or condescension in Emma Hoskins's daughter. Finding none, they saw no reason not to welcome her, and explain that this or that small improvement, if Mr Hoskins could see his way to it, would make their lives slightly easier.

She was grateful to be able to talk to her father in the estate office; the less she visited him at the farmhouse, the less chance there was of bumping into Sid Moffat. But one morning, when she was taking the long way back from the village by the path that skirted Hay Wood, he caught up with her. The expression on his face told her that the meeting wasn't accidental; he'd been watching for just this chance.

'Never see you these days,' he began bluntly. 'Moffats not good enough for you now that you've got so thick with the people at the big house?'

'Don't be silly, Sid; you know I work there,' she pointed out. 'Lady Hester isn't very well, and I don't have much free time to go visiting, that's all.'

''Tisn't quite all: you have time off like everybody else, but you choose to stay away. I'm twenty-eight, Gertrude . . . I've got to know whether I'm to have you or not.'

His eyes travelled over her, and she was uncomfortably aware of the silence and emptiness of the wood behind them. He was gentler-mannered than most of the farmers' sons, and he was her childhood friend, but even so . . . She pulled her shawl closer round her and tried to sound friendly but firm.

'I told you long ago . . . I've no mind to be married. Women can *choose* nowadays – look at Miss Roberts.'

'You're *nothing* like Maud Roberts,' he shouted, suddenly angry with her. 'You look just as a maid should who's ripe to be married.'

She shook her head but made the mistake of smiling at him.

'Don't laugh at me . . . God Almighty, I'll *prove* it to you.' His arms suddenly dragged her against his hard body and, although she tried to struggle, his mouth and hands made a combined onslaught that seemed to be devouring her. He was beyond remembering that this was George Hoskins's daughter . . . she was the girl he'd always reckoned would be his. Gertrude fought, but knew in some cold clear corner of her mind that resistance only excited him still more. It might easily have ended with him carrying her into the dimness of the wood, but the sharp sound of dogs barking round them forced him to lift his head. William Wyndham was running along the path towards them.

'Thought you m . . . might be unwell . . . n . . . needing help,' he panted, above the noise the spaniels were making.

Gertrude, trembling and dishevelled, found it hard to say anything at all, but Sid's flushed face warned her that he was about to forget that he owed his home and his livelihood to the man in front of him.

'No . . . no help needed, sir . . . Sid was just . . . just saying goodbye.' It sounded lame to the point of imbecility, but it was the best she could do.

'I was doing nothing of the kind,' roared Sid, infuriated by this way of describing his love-making. 'But I'll say it now, Gertrude.' He stared at her for a moment more, his expression a mixture of anger, longing and regret, and then strode off in the direction of his home.

She bent down to stroke one of the dogs. Her hands were trembling, and she felt both embarrassed and sad. Sid had been her only friend and, as such, she'd valued him. Now, he was someone else who reckoned Gertrude Hoskins was too set-up for her own good. She'd have liked to make him understand what Lady Hester and Providence meant to her.

'Does Moffat make a habit of bothering you like that?' William's voice broke through her muddled thoughts and the way he said the words 'like that' showed her the measure of his distaste for the scene he'd just interrupted. He lived in a passionless world of his own; of course he would be disgusted by the sight of a man and woman locked together. She wondered why he'd forced himself not to run the other way.

'He meant no harm,' she murmured with difficulty. 'The idea got stuck in his head a long time ago that he would like to marry me.'

'Do *you* have it in mind to marry him?'

87

'No, although it's what my father wants as well; he thinks I belong to the Moffats' farmhouse.'

William looked at her – tall, slender and, despite her ruffled hair and lingering air of agitation, wrapped in some indefinable dignity and grace.

'You belong at Providence,' he said slowly.

'For as long as her ladyship needs me,' she agreed.

He nodded as if it settled matters. 'Come . . . I shall take you home.'

He held out his arm and there was nothing for it but to put hers into it. They'd walked for a moment or two in this way, before she recognized that what was welling up inside her was a dreadful, irresistible need to laugh. She swallowed, coughed, breathed deeply – in vain . . . laughter insisted on being not only seen but heard. It was necessary to stand still because she was unable to walk for the mirth that consumed her. She struggled to grow calm again and eventually smeared the tears of laughter from her cheeks.

'Am I as funny as all that?' he asked stiffly.

'N . . . not you . . . *us*!' She tried to explain. 'It was the s . . . stately way we were walking through the park – just like an elderly couple going in to dinner!'

A frowning expression she couldn't read settled on his face, then it cleared and he said astonishingly, 'A couple . . . that's just what we *ought* to be. You had much better marry *me*, Gertrude.'

She could only imagine that he was making fun of her by way of revenge for her laughter; anger made her forget that he was never unkind.

'I hadn't *better* marry anybody,' she said fiercely.

His smile instantly begged pardon. 'Did that sound impossibly lord-of-the-manorish? It wasn't meant to, Gertrude. What I *should* have said was this: I and my mother, and Providence itself all need you. Could you think of it *that* way?'

She realized she could, easily enough, because in a way it was true, but there were objections all the same.

'My father . . .' she stopped abruptly, then made up her

mind to go on. 'I was going to say my father would be against it, and you'd think I was talking about George Hoskins. So I am because I still think of him as my father, but you'll have to know the truth. My real father is Kitty's father – Daniel Maguire. I'd rather be Hoskins any day.' She said it with a glint in her eye that dared him to disagree.

'Of course you would,' William agreed simply. 'Thank you for telling me, Gertrude. In fact my mother mentioned it in confidence when my sister was here, but she didn't realize you knew. It must have been a . . . painful situation for you – Maguire's other daughter here while you were a . . . a . . .'

'. . . servant at Providence,' she finished for him bluntly. 'I didn't take to her, nor she to me; but perhaps that was to be expected.' She put the subject of her half-sister aside, and fixed her eyes on him. 'I don't suppose you were serious about us marrying; but it isn't a thing you ought to make jokes about.'

He smiled in spite of himself – might have remarked, as James had done once along ago, that she sounded like her governess mother – but said solemnly, 'I never make jokes, Gertrude. I *was* serious.'

'Well, my father wouldn't approve, and nor would Lady Hester, let alone anybody else.'

William looked down his long Wyndham nose. 'I don't find myself much interested in what anybody else thinks. I can't speak for Mr Hoskins, but I believe my mother *would* be pleased. She is very attached to you.'

It was time to get to the heart of the matter, but fearing that she would get nothing but a Wyndham snub for her pains, she shouted at him, 'Providence needs more help than I can give – it needs money!'

'I know, and I'm supposed to find a rich tradesman's daughter. Well, the truth is that if Providence doesn't frighten *them*, they frighten *me*.'

She thought it was probably true . . . as true as her own determination not to marry when it seemed likely that poor Sid would be the only man to offer for her. She knew that he wouldn't do – to that extent Louise had been right in warning her not to make Providence her life, because it would spoil her for a place she *was* entitled to. But marriage to William Wyndham? She tried to think calmly about it. Lady Hester and Providence . . . she'd be able to take care of them better as his wife; there was *that* to be said for it. But against it was William himself – such a kind but hopeless sort of man. All the more reason, then, to take him in hand, said the other voice in this dialogue she was listening to; and what about the idea of going one better than Kitty Maguire and becoming Lady Wyndham? Gertrude prayed that it wasn't the most seductive idea of all; if it was, God would surely punish her.

The indecision in her face seemed to make William unusually forceful. 'I think you *ought* to marry me, Gertrude,' he said firmly.

'I think perhaps I ought to, too,' she agreed at last.

He kissed her cheek, then tucked her arm in his again.

'*Now*, we'll go home,' he said, 'as a couple if the idea doesn't reduce you to helpless mirth once more!'

She stared at him doubtfully, but found herself reassured. His mouth was serious but he had James's trick, after all, of smiling with his eyes.

CHAPTER SEVEN

The news that the new Squire was to marry George Hoskins's daughter sent shock waves humming not only round Haywood's End but the entire neighbourhood. Opinion seemed to be fairly evenly divided as to which of them stood to gain by the arrangement: on the whole, the gentry inclined to the view that Lady Hester's companion was doing well for herself, while the village held to it that it was William who was doing better than they'd expected.

The Moffat family were torn between fear of giving offence to the Squire and resentment that young Sid had been spurned. The outdoor men at Providence like Hodges, the coachman, congratulated her shyly, and although John Biddle tried hard to sound disapproving – 'Won't do to call you young Gertrude any more – it'll have to be ma'am from now on' – she had the feeling he didn't really mind because he knew she loved Providence almost as much as he did. The indoor servants looked knowing about her betrothal, but it was left to the Smithers to be openly hostile.

'Not *quite* what we're used to,' Mrs Smithers pointed out with smiling venom. 'But then, having to be called cook-housekeeper isn't what I'm used to either. In a house like Warwick Castle I'd have a cook under me. Still, if Providence isn't grand, at least I have a free hand here. Smithers and I can't be doing with interference, which is something her ladyship *well* understands.' The threat was thinly veiled but deliberate. They both knew that Gertrude must accept it for as long as Lady Hester still ran the household. If she ever handed over the reins, it would be war to the knife, and they both knew that, too.

The first reading of the banns took place the following

Sunday, to a larger congregation than usual – brought there, Gertrude suspected, by curiosity to see whether or not William had thought better of the idea. She took this theory to Maud Roberts at the rectory and found her practising in the drive on her new safety bicycle. For this perilous but highly enjoyable exercise Maud was got up in her gardening breeches, and Gertrude could see why the more conventional ladies of the neighbourhood were in two minds about Miss Roberts.

'When I walk through the village now I feel like the poor freak woman at Warwick Fair,' she remarked, torn between a longing to talk about her own momentous affairs and a strong desire to try her luck on the bicycle.

'What did you expect? The women don't have much to break the monotony of their lives. Let the poor things have the pleasure of asking each other "if they ever did" several times a day; they'll soon get used to the idea. Have *you*, by the way . . . got used to it?'

Gertrude weighed the question. 'More or less, but my father hasn't. He thinks people should stay where God puts them – only in my case God didn't seem able to make the matter clear.'

'From which,' said Maud thoughtfully, 'I gather you now know Emma's sad story. High time, too; in my view you should have been told long ago.' She relapsed into silence for a moment, watching the face of the girl leaning against the gate beside her. 'Were you worried about Lady Hester's reaction? You needn't have been – I'm quite sure she's delighted to have you as a daughter-in-law.'

Gertrude's frown gave way to a smile that lit her face. 'I seem to think she *is*. She'd have been careful not to hurt my feelings, of course, but if she wasn't happy about it there was no need to kiss me so kindly. I'm to put a penny in the poor-box every time I forget to call her Mama instead of Milady! Still, it's given the tabbies at Barham and Endlicott something to get their sharp little teeth into. I should hate them to have the pleasure of snubbing Lady Hester because of me.'

'They won't. She's an earl's daughter and a Wyndham, not the relict of some twopenny-halfpenny knight! They'll know better than not to receive you *both*, but even if they didn't, it wouldn't disturb Lady Hester . . . she'd leave the correct number of cards and drive away again, unconcerned.' Maud hesitated a moment, then raised a subject she found more interesting. 'I seem to remember you saying once that you wanted to steer clear of marriage. William seems to have managed to make you change your mind.'

'Yes, but not because I want to scramble out of the servants' hall, though that's what dear Mrs Smithers thinks! Maud, I need to belong somewhere. At Providence with Lady Hester to look after, I think I *do*. She needs me, and I'm not sure William doesn't need me, too.'

If it wasn't the accepted reason for marrying, Maud didn't say so, but she was relieved when Gertrude suddenly smiled at her.

'Now can I try to ride your bicycle?'

She and William were married on a soft grey day at the end of November. The ceremony was supposed to be private, but the parish church was full of people curious to see what the new Lady Wyndham looked like. George Hoskins thought she looked beautiful. It wasn't a word his mind was used to applying to people – a new foal was beautiful, or the sight of Hay Wood turning to autumn gold – but Gertrude this morning had to be included in the list of things that gave him quiet joy to look at. If he'd canvassed anyone else's opinion, girls like Daisy James might have said they scarcely recognized the Gertie Hoskins they'd chased to school in this tall slender young woman dressed in pale mauve, with a matching wide-brimmed hat of mauve velour.

Hubert Roberts conducted the marriage service with his usual warmth that seemed to say he positively enjoyed helping to join couples in matrimony, but Gertrude heard his voice as from a long way away. William's quiet responses became fainter still, so great was the distance at which she seemed to be standing from him, watching this ceremony and a girl in mauve who was a stranger to her . . . 'with my body I thee worship . . .' it was a lie, and surely God in Heaven would know? Her chaotic thoughts plunged back in time, like a frightened horse . . . she remembered James Wyndham staring at her in a sunlit courtyard garden, felt Sid Moffat's mouth on hers insisting that she belonged to *him* . . . what was she doing, marrying William Wyndham? The rector's voice prompted her again and she was dragged back from the edge of panic. Her mind steadied under the kindness in his eyes and she was able to remember her name . . . 'I, Gertrude Emma, take thee, William Henry . . .'

They gave no wedding celebration afterwards, because mourning was still being observed for Sir Edward, and made no wedding journey. In fact, nothing seemed to change at all except that she went home to the Great Hall and the dining-room instead of the servants' quarters, and her bedroom was now in the family wing of the house, alongside William's. Their wedding evening was spent quietly with Lady Hester . . . Gertrude sewing, William beginning to read to them from *Bleak House*, but she made little sense of Mr Dickens's great description of a London particular – scarcely heard it in fact, being increasingly concerned with the fog of images in her mind about the night that lay ahead. Anticipation was surely worse than any reality could be, and her smile was brilliant with relief when her mother-in-law suggested calmly that it was time to retire. She helped Lady Hester upstairs, then went thankfully to her own bedroom.

Two hours later she was still undisturbed; her candle had guttered to the point where it must be blown out and it was time to face the truth that she was going to be left to sleep alone. She knew William had come upstairs because she'd heard the uneven floorboards creaking in the room next door as he walked across them, but she was not to be a wife, and the morning's ceremony had been a sham. Her mind skimmed away from the unbearable thought that Kitty's wedding night with James hadn't been like this. She didn't know why William had married her, unless it was simply to keep her at Providence for the sake of Lady Hester. If that *was* the case, she couldn't fairly complain. She'd told Maud Roberts earnestly enough that it was the reason she was marrying *him*. The nervous anticipation of the past few hours went out like her candle, in a smouldering mess of resentment tinged with relief and bitter amusement . . . it was a pity she wouldn't be able to tell Maud that there was nothing to avoid in getting married after all!

'Gertrude dear,' said Lady Hester next day, 'can you think of any reason why a tiresomely dim-sighted, feeble old lady shouldn't allow a young, vigorous daughter-in-law to run her own household? I can't. In fact, perhaps I should move out altogether . . .'

'. . . into the lodge cottage that's quietly falling to pieces?' Gertrude suggested helpfully. 'Or what about that mouldering ruin on the edge of Hay Wood? I wasn't sure whether to mention it or not.' She managed to look serious until she caught her mother-in-law's eye; both of them began to smile, and then to shake with helpless laughter. When she finally wiped her streaming eyes she felt cheerful again. Life was odd, but she belonged at Providence; only a girl who was ungrateful to the point of madness wouldn't find that enough to make life bearable.

'If you're serious about me taking over the household – which I suspect you of suggesting simply because you want to make me feel necessary! – you must be prepared for Mr and Mrs Smithers to walk out,' she said after a moment or two.

'My dear, why should they do such a thing? They *like* being here . . . they've often told me so.'

'Well, I think you'll find they won't like it for much longer.'

Lady Hester couldn't help but notice that her announcement of the change of authority was received in silence, but she had convinced herself that all was well by the time the new mistress summoned up the courage to ask to go through the account books and the storerooms. Mrs Smithers's heavy scarlet face and heavy heaving bosom were equally intimidating. Gertrude did her best to look unconcerned.

'May I ask why . . . *madam*? Lady Hester never saw fit to do anything so demeaning.'

'Lady Hester has been unwell.' The temptation was great to say that she'd thought better of the idea, but if she wavered now, she knew she was lost. 'I don't consider *any* of the duties of a mistress demeaning.'

'*Mistress* . . . fine talk from a servant like the rest of us, and a bastard at that! – someone else's if not the old Squire's,' she interpolated hurriedly, seeing the flash of anger in Gertrude's eyes. 'Well, I shan't stay here to be insulted by the likes of *you*, miss. Smithers and I will go to the sort of house we're used to. We'll go *now*, what's more, as soon as we've been paid what's due to us till the end of the year.'

'You'll be paid what is due up to today, or wait while I make a thorough check of the account books.'

A mixture of hatred and alarm struggled violently inside Mrs Smithers's bosom, but finally she listened to the clearer message of alarm. 'The pittance we get here isn't worth waiting for . . . we'll go now.' She charged out of the room like a maddened elephant, leaving Gertrude trembling and feeling besmirched by malice. She tried to make sense of the account book in her shaking hand, but it was a mess of blotches and crossings-out that defied understanding. The housekeeper hadn't intended that anyone should be able to check the supplies she'd ordered, or the use she'd made of them.

Gertrude didn't know whether to be glad or sorry that William had ridden over to Barham for the morning. By the time he returned Hodges had driven the Smithers to Warwick in the gig, and she had to confess that Providence was without a butler or a cook-housekeeper. The expression on his face wasn't hard to read: this sort of thing hadn't happened under his mother's control, and he feared she'd been high-handed.

'A little rash wasn't it, my dear? Now we are short of

staff. And what about some parting gift for the Smithers? They'd been here for years.'

'They'd also been stealing from you for years . . . my father knows that as well as I do. I paid them what was due to them, and they knew *that* was more than they deserved.'

He looked at her, half-rueful, half-amused. 'You're a redoubtable young woman, Lady Wyndham! I've been frightened of the pair of them for years.'

'So have I! That's partly why I'm so relieved to see the back of them. Now, with your approval, I propose to take over the housekeeping myself. Emmie in the kitchen can be promoted to cook . . . she's been doing most of the work anyway. For the winter at least, with little entertaining to be done, we can manage without a butler; by the spring, young Jem may be experienced enough – it's time *he* was given more responsibility.'

William blinked at this decisive ordering of his household affairs. 'You're full of purposefulness this morning, my dear . . . have you any other suggestions to hurl at me?'

Gertrude took a deep breath. 'Only one more! Your father's hunters, William – they're eating their heads off in the stables, for no other reason than to give Hodges and Artie the job of exercising them. Now that you never hunt yourself, don't you think we should get rid of them?'

'But . . . but Hodges would *hate* having no hunters in the stables.'

Gertrude couldn't decide whether to laugh or weep; in the end she just managed not to shout at him. 'We can't run Providence to keep Hodges happy. William, we live on borrowed money as it is . . . don't you see that we must *economize*? We've got to *save* Providence, not let it slide to ruin.' She was agitated enough now to hurl the other truth at him – that there was no point in saving Providence if there was never going to be anyone to hand it on to – but his pale, set face prevented her; she must let him get used to the present hardships first before he had to exert himself to be a husband. It seemed a long moment before he gave a little shrug that accepted but disapproved of what she'd said. 'Very well,' he agreed coolly, 'I'll speak to Hodges,' and went out of the room.

If Hodges regretted seeing the hunters sold, he was too sensible a man not to know that, like the old Squire, their time had come. One of the maids, truculent Annie, followed the Smithers to Warwick, saying that she could better herself in a house that didn't break her back with its old-fashioned ways. After she'd gone the rest of the staff settled down again. Gertrude consoled herself with the idea that they seeemed happier than before, and the household wastefulness was certainly much less.

As winter closed in upon them, confining them to the house and park and Haywood's End, Lady Hester went serenely through the days, content with her own quiet thoughts if no-one came to visit her, and happy to spend the evenings by the fire in the Great Hall with her daughter-in-law, while William read to them, or played the instrument in the drawing-room next door. When Gertrude's eyes grew tired with sewing, she would listen to William and watch the firelight gleaming on polished wood, or weave stories of her own about the figures in the huge tapestry that covered one wall. It showed a medieval castle on a hill and, with charming indifference to the seasons, a hunt in full cry over meadows bright with summer flowers.

The winter was hard, with snow covering the park for several weeks, but on a morning in early March, the day before her twenty-first birthday, William arrived at the breakfast table dressed in formal clothes.

'Hodges says the roads are clear at last, my dear, so I can attend the council meetings in Warwick. There's enough to keep me busy there for a couple of days but I hope to be back tomorrow evening. Shall you be able to manage with Biddle and Jem while we're gone?'

'Of course . . . Artie can take the gig to the village if we should need anything.'

She watched him drive away with Hodges, and a moment later was overcome by a wave of loneliness and depression that threatened to drown her. It was absurd, at least, to feel lonely when Lady Hester was in her room upstairs, and Emmie bustled cheerfully about her kitchen while Ethel hummed over the task of polishing the stairs. But on a sullenly overcast morning Providence seemed too large and shadowy . . . too heavy with old griefs that made it indifferent to *her* sorrow – that she was nearly twenty-one and, among other slights, her husband hadn't bothered to remember the fact. The only remedy was work . . . she would work until she was too tired not to sleep at night, uncaring whether she slept alone or not.

She was in the dining-room halfway through the morning, standing on a chair to darn a worn curtain, when the clatter of hooves and wheels sounded on the gravel. The noise brought Ethel to the doorway.

'Ma'am . . . there's a carriage jest arrived . . . 'tis this minute gone through to the stable-yard.'

William must have returned; were the roads not clear after all, or had he suddenly felt unwell? She ran out across the courtyard garden, and over the bridge, heedless of the fact that she had no shawl and that the wind cut knife-like through the stuff of her dress. She reached the yard in time to see a man who wasn't William talking to Biddle, while Artie stood happily whispering in the ears of the steaming horses. It was more than three years since she'd seen *this* man at Providence with his new wife. Her first impression was that James Wyndham had aged, grown broader and more completely sure of being a very successful man.

'Gertrude, my dear . . . nice as it is to be welcomed in such a fashion, you shouldn't be out here in this wind.' He was still more easily charming than his brother, she noticed, and still had the trick of smiling with his eyes; she wondered if he was trying to make up his mind how to behave to a sister-in-law who'd been his mother's companion.

'Welcome back . . . is your wife not with you?' She said it with as much composure as she could manage, but it was difficult when the man in front of her stared so intently.

'No, Kitty is not here . . . but let us talk indoors. Is Hodges not around to see to the horses?'

'He's with William in Warwick. Dear John Biddle will be kind enough to help Artie.'

She walked back across the bridge again with James, trying to ignore the sidelong glances that seemed to be measuring the changes in her. 'Your mother will be so happy to see you, James. Perhaps I should warn you, though, that she's frail now and somewhat blind, poor lady. I hope you can give her pleasure by staying a little while.'

'No more than a day or two, I'm afraid. Urgent business brought me to London unexpectedly and I must take the next sailing home. But I couldn't go without a glimpse of Providence and Mama . . . and, of course, my new sister-in-law! I haven't congratulated you, Gertrude.'

They were in the shadow of the long covered porch now, and sheltered from the wind. He leaned towards her and she felt the softness of his mouth and beard against her cheek as she had once before. Colour rushed into her face and when he smiled she suspected him of enjoying her embarrassment. 'On second thoughts, I shall reserve my congratulations for William! What is he doing in Warwick, by the way?'

'Attending meetings of the county council . . . he takes his duties very seriously. The weather has disrupted things so that there is a lot of business to attend to, but he expected to be home tomorrow evening.'

'Good God! – county council meetings sound the last thing in the world my brother would attend voluntarily. It's obvious that I'm sadly out of touch.' It was probably an accident that his eyes lingered on her mouth as he said the words, but she was relieved when he seemed to notice the rest of her. 'I don't object to the effect of the apron . . . it's charming! . . . but perhaps *William* should object. If my mother is frail, you're the chatelaine surely, not the house-keeper?'

'Well, I'm both, as it happens.' She walked ahead of him into the entrance hall, grateful that she had no need to be ashamed of the inside of Providence. It was shabby, certainly, but ordered, cared for, and beautiful. He'd reminded her that she was its chatelaine . . . she had only to behave as such for the brief time he was there and he would go away not knowing the effect he had on her.

'A glass of wine and a biscuit, James, while I tell your mother you're here? She is usually ready to come downstairs about this time.'

He accepted the offer with a little bow, and again she had the impression that he was both amused by her and pleasurably aware of her nervousness. The arrival of Lady Hester, overjoyed at the sight of him, helped her to feel at ease again. After the light luncheon they shared together, Gertrude excused herself on the grounds that there were housekeeping matters to be seen to. They existed well enough, but she would have invented them otherwise. She told herself that she wanted Lady Hester to have all the pleasure of her son's unexpected company. It was true, but not the whole truth. There was a need of her own, which was to avoid James as much as possible and pretend that she imagined the current of awareness that seemed to flow between them. He spoke easily and affectionately to his mother, but all the time she had the feeling he was talking silently to *her*, that contacts were being made between them that she was helpless to prevent, and wouldn't have prevented if she could. She was thankful to hear him say that he would visit old friends while his mother rested.

'Yes . . . Biddle will be longing to see you,' Lady Hester agreed lovingly, 'and don't forget Mr Hoskins, and Matthew Harris, and of course the rector and Maud and . . .'

'. . . Uncle Tom Cobley and all! Dearest Mama, all shall be remembered, I swear!' He led her upstairs to her room, and by the time he came down again Gertrude had prudently disappeared.

Dinner passed happily, and although James's gaze across the table told her that he'd noticed the change of gown into a grey silk that becomingly echoed the colour of her eyes, he seemed content to tell them about his life in America.

But the moment she dreaded came at last: tired by the excitement and exertion of so much conversation, Lady Hester finally admitted that she must retire to bed. It left the two of them alone together in a room that Gertrude had never thought of before as being anything but very large. Its shadowy corners were now lost in darkness, and there remained only the firelit space in which they sat. Desperate for something trivial to talk about, she clung to the opening gambit used by all their afternoon callers.

'It's been a long, harsh winter here . . . no doubt you still find it extremely cold for the time of year?'

'Yes, my dear Gertrude, I believe I do! . . . and thank you, as far as I know my wife and children are in excellent health. Shall we continue in this style, or talk about more important things?'

'Like . . . like Providence, you mean?'

'To begin with. Why are the Wyndhams living in such penury that *you* have to undertake the role of housekeeper? Why no Smithers in the house, and no hunters in the stables? That in itself must be making my father turn in his grave. I know my squeamish brother disapproves of hunting foxes, but even he likes to ride a decent horse occasionally.'

The subject of Providence was a lifeline. She grabbed it, confident that she had the right to speak about something she knew and loved. She could forget the weakness that invaded her every time her eyes met James's, and she might even be able to whip herself into anger with him for failing to understand their difficulties.

'I told you once before that times were hard here, but you didn't believe me – preferred to blame my father instead for being old-fashioned and outworn.' James put out his hand as if to interrupt but she shook her head, determined that he should listen. 'Farming is dying here. My father could explain the reasons to you better than I, but the result is that the income from land declines all the time. Providence is poor . . . in fact mortgaged to a bank in Birmingham. Until times improve we live as unextravagantly as we can, and I am not ashamed to be the housekeeper. What else would you like to know about the way the Wyndhams are forced to live?'

James stared at her flushed face and beautiful, candid eyes . . . she was lovely and courageous and intelligent, and she belonged to *William*! It was enough to make a man rail against Fate, except that Fate wasn't to blame for the wife a man chose for himself. The gods above must be laughing that his hopeless, incompetent brother should have had the wit to take *this* girl, when *he*, before he'd been old enough to know better, had picked plump, pretty, silly Kitty Maguire!

'I hear what you say about Providence,' he murmured, 'but just at this moment I find myself more interested in knowing about *you*. I realize I've made you angry, but I don't regret it . . . you look very beautiful when you're angry.'

Gertrude prided herself on having become competent at a number of things, but dealing with a man such as James Wyndham wasn't one of them. His whole body seemed to be speaking to hers, and she was so terrified that he might discover it by touching her, that she took refuge in anger.

'Who is talking trivialities now? I thought you were concerned to know about Providence. The truth is painful, so you would rather avoid it by paying me meaningless compliments. You *glow* with success, James . . . no doubt believe that you can win whatever you set your heart upon simply by working for it. Well, I must tell you that *we* work too, but it makes little difference to what we're able to achieve.'

'My compliment wasn't meaningless, Gertrude.' His eyes were on her face, and she suspected that he hadn't even listened to her brave little speech. He was so close to her now that she could breathe his clean male smell, and see the network of tiny wrinkles that fanned the corners of his eyes. His hand stretched out to touch her, as if it couldn't help itself; slid gently down her throat, and across her breast, making weakness spread through her like water rippling across grass. If she was to get up and leave him at all, it must be *now*, while her legs would still carry her.

'It's been a long, exciting day, James. N . . . no doubt you're tired too; you've been travelling. I shall say g . . . good night and retire.'

He stood up when she did, but although he didn't attempt to stop her leaving, his smile said she was fleeing the field of battle because she didn't dare to stay.

'I think you *should* retire, my dear Gertrude. The firelight is dangerous, is it not?'

She tried to smile, but hurried to the door like a hare seeking its form. In the safety of her own room, her heartbeat returned to normal. She undressed, washed, and brushed her hair, and adjusted her window casement as usual. Out in the darkness an owl hooted but everything else at Providence was sleeping; the night was the same as every other night except that James was in the house instead of William, and her panic downstairs had been ridiculous. Then a faint tap sounded at her door. She opened it and found James standing in front of her.

'I shall go away again if you ask me to, Gertrude . . . but only if you ask me to.'

She found nothing to say, could only hear the renewed pounding of her heart which she thought he must be able to hear too.

His face was grave in the candlelight. 'Chance has given us a precious opportunity . . . it's for you to say whether we waste it or not. What do you say, my dear . . . shall I go or stay?'

Her eyes answered him even before her tongue found words to say, 'I'd like you to stay . . . oh, James, *please* stay.'

Only afterwards did she realize that he must be a practised lover; for the moment her terrified concern was that he shouldn't find *her* awkward and shy. He found her nothing of the kind because his tenderness led her effortlessly to passion; she responded to his mouth and hands as if her body had waited for just this knowledge and shared delight.

But when she cried out at the moment of fulfilment, he knew the truth.

'Dear God, my love . . . I hurt you! Gertrude . . . why did you not tell me that you were still a virgin?'

She turned her face into his shoulder, and he could feel the wetness of her tears against his flesh. 'Because I was ashamed to say that William has never wanted me . . . it seemed too dreadful a thing to admit.'

James's arms held her now without the fierceness of desire, but with more tenderness than she had known existed in the world. 'He's incapable of wanting anyone, my poor sad brother. If I needed an excuse for what I've done tonight, my dearest, I must have proved to you that the inadequacy isn't *yours*. You were made for love.' He tilted her face with one hand so that she had to look at him. 'Much as I longed to, I shouldn't have come here if I'd known. The precious opportunity was all that I thought it would be and much more, and I shall cherish the memory of it my whole life through, but now . . . the future worries me, Gertrude.'

He looked anxiously at her, her face on the pillow framed in a cloud of dark hair. She tried to smile at him. 'Don't be worried,' she whispered, 'William would tell you I'm full of . . . of purposefulness! I shall manage, whatever happens. But, oh the loneliness of managing without you.'

His arms enfolded her again until he was certain that she slept. Then he gently withdrew and returned to his own room.

CHAPTER EIGHT

She awoke alone as usual, but it was the only thing that linked *this* morning's Gertrude Wyndham with any other that she could remember. Even the room around her, and the sky outside the windows, seemed to shine with a different soft brightness, sharing her own knowledge that she was a woman at last. She lay remembering the feel of James's body against her own; the memory held a threat of future pain, but for the moment she needn't heed it. He was still somewhere in the house, and in a little while she would see him again.

Her face in the mirror looked disappointingly the same; James had touched it and it *should* have blossomed into beauty, if not into a wantonness that would give her away, but she could see no change at all. There wasn't even a trace of triumph in having got Emma's revenge on the Maguires . . . she just looked content to have been loved.

She was in the dining-room when James appeared, and she heard herself say for Emmie's benefit, as a good hostess should, 'Good morning, James – I hope you slept well.'

'Thank you . . . yes.' He smelt of soap and the pleasant pomade he used on his hair, and vitality seemed to play round him like summer lightning, but this morning his eyes didn't smile.

Emmie reported to Ethel in the kitchen that Mr James seemed 'uncommon serious . . . missing his family, I shouldn't wonder'.

Ethel doubted it, having had more to do with Kitty Wyndham when she'd stayed at Providence. 'Thinking of the journey home, if ye ask me. All that water!' She had once visited an aunt at Weston-super-Mare and the sight of the sea had made a lasting impression on a girl who'd never been out of England's midmost shire before.

In the dining-room James stared at Gertrude's entranced face across the table. 'You're not supposed to smile at me like that, you know.'

'I was trying to look like a . . . a well-disposed sister-in-law.'

'Then, my dear one, I'm afraid you were failing!'

He waited while Emmie, having appeared with another tray, bustled out again. 'I've just been to see my mother – to break the news to her that I shall be leaving after luncheon.'

The light in Gertrude's face was extinguished, leaving it pale and sad, but she managed to say quietly, 'So soon . . . must you go *quite* so soon?'

'I must go before William gets home – not because I'm ashamed to face him, though no doubt I ought to be. It's simply that I should find it impossible to talk to him and not remember that he's your husband . . . that he's supposed to be your husband.'

'Very well,' she murmured, 'of course you must go, but your mother will be sad . . .' she stopped abruptly, unable to say what she would be herself.

Silence hung in the room, broken only by the chime of the long-case clock in the corner. It would remind her from now on of this precise moment of time when James had said he was leaving her.

'Kitty is a *Catholic*, you see,' he said suddenly, as if it settled beyond dispute an argument that had been going on in his head. 'She couldn't manage the children . . . couldn't manage anything alone . . .'

'She's your wife,' Gertrude agreed after a moment, 'and I am married to William.' 'Not to flinch' . . . that was what Haywood's End insisted upon; somehow she must manage to smile at him and talk about anything but themselves until it was time for Hodges to drive him to the railway station. She talked, and so did he. They had dealt with Maud Roberts's new bicycle, Matthew Harris's latest grandson, and even the strange man called Arthur Thornley who had taken to visiting Providence, when James sprang up from the table.

'Gertrude . . . I shall explode if I sit here any longer pretending that there's nothing better we could be doing with what time is left to us. A walk round the lake? I suppose not; even the damned snow is against us.'

She understood the frustration that drove him, was about to say that she didn't mind wading through the snow that still covered the park or anything else if he was beside her, when he remembered something else.

'Show me William's paintings . . . the ones Mama talked about last night; at least they'll get us away from these wretched maids bobbing in and out.'

In the empty privacy of the great room where William always worked she waited for James to put his arms round her and kiss away the aching needs her body had now discovered. But suddenly it seemed as if the canvases propped against the walls were what he had come there for. She'd forgotten his instant readiness to be interested in whatever life offered him next – it was his greatest charm, apart from the sheer zest that made him seem twice as alive as other people. He stared at William's paintings and, since pride forbade her to demand his attention, she had no choice but to stare at them too. In looking at them properly for the first time, she made a discovery – picture after picture seemed to sing with light and colour.

James stood for a long time staring at a small canvas simply covered, as far as she could see, in tiny brush-strokes of grey and white paint.

'You're too close,' he said softly, 'come back here.'

She went to stand beside him and saw what he was seeing: the brush-strokes had become a clump of white irises by the edge of the moat against the stone wall of the house; white flowers, grey stone, and water turned to silver by the play of light. It couldn't have been more simple, but even she could see that the effect was magical.

'William talks of certain French artists,' she murmured.

'Impressionists, he calls them. He approves of what they're doing – says painting must take the direction *they're* pointing in.'

'I've seen some of their work in Paris,' James said absently, still staring at the little canvas. 'William obviously does more than just approve; I'm not sure he isn't beating them at their own game.'

'Do you mean someone might want to *buy* such paintings?'

'Not yet, perhaps – the technique is too new. But in time they will.'

Gertrude smiled ruefully. 'I used to think William wasted precious time here that could be better spent on other things! How strange it would be if *he'd* found a way of saving Providence after all. When it comes to selling, I shall have to persuade him to let me do it . . . he would give the paintings away, whereas I shall haggle!'

She was talking too much because she didn't want to talk about paintings at all; she only wanted James to kiss her while there was still a little time. The idea that he might not want to because the night together had been all *he* wanted was almost too painful to bear. She walked over to the great mullion window so that he shouldn't see her tears, but he followed her and the next moment she felt his hands gripping her shoulders.

'Don't weep, Gertrude,' he murmured against her hair. 'I can bear it as long as I don't have to see you weep. Last night . . . it wasn't just selfish pleasure. Knowing you like that was so important that I *can't* regret it. Do you understand?'

'Yes, because I found it important too.' She swung round to face him. 'I can bear it as long as you don't touch me when we say goodbye. And now we shall have to go downstairs. I've just seen Hodges walk across the bridge with William's portmanteau. Something must have brought him home early.'

They found him in the entrance hall, flicking through the letters on the table. She kept a hand on the newel-post of the staircase to support her because her legs were trembling, but she believed that she managed to sound calm.

'William . . . how fortunate that you're back . . . we thought James would have to leave without seeing you.'

It was all the effort she could make and, sensing it, James immediately stepped in front of her.

'It's a brief, unscheduled visit to England,' he said quickly. 'I had to seize the opportunity to come to Providence, but I apologize for not warning you.'

'No apology is necessary.' William sounded surprised. 'Mama must have been delighted to see you, and I'm sure Gertrude has made you welcome in my absence.' His quiet voice laid no stress on the words, but made James feel that *he'd* sounded feverish . . . of course there was no need to apologize for arriving at his own family home. 'Must you go the moment I arrive?' William asked calmly.

Gertrude thought it must be a sense of her own guilt that made everything he said as sharp-edged as a sword. Forgetting that she hadn't given James time to reply, she rushed in with a question of her own.

'What brought you home, William? I told James you weren't expected until this evening.' Hot colour flooded her cheeks, making him stare at her. Now, it seemed to be the worst thing she could have said, but this was what guilt did – destroyed the smallest hope of behaving naturally. If James had had no more practice in a life of deceit, he was feeling just as uncomfortable.

William's glance finally moved away from her flushed face; perhaps she'd only imagined that he'd noticed anything unusual about her.

'I happened to glance in my diary last night. As well that I did, because I found I'd overlooked a momentous date.' Then he turned to his brother. 'You ought not to be leaving us on Gertrude's twenty-first birthday.'

James was suddenly at a loss. 'I'm afraid I didn't know . . . Gertrude omitted to . . . mention the fact.'

Now they were both staring at her. 'I forgot . . . I *completely* forgot,' she muttered. It was ludicrous to apologize for forgetting her own birthday; she could only brazen it out. 'I suppose it couldn't have seemed as momentous as all that.'

'Well, my congratulations nevertheless,' William said with sudden formality. He pulled a small package out of his pocket and handed it to her. She would have given a great deal to be able to take it away . . . to be anywhere but there, trying to ignore the tension that seemed to be growing between the three of them like a spreading stain. But the package was in her hands and William was standing there, waiting for her to open it. When it was unwrapped she found herself staring at a slim, leather-bound volume exquisitely tooled in gold with the title of Elizabeth Barrett Browning's *Sonnets from the Portuguese*. It fell open under her hands, and lines leapt at her from the page – 'How do I love thee? Let me count the ways . . .' Tears clogged her throat, making it impossible even to thank him for so poignant a gift. She was saved by her mother-in-law, carefully descending the staircase. Lady Hester's quiet voice insisted that the day was normal after all.

'William, my dear . . . I should have guessed you intended to get home early! Good morning again, James, and my dearest Gertrude . . . I've been busy behind your back! The rector and Maud are coming to luncheon, but my triumph has been to persuade your father to join us too! I know he prefers to ignore the fact that we're joined by marriage, but today I had to overrule him.' She put her own gift into Gertrude's hands – a jewel-box containing a necklace of delicate antique silver, with an opal glowing in the centre of its pendant. 'It's a Goring family heirloom, my dear . . . I thought it was time it showed to advantage on *you*!'

Left with nothing to say because the day was not normal at all and fast becoming altogether too much for her, Gertrude could only kiss her ladyship's cheek. The gifts clutched against her seemed to reproach her with their kindness. It was a relief to hear the sound of a gig trundling across the gravel of the forecourt, and James seized on it as if he welcomed the interruption too.

'The Roberts,' he said quickly. 'Perhaps I should go and make sure Maud can stop the horse; I seem to remember that she controls it very imperfectly!'

'And I,' William put in, 'shall make sure my father-in-law hasn't gone into hiding somewhere.' He smiled sweetly at them and disappeared in turn.

Gertrude gave a sigh of relief that sounded suspiciously like a sob. 'I'm overcome,' she said unsteadily, by way of explanation. 'I didn't expect anyone to realize it was my birthday . . . even overlooked the fact myself. It's kind of William to understand that my father needs to be fetched.'

Lady Hester smiled at her. 'Dear James is everything that is charming, and William is the kind one, but I expect you'd noticed that!'

With James and Miss Roberts present, there was no danger of any constraint at the luncheon table. Even George Hoskins's shyness melted before Maud's story of an encounter with a pig called Absalom. Dearer than life itself to its owner, the village cobbler, Absalom was normally safely fenced in at the bottom of Mr Martin's garden, where friends were regularly invited to admire him. But Absalom had got bored one day.

'Imagine me bowling along,' said Maud, 'when suddenly the roadway in front of me was full of a very large pig! I stopped *almost* in time, but he took exception to such an unexpected *rencontre*. I assured Mr Martin afterwards that not a bristle of Absalom's snout had been harmed, whereas my bicycle lamp *had* been – it fell off and got stamped on by a very sharp hoof! But to no avail. Martin can quote from the Bible even more freely than Hubert can, and he reminded me in a voice loud enough for the entire village to hear that "a righteous man regardeth the life of his beast, but the tender mercies of the wicked are cruel"!'

William gave a rare shout of laughter. 'Dear Maud . . . I hoped that what he'd said was, "Neither cast ye your *wheels* before swine"!'

The rector bowed his head with mirth at this improvement on the original, and even George had to wipe the tears of laughter from his eyes. Looking from him to James, Gertrude struggled with the knowledge that happiness and pain could exist side by side without drowning each other. The discovery set the seal on a day she would remember always. She had come of age, but the boundary separating her from yesterday had nothing to do with a mere calendar.

Their guests went away when luncheon was over and the four of them waited for the moment of James's departure to come. Conversation eluded them, and gaiety had suddenly disappeared. Gertrude could feel her heartbeats ticking away the minutes, while James stared at the logs on the hearth, and William seemed deep in thoughts of his own. Only Lady Hester made an effort to talk, but for once her choice of subject was unfortunate.

'What is it exactly, James dear, that brought you to London?'

His smile was mocking, even for her. 'I suppose you could say *money* brought me, Mama! Our company was offered the chance of buying into a new steamship line. Transport is the key to future success – the fastest, cheapest transport we can provide. We already hold a stake in the railways that stretch across America; a shipping connection will complete the link that enables us to bring American produce to England.'

'And it will also complete *our* ruin at the same time,' William said with sudden bitterness. 'Don't you realize that cheap American wheat is one of the reasons why our own farming industry is dying?'

James gave a little shrug. 'It's bound to die if it can't remain competitive. Ask Gertrude if any woman with a family to feed would prefer expensive home-grown food to cheap foreign produce. No, *I* shall ask her.' His smile was incautiously tender, reminding her of shared and secret understandings. 'Am I not right, Gertrude?'

He expected that she would think so . . . she *did* think so, and had to admit to it, even though William was frowning.

'Living on labourers' wages, women must buy as

economically as they can,' she agreed carefully. 'What else can the poor things do?'

'Then I hope they can learn to live on even *less* if the man who employs their husbands is forced to give up his farm.' William's cold conclusion seemed to end the subject, but because it was unanswerable it provoked James to rashness.

'Gertrude has been enlightening me about the state of things here. You've been very secretive about our misfortunes, William. Why not have let me know that Providence no longer belongs to the Wyndhams?'

Gertrude saw the flare of anger in her husband's eyes, knew that he thought she had betrayed him.

'It's *mortgaged* . . . not quite the same thing,' he said coolly. 'In any case, the misfortunes mainly seemed to concern me. I suppose that is why I didn't shout them from the house-top.'

She was provoked in turn by the unfairness of it. 'It didn't seem like shouting to explain to *James*, of all people, why the Smithers and the hunters had disappeared. You weren't here to tell him yourself,' she said defiantly.

'No . . . I'm sorry about that,' he agreed in an expressionless voice.

She was silenced, but James came to her rescue. 'Well, you might have asked *me* before putting Providence into the hands of strangers, but it's too late now because I'm heavily committed to American ventures. In any case, if we're to admit the truth, I suppose it's too late altogether. The day of small estates like this one is over. Their only hope is to be turned into private schools or small country hotels, unless rich merchants buy them in the hope of turning themselves into gentlemen!'

'Is that what *you* would do . . . sell Providence to the highest bidder?' William's quiet question seemed born of nothing but a vague impersonal interest in a subject that scarcely concerned him.

'I'd prefer to find some way of making it profitable. But I certainly wouldn't hand on to my son an inheritance that could be nothing but a beautiful millstone hung round his neck.'

'Then how glad I am, my dear brother, that I didn't come to you. I shall redeem the mortgage when I can; meanwhile we manage to live with the shame of it.' Dignity wrapped him round in a way Gertrude had never noticed before. Generations of Wyndhams before him had no doubt called upon just this inherited gift of authority when they needed to and thereby confounded their enemies. Enemies? The word shocked her, but it seemed to describe the hostility that flashed bright as steel between William and his brother.

The conversation languished, but once again Lady Hester did her best to ignore the tension in the air.

'Bring Kitty with you next time, dearest . . . it's sad that she couldn't be with you now.'

'Our son and daughter occupy her at the moment, Mama. Naturally she must be at home with them.'

Gertrude couldn't separate the strands of emotion in the storm of feeling in which she was now being flung about. The grief of imminent loss was only bearable if she refused to accept the way James had just brushed Providence aside.

'I heard the voice of the true Victorian male just then,' she remarked thoughtfully. 'Have you not heard in New York that times are changing?'

He remarked the note of irony and was irritated by it. Gertrude should be in *his* camp; she had no right to forsake him and go over to William.

'Of course murmurs reach us, my dear. Darwin has scuttled the Book of Genesis, the Prince of Wales is doing much the same thing for the morals of his mother's stuffy court, and the old ideas are as dead as the Dodo. In fact, the Industrial Age has dawned!'

'But you are only speaking about the world of men . . . I had *women* in mind. Perhaps even Kitty won't be content much longer to stay your domestic slave at home, while you roam the world in search of profit and . . . adventure.'

The word challenged him to meet the glance of her grey eyes. What she saw in his — the same sadness that lay suffocatingly on her own heart – made her spurt of anger die.

'Kitty is content, I promise you,' he said quietly. She knew that the infinitesimal stress on his wife's name was intended only for her to hear.

At last it was time for him to go. He kissed his mother goodbye indoors, but William and Gertrude followed him out to the stable-yard. Hodges and Artie had the horses harnessed already, to take him to the railway station. From London he would set off on a journey her imagination couldn't encompass, and she might never see him again. All about them the world held out the promise of spring . . . rebirth was in the afternoon's milder air and in the sound of the birds practising their songs for another season. Only the emptiness of her heart spoke of death and dying.

She stood at a distance from James, watching the sunlight glinting on his fair hair, afraid to hold out her hand.

'Goodbye, Gertrude . . . my dear, if there should ever be . . . anything you need, will you promise to let me know?'

Her mouth quivered, but she could only nod to him. It was left to William to step forward and take James's hand.

'Our greetings to Kitty . . . *both* come when you can.'

James scarcely seemed to hear. 'Take care of Mama and Gertrude,' was all he said in reply. Then he climbed into the carriage, Hodges wheeled the horses, and they were away. In a moment all she could see was the back of the carriage jolting over the uneven surface of the drive.

'Let me take you indoors, Gertrude,' William's voice said beside her.

They walked back into the house without speaking. Life would go on, she told herself. It always did, and Providence itself was there to prove it. It had absorbed more griefs than hers during the past four hundred years. She went through the rest of the day with cheerfulness pinned to her face like a carnival mask that could only be removed when she was alone in her room for the night. She lay awake, travelling in her mind with James, pretending that she sat beside him in the carriage, on the train, watched the sea part in front

of them as their steamship drove its way through the waves
. . . but her body was still here at Providence, and her mind
was struggling not to accept the seed of a terrible idea that
had planted itself there. It sprang into life even as she
struggled with it . . . grew and grew, refusing to be
disregarded. There was *one* thing she could do for James,
or perhaps it was William she would be doing it for. It must
be done *now* or it could never be done at all.

Without any conscious decision taken, but driven simply
by the instinct that insisted what she was about to do was
right, she got out of bed, blew out her candle, and groped
her way across the room. A gleam of moonlight fell along
the corridor showing her William's door; all she had to do
now was find the resolution to open it.

CHAPTER NINE

He was sitting up in bed, reading. The room was dark and unknown, but no less unfamiliar to her than William's face in the candlelight. The flame wavered in the draught from the window, throwing his features into a dramatic mixture of shadow and high relief. The expression in his eyes was concealed from her but the coolness in his voice when he spoke made it clear that she wasn't welcome in his room.

'Is something wrong, Gertrude . . . are you feeling unwell?'

'Nothing is wrong – except with *us*.'

He didn't normally hide behind subterfuge, nor pretend that he failed to understand. If he wished not to accept something, he simply removed himself, leaving his opponent with an empty victory. He couldn't do that now. She had a half-hysterical desire to laugh at the embarrassment she had dragged him into, but for once he *did* try to evade the real issue.

'There is no need for our problems to worry you to this extent, my dear. James's talk of our misfortunes has made you a little overwrought. Providence is not about to collapse over our heads.'

She stood looking at him and within himself he saluted the little air of dignity that didn't desert her even in *this* situation.

'I think you know that I was talking about us, William, not Providence. I don't have to be unwell to come to your room, nor wait to be invited. If I'm never to be your wife it would have been more honest to offer me the job of housekeeper.'

The expression on his face reminded her of the very

moment when he'd suggested they should marry . . . she'd just emerged upset and dishevelled from Sid Moffat's arms and William had been disgusted at the sight of them. She thought he was probably disgusted now at having this scene forced upon him. The room felt cold because the casement was open to the night air, but it was despair that was beginning to send tremors down her body. She was going to fail, and the humiliation of it would be something she could never forget. What was left now . . . to apologize for troubling him and crawl back to her own room? She'd rather spend the night where she was . . . collapse eventually with exhaustion, die of pneumonia, anything . . .

'You *married* me,' she shouted desperately. 'I refuse to be ignored.'

The silence seemed to stretch into eternity until he spoke again. 'You don't have to remind me of our relationship. I thought it was understood – that we would take care of my mother and Providence together. I thought *that* was what you wanted, instead of the hot and heady embraces of a man like Moffat.'

'Don't despise Sid Moffat – and don't forget *I'm* not a cool, calm, bloodless Wyndham . . . I'm a *woman*, William.'

She knew she was too shrill, too hysterical, and she was going to fail. Tears that seemed to well up from the sad cold depths of her heart began to stream down her cheeks, and he almost missed the whisper that reached him . . . 'Pity me, please . . . I'm so lonely.'

She was blind to the sight of him moving towards her, but his hands suddenly touched her cold ones and then he led her towards his bed. Still sobbing helplessly, she fell into its softness. The candlelight disappeared, he got in beside her, and his arms cradled her shivering body against the warmth of his own. She was comforted by it, and exhausted by the emotional storms of the day. When she fell asleep at last he remained awake beside her, staring into the darkness.

It was nearly dawn when she awoke, but still not light.

For the first time in her life she wasn't alone, and she knew with certainty that the man beside her lay with the careful stillness of someone who didn't want it known that he was awake. There was one more effort she could make. After a moment she turned towards him, mutely offering her body.

When he took her it was with none of James's masterful tenderness; William was clumsy and hesitant, but the very difference made it bearable. In time, she told herself, she would forget the delight James had made for her, and William would get used to loving her.

Light crept into the room, and he could see her face. 'I wasn't sure, you see . . .' he explained shyly. 'Emma's wasted life might have made you afraid of a real marriage and . . . then there was James!'

'What . . . what has James to do with it?' She could scarcely force herself to ask the question.

'I always used to think that he meant something to you . . . much more than I did, at least. It wasn't surprising . . . a very dashing fellow, my brother James!'

'Yes,' she agreed steadily, then startled him with the beauty of her smile. 'But you're the *kind* one, William.'

Edward George Wyndham was ushered protesting into the world by Dr Markham on a wild January night of the following year. Gertrude knew that he was William's son, but she still owed him, in a sense, to James. No-one else would ever know that it made him doubly precious.

When William came into her room afterwards he had the half-smiling, half-bemused air of a man to whom a miracle had happened.

'Can you picture the happy scene downstairs, my dear? Mama is weeping for joy, your father is patting her and mopping his own eyes, and all the maids seem to be embracing each other in turn and crying at the same time. You would scarcely know that they are all full of joy!'

'Are *you* full of joy, William?'

'I can't describe it,' he said simply. 'Shall we call the boy Ned?'

She nodded, staring at him with grey eyes luminous in the pallor of her face. 'Now we *have* to save Providence . . . for Ned.'

1895

CHAPTER TEN

Ned was almost four years old by the time his second sister, Lucy, was born. She gave her mother and Dr Markham so much trouble coming into the world that he told William afterwards she must be their last child. Gertrude felt exhausted but pleased enough with herself to be able to smile at her husband when he ventured into her room.

'Is she *very* red and squally?' she wanted to know.

'Both at the moment, but Ned has been kind enough to say that she looks all right to him, and Mama insists that the signs of future beauty are there. Predictably, Sybil shows no interest in her sister whatsoever, and is only concerned to make a good impression on John Markham, who looks almost as tired as you do, my poor girl.'

He took his wife's hand, and sat holding it. 'No more children, Gertrude . . . Markham is so definite about that that I must agree with him.'

'Well, for the moment I agree with both of you, but perhaps we can all change our minds later on!'

He kissed her and went away, putting his faith in a doctor's ability to convince where a mere husband couldn't hope to. But her strength took so long to return that she was half-prepared for the doctor's verdict when it came.

'You have three beautiful children, my dear . . . I'm afraid you must be satisfied with them. Another pregnancy will cost you your health, perhaps your life.' It was impossible not to remember Emma's experience of childbirth, and lingering ill-health after it. Gertrude reminded herself of the responsibilities she already had. They couldn't be managed by an invalid. If there was a risk of her becoming *that* she must accept what Dr Markham was telling her, and accept it cheerfully.

'Don't look so worried about having to warn me,' she said, smiling at him. 'I think I'd already decided that I really don't want any other son but Ned, and there's no guarantee that we should only have beautiful daughters in future!'

John Markham smiled in turn, relieved to have found her unexpectedly docile for once. 'I'm happy to agree with you that Ned's perfection!'

'Well, in my eyes he is. Of course he's naughty at times and "powerful stubborn" according to John Biddle! But he's brought us the gift of laughter. William even abandons his precious easel to be wherever Ned happens to be, and Biddle's long face breaks into a smile every time his self-appointed "assistant" arrives. Ned is happy to let Artie walk him round and round the stable-yard on Hercules because his heart is kind and he knows it gives Artie pleasure, but my son's real treat is "helpin' Bi'll". Even at the age of three he touches plants as if he loves them.'

'An inheritance from your father, Gertrude, for all that Ned's beginning to look like a true Wyndham. No doubt there's a dash of George Hoskins in the mixture as well!'

She smiled and nodded, aware that John Markham had not been at Haywood's End at the time of Emma's marriage. It was true that Ned had the fair hair and light blue eyes of his father's family, and Lucy seemed likely to copy him, but from the beginning Sybil had been different, and more difficult – a dark-haired, restless child who wanted whatever she wanted 'now, this minute, please', wept tears of rage when she didn't get it, and smiled entrancingly if she did. Gertrude was inclined to blame her daughter's temperament on the man called Daniel Maguire, whom she otherwise refused to acknowledge as her own father. William smiled and said Sybil reminded him of Louise as a child, so there was no need to despair, because *she* had turned out all right, as Ned would say!

'I despair of nothing except seeing the last of Arthur

Thornley,' Gertrude remarked bitterly, changing the subject. 'William, why does he haunt us so?'

'He says he enjoys seeing his beautiful pieces of machinery actually functioning, but I suspect that what he really enjoys is escaping from his own hellish factories occasionally . . . we shouldn't begrudge him a little of our peace and fresh air.'

'I begrudge him any part of Providence. Having to watch him doing a competitor down would be bad enough, but the spectacle of him exchanging pleasantries with Sid Moffat at the home farm puts me in mind of a spider making up its mind to dine off an unsuspecting fly.'

William shook his head and only told her to remember the parable of the tortoise and the hare. Arthur Thornley didn't seem to worry him, and in the end she aired her anxiety in the estate office instead, where her father still calmly insisted on working for his son-in-law.

'I wish we could make Mr Thornley understand that he isn't welcome here. There must be bits of his machinery littering the rest of Warwickshire . . . why can't he go and watch *them* working?'

'I dare say we're nearest to Birmingham; in any case Sid Moffat enjoys arguing with him. Thornley's a free-trade man of course.' He saw the disapproval in Gertrude's face and felt obliged to argue with her. 'He's part of today's England, my dear, whether you like it or not. What's more, he's cleverer than most and more hard-working. Why shouldn't he climb the ladder?'

'He can climb as high as he likes as long as he stops staring at Providence. By now he must have discovered all its poor sore places . . . counted every loose tile and measured every inch of crumbling stonework. I expect he lives in a shiny new villa himself, stuffed with hot-water pipes and bright with electric light-bulbs. If that's what he wants, let him stay there.'

'It *isn't* all he wants,' George Hoskins said slowly. 'At least, I don't think so. He's a big man in Birmingham, but that isn't enough. He wants to be taken seriously by a wider world than that. To begin with, he must get the local gentry to accept him – that means an estate in the country where he can make a splash.'

Fear constricted her heart, making her take refuge in anger rather than admit to it. 'How can you sound so calm about him? You've always taught me that the land was precious . . . something to be worked with love and care, not grabbed by the Thornleys of this world so that they can boast how many acres they own. You'll tell me next he wants to hoist himself on to a horse and go hunting. The village would laugh itself sick at the sight, much less the rest of our neighbours.'

'I doubt if Arthur Thornley is a man to be laughed at by Haywood's End or anybody else.'

'No,' Gertrude admitted more quietly, 'and *that's* why he frightens me. He's powerful and unscrupulous, and I don't trust him not to find some way of hurting us, if we stand in the way of what he wants.' She couldn't bring herself to say that he wanted Providence, but her father understood.

'This house is in the hands of the bank, but the interest on the loan is regularly paid, and for as long as it is you've nothing to lose sleep over, my dear. Fretting pays no toll, and if you're anxious you'll only upset her ladyship and little Lucy.'

Gertrude smiled in spite of herself. In her father's view Lady Hester and Lucy Wyndham, being made of more precious metal than most, had to be taken care of.

'There's Sybil, too . . . shouldn't we be careful not to upset her as well?'

'*That* independent little morsel will take care of herself. Poor Artie got kicked for his pains yesterday because he wouldn't let go of her leading rein.'

'Well, I hope you smacked her for it.'

'Artie wouldn't have allowed me to do that. "Proper little tartar," he said proudly . . . "just like I remember Miss Louise!" '

'That's what William says – that she's like his sister. But one of these days someone who hasn't got Artie's kind, long-suffering heart will probably kick her back. I can't help feeling that Sybil is going to tackle life by battling with it; everyone who isn't on her side is against her.'

'She won't need to do much battling . . . she's only got to smile to get what she wants. I watched her at it the other day, persuading Matthew's grandson to part with his new whip and top.'

'But that's dreadful . . . didn't you stop her?'

'Oh, I let her have a turn or two at it, knowing she'd soon get bored. When I suggested it was time to give it back, she did, with the air of a duchess making young Andrew a present – so they were both happy!'

'Well, she's a minx, whatever you say,' Gertrude insisted, half-laughing.

'I didn't say she wasn't . . . only that you needn't worry about her.'

Gertrude reverted to the subject that had brought her there. 'You tell me not to worry about Providence, either, but I do. We repay the interest, but not the loan itself. What if the bank decides to foreclose one day and ask for the loan back? What happens to Providence then?' Her eyes were full of an anxiety that he knew she chose not to share with William. It was no wonder she looked thin and tired. An invalid mother-in-law, three small children, and the running of a large, old-fashioned house would have been enough to tax the strength of a girl of twenty-five, apart from the care she provided unstintingly for anyone at Haywood's End who needed help. Providence had always sheltered the village from adversity and so it would continue to do in William's lifetime, whether they could afford it or not; but it was Gertrude who poured out her strength, and asked herself in private whether they could afford such bounty.

'The bank won't foreclose, my dear,' George Hoskins said firmly. 'They know there are more people wanting to sell estates these days than there are takers for them. In any case, banks aren't anxious to push out old families that hold the countryside together. We just have to hang on, as the old Squire used to say, until times get better.'

Gertrude's thin face lit in the smile that made it fleetingly beautiful. 'We must hang on until Ned is able to come to the rescue. I keep telling myself that he's the miracle Providence needs. William loves the house, of course, but he's an artist, not a practical man. Ned's going to grow up like you, a countryman in his heart and in his head. Providence already figures in his prayers, just behind us, but before his dearest friends like Biddle and Moffat and Sam Harris!'

'Well, there you are then, my dear . . . we'll wait for Ned. When he's eighteen I shall be seventy – time to sit back and smoke my pipe, and try not to give him advice that he won't need at all!'

Gertrude felt a rush of affection for this quiet, softly-spoken man who asked of life nothing for himself. All he wanted was to serve Providence, worship Lady Hester, and adore his grandchildren. She kissed his cheek, then smiled because the little gesture flustered him.

'We shall *always* need your advice. Providence would probably have been lost by now but for you, and William knows it as well as I do.'

Despite Gertrude's inability to be more than distantly civil to Arthur Thornley he continued to appear from time to time – like the demon king in pantomime, she complained to Maud Roberts. One day he did more than call at the farm to argue the cause of free trade against protectionism with Sid Moffat – he wrote to the Squire asking for an interview.

It was five years since William had first seen him at Providence. Looking at him, he decided that success had been bought at a high price. Arthur Thornley was noticeably more grey and lined than before, and carried with him the air of a man regularly required to make too many decisions. If his wealth had quadrupled, so had his responsibilities. Tool-making had been added to the agricultural machinery he produced, and more recently a factory making the nuts and bolts and screws that every other industry depended on.

His already strong position in Birmingham had by now grown unassailable.

In the same interval of time his clothes for country visiting had grown no quieter. William tried not to blink at a suit of virulent brown tweed, and courteously ushered his visitor to a chair in the estate office, where he'd chosen to receive him.

'What can I do for you, Mr Thornley?'

'Not to beat about the bush – sell Providence to *me*, rather than to anybody else.'

His heavy face was set in an expression of frowning concentration, as if the willpower he knew he possessed must exert its pull on the man sitting opposite him, as surely as the moon compelled the oceans to ebb and flow.

'I don't have the intention of selling Providence to *anybody*,' William pointed out quietly. 'Perhaps you have got a false impression by listening to Moffat. Countrymen have to be optimists in what they do, but they're often pessimists in what they say.'

Mr Thornley looked affronted at the idea that he could have been stupid enough to have been misled by anybody. 'I don't deal in impressions, Sir William, only in facts. Farming's been dying here for the past thirty years, and your income must have been dying with it. Your tenants are giving up their leases, leaving you with land that *you* can't make pay any more than they could. You keep your farms and outbuildings going at the cost of *this* house . . . it needs money spent on it. Those are *facts*. I'll admit to one impression – that you're dependent on a bank mortgage; but Mr Hoskins is a very close-mouthed man. He doesn't talk about your affairs, in case you're thinking he does.'

'I shouldn't believe you if you said that he did,' William pointed out gently. 'It's kind of you to sum up my situation so clearly, and indeed so accurately, but your facts don't change my answer. There may come a time when the Wyndhams have to relinquish Providence, but the time isn't yet.'

Arthur Thornley's small dark eyes fixed themselves on

the face of the man opposite him. It ought to have been easy to despise William Wyndham. He was a typical remnant of the class that had held on to power too long; it was now outworn, unable to keep what vigour and ruthlessness had once allowed it to grab for itself; but the habit of ownership died hard when it was ingrained through generations. Such families littered the countryside of present-day England like stranded sea-monsters, but it was typical of them that they hadn't even realized their time had come. Stupidity mixed with stubbornness in his opponents angered Mr Thornley because they made a combination difficult to deal with. Instinct told him now that anger wouldn't serve; he must fall back on sweet reason.

'See here, Sir William: first time I called here you told me you were proud of Providence. You belong here and you think I don't; that's true enough, but one of these days it's going to fall to pieces unless someone like me takes it in hand. Why not let go of it now before it does?'

William stared at him, half-repelled by a thrusting man who stood for everything he disliked, half-fascinated by a persistence that ignored the normal codes of social behaviour. It impelled him to an equal rudeness of which he was secretly ashamed.

'Why do you care what happens to Providence? Why not buy some of the land that is now going sadly cheap and build yourself a bright new mansion that *isn't* going to fall to pieces before long? Or am I being stupid in imagining that you want Providence at all? Perhaps it's Wyndham land you're after, so that you can spread the blight of your factories as far as Haywood's End? That's putting it bluntly, Mr Thornley, but you'll forgive me, being a plain-spoken man yourself!'

It brought a gleam to his visitor's eye. The Squire wasn't the milksop he looked after all, and a fight was nothing without giving and taking a knock or two.

'My factories may seem a blight to you, but people can't live on air and a pretty view. They need work and a living wage . . . which, as things stand, they get from *me*, not you.

I won't deny I'd bring another factory this way, and use some of the land you've got out there to build houses for the people I employ. It looks grand and green as it is, I grant you, but it's being wasted. We can't afford idle land or people nowadays. Face the truth, Sir William . . . this is an industrial country now, not an agricultural one, and it's already threatened by foreign competition. We can only stay ahead of the Germans and the Americans by working harder than they do, and by *thinking* clearer . . . not by pretending that it's still 1795.'

William smiled at him. 'I wish you success, Mr Thornley, but for as long as I can prevent it, you're not going to build your factories on *my* land. It's not mine, of course; I simply hold it in trust for my children and their children. Greenness and fresh air and beauty we *must* have, even if we must have your factory chimneys belching smoke as well.'

Thornley pushed the argument away as a dog might shake its coat, emerging from a river. 'I can buy other land if I have to. Providence I want for its own sake . . . and I can't even tell you why. When the Wyndhams can't look after it properly, I reckon it's time for someone else to have it who can.'

William knew an astonishing urge to shout at him. The man was as impossible to get rid of as a burr in a spaniel's coat, but a moment ago genuine longing had leaked out of his voice. This uncouth, bullying human dynamo wanted Providence for what he could do for it, not what it could do for him. The realization made it impossible to be angry with him.

'I can only repeat that the time isn't yet. Forgive me if I say I hope it never will be.'

Thornley nodded, then stood up to go. 'We'll see . . . I'm not normally reckoned a patient man but I know how to wait if I have to. Good day to you.'

William walked with him to the stable-yard and waited courteously for him to drive away. The interview hadn't lasted very long but it had left him feeling tired. A conversation with Arthur Thornley was not unlike a walk in a high wind. He recounted it to his land agent but insisted that Gertrude should not be told, on the grounds that she would persuade young Sid Moffat to shoot Thornley instead of a rabbit when he next appeared at Haywood's End.

A month later their anxiety seemed to be over. The news was all round the neighbourhood that the industrialist had taken Bicton Grange, five miles to the north of Providence on the road to Birmingham.

'That'll keep him happy,' George Hoskins told the Squire.

William shook his head. 'It's only a stop-gap. Mr Thornley has settled down to wait . . . he told me he could be patient if he had to. Now I know what a rabbit feels like with a terrier waiting outside its burrow!'

The arrival of the new family provided the neighbourhood with welcome talk and speculation, but before the end of the year news of a more tragic kind reached Providence from New York, blotting out all other considerations. A long letter from James told them of a street accident in which Kitty Wyndham had been seriously hurt. She had seemed to be recovering, but a sudden relapse had left her dead, and James a widower at the age of thirty-four.

Their sadness for him would have been easier to bear if they could have done something for him and his children. Three thousand miles of land and sea effectively blocked not only practical help but even their knowledge of how his family life was organized. Once loving condolences had been sent, and invitations to bring his children immediately to Providence, Lady Hester could only grieve silently for a son she still missed. William kept to himself the glimpse James had given him of a marriage that left something to be desired, but Gertrude's reactions to the tragedy were much more complicated. She could pretend to no sadness about the woman she had briefly known, who had clearly resented her marriage to William to the extent of ignoring it completely. But, claimed as kin or not, Kitty had belonged to her, and they might one day have come to some sort of understanding. Now the chance had gone for ever and Gertrude was startled to find how much she regretted it.

About James himself, her feelings were even more divided. She had tried to think of him as someone who, like herself, had achieved a sufficient contentment. Usually the memory of him hurt no more than a scar that remained tender to the touch although the wound beneath had healed.

She could tell herself she was a fortunate woman, and mostly believed it. But there were times when quiet contentment wasn't enough. She was still only twenty-five – too young for the passionless life that William had returned to as a result of Dr Markham's decree. It would have been easier to bear if she could have thought her husband suffered too, but she felt he was relieved to be spared the duty of making love to her. Now they slept decorously side by side, and in the night watches her body ached for James.

She had to agree, of course, that he and his children should be asked to come to Providence, but her deepest prayer was that he would choose to remain in America.

CHAPTER ELEVEN

At breakfast one morning Gertrude asked for the use of Hodges and the carriage.

'Shopping in Warwick?' William suggested. 'Or a call on the ladies at Barham that you've been finding excuses for not making?'

She smiled but shook her head. 'I don't avoid visiting Mrs Maynard, even though I can't help feeling that the scandals that attach themselves to the Prince of Wales are better left undiscussed – especially when they're as close to us as the Countess of Warwick! What I had in mind this afternoon was a different call – I thought of going to Bicton.'

William stared at her in astonishment. 'Bicton! You haven't forgotten the Brownings no longer live there? My dear, this is going far beyond the call of social duty.'

'Well, if I go in mid-afternoon I can be reasonably sure of finding that Mr Thornley is pinned inside one of his factories. His wife might be more agreeable.' Gertrude's voice suggested doubt in the matter, but William knew by now when it was fruitless to try to deflect her from what she judged to be right. 'The truth is that I feel rather sorry for the poor woman. Mr Thornley has almost certainly *not* consulted her in the matter of where she would like to live, and if you searched Warwickshire you couldn't find an uglier house than Bicton Grange. On top of that, I'm afraid the rest of the neighbourhood will probably ignore her – as they would have ignored me if your mother hadn't made them welcome me.'

William hesitated, staring at his wife's face. 'If you insist on thrusting your head into the Thornley den, perhaps I should mention that Bicton wasn't his first choice; he had the good taste to want to buy Providence. I had to tell him that it wasn't for sale.'

Gertrude was silent for a moment. 'I've felt it all along,' she confessed finally, 'feared him just because he seemed to threaten us. If Providence would forgive me, I'd pretend to Mrs Thornley that it's an impossible house, dilapidated and uncomfortable; but perhaps that would only make the loathsome man want it more. He longs to get his hands on something that he can transform from what *he* sees as failure into success.'

William smiled at her flushed face. 'My dear, I don't like him any more than you do, but I'm bound to say that there's more to his interest in Providence than a hankering to meddle and "improve"; the first time he saw the house I thought it had put some kind of spell on him, and I knew it for certain the other day.'

'That makes me feel even *more* threatened,' Gertrude said slowly. 'William, my father thinks the bank won't foreclose. If it did, would you consider asking James for help?'

'No . . . he made his attitude clear when he was here, and it's not very different from Thornley's – houses shouldn't become a burden. Nevertheless, James might feel obliged not to refuse, in which case the request would be completely unfair. His life is in America. Why should he exhaust *his* money safeguarding an estate that *my* son will inherit?'

The question was unanswerable and after a while Gertrude changed the subject. 'He looked at your pictures when he was here.' She stopped talking, aware that the moment when they'd looked at the painting of the irises together was sharp and painful in her mind. Then she went on, 'He said that when people had got used to the new style of painting they would want to buy such things. Do you suppose they've had time yet to get tired of winsome beauties, and highland cattle paddling in lakes at sunset?'

He smiled, recognizing the descriptions. 'By no means, I fear. It isn't only a question of time but of education. For as long as people want to cram their houses with overstuffed furniture shrouded in draperies or covered with knick-knacks, they're not going to buy an Edouard Manet for their walls, still less a William Wyndham! By and large, William Morris and his friends are still preaching their "back to Nature" message to the unconverted, and I'm not even sure what *they* think of the Impressionists.'

'Yes, but education has to begin somewhere . . . couldn't we make a start by getting your paintings displayed?'

William gave a little shrug. 'I know of one gallery in London that shows such things . . . it's run by a Frenchman, need I say – a man called Henri Blanchard, in Bond Street. He *shows* them, but I doubt if he manages to sell them.'

'Would you object if we *tried*?' Gertrude persevered. 'At least, if *I* tried; you would be too embarrassed to haggle with him.'

'My worst embarrassment would be to watch him wondering how to refuse with courtesy! That is what he *would* do, my dear.'

Gertrude abandoned the subject for the time being; at least she had now got the name of a dealer, but the matter of what to do with it would have to be thought about a little longer.

She set off that afternoon for a house that was familiar to her. For the Brownings it might have been a sadness to have to dispose of Bicton Grange, but she couldn't help thinking that she would have moved out of it with nothing but relief. It *was* what William called it – a pseudo-Gothic nightmare. Built of bricks that were weathering to an unfortunate shade of yellowish-grey, the house bristled with gables and parapets and curlicues. The eye searched in vain for the relief of some unornamented space where the architect's imagination had failed him; decoration ran riot, inside and out.

The woman who received her looked as if she still hadn't accustomed herself to the plush splendour of her drawing-room. Jane Thornley had the air of someone who had been deposited there by mistake and was hoping to be collected again as soon as possible. She was short and sturdily built, with a pleasantly-featured face and soft brown hair dressed in a plaited coil at the back of her head. Her fawn gown trimmed with rows of brown velvet ribbon was simple but elegant, and an exceptionally beautiful cameo brooch fastened its collar. The new mistress of Bicton was un-expectedly dignified, not least in her efforts to conceal the fact that she wondered what she was doing there. Gertrude found herself hating Arthur Thornley as much on his wife's account as on her own.

'I expect you feel a little unsettled still,' she said with genuine sympathy. 'It's an upheaval, leaving the home one is used to.'

Mrs Thornley's eyes searched her visitor's face and found there nothing but friendliness and a smile that lit it into beauty. Whatever had brought young Lady Wyndham to see her, it certainly wasn't the heartless formality that only waited long enough for a footman to leave the correct number of cards before mistress and carriage drove away again.

Suffocating with the weight of her own loneliness, Jane Thornley forgot the very first rule that governed afternoon calls . . . fifteen minutes' conversation about nothing in particular, to be followed by a return visit of the same duration.

'I suppose you wouldn't take a cup of tea with me now that you're here?' she asked.

Gertrude heard the note of entreaty and promptly nodded. 'I'd be happy to . . . tea always seems to taste better when it's shared. Don't you think so?'

Mrs Thornley's face relaxed for the first time. She ordered tea from the maid who answered the bell, and then said shyly, 'It's very good of you to come. The truth is I've been longing for a bit of company.'

Gertrude's eyes wandered round the huge room. 'It *is* rather large, isn't it?' She was tempted to share with her hostess Octavia Browning's opinion that it would have made an excellent railway station, but it was too soon to know whether Mrs Thornley could see anything funny in Bicton Grange.

'Are you going to miss Birmingham?' she asked instead. 'I have the impression that your husband, at least, isn't country-bred.'

'We've both spent our lives in Birmingham, but Mr Thornley says it's time for a change. He says we'll get used to it in time, but I'm not so sure myself.'

'Why come if you think you won't be happy here?'

'It's for Frank, you see. His father wants him to grow up as good as any other country gentleman. Frank's fifteen now . . . our only child. We'd have liked more, but things don't always work out how you want them to.'

Gertrude guessed that the quiet statement concealed more than Mrs Thornley's own sadness; no doubt she'd been made to feel that the failure had been *hers*, since it couldn't possibly be her husband's.

'Arthur would have been happier with half a dozen, but he's always been kind enough to say quality's better than quantity any day, and that's what we've got in our Frank – quality.'

Gertrude mentally apologized to her absent host. It went against the grain to like anything about Arthur Thornley, but it seemed she had to acquit him of this particular unkindness to his wife.

'We're fortunate in having two beautiful daughters as well,' she said, 'but Ned is *our* only son too, and the greatest treasure we have. I don't know how we shall manage when he goes away to school.'

Mrs Thornley's brown eyes were soft with sympathy. 'We couldn't have parted with Frank – he's at the grammar school in Birmingham. It's different for your boy, of course; I can see he's bound to go away. It makes me thankful we aren't gentry, for all we live now at Bicton Grange.' She looked down at the teacup she was fidgeting with, then let frankness have its head. 'We own this ugly great lump of a house but we don't belong here . . . never shall do. Arthur can't seem to see that, Lady Wyndham, but I do.' The eyes that met Gertrude's steadily were intelligent as well as honest, and full of a desperate appeal.

'Perhaps you don't belong yet, because changes are accepted more slowly in the country. But if you leave out the Earl and Countess at Warwick, the neighbourhood's full of pleasant people who are not especially grand. They've all managed to accept me, who didn't belong either in the sense you mean, although I've always lived at Haywood's End.' She saw bewilderment in Mrs Thornley's face, and proceeded to explain. 'My mother was governess to the Wyndham children, my father is still the land agent for the estate, and I first went to Providence as Lady Hester's companion-help!'

'You don't say so,' Jane murmured, 'and to think I nearly pretended I wasn't at home when Biggs said you'd called. Arthur said Sir William was very stiff with him, and I reckoned you'd be just the same.'

'My husband isn't stiff at all in the normal way, but he dislikes Mr Thornley's factories spreading over the country-side. You must come to Providence and meet my mother-in-law. She's frail now and rather blind, so that leaving the house is a trial for her, but she dearly loves to be visited. *She* will convince you better than I can that there is no reason for you to fear the neighbourhood.'

'That's what Frank says: "You've nothing to be ashamed of, Mam; if they're daft enough to think you're not good enough, feel sorry for them, because it's why they have to sell their houses; they've got more hair than wit!"'

Gertrude thought young Frank sounded remarkably like his father, but she said instead, 'Sons are so full of good advice that they don't seem to stand in need of themselves. Dear Ned is trying to teach me not to be afraid of spiders! My own advice, if it's the slightest help to you, Mrs Thornley, is more practical: don't let your cook get the upper hand because she really *will* sap your confidence, and learn to laugh at this extraordinary house . . . its previous mistress, Octavia Browning, did!'

'Now, laughing at it is something I'd never have thought of,' Jane Thornley said wonderingly. 'I began by thinking I might have to burn it down!'

She delivered the statement in a voice so calmly matter-of-fact that it struck Gertrude as irresistibly funny. She struggled with amusement that might give offence, failed to stifle the laughter welling up inside her, and finally collapsed in the sort of helpless mirth that she sometimes shared with Lady Hester. Her hostess stared at her in astonishment, began to smile herself, and a moment later had tears of laughter running down her face.

'Oh, my dear, I don't remember when I laughed like that,' she gasped eventually, mopping her eyes. 'Even Frank isn't what you'd call light-hearted . . . takes after his father, you see.'

Gertrude agreed weakly that she saw. Her occasional glimpses of Arthur Thornley were of a man who didn't dare see anything comical about life in case he missed an opportunity while he was laughing. When she finally stood up to take her leave, Jane Thornley looked less strained than when she'd arrived. She went back to Providence to report to Lady Hester that Mr Thornley had got himself a wife he didn't deserve.

Her visit the following day was to the rectory, to enlist Maud Roberts in her campaign to introduce Jane to the neighbourhood.

'It isn't too far for you to ride over on your bicycle . . . I think Mrs Thornley would enjoy that.'

'My dear Gertrude, you make it sound as if I performed a circus act for the entertainment of the populace. I shall certainly go, but *not* in my pedalling bloomers – they might shock a lady who is likely to be a pillar of the Methodist Church in Birmingham!'

Gertrude grinned and admitted there was some truth in this. 'Now, dear Maud, that's only my first request. I've got a second one. Will you help me sell William's paintings?'

Miss Roberts was privy to most, if not quite all, of her friend's secrets; she knew, therefore, that a shortage of money was the most constant of the Wyndhams' problems.

'I'll help you do anything you like, but I'm not sure I'm

qualified to . . . purvey . . . I should think that's the word, wouldn't you? . . . purvey modern art.'

'Nobody is,' Gertrude said emphatically. 'That's just the point. It's too modern for people to know that it's what they *ought* to be wanting. We've got to create a demand for William's paintings before a dealer will feel that it is safe to take them.'

Maud stared at her, fascinated. 'Are you about to tell me how we're going to do that?'

Gertrude gave her a blinding smile. 'It just came to me. There's one possible dealer, according to William: a Frenchman in Bond Street Maud, you often go to London . . . could you call and say you're interested in buying a William Wyndham? He won't have one, so there's no danger that he could offer you anything. Then I'll get my father to write – a Frenchman won't know that Haywood's End and Providence are the same place – and I'll ask Octavia Browning to visit the gallery as well. Then before Monsieur Blanchard has had time to forget that several people are interested in William Wyndham, I shall arrive and offer him a painting. The only difficulty I can foresee is that I shall have not the slightest idea what to charge.'

Maud looked pensive. 'I hate to be a wet blanket, but I can foresee more difficulties than *that*. Suppose Monsieur Blanchard, convinced of our eagerness to buy, pursues us up hill and down dale afterwards, offering us whatever you offer him?'

'You don't leave an address – mustn't do, in fact, or Haywood's End *will* crop up rather too often. You just have to say that you'll look in whenever you're passing.' It suddenly occurred to Gertrude that her friend was looking doubtful. 'Dear Maud . . . is it too much to ask?'

Miss Roberts's frowning expression gave place to a charming smile. 'I was thinking of my wardrobe . . . wondering about the correct get-up for an assault on the bastions of art – French bastions at that! I shan't manage to look fashionable, so I must try for the rich eccentric; we must hope that a Frenchman won't know the difference.'

Gertrude wasn't privileged to see the outfit in which Maud nobly endured a visit to her dentist so that she could also call in on Bond Street, but she was given a report immediately afterwards.

'Monsieur Blanchard – charming in the highest degree – was desolated to admit that he couldn't offer me what I wanted, but did *not* admit that he'd never heard of William. In fact, he was so persuasive that I was almost talked into buying a painting by someone called Camille Pissarro instead. I came out having convinced myself as well as Blanchard that I *wanted* a modern painting!'

'Dear Maud, you obviously did splendidly. But there's no need to *buy* a modern painting; we can always give you one of William's.'

'I think it would be an artistic touch if I looked in again, just before you go,' Maud said thoughtfully, 'but the visit will have to be very brief next time; I've almost exhausted everything I can say about the French Impressionists!'

Gertrude grinned, then suddenly looked doubtful. 'William would be horrified if he knew what we were doing; he'd say it was dishonest. But, Maud, it would be such a marvellous thing if we could manage to sell the paintings . . . there are dozens of them. They might educate Ned, even if they didn't save Providence.'

'Don't *you* tell William, and *I* shan't tell Hubert,' Maud said firmly. 'Men are impractical creatures – dear and delightful, but far too wedded to vague principles! In any case, we're doing Monsieur Blanchard a favour, introducing him to an artist he wouldn't have know about otherwise.'

'There is that,' Gertrude agreed. Three weeks later, with her other red herrings safely trailed in front of an unsuspecting art dealer, she was driven to the station and the train for London. William made no objection to her going once she had agreed to be accompanied by Jem Martin, and kindly managed not to say that he felt sure she was embarking on a wild-goose chase.

Bond Street on a sunny October morning was a lively

place, thronged with carriages and fashionably-dressed women. Gertrude quickly lost confidence in her grey alpaca cape and skirt that had seemed elegant enough in Warwick, and regretted the lack of a frilly parasol which seemed an indispensable part of every lady's outfit. She also felt extremely nervous now that Monsieur Blanchard's imposing premises stood before her. One large painting, an antique vase, and some exquisitely arranged flowers completed the window display. It was a world she knew nothing about, and she was probably about to make a complete fool of herself. Still, Maud had found the courage to go inside, and she must do likewise.

A very young and earnest gentleman accepted her card, but took it to his colleague who was in conversation with another couple. The man, Monsieur Blanchard no doubt, excused himself, glanced at the card, and came towards her. She had the extraordinary idea that he was not only amused, but had been expecting her.

'Lady Wyndham . . . how can I help you?' His voice was deep and his English almost faultless. Hair even blacker than her own, and an olive complexion against which his teeth looked very white, gave him an appearance she thought of as exotic. To Gertrude, accustomed to William's dislike of anything but old and shabby clothes, Monsieur Blanchard looked something of a dandy who would consider her a countrified frump! What a pity it was that Maud hadn't thought to warn her about the frilly parasol.

'You do . . . do buy as well as sell paintings?' she asked nervously.

'But of course . . . how else could I operate, madame?'

How else indeed? She blushed for her stupidity, and he realized that Lady Wyndham was even younger than he'd supposed. Her rig was simple, perhaps slightly démodé to the eye of a man accustomed to fashionable society, but Monsieur Blanchard appreciated her appearance never-theless. The effect of a little white frill standing above the collar of her grey cape was altogether charming, and he liked the white straw hat perched forward over her dark hair. He was certain that she'd brought him her husband's paintings and that she was finding it difficult to tell him so. It was curious that Sir William hadn't come himself, but Henri Blanchard enjoyed the curiosities of life and saw no reason not to enjoy a visitor who promised to redeem an otherwise boring morning.

'You are familiar with the new . . . er, Impressionistic . . . techniques of painting, I believe,' Gertrude started off grandly. Monsieur Blanchard bowed but said nothing, and she was forced to go on. 'Then perhaps you would like to consider buying some . . . that is, perhaps one . . . of my husband's pictures?'

'I am ready to consider anything, madame, but perhaps we should withdraw from the gallery for a moment.'

She supposed that it was a French gift to invest a perfectly ordinary suggestion with undertones of licentiousness. The gallery had numerous people in it, and Jem was only as far away as the pavement outside. There was no reason not to walk through the door he held open for her, especially since his face told her he knew the hesitation in her mind and was amused by it. The inner sanctum she walked into was no less sumptuously furnished than the gallery and her spirits began to rise; Monsieur Blanchard was either rich, or successful, or both. She removed two paintings from the folder she was carrying and laid them on his desk; one was a still life of a green glass flagon reflecting light on to an old glazed bowl heaped with grapes; the other was the picture of the irises by the moat at Providence.

The Frenchman was silent for so long that she grew nervous again. It was true that William's work was nothing like the ornate painting she'd seen in the window; if *that* was all Monsieur Blanchard sold, he wouldn't buy this.

'Who taught your husband to paint like this?' he asked suddenly. His voice was brisk, almost harsh, and she felt able to relax. The uneasy moment when she'd felt him looking at *her* had come and gone; she didn't mind at all now that his whole concentration was focused on what was in front of him.

'No one *taught* William . . . he's always painted, since he was a schoolboy . . . he calls himself a dabbler, an amateur.'

'He would, of course, being an Englishman,' Blanchard grunted, still not taking his eyes off the canvases.

'Will you buy them?' She looked down at the irises, then heard herself say, 'At least, perhaps you'd like to buy the flagon one . . . the other is not for sale.'

'Why not, may I ask?'

'Because I've just realized that it's too precious to me. There are similar ones at Providence that you could have instead, but I can't part with this one.'

Monsieur Blanchard seemed to find nothing odd in this, and her heart warmed to him; lesser men might have asked why she'd brought it at all. She was disappointed that he hadn't mentioned Maud's or Octavia Browning's visit. Suddenly he seemed to come to a decision.

'I am glad to have seen these paintings. Normally I should have rejected them for the time being, but it happens that I believe I can sell them.'

Gertrude knew herself confounded. It was one thing to concoct a ruse with Maud; quite another, she now discovered, to allow this unsuspecting man to believe in non-existent buyers. 'Perhaps I could leave this one with you,' she suggested nervously. 'If a client is *truly* interested . . .'

'I know of a lady, a Miss Roberts, who is quite desperate to buy a Wyndham painting.'

'I know Miss Roberts too,' Gertrude admitted. 'She lives at the rectory at Haywood's End.'

'How strange . . . there was another enquiry from that very place.'

'It came from my father,' she said with the calmness of despair. 'He enquired at my request, and so did Miss Roberts. William told me a demand for the new style of painting would have to be created, but he *didn't* tell me to do it like this . . . that was my idea.'

She didn't know what she expected, but certainly not that

Monsieur Blanchard's dark face would be alight with amusement. He lifted her hand in a gesture that startled her and carried it to his lips. '*Mes compliments*, madame . . . when you walked in I think I guessed, but it is a unique privilege to meet an honest woman!'

'William also said that I should be wasting my time in coming. As it turns out, I've probably wasted yours as well; I'm sorry, monsieur.'

She was being appraised again, by a stare that took in more about her than she felt this man was entitled to know.

'In *that* at least, your husband was wrong, Lady Wyndham. No time spent in a good cause is ever wasted. However, the cause is far from won, because people do not yet appreciate the beauty of what I offer them. Some day they will, but for the moment they buy what they are used to – angelic ladies seated at improbable organs, and nymphs strategically draped in white chiffon who stare at themselves in pools . . . they call it *l'Art, mon Dieu!*'

'It all sounds rather hopeless, then,' Gertrude said sadly. 'I need them to buy *now* not when they've grown tired of conceited nymphs.'

Monsieur Blanchard suddenly looked displeased with her. 'Nothing is ever hopeless, *chère* madame; we educate, we wait, eventually we sell. Now, this is how I suggest things arrange themselves. I shall come to see the rest of your husband's paintings. If they are of the same standard as these, I shall arrange to exhibit them . . . perhaps in Paris first of all which though slow, God knows, to appreciate what is new, is not quite so slavishly devoted to antiquity as London. Then, *peu à peu*, the name of William Wyndham becomes known . . . we write a little article here, arrange a little showing there, and so the business goes. But first I must be sure of the quality. What is this strange-sounding Providence . . . a place?'

'Yes, a place . . . but also our home. That shall be a test of *your* quality, monsieur,' Gertrude said, smiling at him, 'whether or not *you* appreciate Providence!' The smile faded from her lips because she saw that he was frowning at her.

'I'm sorry – did that sound impertinent when you seem prepared to go to great trouble to help us?'

'It sounded interesting. Never apologize for offering that, especially to a man.' His eyes lingered on her face a moment longer and then his expression changed again. 'My compliments on the charming hat, madame. Most women insist on balancing a sort of monstrous tea-tray on their heads, laden with stuffed birds and foliage enough to fill a flower vase!'

'Oh, we shall be wearing the tea-trays, monsieur, but in a year or two's time,' she explained solemnly – 'fashion comes late to Haywood's End!'

'Better that it should never come at all. May I keep the paintings for the moment, and bring them when I come to Providence? Do you trust me to do that?'

The conversation had, bewilderingly, become serious again and his question seemed full of a significance that had to do with more than two small paintings.

'Yes, I trust you,' Gertrude said simply.

'Then we understand one another. I shall write to Sir William as soon as I am free to arrange a visit.'

The strange interview was over, and she was relieved to be ushered out into the gallery again and shown to the door. Her hand was bowed over but not kissed again, and a moment later she was blinking in the sunlight, and registering Jem Martin's relief at the sight of her.

'You was gone a long time, milady . . . I was reckonin' I'd better come a-lookin' for ye.'

She shook her head and suggested that he should find a hansom cab instead. Jem was partly right but she had the feeling of having gone far in space rather than time in the company of Henri Blanchard, and now had to retrace her steps to more familiar places.

CHAPTER TWELVE

William was waiting for her when she got home. He thought she looked tired, and blamed himself for not vetoing an expedition that had been bound to fail. On the other hand, he could see no sign of the canvases she'd taken with her.

'You don't like to mention that you left my paintings on the train?' he suggested, smiling at her.

'I left them with Henri Blanchard. He'll bring them back when he comes to inspect the rest.' At the time it had seemed unthinkable not to believe him, but it occurred to her now that William might consider she'd been foolishly trusting. 'He *said* he would come,' she added firmly. The strange mixture of nervousness and excitement that she had felt in the Frenchman's company couldn't be reported on. But, pruned of that, there seemed little left to say about an interview that had made a deep impression on her.

'He wanted to know who had taught you; repeated what *you* had said about people needing to be educated; and muttered something about showing your paintings in Paris if he judged the rest of them good enough.' It was a bald recital of the facts; there was no need to mention also that Henri Blanchard had succeeded in making her conscious of herself as a woman again. There was certainly no need to say that her hat had been his excuse for inspecting her very thoroughly.

Fortunately William's attention was riveted on the word Paris. 'My dear girl, you seem to have done wonders. We mustn't *expect* anything to come of it, of course; Monsieur Blanchard might just have been wanting to get rid of you tactfully! We shall know soon enough, if we have to go and retrieve the paintings ourselves.'

'He said he would come,' she repeated stubbornly. 'I don't think he would take the trouble to say something he didn't mean.'

William stared at her distracted face, sensing that her visit to the gallery had left an impression on her she was unable to forget. It made him curious to meet Henri Blanchard.

'Well, let us hope that your confidence is more justified than my doubt of him,' he said gently.

At the end of a week when nothing had been heard from London, she was beginning to think that William was right; she'd been a gullible fool, and Blanchard was practised in the art of duping women. Then a letter from him arrived, suggesting a visit to Providence the following week. Faith was restored, most magically, in herself and in him!

He wrote briefly to William, suggesting that the paintings should be chronologically arranged for him so that their development, if any, could be observed. Monsieur Blanchard's written English was more stilted than his conversation, his letter conveyed the impression of a busy man who proposed, out of the goodness of his heart, a journey that he suspected would be a waste of time. William replied with his usual gentle courtesy, held out no promise of any visible development, but hoped that Monsieur Blanchard would be their guest for at least one night. At that point Gertrude took herself over to the rectory.

'Maud . . . the art dealer is coming to Providence after all. William is determined not to get excited about it, but don't you think it must mean that the man is at least *faintly* interested?'

'No doubt about it, I should say. How very awkward, though. Your father and I will have to go into hiding . . . I don't think I could bear to bump into Monsieur Blanchard at Haywood's End!'

'You don't have to worry,' Gertrude said baldly. 'There won't be any embarrassment, which is just as well because I want you and the rector to dine with us when he's here.'

'You told him . . . ?'

'Yes – it suddenly seemed unbearably shabby not to when he was about to buy a picture because he thought he had *you* as a ready customer.' She hesitated, choosing her next words carefully. 'You've had more experience of people than I have, but he wasn't like anyone *I'd* ever met before.' Another silence, then she added casually, 'Bond Street was swarming with fashionably-dressed women but he said he liked my old straw hat!'

Maud observed her pensive expression, but said merely, 'I thought you went to discuss art, not millinery.'

'We did, but one thing seems to lead to another with Henri Blanchard. You *will* both come and dine, won't you?'

'Speaking for myself, nothing will keep us away,' said Maud. 'Meanwhile, I'm big with news of my own. I've made the acquaintance of Jane Thornley . . . a nice and long-suffering woman, I thought. But I went one better than you and met "young Frank" as well. He looks just like his father, which is a misfortune, but he had the good sense to watch and say very little – rather remarkable in a boy of that age.'

'I dare say you overawed him.'

'My dear, even I don't overawe a male Thornley; the best you can hope for is to hold your own with them.'

Gertrude nodded, acknowledging the undoubted truth of this. 'My father thinks we can stop worrying about Mr Thornley now that he's got Bicton, but I have the feeling that it isn't as simple as that. Life seems to follow patterns that are prearranged . . . at least, I've found it so. Somehow, I'm quite certain the Thornleys are included in *our* patterns, much as I hate the idea, and it wouldn't surprise me if Arthur Thornley was certain of it, too.'

She went home to spur William on in the herculean labour of sorting out all the canvases propped against the walls of the Great Parlour. By the time Hodges set out for the railway station the following week, the paintings and the house were in the best state of readiness that could be achieved. The November afternoon was soft and overcast, but within doors firelight caught the gleam of polished surfaces everywhere, and Biddle's beautiful late chrysanthemums made pools of glowing colour about the rooms.

The house looked as beautiful and welcoming as she could make it, but Gertrude knew herself to be nervous; as usual, the knowledge made her belligerent. She remembered their guest's smooth self-assurance; Providence might, perhaps, be enough to ruffle it. Henri Blanchard was citified down to his highly-polished boots. He wouldn't be accustomed to the hooting of night owls outside his bedroom window, or a medieval moat, and plumbing which was almost as medieval and only findable at night by candlelight! If none of this shook his metropolitan sang-froid, there remained the poor little ghost in the library! Blanchard would almost certainly patronize William and be bored with the rest of them. She wanted very much to have the public educated, but she wished he wasn't coming.

The reality of the visit was, as is often the case, not at all as she had imagined it. Having persuaded William into his most respectable jacket on the grounds that their guest would put even *that* to shame, she found Blanchard quietly dressed for a country call. It is true that he kissed Lady Hester's hand with inimitable grace, but it was the only touch of foreign-ness that he permitted himself. His greeting to Gertrude was so casually correct that he might have been any English neighbour paying a social call, and she had to admit privately that he seemed much more interested in her three-year-old daughter than herself.

Even when the time came to go upstairs to the Great Parlour Sybil refused to be separated from her new friend, and announced that she would 'go with nice man and look at paintin's too'. Gertrude felt obliged to discover what Blanchard thought of his new disciple.

'We *could* evict my daughter if the "nice man" prefers!'

'Not at all . . . he's much too flattered to be in such rare demand!'

Gertrude didn't believe that the demand was all that rare, but his kindness to a precocious small child was unexpected and pleasant. She thought that, at least until the novelty wore off, he might even be enjoying this sudden immersion in family life. When they'd gone she was obliged to confess to Lady Hester how it came about that Maud had already met their guest; she left her mother-in-law still laughing and forced herself to concentrate on domestic concerns. With everything in the dining-room and the kitchen as it should be, and Sybil finally restored, protesting, to the nursery, she went to her own room to dress for dinner.

Her gown was not new and, like the rest of her wardrobe, had been made for her by the seamstress in Warwick, but its crimson silk flattered her white skin and shining dark hair. She fastened about her throat the necklace of silver and opal that her mother-in-law had given her, and stared at herself in the mirror – far from being a beauty, she decided regretfully, but perhaps not a wife William need feel ashamed of.

Henri Blanchard was alone in the Great Hall, having exchanged his suit for black trousers and a maroon velvet smoking-jacket. He was standing in front of the fire, but turned at the rustle of her skirt. His deliberate scrutiny of her would have been impossible to any Englishman she knew except James Wyndham.

'I'm sorry,' she said quickly. 'William *will* get embroiled with the children. A simple good night always leads to a discussion with Ned on some vital matter that can't wait until tomorrow.'

'I understand how that is, even having no son of my own. I had plenty to think about. You didn't prepare me for Providence – *meant* not to, perhaps?'

'You might have decided not to come if I'd said how old-fashioned it was.' She said it half-smilingly and was disconcerted to see him frown.

'Do you find me so feeble that you fear I cannot exist without my usual creature comforts, Lady Wyndham?' He had moved closer to her to ask the question and she was forced to look at him. The firelight was reflected in his eyes, making them bright but unreadable. His olive skin and black hair against the snowy whiteness of fresh linen made him seem even more exotic than she had remembered, but she had the feeling that he was outside the limits of her experience in more important ways as well. He was still waiting for her to answer his question and she was forced to do her best with it.

'Not feeble at all . . . but I doubt if you are used to a house that lags so far behind the times. Now at least you will understand why I should like to sell William's paintings.'

Blanchard shrugged the idea aside. 'From the point of view of its mistress Providence could no doubt be made easier to run; it could scarcely be made more beautiful.' He stated it, with no wish to please, simply as a truth that was undeniable.

'Thank you . . . that's *your* test safely passed!' Gertrude said lightly. 'Now as to yours for *us* – will you give us your true opinion about William's work, or will you feel obliged to be tactful?'

'I never feel obliged to be tactful! My opinion is this: he must go on working – I understand he's done less lately; nevertheless, there's enough already to merit, in fact to demand, an exhibition. I shall try to arrange it in Paris for next spring.'

Her face flushed with pleasure, but before there was time to thank him, William led his mother into the room and at the same moment Jem ushered the Roberts in as well. Maud, got up grandly for the occasion in a crinoline gown that might have been fashionable ten years before, held out her hand to Blanchard.

'I hoped we wouldn't meet again, but the sins of wrong-doers should, of course, always be discovered! Perhaps you will feel more forgiving towards me if I admit that you almost talked me into buying that little Pissarro.'

Blanchard bowed over her hand. 'Mademoiselle . . . in that case your taste is excellent!' He said it even while he allowed his glance to skim over her antiquated dress, and Maud's smile acknowledged that he'd come off best. From that moment on it seemed to an anxious hostess that the whole evening became imbued with a charmed grace and lightness that made it memorable. Blanchard treated Lady Hester with a gallantry that stopped safely short of ever being overdone, and engaged Maud in a verbal battle of wits that brought a sparkle to her eye. He could talk theology with Hubert Roberts as readily as art with William, but his especial gift seemed to be to include everyone else in the conversation as well and leave them feeling that they had never been so wise or witty.

A paragon of a guest, Gertrude told herself. He found little time to say anything to *her*, but she preferred him concentrating on other people. She didn't know that he found time, at least, to look at her at the other end of the table, registering the black and white and crimson picture that she made. If he'd been able to say what was in his mind – that she and the house she lived in seemed to have stepped out of a more gracious past – he thought she'd have accepted the compliment only on behalf of Providence. His eyes remained on her when she happened to look his way, but there was no reason why anyone else should notice a shared moment of stillness that only ended when he stretched out a hand to lift his wineglass.

The following morning she arranged matters so that he breakfasted alone with William, and then they went upstairs to select the paintings which should comprise his first exhibition. Blanchard declined luncheon, preferring to catch an early afternoon train back to London, and William and Ned were to drive with him as far as the railway station. When the time came to say goodbye Sybil's objections to this arrangement were vocal enough to dominate the situation. With a furious small daughter clasped in her arms, Gertrude found it easier to smile naturally at their departing guest.

'Do you always wreak this amount of havoc when you visit your clientele? If so, I think you should stay in London.'

Blanchard's fingers gently touched Sybil's scarlet cheek before he looked at her mother.

'She's going to be very like you. Will there be a chance of seeing you in Paris next spring?'

'I don't think so. William must come, of course, but I should need to stay here with my mother-in-law and the children.' She was able to say it serenely, as if it caused her no regret. Still holding Sybil, she had no need to offer him her hand, and he thought she didn't regret that either. The wind ruffled her dark hair and he watched her smile as the small girl, forgetting she was displeased with her mother, stroked it into place again.

'There is *every* chance that she will grow just like you,' he said again, as if Gertrude had argued with him, but his voice didn't indicate whether he considered this a fortunate thing or not. '*Au revoir*, madame.'

William helped Ned to scramble up the steps of the carriage, and then Blanchard was ushered in. Except for Artie, whistling as he wandered off to polish harness in the tack-room, she was alone there with her daughter. The wind seemed cold now, making her shiver; it reminded her that it was quite pointless to stand there, looking at a bend in the empty drive.

At Bicton, Jane Thornley was listening to her husband. It was something she often did when he felt talkative. She'd had long practice in reading the signs, knew the moment when some new plan being mulled over in his head was ripe for sharing with her. Mr Thornley wouldn't have agreed that he needed his wife's advice, probably wouldn't have admitted to anyone else that he even gave her the benefit of his confidences, but he knew that she had the instincts of a profoundly sensible woman. More than once she'd turned out to be right when he was wrong, and he was fair-minded enough not to forget the fact. Now, he spread a map out on the table and invited her to consider it.

'Look, Jane . . . a new factory *here* is what I thought.' His finger prodded a spot on the southern outskirts of Birmingham. 'Not too near us, but convenient, between here and the rest of the works. It'll be in full production by the time young Frank's ready to start. Must have something of his own to run eventually, or we'll be getting in each other's road.'

'*Another* factory . . . whatever for this time?'

'Well, I thought of going into munitions, Janey.' He only called her that when he hoped to persuade her of the rightness of something she wouldn't like. He was correct in thinking that she didn't like his latest brain-child.

'No, Arthur . . . surely not guns and such; the world's troubled enough as it is.'

'Just the point,' he said quickly. 'Guns are going to be needed and if we don't make them, someone else will. I take the trouble to find out what's happening in the world, and what's happening is that this country's getting left behind. We've got an army that hasn't been modernized since the Battle of Waterloo – which is why we made such a mess of the Crimea. I can't do anything about the old fools who have the running of things, but I *can* produce weapons that are as good as the ones our enemies are making.'

'Enemies, Arthur?' Jane queried doubtfully. 'Surely not . . . why should anybody hate us?'

'Envy, for a start; we've got possessions other people would like. Don't think we haven't got enemies, and one of these days we may have to fight them. I intend to make a profit, of course – there's no sense in being in business otherwise; but I reckon I'll be doing this country a service as well. *Then* we'll see if the Earl of Warwick still looks down his nose at me, and his Countess gets up protest meetings about my factory working hours.'

'She's a good woman, Arthur . . . trying to help people who are less fortunate, and often at her own expense, I believe.'

'Yes, in between rampaging about the country on her horses, maybe, and bringing scandal on the Prince of Wales! Don't expect me to be grateful for the aristocracy . . . we'd be better off without 'em.'

Jane Thornley stared at her husband aware that an opportunity she had been waiting for had come. 'Arthur,

I'm not happy about you making guns but I can see you're set on it. If I don't argue will you let me do something *I'm* set on as well?'

'Such as what?' he enquired cautiously.

'Make use of this great lump of a house,' she confessed in a rush. 'There are rooms we never even go into, just lying idle.' She brought the last phrase out with care, knowing that it was one of his own favourite arguments.

'What do you want to do in them . . . run a dancing school?'

She didn't even hear the sarcasm, being too intent on what was in her mind. 'I want to bring young women here who can't earn a living in Birmingham . . . there are lots of them, poor sad creatures, too frail or ill to work in your factories. But they can all sit and *sew*, Arthur, and they want work, not charity. I shall set them to making fine underclothes, blouses, and such, but they must have somewhere to work and, until money starts to come in, materials to work with and wages.'

Her husband looked disapprovingly at her. 'Jane, you ought to know the first rule of business by now: it's no manner of good making what you can't sell. What happens when you're knee-deep in fine petticoats?'

'We won't be. I've been talking to my friends at Providence and Miss Roberts at Haywood's End. Between them they know any amount of people, and those people know more people. I reckon we'd be hard put to it to keep up with the demand.'

He stared at her serene face and didn't doubt the strength of purpose that underlay its gentle expression. 'Got it all worked out, haven't you?'

'Yes,' she admitted, 'just like you and your new factory!'

It made him smile, but he wasn't minded to admit at once that he didn't object to the scheme. In fact, he rather liked it. Lady Warwick was becoming a regular nuisance, pestering the life out of men who had more to do with their time than listen to her high-minded philanthropic prattle. There was nothing high-minded or airy-fairy about Jane's idea, but if it worked it would give Thornley's a better name. It might even do a bit of good as well and, being a not ungenerous man, Arthur Thornley didn't object to that, either.

'I'll think about it,' he said eventually.

Jane smiled at him with great gratitude and let the matter rest, but she had herself driven over to Providence that afternoon to tell Gertrude that the school of sewing was as good as under way.

CHAPTER THIRTEEN

Blanchard was as good as his word. William's exhibition appeared in the spring Salon of 1896, and he went reluctantly to Paris to attend it. He was forced there by Gertrude, who insisted that he must make this much effort to get himself known in artistic circles.

'But, my dear girl, I don't *want* to be known. People don't have to be acquainted with my shabby English clothes and my long Wyndham nose to know whether or not they like my paintings. Anyway, Blanchard must understand that I can't be away for your birthday, and the dates of the exhibition clash with that.'

'If we *must* celebrate the fact that I become twenty-six, we can do it when you get back. Mama, *you* convince him, please, that he should go.'

Lady Hester obligingly did so, choosing the argument that her courteous son would find hardest to resist. 'Henri Blanchard is entitled to expect you there, my dear. It would look so churlish to refuse. Who else but you can explain when people ask why you paint in the way *you* do, and not like anybody else?'

'That's exactly what I should wish to avoid, having no answer to the question myself!'

In the end, however, he was persuaded to go, and returned at the end of a week to report diffidently that Blanchard had seemed pleased with the exhibition. About the rest of his visit he was slightly more informative, and a good deal more enthusiastic. He'd spent seven days, and the better part of seven nights, in talking to other painters and looking at their work. There had been very little time left to notice Paris, but he'd seen enough to impress him.

'I shall take you there one day,' he told Gertrude. 'Compared with London, it's more frivolously beautiful – a feminine city, in fact!'

'Let us go by all means, but Paris can wait,' she said firmly. 'What about your *paintings*, William? Did any of them sell?'

He looked vague about a point his wife considered all-important. 'Blanchard seemed to think some of them might go, but I left that side of things to him.'

Gertrude felt no surprise, and could only hope that a dealer in paintings would have remembered that he was there to promote his wares, even if the artist did not. Blanchard would let them know if any of the paintings were going to remain in Paris. She abandoned the subject reluctantly but had news of her own to relate.

'Two things have happened while you've been away. The first was an announcement in *The Times*: Lord Trentham has died. Mama tries not to expect that Louise and her husband will now leave India, but she's allowing herself a little hope, at least. Do you suppose there's any chance of their coming back?'

William considered for a moment. '*Some* chance, I think. Alec's brother inherits, of course, but he's seven or eight years older and apparently a determined bachelor. If he should remain so, Alec must certainly come home.'

Gertrude nodded, then released the second item, which had been agitating her privately much more.

'Your mother had a letter from James yesterday, posted just before he sailed. He expects to be here within a week. It's a business visit and the children are left with their grandparents in New York.' She marvelled at the calm sound of her voice when her thoughts were in turmoil. After thirty-six hours in which to make up her mind, she still hadn't decided whether she longed more for him to come than she hoped that he would have stayed away.

'It will be good to see the poor fellow,' William remarked quietly. 'A pity he isn't bringing the children, though; Mama would have enjoyed seeing them, and Patrick could have got to know Ned.'

The conviction in his voice that this would have been good for James's son made her smile in spite of herself. 'They might have hated each other – cousins sometimes do, I believe.'

'Nobody hates Ned,' William said with certainty. 'Sybil might have been a problem, of course, if Patrick decided that a girl cousin five years younger than himself wasn't worth bothering with!'

'Will she grow out of demanding everybody's attention, or get worse as she gets older?' Gertrude asked anxiously.

William smiled with his usual sweetness. 'You worry too much. If she continues to insist on the limelight, we'll put her on the stage – she can become another Sarah Bernhardt and make the family fortune!'

Gertrude had to acknowledge to herself that she *did* worry too much, because when James reached Providence a week later he greeted her with no more than the easy affection of a man seeing his sister-in-law after an interval of several years. She couldn't prevent herself from staring at him and was saddened by what she saw. Despite a voyage that he insisted had been calm and restful, he looked thin and tired, and beneath surface cheerfulness she sensed a darker strain of tension and regret. How could it have been otherwise? Kitty should still have been alive, in the full flowering of her beauty, to give him comfort and joy.

There was an emotional reunion with Lady Hester, but tears couldn't last long in the presence of Ned – now rising five and greatly interested in the idea, explained to him by William, that he had something called an uncle who was this tall, bright-haired man. Sybil cared nothing for what he was called as long as the nice man who smiled at her should be instantly recognized as *hers*.

'The rest of us could now gracefully retire,' Gertrude explained to James. 'My daughter would be loth to believe that you need any other company but hers!'

'I'm her slave till bedtime,' he agreed, as Sybil established herself on his lap. 'After that we can allow time for other things.'

He spoke bravely at dinner of Kitty's death, saying that the subject must be mentioned between them. His own shock had been great but mercifully *she* had not been aware that she was dying. Patrick and Anita had been disturbed, of course, but a wise God had made children more resilient than adults; they were blessed with doting grandparents and servants who also loved them. Their lives now went on without Kitty, and that was perhaps the most tragic thing of all.

'And business, James,' William enquired eventually, 'how is that?' It wasn't a question it would normally have occurred to him to ask, but it seemed a less harrowing subject than the one they had been discussing.

'Business is up and down – like Tower Bridge, as the Cockney saying goes! We take risks, Dan and I, because that's what we enjoy doing. Some of them succeed, some don't, because we aren't the only fish in the sea and international competition is becoming fiercer all the time.'

'So I'm told. I receive lectures on the subject from a manufacturer in Birmingham, who assures me that we scarcely dare sleep in case some foreign rival should overtake us.'

'He's right, and far-sighted enough to see what a lot of people here simply refuse to acknowledge,' James said soberly. 'But how does it come about that *you're* on lecturing terms with manufacturers?'

'He's a neighbour of sorts. When the Brownings gave up Bicton Grange he bought the property. He's intelligent, hard-working . . .'

'. . . and odious,' Gertrude butted in quickly. 'On the other hand, his wife is intelligent, hard-working and extremely nice. Her only fault in my eyes is that she doesn't disown Arthur Thornley!'

James turned to her with a strange smile. 'Is that what you would recommend, Gertrude . . . disowning a husband?'

She was disconcerted, not so much by the question as by

his manner of asking it, which suggested that she was expected to take him seriously.

'I don't recommend it as a general rule,' she admitted, trying to smile. 'But if you had the doubtful pleasure of Mr Thornley's acquaintance, you'd agree that he's ripe for disowning.'

'Gertrude dearest, I can't agree,' Lady Hester protested, half-smiling, half-serious. 'Beneath an admittedly loud check suit, there is good in Mr Thornley!'

'And he's today's England, my father says,' Gertrude agreed, 'so we must learn to put up with him.'

'Well, likable and good or not, you all make him sound worth meeting,' James commented. 'Does he dine here, or would that be asking too much of the Wyndhams?'

Again there was an edge to the question, this time directed at his brother. William registered it but turned it aside. 'Nothing is too much for your entertainment, James! Mr Thornley shall certainly be invited.'

It didn't occur to Gertrude that her husband had any real intention to do something in the matter, and she intended to do nothing herself. But he reminded her the following morning that Hodges must immediately be sent over to Bicton with an invitation for that evening.

'Why?' Gertrude asked. 'I like Jane Thornley very much, but you certainly don't enjoy her husband's company.'

'Today's England,' William reminded her affably. 'We must at least learn to suffer him gracefully. In any case I think James and he would interest each other.'

'The Thornleys will be offended at the lack of notice and refuse to come.'

'They may be offended but they won't refuse.'

So Gertrude's note was written, apologizing as genuinely as she could for the lateness of the invitation and offering James's brief visit as an excuse for its suddenness. An hour later Hodges returned with an answer: William was at least right to the extent that the invitation had been accepted.

Domestic duties, and the usual daily routines that the children and the house required, enabled her to avoid James without seeming to do so. He spent the day out of doors, riding with William round the estate and visiting old friends in the village. For as long as there were people to talk to and laugh with, he was the light-hearted James of the past, but his expression darkened again as they rode back alone to Providence.

'Nothing changes here,' he burst out irritably. 'The years pass and everything else moves on, except Providence and Haywood's End. I'd swear Matthew's still shoeing the same old horse, and Hubert is probably delivering the same old sermon as when I was here last. It's suffocating! *You* might be able to put up with it, but it would drive me mad.'

William accepted calmly the knowledge that his brother despised him. There was nothing new in that – James had done so ever since they were children. Nor was there anything new in his dislike of standing still when there was some fresh excitement disappearing over the hill in front of him, which could be grabbed by the coat-tails if he ran fast enough. But William hadn't heard quite this note of savage frustration in his brother's voice before.

'You've forgotten that we like our changes to come slowly, James. Things *are* changing here, but I don't know that we're the better for them.'

James gave a snort of disgust. 'Of course not, because you sit and wait for them to happen. Why not try making things happen the way you want them to?'

William was sorely tempted to say that, if appearances were anything to go by, his brother's philosophy had failed to make him a contented man; but he remembered Kitty, and retreated to less hurtful ground.

'You'd be surprised to hear how active we are being! I believe I'm indebted to you for putting the idea into Gertrude's head that my paintings might sell. You can't accuse *her* of doing nothing – I am now the protégé of a charming French picture-dealer, and Paris has just been privileged to see some of my masterpieces!'

'Good God! I hope it could withstand the excitement.' The moment the ill-tempered words were out of his mouth,

James regretted them. If his brother had taken him to task, he would have apologized, but a gentle smile irritated him all the more. 'Don't be so bloody forbearing, William. Call me an unpleasant swine and have done with it.'

'I'd call you anything you like if it would make you less unhappy, but I'm too conscious of my own good fortune,' William said quietly.

'Yes . . . that is the damnable thing about life. Whatever we do, it remains in the end nothing more than that – a matter of good or ill fortune. What we *merit* doesn't come into it.'

'I'm afraid I have to agree with you, but Hubert Roberts wouldn't.'

James thought better of saying that the rector was a fool, and they jogged on in silence for a while.

'Come back to Providence,' William suddenly suggested. 'Heaven knows there's room enough for you and the children; let them put down English roots before it's too late.'

'It's too late already. They must stay where they are.'

The blunt refusal left no room for argument, and William didn't attempt any. With James in his present frame of mind, he now regretted the dinner guests he'd insisted upon. The evening looked fraught with disaster, but all he could do was help Gertrude welcome them as pleasantly as possible.

Jane Thornley came in looking nervous, and William couldn't be sure that his brother wouldn't crush her completely by making it clear that she wasn't worth his attention. Her husband didn't look nervous at all, but there was a risk here as well, because James might easily take it into his head to put a thrusting commoner in his place. But the evening went pleasantly, and William decided that they had the women to thank for it. His mother seemed to exert a charmed spell over Thornley; his harsh voice even became gentle when he spoke to her. Jane Thornley recovered her confidence under the warmth of Gertrude's welcome, and the discovery that her host was unexpectedly easy to talk to.

'I hear from my wife about the progress of the sewing school, Mrs Thornley,' William said. 'There seems to be no doubt that it is already a success.'

'It's a beginning,' she agreed, 'but there's a lot more we should do. Birmingham's better than most other cities, from what we hear, but even so there's hardship enough to break your heart.'

'Much more than can be dealt with by the generosity of people like you. Urban misery is on such a scale now that only effective legislation can deal with it. Laws are coming on to the statute book too slowly, but at least they're coming. The poor and the sick and the homeless are finally being recognized for what they are – human beings like the rest of us, not objects for contempt.'

Jane nodded, surprised and grateful for his understanding. She'd been nervous of meeting Sir William, but at this rate she'd soon be confiding in him what her next scheme was to be – the conversion of most of Bicton's grounds into playing fields for children! She hadn't tried the idea on Arthur yet, but after this evening she thought she would probably feel brave enough to do so.

When dinner was finished and Gertrude had led Lady Hester and their guest to the Great Hall next door, William made up his mind to curtail a male tête-à-tête and the drinking of port, both of which activities he greatly disliked, but the moment they were left alone James abandoned small talk for a topic that interested him more.

'I hear that you're a clever, inventive manufacturer, Mr Thornley. Why stay here to be frustrated by old ways that aren't quite allowed to die, even though they do nothing but hamper people like yourself?'

To William's surprise, Thornley disagreed with him. 'I don't know that things are as bad as all that,' he said consideringly. 'Any road, it's not the old ways that give me trouble so much as the new ones. Working men used to do what they were told without question, grateful to have a job. Now, they're being encouraged to make demands – higher wages, shorter working hours, longer holidays – any excuse will do to get them listening to the trouble-makers. And these don't even come just from their own kind – high-minded members of the upper class can cause even more trouble and often do.'

'Well, speaking as a non-industrialist, of course, I thank God for men like Lord Shaftesbury,' William put in with unusual sharpness. 'The evils that have been uncovered in our mines and factories cry to heaven to be redressed.'

Thornley stared at him. 'There are no evils in *my* factories. I don't employ children, and what women there are do work that is well within their capacity. My people have to work hard; I admit it. I'm a businessman, not a philanthropist. But they get a fair wage, and I arrange my business so that they're not laid off if trade fluctuates and times get hard. Can you say the same for *your* employees, Sir William?'

'As it happens, I can. My labourers don't starve even though farm prices fall or the harvest fails because of flood or drought.'

'Then you'll eventually go bankrupt. *That* won't do them much good in the long run.'

Having successfully provoked Thornley to rudeness and William to anger, James seeemed satisfied. He smiled at them both as he sipped his port. 'I began this conversation with the intention of enticing Mr Thornley to America! It's a big country, and as full of opportunities as it is empty of people.'

Arthur Thornley was not minded to be enticed, nor did he make the mistake of thinking that James seriously wanted him to go. 'I'll stay here, I reckon. Being an Englishman, and proud of the fact too, I'll find my opportunities here.'

James gave a little shrug and it ended the conversation – in Thornley's favour, William thought.

The following morning village affairs took William to Haywood's End, accompanied in the gig by Ned and Sybil, who saw no reason to let him go there alone. With Lady

Hester still resting in her room and Lucy being walked out by the nurserymaid, Gertrude fell prey to James.

'A walk, Lady Wyndham?' he proposed formally. 'Perhaps we should ascertain that the rhododendrons are particularly fine so early in the year.'

She was sadly conscious again, as she had been ever since he arrived, that he was a tense, unhappy man, driven to shafts of ill temper that made him still more at odds with himself and other people. She would have avoided a lonely walk with him if she could, but an unfinished episode lay between them; the time had come to acknowledge the fact. They set off in silence and were hidden by a dense crimson screen before James took hold of her hand.

'If you're about to protest, please don't. It isn't a very serious demand, as yet.'

'I hope none will come that are *more* serious, James,' she said as lightly as she could. 'Why not just enjoy an English spring morning while you have the chance?'

'My first question *has* to be serious. I must know whether Ned is my son.'

She felt her heart stop beating, then go racing on again, pumping blood so quickly round her body that she felt dizzy. She was a fool not to have anticipated that he would ask. Now, she must deal with the question without being prepared for it.

'Ned is William's son,' she said steadily. 'That is the truth, James, whether you like it or not, though there is no reason why you should *not* like it; you have a family of your own.'

'There's every reason,' he said sharply. 'He's the boy I should have had . . . the boy *we* should have had.'

She stood still, the better to marshal her strength against him. Her face was very pale against the darkness of her hair, but he thought she'd grown more lovely . . . and even more desirable now that motherhood seemed to have completed her as a woman. He'd forgotten how beautiful her grey eyes were, fringed with dark lashes, but he remembered a time when they had shone with a passion that matched his own.

'James . . . please don't go on. I understand your sadness

about Kitty, and I grieve for you, but it is useless to talk of *us*.'

His hands pulled her against him, so close that their bodies were locked together and she could feel his breath warm on her face. Her heart seemed to be breaking with pity, but there was nothing she could do to help him.

'You understand nothing, Gertrude. Kitty's death was a tragedy – it was a release as well from the travesty of a marriage. *You* are the woman I should have married . . . you know the truth of that as well as I do.'

'I'm married to William – happily, contentedly married,' she insisted hoarsely.

'Contentedly? I won't believe it. You were made for love and passion; my brother spreads out lukewarm affection with the careful economy of a vicarage housewife spreading fish-paste on charity sandwiches. I'm talking about a real marriage.'

'My marriage *is* real, and it is entirely my own affair. Let us go back, please, James.'

His hands moved up her throat to cup themselves round her face. They held her gently now, and his fierceness had given way to an expression of yearning sadness. 'Come to America with me, my best-loved one. I should take care of you so tenderly, love you so dearly.' His mouth abandoned words and fastened on her own. It was beyond her power to resist. The world around her was blotted out; there was only the joy of being held by him and the pressure of his mouth forcing hers open, so that her whole body felt as if it *must* open to receive him. When he lifted his head at last he was smiling, and his face was transformed.

'*That's* what *our* marriage would be,' he murmured. 'And you've just admitted that you need me as much as I need you.'

She was trembling within the circle of his arms, but summoned a last desperate vestige of self-control. 'How can I help but admit it, when my body refuses not to be set alight by yours. But it changes nothing, James.'

His hands tightened, gripping her cruelly. 'It changes everything. We *have* to be allowed to love each other.' His mouth hovered again just above her own. 'I can convince you, my dear . . . *let* me convince you.'

It was more than her body could withstand – it was convinced already, if her mind was not. She felt him urge her gently down on to the grass. He leaned on top of her, and she stretched out her arms. Her hand touched something and recoiled – the remains of a small dead animal? No, scarcely recognizable, it was an old teddy bear, lost and searched for, and mourned by Ned for months. Discoloured and sodden, it was still his bear and she must take it back for him. Darling Ned wouldn't mind the state it was in. But, dear God, what was she doing here lying beneath James, wanting him to make love to her?

She pushed her hands against his chest, holding him away from her.

'You will have to let me go . . . please, my dear . . . forgive me and let me go.'

He didn't know how or why, but in the moment of being almost sure that he had won, something had changed. She was in control of herself again, and to force her now against her will would be impossible.

'If I let you go, you must promise to listen to me, Gertrude, and *look* at me.' She had closed her eyes rather than see his face with the light of hope dying out of it. 'William isn't the man to contest a divorce, or care whether he's married or not. He has an heir, which is probably more than he deserved. When the time comes, Ned can return here and take up his inheritance, if there's anything left by then.'

She was helped by the knowledge that James was wrong. Her fever had drained away, leaving her only with an enormous sadness and an enormous certainty.

'You don't understand about William. He couldn't survive the loss of the children, even if he could manage without me. And I couldn't leave Providence without them.' Her eyes were luminous with tears, and he watched them gather and spill over her pale cheeks. 'There isn't any way out for us, my dearest.'

His finger gently outlined her trembling mouth. 'I still believe I could make you change your mind.'

'If you did, I should hate you for it, and myself as well. I can do without passion if I must; I cannot do without all that I should have to leave behind – even if I wasn't needed here, and I know that I am.'

James wanted to shout and rage and even weep himself, but none of it would do a particle of good. She was staunch and stubborn, and he would never get over loving her as long as he lived.

He got to his feet and pulled her up beside him. 'Very well, my dear, let us walk sedately back and pretend, even if the effort kills us, that we have merely been admiring . . . what was it we came to admire?'

'The rhododendrons, James . . . so . . . so particularly fine for the time of year . . .' She had to stop because her voice refused to function. This time she didn't protest when he took her hand, but she suddenly pulled away from him to pick up something lying on the ground.

'Friend of yours?' asked James, staring at the dilapidated object.

'Of Ned's,' she murmured.

They walked the rest of the way in silence, and throughout the day said nothing to each other that anyone else could not have overheard. With an effort that perhaps nearly did kill him, James managed to be gentle with his mother and polite to William, but he left Providence the following morning, and Gertrude felt almost certain that they would never see him there again.

CHAPTER FOURTEEN

Lady Hester was becoming too frail to make the journey to the parish church but Hubert Roberts brought the sacraments to Providence each week, so that she might continue to receive Holy Communion. The chapel room had been consecrated long ago, but he would have come in any case to minister to a woman he regarded as embodying the goodness that his Lord required. Afterwards he would stay to a luncheon shared with Gertrude, and with the ease of old friends who were tolerant of each other's prejudices, they would wrangle about any topic that came to mind. But on the day following James's departure he sensed that both women were deep in reflections of their own and had to keep reminding themselves that he was there and must be talked to. Lady Hester, especially, looked sad and he supposed that she feared she'd said goodbye to her son for the last time.

When Gertrude excused herself and left them alone he decided to avoid the subject no longer.

'I don't think I could tempt you into an argument today, even about *my* Anglicanism versus your Tractarian sympathies! You are missing James and, alas, I cannot shrink the Atlantic ocean for you.'

She smiled ruefully at him. 'Forgive me, Hubert. I meant *not* to seem gloomy! I was certainly thinking of James, but it's a more complicated matter than simply missing him. The truth is that I was relieved as well as sad to see him go. It seems a strange and terrible thing to think, much less to say, about someone I love as dearly as I love James.'

'Would it help to tell me why you think it?'

'Yes . . . perhaps I should feel less guilty if I confessed it to you. All through James's visit I was reminded of him as a small boy, with his mind fixed on something that he wanted but had been told he couldn't have. No argument that the thing belonged to someone else could ever convince him that he shouldn't be allowed to take it, simply because *he* wanted it so badly.' She stopped talking, having conjured up the past so vividly in her mind that the rector was forgotten again.

'You think he hasn't changed . . . that there was something he wanted this time?' he prompted her gently.

'Yes, if you can call happiness a thing. But he went away without it. I am exceedingly thankful about *that*, but my fear is that he won't know how to cope with such a bitter disappointment. Coming on top of Kitty's death . . .' her voice was clogged with tears which she couldn't allow herself to give way to in front of her friend.

He took her thin blue-veined hands in his own warm ones. 'My dear, I don't think there is any need for you to agonize about James. You are remembering him as a child, but he hasn't reached the age of thirty-four without learning how to live with disappointments. By the time you see him next . . .'

She interrupted him by shaking her head. 'Gertrude once said she thought of Providence as holding out its arms to give comfort. I wish we could have shared its healing grace with James, but he won't come here again.' She spoke with such certainty that he knew it was pointless to argue with her. Before he could say anything at all she smiled to show him that her momentary distress was over. 'You were right to remind me that he's his father's son, not a weakling. No doubt he will have learned much more than I give him credit for.'

When Hubert went back to the rectory to report that Lady Hester was in lower spirits than usual, Maud lost no time in pedalling over to Providence to see her. Of the two women there, however, she thought it was Gertrude who was having to make the greater effort to seem cheerful. She smiled at Lucy sitting on her lap, but not even the little girl's enchanting ways could quite dispel the shadow in her eyes. Maud chose to plunge briskly into a subject that was likely to seize Gertrude's whole attention.

'I saw Jane Thornley yesterday. The sewing school is now in full swing and supply is soon going to exceed demand unless we can find some regular source of orders. I've exhausted all my friends with daughters needing wedding trousseaux, and we've used up the Wyndham connections as well. I think it's time we considered opening a shop in Warwick.'

Gertrude thought about the idea and countered with a suggestion of her own. 'Better still, why don't we try to interest a shop that already exists – preferably in some smart part of London? Somewhere new and fashionable, like Liberty's emporium.'

Maud's imagination toyed with the idea of walking into its premises in Regent Street with an armful of petticoats and chemises. She knew herself ready for most things, but perhaps not for that! 'They sell exotic merchandise – silks from India, Kashmir shawls . . . that sort of thing,' she objected. 'Are they going to be impressed by home-made underclothes?'

'Why shouldn't they be? We *know* these garments are exquisite, and if they don't stock such things already, so much the better; we shall have no competition. Regent Street must be the haunt of fashionable women, and they're just the sort of clients we need.'

Maud could see no help for it: Gertrude with the bit between her teeth, as now, was scarcely stoppable; Regent Street it would have to be. 'You'll want an accomplice, I suppose, in this venture?' She made a brave attempt to put enthusiasm into her voice, but couldn't help feeling relieved when the offer was refused.

'One of us at a time is enough. If they turn me down, you can try somewhere else.'

She set out for London a week later, escorted there by William who was going to visit Henri Blanchard. Her own mission called for the best impression she could create, and she dressed for the occasion with care. William failed to observe that she had done so, but she wasn't unduly discouraged by this since he never noticed what she or anyone else wore.

'Do I at least look like a woman of means and influence?' she asked, even though his opinion would be of doubtful value.

He took the trouble to observe her carefully, and then smiled. 'You look like everyone's idea of a young and beautiful duchess!'

'Well, *that* should do it, then,' she said cheerfully. Her tightly-fitting coat and skirt were of the same colour as her hat of dark green velour. It was severely shaped like a gentleman's bowler, but a cream ostrich feather curled seductively over its brim, matching the cream ruffles of her muslin blouse. For good luck, she had fastened to the ruffles a topaz brooch borrowed from Lady Hester. Though not aspiring to be mistaken for a duchess, she felt at least that the gentlemen at Liberty's couldn't despise her.

William's hansom cab deposited her at the doors of the shop, and it was arranged that she should rejoin him at the gallery. He would give her luncheon, and then they would take the train home again together. She arrived in Bond Street an hour later, flushed with triumph, to find herself face to face with Henri Blanchard instead of William. They hadn't met since his brief visit to Providence. During that time he thought he had been successful in persuading himself that he had no interest in pursuing his acquaintance with Lady Wyndham. Watching her come towards him now, he acknowledged that his efforts had been in vain. He liked her looks, the way she walked, and the smile she offered his assistant for opening the door for her.

Gertrude was so pleased with her morning's work that she'd almost forgotten how uncertain she felt in the company of Monsieur Blanchard. Now, with his slow inspection of her, she was reminded of it. She insisted to herself that it meant nothing. He was always examining the paintings that were put in front of him, and this automatic scrutiny had become a habit with him.

'Good morning,' she said quickly. 'I thought I was supposed to find William here.'

'A brief errand, madame . . . a matter of paints and brushes urgently needed, I understand. He will soon be here. I was told about your own venture this morning, and surmise that it was successful, because your mouth cannot quite keep from smiling.'

She was nervous all over again: the man had a way of ignoring the conventions that made it almost impossible to keep him at the distance she felt she needed between them. 'The morning was most successful,' she agreed primly. A detailed description of the merchandise she'd been offering would lead to the sort of embarrassments she felt he would positively enjoy. She stared round the gallery as an alternative to having to meet his too-insistent gaze. 'Surely that's one of William's paintings over there?'

'Yes, I display them now, one or two at a time. The process of education has begun, you see.'

She remembered that they had cause to be grateful to him, and found courage enough to turn towards him with a smile. 'William talked a great deal about the gifted painters he'd met in Paris, but all he said about his own part in the exhibition was that you'd seemed sufficiently satisfied with it.'

'Sufficiently?' Blanchard considered the word with some care. 'Yes, I am prepared to say that much,' he agreed coolly.

She knew that she'd been deflated deliberately, and felt angry on William's behalf. 'We are not to get over-excited by a small success . . . is that it? You are being a little cruel only to be kind!'

If he registered the ironic note in her voice, he took no notice of it. 'I am not in the habit of being kind. Your husband is a good artist, but he will become an even better one if he is not allowed to be satisfied with what you call his small success.'

She had been rebuked by a man who knew what he was

talking about. He watched her face flush with colour beneath the sweep of that absurdly charming ostrich feather and knew he'd been unnecessarily severe. If he wasn't kind, nor was he dishonest either, especially with himself. Rancour had tinged his little speech just now, although he had nothing in the world to complain about. His permanent home was a converted mill outside Paris, which he cherished, and although the gods hadn't blessed him with the divine creative spark, he didn't underestimate the genius he *did* possess for fostering the talents of other men.

But for the moment, while Gertrude Wyndham stood before him, it was difficult to remember that he liked her husband. The inheritance of Providence and a very considerable gift should have been enough for one man, but the Fates had seen fit to give him this woman as well. Blanchard had to remind himself that he'd never wanted a wife – never sought one among the numerous women who liked to call themselves his friends. Charming as they might be to dine or even sleep with, they either palled after a while, or began to make demands he considered unreasonable for one human being to make of another. No, he certainly didn't want a wife, but he'd have liked to discover how long it would take for Lady Wyndham to bore him.

She was looking round the gallery again, not at the pictures being displayed, but at his clientele. Elegantly-dressed men were accompanied by fashionable wives – exactly the sort of women who would be certain to wear expensive, hand-made underclothes. She gazed wistfully at them, unaware that Blanchard gazed at her.

Then he forestalled her. 'No, madame, I regret infinitely, but I do *not* propose to advertise your petticoats among my customers . . . they are here to buy *objets d'art*!'

She blushed to have had her thoughts read so accurately, but looked regretful all the same. 'I can see that it wouldn't be quite suitable, but it's a waste of a golden opportunity. I wonder . . . could you at least bring yourself to mention the petticoats to your circle of . . . of women friends?' She didn't doubt that the circle was large; he was not conventionally handsome, but his confident air spoke of a man whose success with women came easily.

The expression on his face made her realize, too late, that she had been impertinent. It was one thing to suppose privately that he was on intimate enough terms with women to advise them where to buy their underclothes, it was quite another to say it to his face. He was a Frenchman, of course, and Frenchmen were known to order these matters differently, but nevertheless . . .

'Quite so, madame,' he said, reading her thoughts with perfect accuracy again, 'we are not as the English are, although I suspect you didn't intend it as a compliment!'

She was made aware of the shortcomings of Haywood's End as a training ground for this kind of verbal battle; exhilarating it might be, but she was breathless already and must disengage while there was still time.

'I was at fault, monsieur,' she confessed simply. 'It's just that you look . . .' she floundered to a halt again, on the very brink of making matters worse.

'Look . . . ?' he queried with interest.

'Like a man who is experienced in such matters,' she told him finally, giving truth its head.

She didn't know whether he was offended or not because he bowed gracefully, but had no time to say anything before the gallery door opened. William hurried in, with his arms full of parcels. He saw them standing apart from the other people there and might, at any other time, have sensed the fact that they were unaware of not being alone, but he was anxious to apologize.

'My dear, I'm so sorry . . . I kept remembering things I needed. You look . . . rather excited, I think. Does that mean you were successful this morning?'

She nodded, smiling at him with unusual brilliance. 'Very successful . . . I'll tell you about it over the luncheon you promised to give me.'

Blanchard walked with them to the door, confirming some arrangement already made with William. Then he held out his hand to Gertrude. '*Au revoir*, madame . . . I should have mentioned that *this* hat is even more charming than the one before; there seems, however, to have been so much else to talk about!'

She registered the glinting amusement in his face, and was regretfully aware that her own was pink with embarrassment. If she was ever forced to meet him again she would see to it that she ventured nothing more than a remark about the weather; surely not even Henri Blanchard could invest *that* with some sophisticated innuendo.

William hailed a hansom cab and during the drive to the restaurant she forced the last fifteen minutes out of her mind by plunging into an enthusiastic account of her visit to Liberty's.

'The floor-walker was supercilious to begin with, once he realized I hadn't come to see the manager in order to complain. The manager was courteous but lukewarm, but then the lady buyer was summoned to attend. She, dear, kind, clever soul, saw instantly that nothing could be more beautiful than the garments I was offering her. After that it was quickly settled. Jane now has to send them a trial consignment, and as soon as they arrive we must encourage everyone we know in London to go to Liberty's. I really don't see how we can fail.'

William looked impressed. 'Well done, my dear. Mrs Thornley is a splendid, resolute woman but I don't somehow see her storming the citadels of Regent Street in quite such a triumphant fashion. Perhaps the hat had something to do with it – it certainly seemed to have impressed Blanchard!'

'He talks for effect; it means nothing,' she said hurriedly.

'Really? I remember you saying once that he wouldn't bother to say anything he didn't mean!'

'I exclude stupid compliments, of course.'

William smiled at this unusual loftiness but let it go. 'Well, I'm sorry that I left you with him for so long, especially if my impression is correct that you don't like him.'

He made a question of it and she was obliged to answer.

'I don't think I know whether I like him or not. All I *am* sure about is that I haven't met anyone else quite like him.

That may simply be because I haven't met any other Frenchmen.'

'They don't all ignore the usual social rules in the way that he does,' William felt obliged to concede. 'Blanchard insists on going straight to the heart of the matter, but I rather like that myself. His reputation stands very high in the art world, and I've learned from other people, not from him, that his own wealth has saved a number of good artists from starving until he could get them safely launched.'

Gertrude accepted this new light on him in silence. Then she said, 'He thinks *you're* good, but he probably didn't tell you so. You are to be spurred into becoming even better by being kept short of praise. About that I think he is wrong. People *need* praise, warmth, encouragement . . . how else can they measure the success of what they do?'

'I suppose, in the case of struggling artists like me, they must rely on Blanchard to tell them! Five of my paintings remained in Paris, by the way, and he has definite commissions for two more.' William tried to sound casual about it and almost succeeded, but the expression on Gertrude's face made him smile.

'Commissions! William . . . how grand and professional that sounds.'

'It also sounds terrifying,' he admitted. 'But I find that Blanchard's certainties are catching! If he thinks I'm capable of doing what his clients want, then I can and must and shall.'

'Of course . . . but it makes Monsieur Blanchard dangerous as well. Suppose he expected of you something that was wrong? You might still have the same compulsion to obey.'

She offered the possibility so gravely that he was reminded again of the fact that she didn't seem to like or trust his patron. He didn't know why because, with the exception of poor Arthur Thornley, in whom she could find no saving grace at all, she was generally inclined to think well of people.

'No cause for anxiety, my dear,' he pointed out gently.

'He's not going to ask me to rob the Bank of England or paint a counterfeit Rembrandt!'

'True.' She smiled and said nothing more, but it occurred to her that something else made Henri Blanchard dangerous as well. She hadn't once thought of James since walking through the gallery door.

CHAPTER FIFTEEN

Lady Hester often prayed for James in the quietness of the chapel room. She'd shared her anxiety about him with Hubert Roberts, but it was as far as sharing could safely go; she would normally have talked to her daughter-in-law, but she was convinced that it was Gertrude whom James had wanted to steal from Providence. As often as she prayed for him, she also thanked God that their life at Providence had been left intact, but it had been bought at the price of James's happiness and perhaps of Gertrude's as well. A half-blind woman was at a disadvantage when it came to seeing things but, with other senses sharpened, she couldn't miss her daughter-in-law's struggle to seem cheerful. One day she might be able to tell her so, but for the moment she could only share James's rare letters with Gertrude and accept her pretence that she had nothing but a mildly affectionate interest in them.

Before a cool wet spring had merged into the summer of Victoria's sixtieth year on the throne, distracting news reached them from another quarter of the globe. One, at least, of Lady Hester's dearest hopes was going to be realized: the Trenthams were coming home from India. Gertrude did her best to share in the excitement, and confessed only to her father that she didn't look forward to Louise's return.

'What's amiss about it, lass?' he asked quietly. 'Seeing that the visit will give her ladyship more pleasure than anything else in this world, I'd have thought you'd be glad about it.'

'Of course I'm glad for *her*, but it's not a visit – they're leaving India for good.'

'They'll not live at Providence, if that's what bothering you. Miss Louise will be wanting a home of her own.'

'There you are . . . *Miss* Louise,' Gertrude burst out. 'That's what's wrong! It's how we think of her still, you and I. And I can tell you how she thinks of *me*. I'm little Gertrude Hoskins, her mother's companion-help, who ought by rights to be on the servants' side of the green baize door.'

George Hoskins stared at his daughter's troubled face. She was too thin, and her face was tautened by some inner stress that only occasionally found release when she was playing with her children. He doubted whether Louise Trentham was the sole cause of her unhappiness, but the rest of it she didn't choose to share with him and he must leave her to cope with it alone.

'You're letting yourself get bothered, my dearie, and not seeing things clear. How should you know *what* Louise Trentham thinks . . . you haven't seen her for six years. In any case, you fit the part of Lady Wyndham real snug by now; she'll see that as well as the rest of us do.'

'That's *exactly* how she'll see it – I'm playing a part I'm not entitled to.'

'Now you're talking nonsense, lass. You've more than earned the right, seeing that it's you who holds Providence together.' He hesitated for a moment, choosing words even more carefully than usual. 'I fancy it's *me* you're bothered about, in case she forgets I'm William's father-in-law and still refers to me as "Hoskins" in the way she used to do. Well, it won't trouble me if she does, so there's no call for *you* to go getting on your high horse about it.'

Gertrude looked at his calm face and knew that he spoke nothing but the truth. He'd lived long enough to be sure of his own worth, even though he would be too modest to put the assessment nearly high enough; for as long as he knew himself to be Lady Hester's friend and the confidant of Gertrude's children, no-one else's opinion troubled him.

He smiled suddenly, thinking of his grandson. 'Ned'd be very put out if I was a gentleman of leisure instead of land agent in the estate office. He sits there drawing Moffat's plough horses to keep me company while I'm doing my paperwork; he says I might get lonely otherwise!'

Gertrude was forced to smile. 'Oh, *he* knows what he thinks about things. Providence belongs to his father, but *you* take care of it. And dearly as he loves William, that makes you even more important in his eyes!'

She abandoned the subject of Louise without mentioning the real grounds for her anxiety. The only response from India to the news of her marriage had been one very cool note of congratulation. It had said as clearly as anything could that the new mistress of Providence was bitterly resented. Gertrude still remembered the walk back from the churchyard one Christmas morning that she'd shared with Louise. For the length of it they'd been equals because Louise had chosen to step down to her level, but the manoeuvre in reverse wasn't acceptable.

The cavalcade reached Providence halfway through the month of June, without Alec Trentham, who had been left behind in Delhi to finish training his successor. Meanwhile, Louise, Harry, her daughter Charlotte, and the nurse, together with a separate coachload of luggage, were driven into the stable-yard.

In the first moment of catching sight of her sister-in-law, Gertrude's apprehension gave way to pity. It was more than time Louise came home to a gentler climate. She was still only thirty-two but looked ten years older. Colour and vitality had been absorbed by the burning heat. Her fine English skin was lined and stretched tightly over her bones; she had the fragile wrists and ankles of a child.

She embraced her mother and kissed William; then, while they greeted the children, she stopped in front of Gertrude, slowly extending her hand.

'You are looking well . . . being Lady Wyndham seems to suit you, but I hope poor Sid Moffat recovered from his disappointment.'

'We suppose that he did, seeing that he recently married Matthew Harris's daughter.'

Louise looked round the yard before returning her gaze

to the unexpectedly composed girl who stood in front of her.

'I don't see your father, Gertrude. Has *he* not moved into Providence as well?'

'He still lives at the home farm,' she explained quietly. 'By his own choice, in case you are thinking that I prefer to keep him hidden there.' Their eyes met with the kiss of sword-blades saluting. Gertrude knew that her father had been wrong; and she was the more resented because she'd learned so successfully how to look and sound like the woman she was supposed to be; Louise might have forgiven her if she had not.

Mrs Trentham had one more shot to fire. 'My dear Gertrude, of course Mr Hoskins must be allowed to live where he feels most at home.' Then she smiled sweetly and turned her attention to the servants who were staring at the mountain of luggage being handed out of the second carriage. They were flung clear, firm orders, and in a short space of time the hired carriages that had brought the visitors from the railway station were rumbling away along the drive. Louise had had much practice in giving commands, and Gertrude decided that whatever else her family went short of it wouldn't be competence in the ordering of their affairs . . . what a loss she must be to the Empire! It was to be hoped that a small green rainswept island would be big enough for her after the continent she had known.

Feeling slightly ashamed of this tartness, Gertrude watched her son making up his mind about his cousin; Harry, five years older, was taller, but not so compactly sturdy. He'd forgotten Hodges and Artie, but he remembered the pony on to whose broad back his grandfather had once lifted him, and stroked Hercules's old grey nose, unaware that he was being observed. Then Ned went to join him; his new cousin looked all right, and it would be nice to have a change from girls. Sybil, now nearly five and therefore two years younger than Charlotte Trentham, was taking longer to make up her mind. It might be necessary to make a fuss to establish who was in charge, or it might not. For the moment she only stared at Charlotte, but smiled entrancingly at the tall pale woman she was to call Aunt Louise. She was already aware that it paid handsomely to keep on the right side of the grown-ups.

The confusion of arrival was over and the children settled in their strange new quarters before there was time for much conversation. At dinner that first evening Lady Hester was anxious to know how long they could all stay at Providence. 'Surely until poor Alec gets back?' she suggested hopefully.

'If William can put up with us that long, Mama . . . and Gertrude, too,' Louise remembered politely as an after-thought. 'But I must start looking for a house in London . . . Alec won't want to be bothered with that.'

'In London? My dear, aren't you going to live at Somer-ton?'

'As little as possible! I scarcely know Alec's brother, but they never got on as children, and are virtual strangers now. By all accounts, however, Richard is a frightfully pompous bore! We shall have to go occasionally, of course, so that Alec can become familiar with the estate . . . it's why we've come home, after all.'

'But, dearest, what will you find to do in London?'

'Alec will represent Somerton's borough in the House of Commons, and I shall become one of those political hostesses who wield immense power behind the scenes! I rather like the idea, as a matter of fact.' She stared quizzingly at her brother across the table. 'Being Trenthams, we shall be on the Whig side, of course . . . doubtless not where *your* sympathies lie!'

William smiled sweetly. 'You mean to imply, I suppose, that I'm bound to be a Tory. Well, let me tell you that I have no political sympathies at all, being disenchanted with the whole tribe of politicians. The clever ones are likely to be self-interested rogues; the rest are worthy but in-competent. The country loses no matter which are in power.'

'Disenchantment indeed! All the more reason to have someone like Alec in Parliament, who is neither venal nor

188

stupid. In any case, he must do *something* except wait to step into his brother's shoes, and so must I. I've long outgrown the rural excitements of chasing foxes and calling on the sick with bowls of soup! We shall eventually have to settle down to English country life again, but it's a vegetable existence, to be deferred as long as possible.'

Gertrude did her best to remember that Louise was newly torn from a way of life she had greatly loved; allowances had to be made for an arrogant, viper-tongued woman who was also unhappy. Even so . . .

'You haven't had time to discover that your "vegetable existence" may be out of date,' she remarked with gentle malice. 'The countryman is no longer despised for his obsession with muck and mangelwurzels; on the contrary, the rustic life is now seen to hold the key to health and sanity, while towns are hotbeds of disease and vice from which anyone rich enough to escape does so!'

Louise turned to speak to her for the first time since they'd sat down to dinner. 'My dear Gertrude, I'm not proposing to live in some hellish Birmingham slum. We shall find a house in the metropolis. There *is* a difference, you know.'

'You are right to point it out,' Gertrude said gratefully, 'since I'm so little acquainted with either.'

Louise was nettled by the smile that touched William's mouth for an instant, as well as by her sister-in-law's unreasonable self-possession. She abandoned them both and turned to her mother instead. 'I suppose our neighbours are just the same . . . ?'

'Not quite. Since Lord Brooke succeeded to the title at Warwick, the town has often been graced with the presence of the Prince of Wales – the new Countess is a particular friend of his,' Lady Hester said drily. 'The Maynards are still at Barham, but the Brownings had to give up Bicton Grange. It was sold to a Birmingham industrialist.'

'Whom, presumably, we do *not* entertain?'

'Whom, as it happens, we *do*,' her mother said calmly. 'No doubt you will meet the Thornleys before long. James did so when he was here and found them interesting.'

'Well, I hope I shall be able to survive so much honour!' She was aware of the reproof in Lady Hester's face, and felt obliged to apologize. 'I'm sorry, Mama; I'm afraid that sounded very sour. You must forgive my ill-temper, which comes of missing India. Home leave is delightful, but the knowledge that I've left India for good is scarcely bearable . . . no doubt I shall get used to it in time.'

'No doubt, dear,' her mother agreed, forgiving her immediately.

The children had less difficulty in settling down. They soon accustomed themselves to the lush greenness that now surrounded them and to English rain more gentle than any they had known; they learned to find their way about, inside the house and out of doors, and quickly forgot to be surprised that they were waited on by servants as pale-skinned as themselves.

Charlotte, unsure of herself and missing her father, attached herself to William first of all, but when she discovered fat, laughing Lucy in the nursery she was happy to be enrolled as a willing slave. She couldn't understand Sybil's flagrant exhibitionism, much less compete with it, and as soon as Miss Wyndham realized this she graciously consented to adopt her shy cousin. Ned reckoned Charlotte less troublesome than his sister and kindly offered her those of his treasures he thought she might like. But his special friends were for sharing with another male – Harry was given the privilege of meeting Grandpa Hoskins in the estate office, Biddle amid the earthy enchantment of his potting-sheds, and Matthew Harris at the forge. If these attractions palled, there were Moffat's plough-horses to be visited, and the whole kingdom of the stable-yard at Providence itself.

One morning when William had set off early for a meeting in Warwick and Gertrude had to face her sister-in-law alone across the breakfast table, she felt obliged to apologize. 'I hope you don't mind seeing so little of your son? I hadn't realized before how much Ned would have enjoyed having a brother.'

Louise looked surprised. 'I saw even less of him in India. Let Ned make the most of his company now . . . Harry will go away to school at the end of the summer. He's late in going to a preparatory school, but two years there will have to be enough to prepare him for Eton when the time comes.'

She surveyed Gertrude deliberately across the table. 'Unlike me, you've improved, much as I dislike having to admit it.'

'There was no need to, even if you were kind enough to think so,' Gertrude pointed out.

'I'm never *kind*, as you call it, but I do try not to be dishonest. That's why I didn't go into transports of delight when William married you. I expect you noticed.'

'I could scarcely fail.' Bluntness, Gertrude thought, might as well be met with bluntness since she had so little to lose. She saw the glint in Louise's pale eyes and braced herself for whatever might be coming next.

'James and I used to think that William would never marry . . . what happened? Did *you* ask him?'

Gertrude hung on to her temper with an effort she hoped the heavens were applauding. She even managed to smile. 'As I recall the occasion, asking didn't come into it; your brother *told* me that he thought we'd better make ourselves into a couple . . . so we did.' It was the truth as far as it went, and she didn't have to admit that she *had* had to ask William to make her a wife.

Louise nodded. 'Yes, that sounds like him. As a family, the Wyndhams can't be said to err on the side of hot-bloodedness – although I think I might have to exclude James.'

Gertrude couldn't allow her to sit dissecting James. Rather than have to listen, she plunged into an impertinence of her own. 'Knowing that you would resent me being here, I wasn't looking forward to your visit, even though I knew it would give Mama pleasure.'

'She's not as pleased with me as all that,' Louise acknowledged with unexpected ruefulness. 'I've been taken to task for not being more sisterly to you! My dear mother thinks we should all have her ability to love everybody . . . she even seems to have taken the egregious Mr Thornley to her heart, but by the sound of him *that* will defeat me, however much I try with you!'

'Don't feel obliged to try to hard with me. You're not bound to like your brother's wife *whoever* she might be, and I can see that it's especially hard for you to have to change from despising little Gertrude Hoskins to liking her!' Gertrude said tranquilly.

George Hoskins's daughter had no right to look as if she didn't care one way or the other whether she was liked or not. Louise was irritated again and wanted to disturb such unnatural composure.

'James was here recently, I gather. Mama didn't seem entirely happy about his visit, although she did her best to pretend when I asked her about it. Did you fall out with him? His letters to me have never once mentioned you . . . which is rather odd. James, like Mama, normally loves everybody!'

Gertrude forced herself to meet the pale, inquisitive eyes that watched her across the breakfast table. If she died in the attempt, now was the moment when she must try to sound unconcerned. 'His letters here don't mention *you* as I recall; but no doubt he shares your opinion. I'm rather relieved that he *doesn't* mention me. If I figure in his memory at all, it's probably as the Hoskins child in black boots and pinafore!'

'Most likely,' Louise agreed carelessly. Balked in that quarter, she remembered another cause for resentment. 'I gather you know London a good deal better than you admitted to. Mama says you've stormed the capital and found a dealer there for William's paintings . . . brave of you, my dear, especially when I gather that he's a fascinating Frenchman into the bargain!'

It was more bearable to be quizzed about Henri Blanchard

than about James, but Gertrude was beginning to tire of suffering her sister-in-law; one more jibe and the whole company of saints wouldn't be enough to prevent her telling the woman so.

'I haven't noticed whether he's fascinating or not,' she said coolly. 'French he certainly is. All that matters to me is that he's disposed to think highly of William's paintings and will sell them as well as he can for us.'

Louise gave a little shrug. 'I thought William painted for love of art, not for love of money.'

'He does . . . but we happen to need money as well,' Gertrude snapped, 'since we cannot live on air. When you are living in London you can frequent Monsieur Blanchard's gallery, and make up your own mind about him. If, as well as deciding how fascinating he is, you'll also be kind enough to take potential customers there, your visits will be even more worthwhile from our point of view.'

'Yes, my dear Gertrude,' Louise said meekly, amused rather than put out by this onslaught, and there the conversation rested.

Several weeks before the Trenthams' arrival William had had to be prodded by his wife in the matter of the Queen's Diamond Jubilee.

'Must we do anything?' he'd asked plaintively. 'Yes . . . I suppose so, although I am not sure what we have to celebrate except the astonishing longevity of the Queen.'

Gertrude had stared at him in astonishment. 'What can you mean? No-one else will find it difficult to shout hurrah. We own a vast trading empire, the rest of the world buys our manufactures, and our Navy has control of the seas. Is that not enough for a small island to celebrate?' She was pleased with herself for stating the truth so succinctly, without falling into the error of over-arrogant pride that even someone as Empire-minded as Rudyard Kipling was beginning to warn them against.

William had looked unimpressed. 'You've just described the common view of our situation, but I could paint a different picture for you. Our far-flung "possessions", as everyone likes to call them, can't be held for long against the will of subject peoples and the envy of contending powers. In the long run I'm afraid we shall find that those territories are likely to give us considerably more pain than profit. At home, there is just as little to be complacent about. America, Germany and Japan are already competing for our foreign markets; eventually they are bound to overtake us, but even that isn't the worst of it. We have won industrial success at the cost of killing our agricultural industry . . . we are now dependent on imported food to feed a population that has doubled since Victoria came to the throne.'

Gertrude had never heard him speak so sombrely before. She'd stared at the future through his eyes for a moment and found it frightening. Providence was threatened, of course, as a result of the very things William had described, but it had never occurred to her that England itself was anything but impregnable. Her thoughts flew to Ned and she contemplated the unstable world in which *he* might have to try to preserve Providence. Imagination was depicting a dreadful scene in which the park was black with starving factory workers storming the house as if it were the Bastille, when William's voice penetrated the nightmare.

'My dear girl, there's no need to look quite so tragic . . . disaster isn't going to overtake us immediately, if at all, and certainly not before we have to celebrate the Queen's anniversary! What do you suggest we do?'

She had blinked and brushed terror aside, mumbling 'something mainly for the children . . . a fair and sideshows on the green . . . and tea, of course, for everybody.'

Thus it came about that under a hot June sky everyone at Haywood's End sat down to an alfresco tea as the guests of the Squire. Around them the perimeter of the green was lined with as many booths and sideshows as could be crammed in, and a perspiring brass band blew its heart out in honour of the Queen.

When tea was over and the fun was getting faster and

more furious, Louise drove her mother back to Providence in the gig, leaving Gertrude and William to bring the children when they could be persuaded to leave a Punch and Judy show, in which they were engrossed.

The courtyard garden seemed a miracle of cool quietness after the village hubbub, and Louise returned to it when she had seen Lady Hester safely to her room.

She was astonished now to find two strangers there – a grizzled, pugnacious-looking man in a loud suit, and a youth who clearly belonged to him. A suspicion of the man's identity was already crossing her mind when he offered her what she supposed was meant to be an ingratiating smile.

'Evening, ma'am – Arthur Thornley's the name, and I dare say you're Mrs Trentham, the lady from India.'

CHAPTER SIXTEEN

Mr Thornley stopped smiling. He wasn't a man to waste anything, even bonhomie, and the thin, colourless Long Meg now staring at him seemed unlikely to smile back. She wasn't even impressed by the fact that he'd guessed she was the Squire's sister.

'If you were looking for Sir William, you'll find him with the rest of Haywood's End on the village green,' she said coldly.

'I know . . . we've just seen him there; that's to say, me and my son – young Frank.'

The boy ducked his cropped head, then resumed an unblinking stare that seemed too adult for the age Louise took him to be. She found the silent, watchful boy as repellent in a different way as his father, and proposed to make no secret of the fact that she regarded them as impudent intruders.

'If you don't wish to see my brother, I'm not sure why you're here. Local people are permitted to walk through the park but they do not, as far as I know, normally cross the moat uninvited.'

It was open warfare, and recognized as such on both sides. The glint of battle shone in Arthur's small eyes; there was no pleasure in a fight where courtesy tied the tongue of his opponent, but by the sound of her, Mrs Trentham didn't propose to have much truck with courtesy.

'Ah, now *there* I have you, ma'am,' he said happily. 'I asked the Squire if I could give Frank a squint at Providence, seeing that he's never been here before. So, in a manner of speaking, we *are* here by invitation.'

He'd put her in the wrong and enjoyed doing it, but she

didn't intend to apologize. William and her mother must be insane to permit, much less encourage, such a man; he'd have been inside the house by now if she hadn't come out into the garden. They were both considerate and gentle by nature, and a little lacking in steel. Thornley's kind of effrontery could only be met by equal rudeness, and Louise had no objection to supplying it on their behalf.

'You now own Bicton Grange, I understand. No doubt it's rather different from anything you've lived in previously in Birmingham?'

'You're right there,' he said, full of delighted admiration. 'I don't know how you guessed, but I wasn't reared in an old country mansion, and nor was Mrs Thornley if it comes to that. Still, we're getting used to it.'

Louise wished that she could induce her lip to curl – at this point it was surely what was indicated, but imagination was getting the better of her. She saw in her mind's eye a picture of this man and his suburban wife amid the hideous Gothic splendours of Bicton; the worst she could say of both was that they deserved one another!

'I don't think I should call the Grange old,' she pointed out next, 'at least, not by any standard worth mentioning; it was built in a moment of architectural madness by Mr Browning's grandfather.'

It was a palpable hit, but they were about to bleed on both sides. 'I'm not saying we'd have *chosen* Bicton, but your brother wouldn't sell me Providence . . . which is a pity, seeing that I'd have been able to do better for it than he's done.' As if by chance his eyes fixed themselves on the crumbling stonework of the mullioned window beside him. 'Old houses need a deal of nurturin', ma'am, whether or not you try to bring them up to date a bit inside as well.'

For an uncomfortable moment she saw Providence through his eyes. She couldn't deny its outward signs of neglect, nor its backwardness in the matter of amenities. Stupid she'd been, not to enquire further into Gertrude's determination to sell William's paintings. It made her go on the defensive with Thornley now, but angrily so.

'My brother has much else to look after besides this house. Perhaps you have yet to discover the responsibilities of being a landowner . . . or perhaps they're something you don't intend to accept? There will be roads and tenants' cottages to repair; the school board will look to you to help provide the teacher's wage; and the vicar will sadly draw your attention to the state of the church roof. You probably have no idea of the hundred and one things you will be expected to take care of, apart from your own property and your family.'

Anger brought her worn face to life, renewing its colour and sparkle. He reckoned she'd even look young again if she could live in a constant state of rage. Still, it went against the grain to have her take him for a fool.

'I know all about my responsibilities, and I accept them,' he said bluntly. 'What's more, I happen to have a few that don't trouble Sir William.'

'Your factories, you mean? Well, you employ people to do the work, and no doubt they provide you with handsome profits.'

'I make sure they *do*, but it's not as simple as you make it sound – not by a long road.' He thought she was just the sort of woman to read him a lecture about child labour, or the evils of strong drink, or evening education for the working man . . . she and her ladyship over at Warwick Castle would get on a treat. But Louise wasn't interested in his factories, or his difficulties; she simply wanted him to go away, but she refused to leave him there as if he had the right to come and go at Providence as he pleased.

'I expect I have a lot to learn about the art of being an industrialist, but I mustn't keep you. "Time is money" . . . isn't that the sort of thing you would be likely to say? If you've finished showing your son round, I'll bid you both good afternoon.'

'No hurry, ma'am. The factories are closed today, seeing that it's a public holiday for the Queen, God bless her, so I'm not losing anything by standing here enjoying this little chat.'

She realized that he was a foeman worthy of her steel. It was hard to get the better of a man who caught his opponent's arrows in midflight and simply reversed them. Then, as if he'd suddenly decided to take pity on her, he smiled at his silent son. 'All the same, Frank boy, it's time we collected your mother. If I know her, she'll have emptied her purse by now, paying for the village youngsters to have a whack at every sideshow.'

His thick body, rather too tightly encased in a suit of brown checks, bent towards her in a perilous but gallant bow. 'We'll be off, Mrs Trentham . . . good day to you.' They were nearly at the bridge when he was struck by an afterthought. 'Dare say Lady Wyndham's told you about our new line – ladies' petticoats and chemises! No need for you to go buying 'em anywhere else . . . Thornley's the name!'

She couldn't frame a sentence fast enough that would slay him once and for all. He had a moment in which to enjoy the expression on her face before he followed his son across the moat.

Five minutes later, in Lady Hester's room, she was demanding to be spared any further acquaintance with the new owner of Bicton.

'You're too late, dearest. Gertrude has invited them to dine here, with the Roberts, specially to meet you.'

'Then I suppose I must look forward to him thrusting samples of his wretched underwear under my nose at the dinner table. The man is capable of even that.'

Her mother smiled, but chose to answer seriously. 'I think he's capable of almost anything. Appearance apart, I find him rather admirable.'

'Well, so do I *not*! He's bound to exploit his workers and grind their faces in the dust . . . how else has he got so rich?'

Lady Hester shook her head. 'Workers are not so easily exploited now, I'm thankful to say, but in any case I believe Mr Thornley's reputation to be very good. He's been teasing you, though, dearest. Unless you want machinery and munitions, his factories can be of no help to you. It's Jane

Thornley's poor handicapped women who make underclothes, and they're not wretched at all but very beautiful.
Her way of doing good with her husband's wealth is to
bring the women to work at Bicton every day. She gives
them congenial, well-paid employment instead of the grudg-
ing charity they would receive from the Poor Law Board.'

The knowledge that she'd been taken at fault made Louise
no better disposed towards a man who'd enjoyed misleading
her.

'Well, let us agree that Mrs Thornley's idea is admirable,
Mama, but if *we* are to feel obliged to buy whatever her
women make, we shall soon have petticoats enough to last
a lifetime.'

Lady Hester knew that she was about to mortify her
daughter still further, but her dear Louise hadn't changed
. . . she would *insist* on rushing her fences!

'We aren't obliged to do anything of the kind, although
it's true that we began by coercing our entire acquaintance!
After that Maud wanted to open a shop in Warwick, but
Gertrude had the idea of going to London to see someone
at Liberty's new emporium in Regent Street, and she
persuaded them to accept a trial consignment. We were
anxious at first, but now they are happy to take whatever
Jane Thornley sends them.'

Louise took her disgruntlement over to the casement
window in case even her mother's poor eyesight should
glimpse it. Outside lay the sunlit park, and beyond it a
further sea of green upon green, broken only by the square
grey tower of Hubert's church. She'd loved it all once upon
a time, and must learn to love it again. As long as her heart
hankered after what it could no longer have she would
remain blind, not only to England's loveliness but to many
other things as well; being blind, she would rush headlong
into errors that had to be apologized for, as now.

'Gertrude seems to have had quite a lot of useful ideas,'
she said after a long pause. 'Perhaps you should have told
me sooner.'

'Perhaps you should have waited longer before making

up your mind that she wasn't a fit wife for William . . . that *is* what you thought, isn't it, dearest?'

'Yes, and if we are to be honest with each other, Mama, I still think they are ill-matched. I don't, in justice to myself, say that to be unkind. It won't necessarily be William who suffers in the long run . . . I'm beginning to suspect that it will be Gertrude herself.'

The change in her mother's expression told her she'd stumbled on a truth that had already been recognized. She remembered her mother's reticence about James's visit, and Gertrude's obvious disinclination to talk about him – as marked as *his* omission of her name in the letters he'd sent to India. Was it James, or someone else, causing the sadness her sister-in-law was doing her best to hide? Louise didn't expect that her mother would say, even if she knew.

Lady Hester finally answered her. 'Most couples are ill-matched to some extent, even when they can choose their partners. William and Gertrude have the great advantage of liking each other. Once passion has been spent, and it always is eventually, liking is the saving grace of marriage.'

The word 'passion' seemed startling on her lips. Louise hadn't expected it; nor could she visualize William being roused to anything resembling it. If Gertrude had succeeded *there*, then she was truly remarkable. She would have liked to say so, but the subject had an element of danger in it. Once started, where might such analysis not take them? There was Hester Wyndham's marriage, for example, to a man who had surely never been passionate about anything but horseflesh; there was her own calm coupling with Alec. It had worked well enough, but Louise was aware that neither of them had found the world well lost for love. She'd suggested glibly to Gertrude that the Wyndhams were cold-blooded . . . but perhaps it was even true?

Abruptly, she abandoned the subject. 'There was a witness to my interview with Mr Thornley . . . "young Frank"! If you haven't had the pleasure of his acquaintance, I can tell you that he doesn't speak. He merely fixes you with an unblinking stare that is extremely unnerving.'

'Gertrude has met him at Bicton. She's convinced that he's bound to become even more successful than his father, whom she dislikes quite as much as you do. Her strong suspicion is that he's waiting for the chance to steal Providence from the Wyndhams.'

Louise thought *that* might be true as well. 'Why entertain him here then?'

'She embraces the military theory that her enemy is best kept in sight! Apart from that, she feels sorry for Jane Thornley. William's motive, I am afraid, is less laudable – he enjoys matching Mr Thornley against Maud Roberts. So far I think their honours are roughly even.'

Louise smiled suddenly. 'I withdraw my objection to the dinner party . . . it sounds interesting!'

It turned out to be even more interesting than usual because Gertrude prevailed upon her father to attend, to complete her numbers at the table. She wasn't certain whether he agreed to give her pleasure, or to convince her that Louise Trentham and the Hoskins could, like the wolf and the lambs, lie down together.

The conversation turned inevitably to the burning topics of 1897 – imperial expansion, trade, and the decline in agriculture. William aired his view that no short-term benefits could outweigh the problems of having a far-flung empire, and was seconded more forcibly than usual by his father-in-law. Arthur Thornley was loudly vocal in support of his Birmingham hero, Joseph Chamberlain, now in the House of Commons and Colonial Secretary in Lord Salisbury's cabinet. ' "Learn to think Imperially" . . . that's what Joseph says, and he's right. Each colony acquired in the name of the Queen means another market for us,' he said emphatically. 'And it's no good telling me that England can live without foreign markets.'

Hubert Roberts agreed with him, but for a different reason. 'I hope we have more to offer than manufactured goods. Surely civilizing influences can follow trade – perhaps even help to justify it?'

Mr Thornley refused to accept such pacific support. 'I don't mind us teaching them to be less heathen, but trade doesn't *need* justifying. Like it or not, we're a manufacturing nation; we need every market we can grab hold of before someone else grabs it first.'

'And why?' George Hoskins wanted to know. 'Because, thanks to people like you, agriculture in this country is being allowed to bleed to death, and we can't feed half of our population.'

Thornley shrugged. 'We can't do everything – it's a small country we've got. But we can't put the clock back, either. It's the future we have to think about, and my idea is that we have to think *big*!'

' "A great empire and little minds go ill together",' the vicar quoted, smiling at him.

'True enough; whoever said it knew what he was talking about.'

' ". . . God who made thee mighty, make thee mightier yet" ', Louise contributed, only half-ironically. She was reluctant to find herself in Arthur Thornley's camp, but fresh from India how could she not be Empire-minded? He smiled at her and nodded as a teacher might at a backward pupil who had unexpectedly shown promise.

Maud entered the lists in support of William and George Hoskins. 'Our bible-quoting village shoemaker isn't here, but if he were I can tell you what he'd say – "Pride goeth before destruction, and an haughty spirit before a fall"! I think it's high time England watched out for a haughty spirit which, apart from anything else, must be exceedingly irritating to her neighbours on the Continent.'

Arthur turned to her in triumph. 'Why do you think I'm in the business of making munitions, Miss Roberts? Of course they envy us – want our territories and our trade – but properly armed and properly confident of our right to govern, we needn't let faint-hearted, bible-thumping village cobblers hold us back . . . begging your pardon, Vicar!'

Gertrude stared at him across the dinner table, wishing that he didn't remind her a little of James. For both of them failure was only another way of saying that not enough effort had been made to achieve success.

'Your argument is beautifully tailored to suit *you*,' she pointed out, when the others seemed to have been silenced, either by his conviction or their own reluctance to attack a guest. 'You manufacture things, therefore you must have people to sell them to; you're an Englishman, therefore you are fitted by Heaven to tell these people what to do; being English, you are bound to be right, and if they don't wish to buy or to be ruled, they are not only wrong but ungrateful as well.'

If anything, her victim looked pleased with this summing-up. 'You've put it in a nutshell,' he agreed. She thought it was like trying to spear an armadillo with a feather.

William smiled at her from the other end of the table. 'My dear, there's no gainsaying a man who embodies all the virtues of Victoria's England – sublime confidence, energy, and a belief in self-made success that practically amounts to a new religion!'

Thornley stared at his host. 'If you weren't so civil, Sir William, there'd be things you'd put on the other side of the scales. I'd accept them, as well as what you've just said.'

It seemed to end the discussion, but William had the conviction that they would all remember it. The time might come when events would remind them that, at least in the matter of needing weapons, Arthur Thornley would be proved right.

CHAPTER SEVENTEEN

Alec Trentham's departure from Delhi was twice postponed by the local feuds, famines, and skirmishes that serving officers of the Raj were required to deal with. Before he finally reached England Harry had been parted with difficulty from his friend at Providence and sent to school, and Louise was completing the business of renting a house in London. If it proved suitable for their needs, they could buy it when they wanted to. She rejected William's well-meant offer of help, saying that she was accustomed to handling such matters. Gertrude offered no help at all, explaining to her husband that daughters of the Empire were probably accustomed to do much more than ensure a roof over their families' heads. He smiled but looked regretful as well.

'Mama is right – you and Louise still merely suffer one another. I'd hoped you might become friends.'

'Friendships don't come by hoping. We don't seem able to progress from where we were fifteen years ago; *she* can't forget that my mother was her governess, and *I* remember that she despised my boots and village-school pinafores. So we merely play politely at the business of being sisters-in-law. Jane Austen has hit us off exactly – "Pride and Prejudice"!'

She was surprised, therefore, when Louise proposed accompanying her to London one morning. The tenancy of the house in Cadogan Square was settled, so presumably boredom rather than business was the reason for a suggestion that Gertrude would have preferred to refuse.

'I'm only going to haggle at Liberty's,' she pointed out bluntly. 'Jane's girls need a change from making underclothes and are starting on beautiful blouses instead; but before they get any further, I must make certain that we can sell them.'

If she'd hoped that this would put Louise off, it didn't succeed. 'I'm bound to have had more practice at haggling than you . . . it's obvious that I must come.'

Gertrude told herself firmly that her sister-in-law's intentions were good, even if her manner of putting them into words couldn't fail to give offence. They set off on an October morning that reminded her of the day a year previously when she'd first walked into Blanchard's gallery. For something to talk about on the journey, she described the visit. 'I was very nervous; aware of looking a dowd, and mortified by the discovery that I was as good as naked in Bond Street without an elegant parasol! Maud had forgotten to warn me about that.'

Louise smiled, remembering the vicar's sister. 'You mean Maud had forgotten to notice. However, Monsieur Blanchard must have been sufficiently impressed by William's paintings not to hold it against you . . . or was it, by any chance, *you* he was impressed with?'

Gertrude recognized the thrust as being deliberate. Although she scarcely knew why, it was clear that Louise was curious about her and her unexpected marriage to William. The peaceful stay at Providence had restored her energy and now she was looking for something to direct it at; studying her odd sister-in-law was better than doing nothing at all. Gertrude did her best to give Louise's curiosity nothing to feed on, but she was nervously aware that James was suspected of being involved in the situation. Anything would be better than to have her stumble on the truth; and a disconcerting Frenchman could scarcely fail to tempt her on to a false trail.

'Monsieur Blanchard *might* be impressed if Helen of Troy combined with Shakespeare's idea of Cleopatra walked into his gallery. For want of *that*, he likes to amuse himself in this country by being excessively French! I can't imagine what he does in France to draw women's attention to himself, assuming that millions of other Frenchmen behave like him over there.' She felt slightly ashamed of herself, remembering his kindness to Sybil, but he was too good a red herring to be wasted for the sake of truth or principle.

'I'm not sure what being "excessively" French means, so perhaps it's time I found out,' Louise murmured. 'When we've talked Liberty's into submission perhaps we should visit Monsieur Blanchard's gallery. In any case, I should like to see William's artistic efforts actually on display.'

Gertrude swallowed irritation at her sister-in-law's choice of phrase, and tried to think of some excuse for not going to Bond Street that wouldn't harden Louise's determination to go at any price.

'As you wish,' she said finally, having failed to think of any excuse at all. 'Blanchard himself is not always there. According to William, he spends a lot of his time in Paris. But you can always see William's "efforts" at Providence.'

'Not the same thing at all,' Louise insisted with her usual accuracy.

She *was*, Gertrude admitted to herself afterwards, a great help in extracting an excellent price from the shop for Jane's sample blouses. No-one seeing Louise's elegant dress and elegant Wyndham nose could have supposed her to be doing anything so degrading as haggling; she merely looked so disdainful at the first price suggested that it was hastily revised upwards by a shamefaced buyer.

When they got to the gallery Gertrude saw Blanchard at once, in conversation with a client. The discussion was conducted in French, and the client was clearly enjoying herself. Gertrude thought his pearl-grey suit might have been chosen deliberately to flatter his swarthy skin and black hair – *had* been chosen, she amended silently; he was as vain as a peacock, as well as being excessively French.

She led Louise to one of William's paintings and they were still studying it when Blanchard spoke behind them. 'Forgive me, mesdames, for not being free when you arrived.'

Gertrude turned to her companion. 'Louise, may I present

Monsieur Blanchard . . . William's sister, monsieur, Mrs Trentham.'

She watched him examining Louise and felt thankful to be offering him someone else to stare at. It was understandable that a faint, becoming tinge of colour had crept into her sister-in-law's cheeks under this treatment. Gertrude supposed it to be caused by indignation, but Louise was well equipped to fight her own battles. She smiled impartially at both of them, waited long enough to explain that Mrs Trentham had just returned from a long sojourn in India, and then wandered away. Blanchard could discover unaided Louise's total ignorance of Messrs Monet, Pissarro, and Degas, and she could find some way of dealing with his Frenchness.

Gertrude hoped that a small red label in the corner of one of William's paintings signified that it had been sold, and Blanchard's young assistant was eager to confirm that this was so. They were still deep in conversation, happily telling each other how clever William had been in depicting the moat and bridge under snow, when Blanchard interrupted them.

'Clever, yes . . . but nevertheless I wish him to try again. It's the most difficult thing of all – white on white. He's not yet master of it.'

He smiled at the expression on Gertrude's face. 'You wish to point out to me, no doubt, that I couldn't accomplish it at all? You are right, of course, but I am your husband's mentor, am I not?'

She nodded, aware of her usual difficulty with him; it was impossible to keep him from walking clean through all her defences because she could never tell from which direction his assault would come. 'What have you done with Mrs Trentham?' she asked, remembering that Louise was supposed to be keeping him occupied.

'She was ready to leave a moment ago, but has just been greeted by an acquaintance.'

Across the gallery Louise was now talking to Octavia Browning.

'A former neighbour of ours,' Gertrude said without thinking, then blushed at a memory best forgotten.

'Quite so . . . I shall soon persuade her to buy something – perhaps the little Pissarro that Miss Roberts coveted!'

His smile was not unkind, and she was visited by the strange idea that it would have been pleasant to have him as a friend. She went over to Louise and Octavia, and five minutes later when they took their leave, Blanchard was already embroiled with someone else.

Louise offered no opinion of him on the journey home, seeming deliberately to choose to talk of other things. Gertrude failed to decide what this silence meant, and referred instead to their surprise meeting with Octavia. 'The Brownings seem to have a vast acquaintance in London. If you know few people there to begin with, it's a situation Octavia will be happy to remedy for you.'

'I think I should prefer to remedy it for myself, but in any case Alec has a lot of London connections.' She gave an odd little smile, then added, 'I can contribute one interesting acquaintance myself – Henri Blanchard!'

Gertrude looked thoughtful. 'William happens to like him, but I can see that husbands, in general, might not.'

'Mine in particular will undoubtedly hate him, being stiffly correct at all times and suspicious of any foreigners whom we do not rule!'

'Then your acquaintance with Blanchard will scarcely prosper.'

Louise smiled faintly. 'Perhaps not, but then again it might!'

Alec Trentham arrived home in time to take his family to spend Christmas at Somerton. Having decided that this was the correct thing to do, he ignored Harry's pleas to be allowed to stay at Providence, and Louise's obvious disinclination for her brother-in-law's company. Afterwards, when they were briefly back at Haywood's End, Gertrude tried but failed to get to know Major Trentham.

'He's so smooth-surfaced that I can't get a grip on him,'

she explained to William. 'Outward forms of behaviour – all very diplomatic, ceremonial, and totally discreet – have polished him into anonymity!'

'Service gloss . . . you can hardly blame him for it and I dare say it will wear off in time,' her husband said. 'At the moment he still thinks and behaves like the rest of his kind – he's the distilled essence of every younger son who's ever gone East to serve Victoria's Empire.'

Gertrude nodded, wondering whether Louise, too, found him worthy but extremely dull. She had certainly been right in saying that he wouldn't approve of Henri Blanchard.

The Trenthams settled into the house in Cadogan Square, and at the next Somerset by-election Alec was returned without much difficulty as the new Member. The Liberals were still in opposition, so that there would be no great opportunity for a new recruit to the Party to make his mark; but Gertrude didn't doubt that Louise would see he took the opportunity when it came. Meanwhile her letters to Lady Hester casually mentioned dinners carefully given and received, little soirées and large receptions attended, and weekend house parties in the country more, or less, enjoyed. Alec made a successful maiden speech, boldly attacking French colonial marauders in Africa who were menacing Kitchener's plans to reconquer the Sudan.

'If it's right for Kitchener to be there, why is it wrong for the French?' Gertrude asked William.

He did his best to explain. 'Something to do with the Sudan being contiguous with Egypt, I fancy, and the Suez Canal, which is the lifeline to our Indian Empire. You'd do better to ask Arthur Thornley . . . he's our great colonialist!'

To Gertrude, immersed in the daily struggle to take care of her family, Providence, and Haywood's End, Louise's life in London seemed to belong to a different world. She envied her sister-in-law none of it, not even the triumphant presentation to the Prince of Wales. When the House was in recess, the Trenthams frequently travelled abroad, and to Ned's intensest joy this meant that Harry and Charlotte spent almost all their holidays at Providence.

Lady Hester took no pride in her daughter's grip on the highest rung of fashionable society's ladder – in fact, she bluntly deplored it when Louise paid her a rare visit.

'Dearest, of course I'm glad that Alec's new career is being so successful, but if the half of what one hears is true, the society you now frequent is extravagant, idle, and immoral . . . and regrettably it includes the heir to the throne. I wish you *didn't* have to be involved in it.'

'Mama . . . this is 1898, not 1858. Albert the Good is long since dead, and his stuffy morality has been abandoned along with our crinolines and steel corsets!' She thought it would give her mother no comfort to add that any wrong-doing was allowed as long as it was done discreetly; the only sin punished by society was that of being found out. Lady Hester listened for what was carefully *not* being said, and wondered whether she was right in thinking her daughter less than satisfied by her glittering social life.

'I suppose you couldn't come with the children this summer?' she suggested wistfully. 'I can see that Alec has to remain in London, but must you do so . . . would he miss you dreadfully?'

Louise smiled brightly. 'I doubt if he would miss me at all. I am a political grass widow. I should have remembered that he never does anything by halves. For as long as he is concerned in politics, he's wedded to Westminster!'

'Could he not find something else to do?' her mother ventured . . . 'something that would make you less unhappy than I seem to feel you are?'

'Mama dear, your usually reliable antennae are confused! I'm not at all unhappy, merely a trifle tired, that's all. Alec would hate to give it up until he's had a chance, as he says, to do something! His sole fear is that Richard Trentham will die before there's been a change of Government and he can be offered a place in the next Liberal cabinet.'

Her mother did her best not to wince; she disliked Louise's new-found brittle humour, but accepted humbly that she was out of date. The morality of fifty years ago was to her liking, not the present-day *laisser tout faire*; but, as everyone was at pains to tell her, the clock could not be put back.

Louise deliberately changed the subject, choosing the new topic with a gambler's instinct for courting danger.

'William's paintings, Mama . . . I gather from Blanchard that they are beginning to sell quite well. He, by the way, is part of the fashionable society you disapprove of . . . one sees him everywhere.'

'I think William both likes *and* disapproves of him.'

'Why should my dear unworldly brother disapprove of someone who does a great deal of good for him professionally?'

Lady Hester found this subject even more distasteful than the previous one, but there seemed no way of avoiding an answer to her daughter's question. 'He is grateful for *that*, of course, but my impression is that he finds Monsieur Blanchard too attractive to women. I found him delightful myself when he came here, and it's scarcely likely that I was made to feel the full effect of his charm! Unleashed, so to speak, on a woman of his own age, I can see that the result might be . . . considerable. Gertrude avoids him as much as possible, grateful as she is on William's behalf.'

'And you think *she's* aware of temptation?'

Lady Hester frowned at the suggestion, but answered calmly. 'Not at all; she has simply found Monsieur Blanchard a little too . . . too French in his behaviour.'

'Dear Mama, you, and my sister-in-law as well obviously, are deliciously behind the times. You're buried the year round at Providence and simply don't know how the rest of the world behaves now. Manners are somewhat freer than they were.'

'I dare say, dearest. I don't like them as they *are*, but that only goes to show that I'm a confirmed early Victorian!'

The following year there was more to think about than changing manners, declining morals, and the sort of scandals that continued to surround the name of Oscar Wilde, recently released from prison. Just as the pillars of Victorian society – thrift, decorum, and hard work – seemed to be tottering towards collapse, so did complacency about the Empire die in the muddled bloodshed and bitterness of the Boer War.

Ned came home with William from Warwick one day with his eyes full of excitement.

'Mama . . . we saw soldiers, lots and lots of them – marching off to fight for the Queen, Papa says. I should like to go too.'

Gertrude didn't make the mistake of saying that she was thankful he was too young by at least ten years to do anything of the kind. She merely permitted herself to look disappointed.

'I thought you wanted to stay here and be a fine farmer, like Mr Moffat.'

Ned considered the problem for a moment. 'I shall, later . . . but perhaps I could have some fighting first?'

She wasn't to know that his words would surface in her mind long afterwards with the most bitter painfulness. Now, there was the big globe in the library to be looked at, so that Ned could find thereon a place unimaginably far away called the Transvaal; and there was Sybil to be argued with until she agreed to help him rechristen the moat the Orange River.

What began in the rosy confidence that an impertinent uprising by two Boer republics could easily be suppressed took three years to end. Before it did so Victoria was dead, and all the majestic certainties of her reign died with her. Edward had had time enough and more in which to become known and liked by his subjects but, with his mother's burial at Frogmore on a cold February day in 1901, the sun seemed to have set in the Imperial sky.

The war in South Africa dragged on, but when the Treaty of Vereeniging was finally signed the following year William still looked so grave that Gertrude was impatient with him.

'Surely an end to the fighting is something to be thankful for?'

'Of course, but the job's only been half done. The settlement does nothing to prevent a confrontation that will certainly come – not Boer against English, but black against white, and *that* will probably be more terrible. The enfranchisement of non-whites is to await "representative" government; it will therefore wait so long that it will come too late, if it comes at all.'

Gertrude nodded, aware that in such matters her husband's views were to be trusted. But her own anxieties lay much nearer home. Lady Hester was growing frailer every day, the time when Ned must be incarcerated in a preparatory school before going to Rugby could no longer be delayed, and she was almost certain that, in London, Louise was becoming ruinously involved with Henri Blanchard.

CHAPTER EIGHTEEN

By the time it was clear that James should be urged to make the long journey to Providence, a summons was almost too late: Lady Hester's slow and gentle journey into the shadows had accelerated. Watching her, Gertrude thought it was as if she'd decided to speed the mournful business of dying, not for her own sake but for theirs. Sitting with her one wintry afternoon, as usual, Gertrude was suddenly overwhelmed by the fear that the woman she had grown to love so deeply might even now be slipping away from her, beyond the point where return was possible.

'Mama . . . stay a little longer,' she said desperately . . . 'just a *little* longer . . . I don't see how we can manage without you.'

Lady Hester's thin fingers moved in her own, now holding them instead of being held. 'Dear child, you manage beautifully . . . always have done, ever since you first came here and frightened Edward into good behaviour with your little book! I can leave everything in your hands . . . contentedly.' Her voice faded to a thread, then strengthened again. 'You and James, dearest . . . was it *very* bad? I've always wanted to say that I knew, but didn't in case it made things worse.'

Gertrude tried to smile at the frail, beautiful woman who lay watching her. One last effort was needed so that she might be reassured. 'Well, it's all right now . . . long over and done with; and never more than a mistaken idea of happiness anyway. Everything's all right, except the thought of losing you.'

Lady Hester smiled and in that moment her face seemed to regain the brightness of youth. 'No need to be sad, dearest

. . . Hubert knows I'm very curious about what happens next!'

She died a week later, and was carried to her resting-place in the churchyard by William, George Hoskins, Biddle, and Hodges. Alec Trentham refused to share the privilege, telling his brother-in-law that it belonged to the old friends who had known her for nearly a lifetime. When William told Gertrude about this she took her first real step towards liking Louise's husband.

Ned and Harry came home from school to attend their grandmother's funeral, but Sybil, Lucy and Charlotte were left at Providence under the eye of the governess, Miss Lacey, who had recently joined the household. Afterwards Ned grappled by himself with the terrifying difference between a vague idea that people eventually had to die and the actuality of having someone that he loved taken away from him. Sybil's reaction to the mystery was to talk even more than usual.

'Mama . . . Granny was restful, wasn't she . . . always sure of things? I'm usually in a muddle, but she never was. Does that come of being very old or very wise?'

Gertrude smiled at her puzzled daughter. 'She wasn't very old, my darling, but she was certainly wise. I think her secret was that she'd decided what was important in life. The rest of us waver about, and keep changing our minds.'

Sybil thought about this and eventually nodded. *Her* mind never told her the same thing for more than ten seconds at a time.

'Ned remembered what the rector said about Granny . . . she was "lovely and pleasant in her ways". I'd like someone to say that about me, but I don't suppose they will. I heard Ethel tell Emmy I was a holy terror.'

Gertrude thought she sounded not entirely displeased by the idea and tried to instil a small doubt in her daughter's mind. 'Never mind, I dare say you'll improve as you get older.'

'Miss Roberts keeps reminding me at Sunday school that "the meek shall inherit the earth, dear Sybil". I think Lucy may grow up meek all right, but I don't want to . . . it sounds feeble to me.'

'Meek means being like Granny, courteous and kind; but *she* wasn't feeble.'

Suddenly the word 'wasn't' fell on Sybil with the weight of something dreadful but unalterable; the thing that had happened was true, not a game they could stop playing . . . but she couldn't be meek about death, either. 'Granny *shouldn't* have died,' she shouted, her face scarlet with rage. 'She should have stayed here with *us*.'

'I know, my darling, but she was tired and wanted to go to sleep.' Gertrude waited a moment, then offered her daughter something other than death to ponder. 'Ethel thinks you're a fiend because you speak to her sometimes as if a servant's feelings don't matter.'

Sybil looked genuinely puzzled. 'Yes, but they can't matter so much, can they? Servants are stupid and have to be told what to do – it's what they're here for.'

Gertrude thought it might have been the voice of a young Louise Wyndham talking. She'd often wondered when the time might come for her to say what she was about to say now, but the moment had finally chosen itself. 'Ethel's feelings matter quite as much as yours. I happen to know, because I first came to Providence as a kind of servant myself. Once, although it wasn't my job, I had to help a lady dress. I didn't do it very well and she shouted at me as if I wasn't a human being much the same as herself. It happened a long time ago, but I've never forgotten it.'

Sybil's face had paled, but now suddenly flushed with colour again. She was going to be very attractive . . . and her mother was reminded of what Blanchard had once said – 'She's going to grow up just like you'. It was impossible to guess what Sybil would say now. Ned would have hugged her and said, 'Stoopid woman . . . don't mind *her*, Mama', but her daughter was nothing if not unpredictable. For the moment she seemed to be deep in thought.

'Emily Maynard said something once that I didn't understand,' she muttered finally. 'She sniggered about it and I had the feeling that I ought to hit her on her silly turned-up nose.' Sybil frowned over a wasted opportunity, then grinned entrancingly. 'Never mind – she's so stupid, I'm bound to get another chance!'

Gertrude reported the conversation to William that evening, saying that, apart from taking her daughter's mind off death for a little while, it hadn't seemed to make much impression on her.

'My dear girl, what did you expect?' said William, smiling at her. 'Like any other child, she's really only concerned with herself. Nothing changes the important thing that she's who she is – Sybil Wyndham of Providence. She'd much rather be that than Emily Maynard, whose family built Barham a mere two hundred years ago! If that weren't enough, it's plain to see that *her* mother is kind and clever and beautiful. Mrs Maynard, though doubtless kind, is just as obviously silly and plump!'

Gertrude smiled in spite of herself. 'Thank you for the charming compliment, dear sir! All the same, you make our daughter sound like an analytical monster.'

'I think I make her sound like a ten-year-old female, who perhaps sees things a little more clearly than most.'

Gertrude accepted the truth of this, then her face grew sad again. 'I wish we could have let James know in time about today. It might have comforted him to be here, to see how dearly his mother was loved.'

'I'm afraid the man who really needs comfort is your father . . . he's bereft without her. Looking at him this morning, I kept remembering something: ". . . allow this aged man his right, to be your beadsman now that was your knight". I think that great and good gentleman was both knight and beadsman to my mother.'

Gertrude smiled tremulously at her husband. 'I wish he could hear you say so.'

They sat quietly for a while, in a shadowy room lit only by the burning logs on the hearth. In the flickering light he thought she looked desperately tired, as well as sad. 'It's been a difficult day, my dear . . . why not go to bed?'

'I'd go if I thought I could sleep . . . as it is, I'd rather stay here talking to you. When I saw the Thornleys in church this morning I was reminded of something Jane said recently. Her husband's new factory is almost ready to go into production, turning out countless numbers of dreadful weapons. Who needs such things?'

'I'm afraid we do. Germany is probably ahead of us as it is, but she can't be allowed to get *too* far ahead.'

'But, William, the Kaiser is the King's nephew! I thought it was France we'd always feared.'

'My dear, it's true that France has traditionally been our enemy, but since 1870 *Germany* has been in command of Europe, not France. Bismarck's brilliant diplomacy and a brief, successful war have left the Germans very sure of themselves – they now believe that arrogance and military strength can win them anything they've a fancy for.'

'You mean that we're going to have to *fight* Germany one day?'

William shook his head. 'No, although judging from the pages of Mr Harmsworth's *Daily Mail*, you might well think that the entire population of this country can scarcely wait to sink its teeth in German throats. No, it's simply an elaborate and costly game of bluff we're playing.'

Unaware that her husband had no faith in it himself, Gertrude accepted the quiet statement, because her mind had turned to another anxiety. 'I wish we'd insisted on Louise staying here for a day or two. She looked so strained and sad this morning.' Gertrude felt sure that more than grief for Lady Hester had caused Louise's face to look strangely, beautifully tragic beneath a toque of dark fur. She was like a leaf blown about in a storm; she was Tolstoy's Anna Karenina, governed only by emotions that had run, for once, out of control.

William gave a little shrug. 'Insisting would have done little good; Louise has a mind of her own, and will only listen to advice if it matches what she's already made up her mind to do.'

He was right, of course, but it did nothing to ease

Gertrude's steadily growing anxiety about her sister-in-law.

Ned was to return to school the following morning. When she went to his room to remind him that it was almost time to leave, he was staring out of the window. He looked older, suddenly, and more grave. His eyes under a thatch of hair that was darkening to brown were thoughtful. They were the pale blue eyes of the Wyndhams but, as always, she felt a secret twinge of pleasure that he had *her* short, blunt nose! For once he didn't smile, as he usually did when he caught sight of her.

'Papa told me about the bank owning Providence,' he said abruptly. 'I think I sort of knew something was wrong . . . Grandpa Hoskins often says we can't do needful things "until times get better, do you see, Ned"! It's going to be all right, though, when I've finished school, Mama. I've got lots more ideas than dear old Moffat.'

She tried not to weep because it would upset him, but her heart seemed to be breaking with love. Instead, with a great effort, she was able to smile. 'Everything will be perfect when you're here for good; meanwhile, my darling Ned, it's time for you to leave.'

In a pleasant candlelit apartment in Pont Street, Louise sat dining, with the outward air of a woman who was happily content. But something was wrong . . . had been increasingly so for several weeks, and tonight she was sure of it. Henri had held and kissed her when she arrived, but she was almost certain that the embrace had been simply habitual. Usually, by now, the servant would have been dismissed and they would have retired to the room next door – her need matching his desire, both flaming into the sort of passion that her body hadn't known existed before. But this evening when she found an excuse to touch his hand, he withdrew it and her fingers were left empty. She laced them round her wineglass to stop them trembling, looked up, and found him watching her.

'Louise, *ma chèrie*, I'm going back to Paris very soon,' he said suddenly.

'A visit . . . to see the chestnut trees in bloom?' she tried to ask lightly.

'Not a visit; I am going for good. I shall send someone else to run the gallery in London.'

Her hands released the glass and stretched themselves out towards him across the table, but if he noticed the gesture he ignored it. 'May I come with you?'

'No . . . I am going alone.' His voice was gentle, almost persuading her that even if she heard correctly what he was saying, she need not be alarmed by it.

'You . . . you don't mean it,' she murmured, and saw him nod by way of reply. 'Henri, you *can't* mean it.' Her voice roughened; a terrible fear was growing in her heart. 'I can't be left behind . . . I should die without you.'

She could see only pity in his face, and perhaps a faint disgust that she should be ignoring the rules of an illicit love affair. Mutual pleasure discreetly enjoyed, and mutual acceptance of a graceful ending when it was time to say goodbye – those were the ground rules, well known and meticulously observed, even by His Majesty the King, in such affairs.

'Are you going because of me? Is that why I am not to come? Tell me, Henri . . . say *something* to make me understand.'

Blanchard's hands closed over hers. 'I'm not sure that I *can* make you understand. We have enjoyed being lovers, have we not? But an *affaire* is not like a marriage, you see. It begins as a little seed of desire, grows, blossoms into passion joyfully given and received, dies because its soil is shallow, and gently disappears.'

'*Our* passion hasn't died . . . it can't have done. I won't believe it. My dearest, say I'm right . . .'

'Listen to me, Louise. You are married to a man in public life. Even if Trentham agreed to a divorce, his career would be ruined. If he did not, and you spent the rest of your life as my mistress, *you* would be ruined, here or in Paris.'

Her eyes, blazing like aquamarines in the pallor of her

face, pleaded with him. 'Then stay here . . . let us go on as we are.'

'I want to return to Paris; I am tired of living in London.'

'You mean you're tired of *me*. Say it! I want the truth, Henri.'

His beautiful hands sketched a gesture she was familiar with. His hands were known too, and loved, and they had caressed her body into charmed delight. 'The truth is that you are becoming indiscreet. I prefer the world *not* to be allowed to guess so easily that we are lovers.'

A bitter smile touched her mouth. 'No doubt it damages your success with women buyers in the gallery.'

'It damages *you*, my dear,' he answered gravely.

In the silence of the room she could hear a church clock chiming in the distance . . . waited to count its strokes, as if it mattered to know the time. 'When do you leave?' she whispered.

'Tomorrow . . . I didn't tell you before because . . .'

'. . . you didn't wish me to be destroyed until the last possible moment. Such thoughtfulness, my darling . . . it is one of the things that make you irresistible to women!' She saw the expression on his face, and her voice faltered. 'I'm . . . I'm behaving very badly, am I not? I should smile and kiss you goodbye, and glide away to my next little affair! I won't kiss you, but the rest perhaps I can manage.'

She moved to the sofa where her evening cloak had been thrown down and flung it round her shoulders before he could reach her.

'I shall see you to a cab . . . or walk with you,' he said quickly.

'No, I prefer to go alone. *Bonne chance*, Henri!' A moment later she had let herself out into the lamplit dusk. The evening had grown misty as darkness fell; the gaslights bloomed like tiny golden crocuses veiled by gauze, and the familiar road she had to cross had become an unknown highway . . . as frightening as her own life had just become. She was lost . . . oh, God, which way to go? She closed her eyes against drowning waves of despair . . . heard the clatter of hooves and wheels, and a voice that shouted at her, jerking her eyes open again. She was in the road, and something loomed above, almost upon, her. The instinct to fling herself out of the way came nearly too late, but a moment later she was huddled in the gutter, and a passer-by was bending over her. It would have been easier to stay where she was, to refuse to make any kind of effort ever again, but a strange voice kept asking if she were all right, and a rougher one, presumably belonging to the driver of the hansom cab, was repeating over and over again, 'S'truth, guv, the lady just stepped clean orf the pavement in front o'me.'

'I'm not hurt . . . just a little shaken,' she heard herself say. Faintness washed over her, but she bowed her head, and then succeeded, with the help of the concerned passer-by, in standing upright again. 'I am perfectly all right, and it *was* my fault. I have only a few yards to go to my home.'

The driver walked thankfully back to his cab, still muttering his incantation, and the elderly man to whose arm she was clinging insisted on supporting her as far as her front door.

'You've been very kind . . . now I shall be able to manage,' she murmured. He raised his hat and walked away, and she let herself into the sleeping house. The servants were downstairs out of the way, Alec was at Somerton, attending a meeting of his constituents. She had refused to go with him and he had left angry with her. If her heart would oblige her by refusing to go on beating during the night, she need never face him again.

She was still alive next morning, but so sunk in misery as to be indifferent to the pain of the wrenched ankle and shoulder she had fallen on. Her maid was brusquely told to leave her undisturbed, but some time later the door opened and she summoned enough energy to lift her head and shout at the girl. It wasn't her maid who walked into the room, however.

'Oh, God . . . *you*! Go away, Gertrude . . . I find myself

unwell this morning . . . you should have been told I wasn't receiving visitors.'

'I'm not a visitor . . . I'm your sister-in-law, remember?'

Louise wanted to say that she'd never been able to forget the fact, but the hurtful words couldn't be forced out of her mouth. She felt deathly cold, even while waves of feverish heat swept over her body. If only she could die.

Gertrude sat beside her on the bed, trying to pretend that she wasn't shocked by her sister-in-law's haunted face. 'I came because I've had the feeling lately something was wrong. This morning the feeling was so strong that I couldn't stay at Providence. William was in Warwick, so I left a note explaining that I had to make an urgent visit to London. What can I do, now that I'm here?'

Louise shook her head, then winced because the movement jarred her hurt shoulder. 'It's kind of you, but all I need is to be left alone . . . go away, please, Gertrude.'

'I'll go when you tell me what's wrong and I'm convinced I can't help you. Why are you here alone in this state?'

'Because Alec is away. There's nothing unusual about that, and the only thing that can be said to be wrong is that my lover, finding me an embarrassment, is now on his way to Paris without me! Are you now sufficiently convinced that you can't help me?'

'It's Blanchard, isn't it?' Gertrude asked gently. 'I don't suppose anyone else would guess, but I saw the glance you exchanged one day in the gallery.'

'And saw *what*? Desire, lust, passion? Surely nothing *you* could possibly recognize, my dear, virtuous sister!'

'I'm aware of those things,' she replied gravely. 'All I can see now, though, is your dreadful unhappiness. Let me take you back to Providence; it's a healing kind of place.'

The spark of malice died out of Louise's face, leaving it tragic again. 'It can't heal me of loving Henri; or soften the humiliation of knowing that he couldn't wait to be rid of me.' She stared at Gertrude for a moment. 'What did *you* need healing of . . . the rare excitement of being William's wife? I told you once that the Wyndhams were cold-blooded.

I was right about him, but too thorough at proving I was wrong about myself. I wanted to be properly alive . . . now I'd rather be dead.' Tears shone in her eyes, brimmed over, and poured down her white cheeks. Gertrude slipped to her knees beside the bed and wrapped Louise's shivering body in her own warm arms, waiting for the storm of weeping to pass.

Finally, she said, 'You've loved and been loved in return; there's no humiliation in that unless you insist on finding it. Blanchard has gone because he could see no other way out for himself and the wife of Alec Trentham; there's no humiliation in that, either. You're left with the pain of losing what you loved, but that you can slowly recover from if you want to.'

'How do *you* know?'

'Because I had to get over loving James.'

Louise lay watching her. 'I thought . . . no, I *knew* there had to be someone other than William. You could have gone to James when Kitty died. Why didn't you?'

'The price was too high – William's peace, the children's happiness, even Providence itself. Will you come home with me now?'

Louise shook her head. 'If I'm to fight my battle anywhere, it must be here. In any case I doubt if I could hobble downstairs at the moment. I wrenched my ankle and shoulder, getting out of the way of a hansom cab last night, and I'm suffering a little. I expect that's why I wept over you in such an embarrassing manner.'

'I realize that you don't make a habit of it,' Gertrude agreed, smiling at her. 'Now that I know you've hurt yourself, I shall take the liberty of sending your maid to summon the doctor. Meanwhile you would also be better for a little nourishment, I think; you look much too fragile.'

When she came back into the room, Louise almost smiled at her. 'You're almost as bossy as I am!' Then her expression changed again. 'There's one more thing I need to say to you. I knew right from the beginning that it was *you* Henri wanted. It made me determined that he should prefer Louise

Trentham instead. I know now, of course, that I never succeeded in convincing him. I ought to hate you for it but somehow I don't.'

Gertrude bent down to kiss her cheek. 'Nobly said, but I doubt if his interest in me went much beyond an impersonal curiosity in a female he found odd and slightly amusing.'

'You're wrong, but we won't argue about it. It doesn't matter now *what* he thought.'

Gertrude wanted to weep for the desolate note in her voice; wanted to hate Henri Blanchard for reducing her proud, confident sister-in-law to this pain-racked, lost creature. She hadn't anticipated staying in London but was still making up her mind whether Louise ought to be left alone when the problem was settled for her.

'You can go without fearing I shall throw myself at the next hansom cab I see. Having discovered in myself an unexpected talent for affection, I shall try to offer it to my family, and good will thus come out of it! You see – I spare you the bother of giving me the little homily!'

Gertrude's own eyes filled with tears. 'Louise dear . . . it *will* get easier; I promise you.'

By the time she left the house the doctor had called, and Louise was not only comfortable but was mistress of herself again. 'I'm glad you've seen me beaten – you can't ever again have the silly idea that we aren't equal,' she said when Gertrude was about to depart. 'I shan't hurt Alec by telling him the truth, by the way . . . keeping it to myself is no doubt part of my punishment.'

Gertrude nodded. 'Come and spend Easter with us . . . I only ask, of course, so that Ned can have Harry's company!'

'You lie a little, I think, but thank you . . . thank you, dear Gertrude.'

She arrived back at Providence in the early evening, tired to the point of exhaustion. William was in the Great Hall when she walked in, and his pale face changed colour at the sight of her.

'I didn't expect you back,' he said in a strange, cool voice that puzzled her.

'I left a note for you, explaining that I had to go to London. Did you not see it, William?'

'Yes, but I wasn't sure what it meant.' He turned towards the stone fireplace and began tracing the Wyndham arms engraved in the stone. 'Blanchard wrote to me a week ago that he was leaving London, but would continue to watch over my career from Paris. I couldn't bring myself to tell you. Blanchard felt something for you, and I was afraid you . . .' He turned to face her. 'I knew he was going today. When I found your note I was half-demented. I couldn't decide whether you would listen if I rushed after you . . . whether it was already too late, or even whether I had the selfish right to implore you not to go . . .' His voice was suspended, and she crossed the room to put her arms around him.

'You know what Ned would say – stoopid! I don't want Blanchard *or* Paris; I simply want to stay here. My visit to London was to see Louise. I had so strongly the feeling that something was wrong that I couldn't *not* go. I'm glad I did. Alec was at Somerton, and she'd had a mishap in the street. Some minor injuries but nothing very serious, the doctor says.' She hesitated a moment. 'Louise has been unhappy of late, William, but I have the feeling that she will slowly recover now.'

'And I have the feeling that I'm not being told the whole, but I shan't ask to know more.' His eyes still searched her face. 'Was it true what you said just now, about wanting to stay here?'

She didn't look away from him, and her eyes were truthful. 'I only want you and the children and Providence.'

'I've never been quite sure . . . always felt we might not be enough for you,' he murmured. 'But you're so very precious to *me*, my dearest girl.'

Her tired face was lit by a smile of luminous beauty. 'Dear William . . . do you realize you've never said it before?'

'I've wanted to, often; but after Markham's grim warning

when Lucy was born, I've been too terrified to touch you in case careful self-control went up in flames.'

She wanted to burst into tears . . . years of what James had called lukewarm affection imposed on them both unnecessarily. 'There's a thing called contraception . . . so respectable nowadays that it's even written about in the *Fortnightly Review*! Don't you think we might learn how to make use of it?'

William's smile answered her. 'Oh, my dear . . . I rather think we must.'

His arms held her close to him and she said a final goodbye to James in her heart. She hoped God would be merciful and allow Louise to forget Henri more quickly.

'I asked Louise to spend Easter with us, my dear . . . Providence will make her its usual gift of healing grace, I'm sure.'

'It's the gift of you and Providence together,' he insisted. 'No unhappiness can withstand it.'

1910

CHAPTER NINETEEN

In retrospect, the first decade of the new century seemed to Gertrude's children the last of the sunlit years. At the time, they and their Trentham cousins were only aware that the little world of Providence was bathed in the golden glow of peace and stability. The Boer War and its shaming saga of ineptitude and near-defeat had become a memory, useful only as a spur to shock the Government into starting to modernize an antiquated army. Fortunately there was no need of an army that did more than *look* like being capable of fighting; the intricately woven mesh of alliances – England, France and Russia balanced against Germany, Austria and Italy – held Continental peace secure.

In the tranquillity of Haywood's End there should have been nothing to disturb the certainty that God was in His heaven and all was right with the world but, having reached the thoughtful age of eighteen, Ned sometimes wondered whether all *was* right with a world that seemed woefully uneven. He was on the joyous brink of leaving Rugby and life stretched out in front of him in a prospect that seemed challenging but entirely good as far as Ned Wyndham was concerned; only the prospect wasn't so happy for everybody else. In the spring of 1910 he couldn't miss the rumblings of a widespread discontent, or the smell of violence that was beginning to taint the air.

After careful thought he chose his confidant; Mama and the girls, being female, mustn't be alarmed; Papa, busy painting more often than not, wasn't to be disturbed; and his friend Harry was now a dashing fellow too busy to stop and ask himself the whys and wherefors of life. There remained Grandpa Hoskins – white-haired now and a trifle stooped, but still the friend whose counsel Ned valued most.

Before going back to school after Easter for his last term, he took his usual seat on the wide window ledge in the estate office one morning, not sure what it was that he had come to say.

'Morning, Ned . . . going to the top meadow? Young Sid's sowing oats there today.' George Hoskins doubted if this information was what Ned had come for, but it would serve to launch a conversation he seemed reluctant to start.

'I know. I said I'd go and help. Gramps . . . do you reckon it's fair, us owning Providence? I can't help wondering sometimes whether things shouldn't be shared out a bit more. We drove through Birmingham yesterday . . . so many human beings crammed into hovels we'd be almost ashamed to keep the pigs in, and children playing in stinking alleyways, with not a blade of grass in sight. When I look at everything we have here, life seems very unfair.'

His troubled face warned George of a crisis of conscience that must be handled gently. 'Life *is* uneven, Ned, but I doubt if sharing out bits of Wyndham land as far as they'll go round will do much to make it less so, if that's what you've got in mind. Men go where they can work, and where they go, their families must go too.'

'Yes, and that means crowding them into industrial towns, but do the towns need to be so hideous? England's rich; why can't its wealth be used to give people houses that are fit to live in, and green spaces here and there so that their choking lungs can breathe fresh air?'

'These things have been too long in coming, I grant you, but the Government *is* getting to grips now with problems that have been building up for generations. It's work for the lawmakers, Ned; not for the individual efforts of people like you. Thinking of going into politics, like your Uncle Alec?'

Ned's face broke into a grin. 'I'm not thinking of doing anything but staying at Providence, but it seems too easy in a way. P'raps I ought to go out and slay a few dragons first . . . I could start with Mr Thornley, seeing that he's nearest!'

George took the last thing first. 'I've no doubt there are

employers who ought to be slain, but Arthur Thornley isn't one of them. There's nothing wrong with the way he and his son run their factories, and there's no reason why clever, hard-working men like them shouldn't get rich – in fact there's every reason why they should, as long as they don't cheat or ill-use their workpeople.'

Ned was distracted for a moment from the matter in hand. 'Frank Thornley's a strange chap – hardly says a word, but takes everything in. The only one who rouses him to talk is Sybil, simply because she gets him so angry that he can't help himself. I think he despises Harry and me . . . he thinks Harry's some kind of toy soldier playing a game, and he reckons I'm just waiting for Providence to drop into my lap when I ought to be carving out a future for myself.'

Aware that the conversation wasn't over yet, George allowed himself the luxury of filling his pipe. 'Ned, you have to remember that young Frank is a town man, for all that he's lived at Bicton for years. He's a magician when it comes to designing bits of machinery, but he doesn't know about working the land and trying to make it pay without tearing the heart out of it. He doesn't begin to fathom the mysteries we spend our lives trying to understand. England needs people like Frank Thornley, always thinking up a new idea; but there's nothing wrong with people like *us*, preserving what's already here. With your father's permission, we'll go into all the figures soon, but you know some of the problems already. Keeping Providence safe and sound will take all your energy when the time comes; but it *must* be preserved if we're to hand on to children not yet born something more than smoking factory chimneys and slag heaps.'

'That's exactly what Papa says,' Ned remembered thoughtfully, 'and the odd thing is that I think old Mr Thornley agrees with him, even though he's proud of his rotten chimneys too!' He stood up, staring out at the springtime beauty of his father's land. 'Still, we *are* lucky, Gramps, and I can't help wondering what we've done to deserve it. Perhaps it's what we may *have* to do. Harry repeats things sometimes that he picks up from Uncle Alec.

Apparently international crises keep swelling up like tar bubbles on a hot day, and although they seem to go plop without doing any harm, it's not to say they always will.'

'Harry's a soldier, bored with changing guard at Windsor Castle; I've no doubt he'd wish a little war on us if he could, just to liven things up.'

Ned grinned at the unusually acid note; he was aware that his grandfather faintly disapproved of Harry, whose newly fashionable motorcar not only tore up the surface of the drive but coated the hedgerows in a layer of white dust and frightened the horses.

'Coming to the top meadow, Gramps? It's too good a morning to be in here adding up accounts.'

'It happens that accounts have to be added up once in a while,' George Hoskins pointed out austerely, then spoiled the effect by smiling. 'I dare say I'll be along to see you don't make a mess of it.'

Ned finally took himself off, whistling as sweetly as a blackbird; he couldn't put the world to rights single-handed, but he *could* help Sid with the sowing. His grandfather spread out the accounts, but thought instead about what they'd just said. Life in Edward's England *was* uneven; not a doubt about that. The extremes of wealth and poverty were there for all to see. The very idle rich consumed time and wealth in a mindless pursuit of pleasure, while the very hard-working poor consumed life and health in the satanic mills and mines that pockmarked the country. George thanked his God that Providence knew neither of these extremes. Life was still dictated by the slowly revolving pattern woven by the changing seasons of the year. Whatever happened elsewhere, at Haywood's End winter ploughing, spring sowing, haysel, and harvest-time marked the turning of each year. So he hoped it would always be, world without end.

The first crack in the shining surface of expected things came almost without warning. When King Edward paid his usual spring visit to Biarritz that year he came home visibly

234

unwell, only to die a few weeks later. The people in the valley hadn't had occasion to see in person a monarch whose taste had mostly been for other than country pleasures, but all the same they reckoned his time shouldn't have come quite so quickly. Sixty years had been a longish wait for a throne he only sat on for nine years. Still, by all accounts, his burial at Windsor Castle had been a grand and seemly affair, with kings coming from all over Europe to walk behind his coffin to St George's Chapel. Haywood's End took a little of the credit for this – hadn't young Harry Trentham been right there, rubbing shoulders with the poor King's nephew, the German Emperor? It was almost as good as being there themselves.

When it was over Harry came back to Providence, as he usually did when he had off-duty time to spare. Gertrude welcomed him and listened to his account of the funeral, but couldn't help sighing when he'd rushed away with Sybil to play tennis at Barham Manor. The sigh was heavy and William realized that he was meant to notice it.

'You're looking mournful, my love, and I doubt if it's on account of his late Majesty. My guess is that, fond as you are of Harry, you wish he would spend more of his time with Alec and Louise in London and less at Haywood's End. Are you afraid he'll dazzle your son into wanting a military career? Short of chaining Ned to your father's desk in the estate office, there's nothing we can do about it, I fear.'

Gertrude smiled but shook her head. 'I'm not worrying about Ned. The charms of being a dashing Life Guards officer don't compare with the siren song that Providence sings in his ear. I'm worrying about my poor vulnerable daughter.'

'You mean *Sybil* wants to be a dashing . . . no, that *can't* be what you mean!'

'William, be serious; Sybil is perfectly content to be what she is, and she is *never* vulnerable. Harry is merely a convenience, to be made use of to the greatest extent that he will allow. I was referring to Lucy.'

'But she's only fifteen; a schoolgirl still, under the eye of that martinet upstairs who terrifies the life out of *me*, and presumably has much the same effect on Lucy.'

'Miss Lacey is deceptive . . . all stiff shirt-front and a heart as soft as dough underneath. She never managed to exert the slightest discipline over Sybil, and I doubt if she's doing much better with Lucy. Sybil flatly refused to learn anything that didn't interest her and although Lucy is too kind to do that, she just smiles sweetly and thinks most of the time of something else.'

'And you fear she's thinking of Harry?'

Gertrude nodded. 'No doubt you see him as a pleasant young subaltern, perhaps a little less vain than most. I can tell you what Lucy's imagination makes of him . . . he's the knight in shining armour, who is required to perform deeds of valour before he carries her away on his white charger.'

'You doubt if Harry is capable of deeds of valour?'

'He may be young Lochinvar himself, but he'll never notice poor sweet Lucy. I don't think he realizes it yet, but he's falling in love with Emily Maynard.'

William stared at her, fascinated by this example of near-occult divination. 'My dear, an uncomprehending male wouldn't dare argue with you, but how do you know?'

'It's obvious. He pays a lot of attention to Sybil, with whom he is *not* in love, simply in order to have the excuse of taking her to Barham. Less obviously, he talks readily about everyone else of our acquaintance, but he never mentions Emily!'

'If you're right, I imagine it will irritate one daughter quite as much as you think it will break the heart of the other. Emily is a dear friend, but Sybil also regards her as a hopeless duffer.'

'That's why they're such good friends,' his wife explained patiently. 'Sybil has to lead. She'd soon get tired of someone who competed with her on level terms. Give her a friend or a sister who needs telling what to do and she's perfectly happy.'

'Well, I'm afraid it's quite useless to worry about Lucy. With all the love in the world for them, you can't protect any of your children from the dangers of life, and presumably falling in love with the wrong young man is the most likely danger of all for a girl.'

Gertrude accepted the truth of this but continued to frown. 'The strange thing is that it was Sybil I used to worry about. Even when my father pointed out years ago that there was no need, I continued to agonize over the scrapes and problems she was bound to fall into. But Lucy is the vulnerable one, after all, wanting to love everybody and endowing them with such impossible virtues that they're bound to end up disappointing her.'

William nodded, on firmer ground now that they were discussing a trait even he could recognize in his daughter. 'Shall we take her with us to the Continent, after all? It might take her mind off Harry.'

'She'd come so reluctantly that it wouldn't take her mind off anything. I think we'll let the present arrangement stand. A visit to London is excitement enough, and she loves being with Charlotte.'

So it was that at the end of June the family set out from Providence – Lucy to be left in London with her Aunt Louise, William and his wife shepherding Sybil and Emily Maynard to a Swiss finishing school. Gertrude had long ago envisaged the need for this rounding-off of her daughters' education, without seeing how it was to be accomplished until William's paintings had begun to earn them money. The school in Lucerne had been warmly recommended by Maud Roberts as a place where English cygnets could safely be turned into swans.

William and Gertrude broke their homeward journey in Paris, where the most recent of his paintings were being exhibited. On the way from Lucerne Gertrude was so unusually abstracted that he imagined she was remembering a weeping Emily and a scowling daughter left behind.

'My dear, you're worrying again. Don't you have confidence in Maud's seminary? It looked delightful to me.'

Gertrude smiled suddenly, thinking of the glance Sybil had exchanged with the formidable woman she was being entrusted to for the next nine months. 'I have *every* confidence in Mlle Lebrun. Sybil was immediately aware that she'd met her match, which is why she looked so reproachful when we left! She'll have settled down by tomorrow, and under her bossy wing Emily will soon be all right as well.'

'Then you can forget your family for a little while and enjoy Paris with me.'

She agreed, cheerfully enough, and he was moved to notice as he did once in a while that she looked absurdly youthful still. Under a charming toque of white silk roses her hair remained lustrous and dark, and the years had been kind in merely defining the bones of her face more clearly. In repose she looked a woman, elegant and poised; smiling, she was Sybil again, with all her daughter's vivid enjoyment of life.

'If I'm quieter than usual, it's because I'm excited,' she explained solemnly. If not entirely true, it was all the truth she could admit to. A woman of forty, with daughters almost grown up, had no right to be in the grip of an attack of nervousness. It was more than ten years since she'd last seen Henri Blanchard, and on the whole, much as she wanted to visit Paris, she would have preferred never to meet him again. Louise's return to peace of mind after her *affaire* with him had been slow and painful. Gertrude had known that it was scarcely fair to blame him entirely, but she doubted if she would be able to meet him without remembering her sister-in-law's anguished face the day he'd left London. There was something else too, but she proposed not to recall even to herself what Louise had finally admitted to.

They reached Paris late in the evening and were driven from the Gare de Lyons to the hotel Blanchard had recommended – the Hotel Bristol in the Faubourg St Honoré. There was a glimpse of the river, and the grey towers of Notre Dame, then they were driving across the imposing spaces of the Place de la Concorde. The hotel was comfortable, Blanchard had said, and being situated on the

Rive Droite was conveniently placed for the galleries that specialized in displaying modern art.

When they set out next morning Gertrude was so genuinely excited by Paris itself that she gave almost no thought to Blanchard, waiting for them at his gallery in the boulevard Haussmann. There *was* a different feeling in the air, as William had told her long ago. London's citizens went soberly about the business of living; here, where no doubt people had to work equally hard, time was found as well to saunter in the parks and gardens, to stop and stare, and above all, it seemed, to talk! She dawdled along, intrigued by two men whose hands, eyes, whole bodies even, were being used in the course of a spirited conversation.

'They talk here as if they enjoyed doing it,' Gertrude observed. 'At home we seem to converse only as a necessity. What do you suppose *they* were discussing . . . some matter of life or death?'

'I would guess food, women, and politics, probably in that order, though not so very long ago they might have been arguing about Gustave Eiffel's new tower. I must take you to see it because it's an astonishing construction that divided Parisian opinion for years. Many people thought it the ruination of the city's beauty, but Henri wasn't one of them. He has an odd affection for it.'

Gertrude nodded, prepared for Blanchard to be different from the rest of the world. Remembering his gallery in London, she was also prepared for the richness of his Paris setting, in an hotel of perfect eighteenth-century proportions. Looking at it, she had so strongly the sensation of stepping back in time that it was disconcerting to find him waiting for them dressed with his customary modern elegance. She smiled at him from under the curving brim of a cream straw hat, decorated only with a wide silk ribbon and a single scarlet rose. Her jacket and skirt of plain cream linen had the same elegance born of extreme simplicity, and a silk cravat the colour of the rose in her hat added a small and charming note of gaiety.

'Good morning, monsieur . . . in these surroundings I expected to see you in powdered wig and a suit of claret-coloured velvet!'

Blanchard bowed over her hand, holding it 'for as long as all may, or only a moment longer'. The words spoke themselves in her mind, disconcerting her.

'Had I known, *chère* madame, I would have done my best not to disappoint you, which would have been only fair seeing that *you* do not disappoint me.' The compliment was even more disconcerting because she'd forgotten his habit of ignoring all known conversational rules. He said what he wanted to say, and the gap of years since they'd met was as unimportant as the normal social gambits. It was a relief when he turned to greet William. Watching them, it occurred to her that they liked each other. In most ways as different as two men could be, they nevertheless shared not only a passionate love of painting but also the unacknowledged conviction that the most important thing in life was to be civilized. When Blanchard turned back to her she was still thinking about it.

'Now, with William's permission I shall ignore him and take *you* on a tour of my treasures. No delicate Fragonard ladies losing their slippers on swings – beautiful in their way, of course, but I leave such things to other dealers. Instead I'll show you the young women Degas painted; I hope you don't find them out of place in these antique surroundings?'

Gertrude looked at the canvas he was pointing to – it showed a girl bent in a dancer's graceful posture while she tied the strings of her ballet shoe; around her the skirts of her dress made a cloud of filmy white.

'She's enchanting, and couldn't be out of place anywhere.' Gertrude glanced along the other paintings hanging on the same wall and made a discovery. 'They're all beautiful, but in the same simple way – not deliberately posed or prettified, but painted just as they are.'

Blanchard smiled and she had the heart-stopping sensation that he had kissed her. 'Exactly, *très chère* madame;

the technique is interesting – colour built up on the canvas, not mixed on the palette; but that isn't what counts. It's the ordinary turned into the *extra*ordinarily poetic simply by the intensity of the painter's vision. Your husband has that kind of vision too; it's why I'm certain he'll be judged a true artist, perhaps even a great one eventually.'

She looked across the room and smiled at the sight of her true artist deep in conversation with a small bearded man whose finger jabbed excitedly at the canvas in front of them. They were joined by someone else and the conversation continued, even more emotionally than before.

'I can safely say that William has forgotten I'm here,' she said, sounding unconcerned about it. 'But that doesn't mean that *you* have to devote your morning to keeping me entertained, monsieur. Please leave me; I shall be happy to wander about on my own.'

Blanchard stared at her unsmilingly. 'I arrange life always so that I do what I want to do. Since *you* are here at last, that means talking to you. How is the small female Wyndham whom I did succeed in impressing?'

Again she ignored what couldn't be commented upon and fastened instead on the subject of her daughter. 'Sybil is small no longer, and harder to please than she was – though I don't mean to suggest that you would no longer impress her! We left her with a friend from England at a finishing school in Lucerne, not entirely convinced that she would be able to get her own way to the extent that she's been accustomed to.'

'And William's sister . . . Mrs Trentham . . . how is she?' He asked the question without much sign of interest, and certainly without any embarrassment. For the space of a moment or two she felt angry enough to try to shatter an air of confidence that seemed altogether unbearable. But even if she could have brought herself to refer to his *affaire* with Louise, he might have been flattered to know that he'd almost managed to destroy a woman whose self-assurance was normally as complete as his own.

'My sister-in-law took some time to accustom herself to

London,' she said at last, choosing words with care. 'It wasn't much like life in Delhi, and nothing at all like Haywood's End. But Alec Trentham is now a junior minister in the Liberal cabinet, and she is very busy being a political hostess – happily busy, as far as I know.'

Blanchard didn't avoid the candid grey eyes fixed on him, which said more than she'd permitted herself to put into words.

'You know about us, of course . . . *ça se voit*. Do you blame me for hurting her?'

'I wanted to . . . tried to,' Gertrude replied honestly, 'but I had to accept that Louise must have known from the beginning how matters would end. Apart from that, the experience wasn't all loss, either. It made her discover her own frailty, which is something we all have to do. The result is that she's more tolerant now of other people's weaknesses.'

He nodded but didn't seem interested in Louise's discoveries. 'I ask myself what has been the frailty *you* have had to recognize. Shall I embarrass you by saying that I wish your weakness had been me?'

She turned her head away so that all he could see was the delicately moulded line of her cheek and jaw under the brim of her hat. Embarrassment seemed an inadequate word for the emotions taking charge of her. 'There must be many other people here whom you should talk to,' she suggested hurriedly. 'Should we not rejoin them?'

'I'm not interested in the other people here . . . in any case they would hesitate to interrupt our contemplation of the best canvas Manet has yet painted.' He stood sheltering her from the view of the rest of the gallery, and encircled her gloved wrist with his hand. 'Gertrude, look at me, please.' Reluctantly she did so and saw that his expression was not only serious but sad. 'I have made it a rule to do as far as possible the things I wanted to do, and never to waste time repining over those that I didn't achieve. Now my rule is in ruins because I *have* to regret that I've had no chance to succeed in loving you. I shall die regretting more than anything else in this world the fact that I never knew what it was to make love to you.'

The murmured words were low, but reached her with the intensity he found in his Impressionist paintings. When he finally released her wrist she cupped it in her other hand without knowing that she did so. The people around them might not have been there for all that she was aware of them. William might have forgotten her, but not more completely than she, for the moment, had forgotten him. There was only the man standing in front of her, and the sensation of burning in her wrist where his hand had held her, and the impossibility of knowing how to answer him.

'Are you about to protest, feel insulted, insist that I should be whipped for saying such things to the wife of a man who thinks of me as his friend?'

He saw a faint flush of colour come into her cheeks, but she didn't look away from him.

'You *are* William's friend,' she said quietly. 'As for me, how can I feel insulted because I've been found worthy of loving?'

A smile touched his mouth, died again an instant later. 'I should have known that you wouldn't say what any other woman would feel obliged to say in the circumstances. Gertrude . . . your children are almost grown-up, and William's career is firmly launched. Would you consider leaving him and Providence? In French perhaps I could persuade you with words of my own . . . in English I must borrow from one of your own poets . . . will you "live with me and be my love", and *not* tell me how absurd this is when we have not seen each other for ten years?'

Her eyes had the soft shine of tears in them, but she shook her head. 'The question ought to be absurd, but isn't. In English or in French, though, the answer has to be the same. Even if the children and Providence didn't need me still and I think they do, and even if I could hurt Louise and I wouldn't be able to, there remains William. I could hurt him least of all.'

'In that list of people who must be considered you don't

mention the needs of a woman called Gertrude Wyndham. Will *she* not be a little . . . just the smallest degree . . . hurt if you think only of them?'

'I think . . . I believe she will.'

In the silence that fell between them she saw his mouth touched again by a smile that glimmered briefly and left his face sad. 'Thank you, you're honest, and it's the rarest virtue of all in a woman. Now, shall we abandon Manet's water lilies, beautiful as they are, and go back to the everyday world?'

Half an hour later she left the gallery with William and they spent the rest of the day looking at the things everyone goes to Paris to see. In the evening they were taken by Blanchard to dine and watch a performance of *Manon* at the Opéra, but all the time he was an impeccably-behaved friend and host. She had no way of knowing what it might be costing *him* to listen calmly to Massenet's music that poured over them in a sumptuous lyrical flood, but knew herself to be continually on the verge of tears. She was as much aware of him as of the music, sitting just behind her so that she and William might have the best view from their stage box. As the performance ended, he leaned towards her and she felt his mouth touch her bare shoulder in the darkness. The brief kiss, if that was what it could be called, said many things, and the most painful of them was a goodbye that she recognized to be entirely final.

When the house lights glowed into life again William peered at her tear-wet face but didn't seem surprised.

'My dear . . . I felt almost like weeping myself, it was so heartbreakingly beautiful.'

She nodded without speaking, and all three of them left the theatre without finding anything more to say.

William went again to the boulevard Haussmann next morning, to confer with Henri about some new commissions, but Gertrude excused herself from going with him. There were small gifts to be taken back for the servants at Providence, and these she insisted she would enjoy struggling on her own to acquire. They left Paris without the occasion for her to have to see Blanchard again.

On the train journey back to Calais William suddenly looked up from the journal he was reading.

'You're quiet, my love, and looking a little sad. If you've grown so attached to Paris that you hate leaving it we must repeat this visit.'

She shook her head. 'Once was perfect, William, but I shan't want to come again.'

He returned to his magazine, but then interrupted his reading again. 'Will you remember to tell Sybil when you write that Henri may call at the school when he next goes to Lucerne? She won't remember him, of course, but a visitor is always pleasant, even one less distinguished-looking than Blanchard. He couldn't fail to send up her stock considerably with the other girls!'

Gertrude heard herself agree calmly that he was doubtless right, and that she would certainly remember. They had spoken of frailties, she and Henri. Her weakness over James had finally been confessed to Lady Hester, but *this* near-despair when she had taught herself to be satisfied with her life was scarcely bearable. She even envied Louise a knowledge of Henri she didn't have herself, and that seemed to be a final humiliation.

When William spoke again she had to ask him to repeat what he'd said.

'I remember that you used to be rather wary of Blanchard, perhaps because he seemed rather richly foreign in London! In Paris, surely, you must have found him charming?'

Gertrude heard the sound that was forced out of her – half-laugh, half-sob; saw the puzzlement in her husband's face, before she turned away from him to look out of the carriage window.

'As you say, in Paris he is . . . very charming!'

CHAPTER TWENTY

The world seemed to have narrowed, but the echo of the word in her mind shocked her. An old stone house slumbering within its ring of silver water, and the lush greenness of the valley – she had never thought of them as a cage before. The memory of Paris, and a less ancient house, and a man with sad, knowledgeable eyes would soon be no more than another strand in the design that Fate spun for her – a strand that provided a precious gleam of brightness, but wasn't part of the repeating pattern that made up daily life. *That* was the ritual that had seemed satisfying enough until a few weeks ago; it meant caring for Providence to the best of her ability, loving her family, and helping her friends and dependants when necessary. All these things she still did, but they had become a joyless duty.

She went to Barham to report that Emily had been safely deposited in Lucerne; shared Maud's concern about a local difference of opinion that threatened to split Haywood's End in half; listened sympathetically to Jane Thornley's constant fear that Arthur would kill himself with overwork; and even managed to persuade Emmie in the kitchen that they could manage a *little* longer without a more modern cooking-range. Gradually the ritual brought its own comfort. She was calm, she was cheerful; she could tell herself that the worst was over.

Then one morning Sybil's weekly letter was full of Papa's friend, Henri Blanchard, who had called and been permitted to take her out to tea. Gertrude re-read the letter, went to the courtyard garden to pick flowers for the chapel room and found herself too blinded by tears to see anything at all. She stood with her eyes closed, waiting for the moment when the pain that had clamped her heart would agree to let her go. The crimson Étoile d'Hollande climbing the wall beside her poured out its scent into the warm still air, and the only sound came from the bees raiding the lavender that made a mauve edging to the paths. The peace of Providence, 'dropping slow', would rescue her if she allowed it to. When she opened her eyes again someone was standing a dozen paces away . . . her friend, Maud, whose long plain face was gentle and filled with kindness.

'I didn't interrupt – you looked deep in something – thought, or perhaps even prayer. It always seems to me that God is very near in this enchanted garden.' She made no reference to the tears that lingered on Gertrude's face, knowing that they weren't meant to have been observed.

Gertrude nodded. 'Yes, God and the grace of Providence seem almost one and the same thing out here.' She scrubbed her wet cheeks with the back of her hands and saw Maud begin to smile.

'That's exactly what little Gertrude Hoskins used to do . . . when she was ten years old and struggling with some small tragedy!'

'Not a tragedy this time . . . I was saying goodbye to something – youth, I think. But, as Sybil used to say with dignity after a shaming bout of tears, "I'm perfickly all right *now*, thank you"!'

Maud saw no need to argue the point. 'How is my entrancing minx of a god-daughter – keeping England's end up with Mlle Lebrun, I hope?'

'Honours roughly even, I'd say, but this morning's letter didn't mention her adversary. It was full of a visit she'd received from William's dealer friend, Henri Blanchard. He arrived in a blaze of motoring glory to take her out to tea. My daughter is now happily sure of being the envy of a bevy of maidens whose minds are supposed to be on other things!'

Maud found that she remembered William's dealer friend very vividly, and the expression on his face when he'd looked across the dinner table at Gertrude – years ago, that had been, but the picture remained clear. There had been a meeting recently in Paris, and Maud thought perhaps she knew what Gertrude had been saying goodbye to. Like her friend's tears, it wasn't to be commented upon. Instead, she said, 'No sign of Ned – surely he's home from Rugby by now?'

'Yes, but Harry suggested a walking tour of the Highlands and we talked him into going. Ned was anxious to start serious work here, but there's time enough for that and he's rather missed Harry's company in recent years.'

'Did Lucy enjoy herself in London while you were away?'

'Moderately, I think, but she seemed glad to come home. She found London too big, and her aunt's friends rather too grand and frightening. Providence means as much to her as it does to Ned, but what she needs above all is to be with people who know and love her. Sybil at the age of five regarded a room full of strangers as an enjoyable challenge; Lucy at fifteen still finds them an ordeal.' Gertrude frowned over the thought. 'It makes her future something of a problem. Dear Miss Lacey does her best, but I don't know that she manages to teach Lucy much except charming manners and her own passion for the novels of Sir Walter Scott!'

Maud couldn't help smiling at this regretful statement. 'Well, perhaps there's more to learn, but she could make a worse start than that! Lucy's not clever like you, nor adventurous like her sister, but so loving and lovely that I don't think you need worry about her future. Some worthy young man's bound to mark her down as a beautiful, biddable wife . . . and if *he* doesn't, his mother surely will!'

Gertrude smiled and agreed. It didn't solve the problem of a girl who'd set her too-loving heart on Harry Trentham, but she saw no need to tell Maud that.

Ned came back at the end of a fortnight, sunburnt, footsore, and happy. Poor old Queen Victoria had been quite right, he said, to get attached to Scotland. It was a splendid place; but as a prospective landowner himself, he hadn't approved of quite so much of it being in the hands of men who visited it once a year purely for the pleasure of slaughtering grouse and deer. Harry hadn't seen anything wrong with this, but it seemed to be the only point on which they'd fallen out. Gertrude watched Lucy's face, eloquent of the struggle to agree with Ned without disagreeing with Harry, and wished unavailingly that she could spare her daughter the agonies of growing up.

Ned settled down to work with George Hoskins, too immersed in the problems of the land and the responsibilities of owning it to be much concerned about events outside Haywood's End which seemed to some people to be threatening the very fabric of England's law-abiding life.

At Bicton, Jane Thornley thought her husband grew daily more tired, and her son's face more set and old as they wrestled with the problems that beset industries. Already Frank looked ten years older than his actual thirty years. The factories ruled their lives, and she began to hate them so much that one morning she felt compelled to say so.

'Hate them? You're talking daft, Janey.' Arthur sounded more disappointed than angry, that after all their years together good commonsense should now be deserting her. 'Factories are this country's lifeblood, lass; don't ever forget it.'

'And if they're the death of you, I won't forget *that*, either. You're worn down with the worry of it all, and Frank's done nothing but study and work since he was a boy at school. There are other things in life and he ought to know something about *them* too.' Anxiety for her family suddenly thickened her voice with tears. However the rest of the world saw Arthur Thornley, and she knew there were those who didn't value him properly, to her he was a giant among men; and Frank was their only child – irreplaceably dear. Both of them spent more hours of every day in those damnable, all-demanding factories than they spent out of them, and the problems only seemed to be getting worse.

'Now, Janey, there's no need to take on so.' He said it with the gentleness that only she aroused in him. 'Granted things have been difficult these past few months, but we can stand a bit of wear and tear, the lad and me.'

'*Lad!*' Jane shouted. 'Arthur, *look* at him; he's an old man already.'

Her son chose this moment to walk into the breakfast-room and she flushed scarlet with the shame of losing control of herself and the fear that he might have guessed whom she was shouting about.

There was a moment's silence while Arthur did what he'd been told and looked at Frank more carefully than usual: Jane was exaggerating, but there was a bit of truth in what she said. There was nothing handsome or remarkable about his son's face: clean-shaven, square chin, beaky nose on which spectacles usually rested, sandy eyebrows and short-cut hair. Frank Thornley almost went out of his way to mislead you into thinking there was nothing remarkable about *him* either, but Arthur knew better. His son was a good sight cleverer than most, and stubborn into the bargain; not a man to be bullocked against his will. But it was true that he was beginning to look tired.

'Your mother thinks you work too hard,' he remarked, apparently to the kipper on the plate in front of him.

'And what does she think about *you* . . . that you sit all day with your feet up, I suppose.' Frank helped himself to food from the sideboard, then sat down at the table. He caught sight of his mother's face and realized that the conversation wasn't over. She didn't often assert herself, but when she did it was as well to listen. He took off his spectacles and laid them beside his plate; they were a necessary evil, but he hated them and blamed them for the fact that he found it difficult to get to proper grips with other people. Giving them orders wasn't a problem; getting to know them was.

'If you're about to say things have been difficult lately, don't bother; I've heard that from your father. I know all about the miners going on strike and unsettling other men, and about the ones who call themselves Socialists. But now that I've started, I'll say it all. We moved here so that you could grow up to become a country gentleman. There are horses outside you never ride, pheasants you don't shoot, and grounds you scarcely walk in. For all the good Bicton's done you, we could have stayed in Birmingham.'

'So we could,' he agreed calmly, 'but you wouldn't have got your sewing women started, or played fairy godmother to every child for miles around; and you certainly wouldn't have made friends with women like Lady Wyndham.'

'I'm talking about what *you've* got out of it!' she cried. 'I never thought I'd say it, but I *like* this ugly great place now. I'd like it even more if you and your father would enjoy it too.'

Arthur was moved to intervene, out of a craven desire to keep his wife's attention away from himself. 'I dare say what your mother really means is that you ought to take the time to find a wife, Frank. Women are all the same – think it doesn't do to let a man stay a bachelor too long because he gets powerful set in his ways.' He looked guilelessly at Jane, knowing that although she'd never have brought herself to say so, she *was* beginning to be afraid she would never have a daughter-in-law to help and love. 'If you don't watch out, lad, she'll have you offering for hoity-toity Sybil Wyndham!'

'No, she won't,' Frank said definitely. 'That's one noose I *shan't* be putting my head into. I'd rather take anybody – Alice Sykes, even – at least she wouldn't argue me to death.'

'True, on the other hand she'd not be what you could call a lively partner,' Arthur pointed out. Since Widow Sykes, the lady in question, had given up conversing with the male sex in case she should find herself talked into marrying one of them again, Jane Thornley could be pardoned for thinking she was not being taken seriously.

She stood up, torn between tears and laughter. 'You're making game of me, so that I'm to think I needn't worry about the pair of you. Well, I do worry, even though it won't do a ha'porth of good.' She smiled tremulously and left the room, knowing that they'd be talking business again the moment her back was turned.

Frank pushed his plate aside and helped himself to coffee. 'Mother's right . . . it's time you let up a bit.'

'If you're about to point out that I'm not as young as I was, I know that; and if you're going to add that Thornley's can do without me, I can tell you I'll take it right unkindly.'

Frank's face broke into the smile that nowadays came rarely. 'I wouldn't be so daft as to say anything of the sort – the factories still belong to *you*. All the same, a day off now and again wouldn't hurt you.'

'When things get easier. Now, lad, what's to be done about Albert Simpkin? Seems to me we lose whichever way we go. We'll be getting the same strike trouble as the industries in the north if we let a union in; if we don't, people like him will keep good labour away from us.'

Frank shook his head. 'They'll only keep bad workers away, and *them* we don't want in any case. The men know that we pay them over the odds and take care of them in hard times. Troublemakers like Simpkin must be shown the door. We're not going to have Marxist shop stewards telling us how to run our factories. Bad employers have brought trades unions on themselves, I reckon.'

Arthur Thornley nodded. 'All right, we'll go our own road, same as we always have.' He poured himself more of the black stewed tea he insisted on instead of coffee, and opened the *Birmingham Daily Post* waiting on the table in front of him. Over the top of it he glanced at his son. 'Your mother's right about the wife business . . . we'll be needing a good lad to carry on Thornley's when the time comes.'

'I know that . . . I'm keeping it in mind.'

'You weren't serious . . . about Alice Sykes? It'd be like having a deaf mute in the house.'

His son refused to be drawn. 'You'll have to wait and see, like mother!'

With the hornet-tongued Sybil Wyndham safely out of reach in Switzerland, he didn't object to driving Jane to Providence the following day – a Sunday, when he never attended church, and rarely went to the factory. He deposited his mother at the bridge across the moat, and drove the dog-cart round to the stable-yard. Through the open postern gate he could see the lawn beyond, and Ned patiently trying to persuade his younger sister that a tennis racket was better held in one hand than two.

'I know, Ned, but I can thump harder with both hands . . . look!' Unaware of Frank Thornley coming up behind her, she gave a demonstration of her own technique with a tremendous swipe that took him by surprise. He jumped back, but not before the edge of the racket caught him on the temple and dislodged his spectacles at the same time. In the midst of real distress, Lucy noticed that he looked very different without them . . . less unapproachable, and more nearly of a generation not so far removed from her own.

'Mr Thornley . . . I'm so very very sorry . . . I'd no idea you were there . . . your spectacles . . . have I broken them?' Her soft voice poured a mixture of agitation and balm over the throbbing of his head; almost on a level with his because she was tall for her age, her blue eyes were huge with concern.

'Nothing to worry about . . .' He retrieved the spectacles she held out to him, put them on and removed them again because they pressed against the swelling already beginning to come up on the side of his face.

'A cold compress,' she said with the experience born of her brother's innumerable childhood brushes with unyielding objects. 'I'm sure *that's* what is needed.'

Ned grinned at Frank. 'You may as well go quietly . . . you're probably not aware of it, having no sisters, but girls *will* be Florence Nightingale, given the least excuse!'

They went towards the house together, Frank thinking that he felt not only slightly dizzy with the throbbing in his head, but also slightly absurd. The only mercy bestowed on him by Heaven was that Sybil Wyndham wasn't around to watch this ridiculous procession and be wickedly amused by it. There was no doubt that the cold wet cloth Lucy applied to his head was comforting, and he found unexpected pleasure in watching the gravity with which she went about the business of wringing out a fresh cold flannel.

She still wore the calf-length dress of a schoolgirl, and her hair hung down her back in a plaited rope the colour of . . . what? He could only think of a wheatfield ripe for harvesting with the sun burnishing it – gold turning to bronze.

'How does it feel now?' she enquired anxiously.

He forbore to say that little rivulets of water now trickled down between his collar and his neck. It was a piece of self-denial that would have surprised even his mother. He was more gentle with Jane than with anyone else, but forbearance wasn't a quality she would have claimed for him. 'It feels better . . . almost normal, in fact . . . Florence Nightingale has done very well! Is that where your future lies – in nursing?'

Lucy shook her head. 'It might if I could do it here, but I can't leave Providence . . . I'm going to stay and help Ned.' She would leave Heaven itself and descend like Persephone to the nethermost regions of the underworld if Harry were to invite her to go with him there, but that was her own heart's secret.

Frank turned to the boy who sat on the windowsill, kept there by some instinctive feeling that to leave their battered guest to his sister wouldn't have been a courteous thing to do.

'You're set on taking over from your father,' Frank said, 'even though . . .' he hesitated, aware that he couldn't find a tactful way of ending the sentence.

'. . . even though, according to that old battle-axe Lady Bracknell, "land has ceased to be either a profit or a pleasure"!' Ned finished obligingly. 'Yes, but Oscar Wilde was only half right, or trying to be funny at the expense of truth. It *is* still a pleasure . . . always will be for people like Sid Moffat and me. There's something about the land, you see . . . especially if it happens to be yours.' His fair skin flushed in case the man in front of him might think he was trying to say Bicton didn't properly belong to the Thornleys.

Frank smiled at him unexpectedly. 'I dare say it's much the same feeling as I have about my father's factories, except that in our case, at the moment, there isn't much profit to be had and even less pleasure.'

'Strikes and things, you mean? Men turning ugly and starting to believe that violence will get them what they ask for if they can't get it in any other way? My father says nothing justifies violence, but I don't altogether agree with him. If people with the whip hand won't listen to them . . . won't give them a living wage or housing that isn't insanitary and rat-infested . . . I can't see why they *shouldn't* take the law into their own hands.'

This time he'd forgotten tact completely. As well as having a sore head at Lucy's hands, Frank Thornley must recognize himself as one of those very employers who could be said to hold the whip hand. Still, it seemed necessary to say that there *was* something painfully wrong with a society that allowed a tiny fraction of its members to live in idle luxury while the rest sweated out their days in drudgery or desperate want. Ned didn't yearn to lead a revolution, or even to take part in one, but he was faintly ashamed to know of himself that this was so.

Frank gave an inward sigh, aware that the role of wicked exploiter of the poor must seem to fit him and his father like a glove. How else, Ned Wyndham would be saying to himself, had men like the Thornleys made themselves wealthy in the space of a couple of generations . . . and why, being the urban upstarts they were, should they lord it at Bicton or anywhere else while the *real* gentry scraped along, trying to conceal poverty and hang on to their crumbling inheritances? In the normal course of events he wouldn't have troubled to argue with a boy who hadn't yet grown out of the half-baked idealism that came with adolescent spots, but something in Ned Wyndham's argument was too dangerously wrong not to be put straight.

'*Nobody* in this country can be allowed to take the law into their own hands,' he said emphatically. 'The fact that there are plenty of people trying at the moment – people who ought to know better – only confirms what I say. When a country no longer respects its own laws, let it improve them by all means – but by all *constitutional* means! To say that the laws no longer matter if you happen not to like them . . . *that's* the road to hell and disaster.'

Lucy had been listening, wide-eyed, to the conversation. It reminded her of a lecture from Charlotte when she'd been staying with the Trenthams in London. The subject of the suffragettes who were seriously embarrassing her uncle's colleagues in the Cabinet had often come up for discussion in Cadogan Square. No more than Ned did Lucy wish to number herself among the revolutionaries . . . one morning she'd seen some of the women who'd chained themselves to the railings outside the House of Commons, and the sight had seemed to her immeasurably shocking. But she had the feeling that she *ought* to have joined them, and that Sybil would have found some way of chaining herself that would have defeated anyone's attempts to get rid of her.

'I suppose you think the suffragettes are wrong, too,' she said more sharply than she meant to, because attracting the opposition of this unknown and forbidding neighbour wasn't like arguing with Ned. 'It's all very well for a man to say "change the laws, don't break them". Women are not allowed to make them, or change them. They've tried and tried asking peacefully . . . now they're entitled to break windows . . . and burn things . . . until someone listens to them.' It was Charlotte's argument, repeated as well as she could remember it, but it seemed to lack fire when delivered at secondhand.

She was flushed with the effort of talking to Frank Thornley at all, and even Ned was staring at her . . . little Lucy with the bit between her teeth. He was afraid she was about to be demolished, and knew he'd have to weigh in himself on her side, despite the fact that he had only a little sympathy for the idea of giving women anything as dangerous as a vote, and no sympathy at all for the brawling, undignified creatures who demanded to be manhandled and ill-used.

Frank had, to his own surprise, no desire to demolish her and heard himself say something that completed his astonishment. 'It's as wrong that men should suffer under bad laws as it is that women should have no say in making them. They are bound to be enfranchised before very long, because piece by piece the traditional framework that has kept them subordinate to men is being dismantled. But if nothing justifies violence, certainly nothing justifies stupidity . . . and it *is* stupid to inflict their mindless campaign on the only men who are in a position to give them what they want – that is to say, the members of the Government who alone can bring in the necessary legislation. Without the violence which has turned people against them, they would have had the vote before now.'

She had heard Uncle Alec say exactly the same thing. Perhaps Charlotte would have been able to make some devastatingly sensible reply; but if she *had* produced the necessary clincher, Lucy couldn't remember what it was. Greatly to her surprise, and even more to her relief, it didn't seem to matter at all. Still clutching his spectacles in his hand instead of frowning at her through them, Mr Thornley was smiling in a way that left her not feeling stupid; in fact his face seemed friendly, almost pleasant. It was strange that biffing his head with Ned's racket should have produced this unlikely result! Now, though, she was uncertain about what to do with him next. She looked hopefully at her brother and he didn't disappoint her.

'A cup of tea . . . I think *that's* what you ought to be offering,' Ned suggested. 'If we were to beg some off Emmie in the kitchen, we'd get fruit cake as well, instead of delicate drawing-room sandwiches!'

Lucy looked dubious, but before she could point out that their visitor properly belonged with the sandwiches, Frank Thornley heard himself make his own choice. It was as out of character as the rest of his behaviour had been for the past hour. 'Cake in the kitchen, please.'

She smiled with ravishing sweetness. 'Then I'll go and warn Emmie, Mr Thornley . . . she'll get a bit flustered otherwise.'

Mr Thornley . . . it brought back common sense again,

and the recollection of his true age and his aching head. God alone knew what madness had got into him a moment ago. He waited for her to run out of the room, then said abruptly to Ned, 'I think I'll change my mind. I'll leave the tea and cake to you and take a walk in the fresh air instead. Don't come with me . . . I can find my own way outside.'

He walked out of the room, leaving Ned feeling snubbed and determined not to go after him. Funny . . . just for a little while it had seemed as if they'd both been wrong about him . . . but Thornley was a piggish sort of fellow after all.

CHAPTER TWENTY-ONE

No more was heard at Providence of Henri's occasional visits to Lucerne because Sybil found that she didn't know how to write about them. For the first time in her life she seemed not to be in control of things. Her father's friend was painfully intriguing – not simply because he was more worldly and cosmopolitan than anyone else she knew, and demonstrably more intelligent than the young men like Harry whom she'd grown up with – but because she had the feeling that the most important part of him was held aloof from her. He was kind but elusive, teasingly affectionate but unimpressed. His first call at the school was repeated whenever he came to Lucerne to visit a sick painter there, but always he seemed to come looking for someone else, and went away each time disappointed that he had only found Sybil Wyndham. Her letters to her mother didn't mention him because she felt a failure; there was nothing to boast about in that.

It was hard to fail with *him* of all people, and harder still to understand why she did so. She'd been quick to see that there was much to be learned from Mlle Lebrun, and she was ready to be taught by anyone who had something of value to teach her . . . her mother could do it at home, and so could Godmother Maud, though not dear dim Amelia Lacey. Unlike Emily, who found the abundance of irregular verbs too great an obstacle to progress, Sybil had quickly got on working terms with the French language. She hadn't Emily's red-haired, white-skinned beauty, but knew the appeal of her own vivid looks, and made the most of a flair inherited from her mother for dressing elegantly. She knew instinctively when a colour or line was wrong, and Henri had even been moved to say that it was no hardship to be seen with a demoiselle so very *comme il faut*. But all the same she knew he didn't take her seriously.

On a Saturday afternoon of late autumn when Mlle Lebrun had again agreed that she might be taken out to tea, they finally left the elegant lounge of the Schweizerhof and walked down towards the lake. The first lamps were being lit on the other side of the water, and the far end of the old covered Kapellbrücke was already hidden in the mist. On their side of the lake a last gleam of light caught the trees behind them, and dying leaves floated down to speckle the surface of the water. It was beautiful but melancholy, and she shivered, sensing in the quiet man standing beside her the same autumnal sadness.

'Too cold for you, *petite*?'

'No, I was just thinking that I don't like this dying season.'

'At eighteen, I don't suppose you do, and probably nor did I. Now, it seems to suit my declining years!'

'Why do you say that?' She was angry with him, because he insisted deliberately on a difference between them that she preferred not to recognize. 'As if years mattered . . . some people are born old, others are still young when they die.'

He smiled at the spurt of temper which was typical of her. She would go through life fighting anything she feared, instead of fleeing from it as most people did. 'I agree with you as far as mental outlook goes; age need have nothing to do with that. But the spirit ages with experience, and that is the difference between us. Your spirit is young and ardent, mine is . . . a little tired.' His deep voice, that had the power to transform ordinary English words into something beautiful in her ears, sounded full of sadness.

'Is it the poor sick painter you come to see who makes you unhappy?' she asked.

He turned to look at her, aware that she wanted him to deny that he was unhappy, because they were watching the falling leaves together, and aware of much more about her besides. She was so nearly a younger version of Gertrude, so eager for life, and so convinced that it must yield up all its treasures for her. Only pain hadn't yet come, as it had surely come to her mother, to teach her that life offered or withheld, as it pleased.

'*Waste* makes me unhappy,' he said finally. 'There's so much of it in this imperfect world.'

She was almost sure he wasn't only talking about the dying painter, but before she could steel herself to ask, he glanced at his watch, and smiled at her. 'Time to go back, *ma chèrie* . . . Mamselle will imagine I've abducted you.'

They turned away from the lakeside, and walked in silence to the school. He kissed her cheeks, French fashion, when he said goodbye, with the kindly affection she thought he would have offered a niece who had been given a treat and not been troublesome. The pain of it was so great that at last it had to be shared with Emily.

'All part of your education in the school of life . . . that's what Mam'selle would say,' remarked Miss Maynard, pleased with herself for having got the better of Sybil for once. 'Though if she knew that you were flinging yourself at Henri's head she wouldn't let you go out with him at all.' Then she caught sight of her friend's face and quickly apologized. 'Sorry, Syb . . . I thought we were funning. Why be in such despair? You're bound to go on seeing him if he looks after your father's paintings.'

'No, he never goes to England now,' Sybil said desolately. 'He said it once in such a way that I think there must be a special reason.'

'A duel, you mean? Or perhaps he compromised a duchess and had to flee the country for ever!'

Sybil was beginning to wish that her sore heart hadn't led her to confide in Emily. Duels hadn't been fought for ages past, but it had occurred to her only too often that some tragic love affair would have left her dear elusive Henri the onlooker on life she felt him to be. She had no patience with mere onlooking; life was for getting involved in, though already she was beginning to see that experience might have to be dearly bought.

As autumn merged into winter she saw almost nothing of him, and his only letter briefly reported that the Swiss artist had died. She spared a moment of regret for the lost painter, but couldn't help but think much more about herself. What, if anything, would bring Henri to Lucerne in future? She could recall his face and the sound of his voice without seeing him, but the memory of half a dozen shared pots of tea couldn't sustain her indefinitely. When it was almost time for her to leave Lucerne, she took to praying that he would at least come to say goodbye, but he didn't do so; she had the feeling that he *deliberately* didn't do so. Instead, a formal note expressed his thanks for their pleasant outings, and accompanied the gift of a small, exquisite glass paperweight, with the colours of the sea imprisoned inside it. She wept over it, and didn't show it to Emily.

They set off just before Easter, she, Emily, and several other girls returning to England, with Mlle Lebrun's parting injunction ringing in their ears. She expected them to comport themselves en route for London in a way that would do nothing but credit to the institution that had cherished them for the past nine months. Delivering this Parthian shot, her eye fell on Miss Wyndham, well-known for her propensity for leading others astray. In normal circumstances Sybil would have accepted the remark with a dazzling smile that turned it into a compliment, but at the moment she had no heart for rebellion.

Emily's parents met them at the station at Victoria, after a boringly uneventful journey, and drove them home to Warwickshire. For a day or two it was enough to be back. Providence was at its most beautiful in the spring, her family were dear, and all her friends delightful. Within a week she'd bitten Lucy's head off, quarrelled with Ned, and been sadly impertinent to her mother.

It was her godmother who found her one bitterly cold afternoon sitting alone in the empty church, with tearstains on her cheeks.

'I'm glad you feel like weeping too,' Maud said calmly. 'When an April day is as bleak as the middle of January I think we have cause to bewail. What about tea and toast by the fire at home?'

Her god-daughter consented to accept the offer. They were settled in Maud's little parlour at the vicarage, with the tea things beside them, before Miss Roberts said, 'Do you want to tell me what's wrong, or not? Nothing's worse than being made to feel obliged to talk if you don't want to.'

'I think I'd like to.' There was another silence before she said tragically, 'My family hate me, but at the moment I can't say I blame them.'

Maud realized that this was *not* what needed to be said; it was the necessary preliminary before they got to the heart of the matter, with a little help from her.

'Providence is too peaceful, Haywood's End is a rural bore, and your dear ones don't understand that you're too young to be buried alive in the wilds of Warwickshire. Is that it?'

'Well, I suppose it might have been, except that dear Mama has already exerted herself and persuaded Aunt Louise, who doesn't like me above half, to bring me out in London this season.'

'Perhaps you're also bored with the thought of a London season?' Maud suggested.

'Of course not; at least how could I be until I've tried it? But last year the prospect would have filled me with joy; now I don't seem able to be joyful about *anything*.' She stared at the fire, forgetting her buttered toast, and Maud perceived that matters were indeed serious.

'Tell me, if you want to,' she suggested gently.

Sybil gazed at her with Gertrude's candid eyes, and they were filled with pain. 'It hurts, doesn't it, loving someone?'

The sad little question raised an echo in Maud's mind. She remembered another question that had been put to her long ago, by a girl who'd asked 'is it *very* difficult not to get married?' She banished the memory and tried to deal with the present problem.

'If, as I suppose you mean, does it hurt to love someone who doesn't seem to love *you*, I'm afraid the answer's yes. I could tell you that, even so, the experience wouldn't be wasted, but at the moment I doubt if you'd believe me.'

'Henri seemed to think that life *was* full of waste.'

'Henri Blanchard, I suppose we're talking about?'

Sybil blushed, aware that she had given herself away, but there was a certain relief in sharing the secret of her sadness. 'He used to call at the school when he visited an artist in Lucerne. I was allowed to take tea with him in a very dignified hotel, and then we would go for a very dignified stroll by the lake.' She hadn't meant to weep, but tears gathered and brimmed over. 'Then he stopped coming . . . didn't even come to say goodbye.'

Maud felt with some asperity that it was a pity he'd gone at all. Unvain men who didn't realize the damage they did were almost as bad as those who did realize it but were vain enough to go on causing damage just the same.

'You knew him here,' Sybil mumbled. 'Did he . . . was he . . . attached to someone?'

Maud thought for a moment, trying to decide how to reply. 'I think he was,' she said at last, 'but the lady was already married. He left London and didn't return.'

Sybil's eyes were fixed on her face. 'Will you tell me who the lady was?'

'No . . . it doesn't matter now,' Maud said gently.

There was a little silence in the room, then her god-daughter murmured surprisingly, 'I think perhaps I know.' She stared at the uneaten piece of toast still clutched in her hand as if she couldn't remember how it had got there. Maud busied herself pouring tea and decided that it was time to talk of other things. She had to work quite hard, but finally succeeded in making Sybil laugh with an account of her own début in the days when Queen Victoria's stern eye still monitored the standards of London society.

Afterwards Gertrude confessed to her husband that it was a relief when their elder daughter, with a London wardrobe hastily assembled, left them again for a three months' stay in Cadogan Place.

'Do you think so?' he asked diffidently. 'I rather miss her myself. Mlle Lebrun seems to have worked wonders. Sybil now knows much more about the history of European politics than I do, and she can talk intelligently about the difference between Duccio and Delacroix! She was even kind enough to take an interest in *my* paintings, which shows true daughterly affection as well as excellent taste!'

Gertrude smiled, but felt obliged to explain. 'I don't mean to say that I shan't miss her, but she's restless and moody and quarrelsome, apart from being intelligent and well-informed and full of excellent taste! We have a breathing space while Louise takes charge of her, but I keep wondering what we should do with her after that.'

William stared at her, rubbing his nose thoughtfully. 'I thought what we expected to do was marry her off to someone . . . isn't that what this expensive coming-out charade is all about?'

'It's what most parents expect, but it won't do in her case. She came home from Switzerland with something on her mind which she chose not to share with me. All I'm certain of is that she won't be satisfied with marriage to a conventionally suitable young man.'

Unable to suggest anything himself, William's glance wandered back to the easel set up in the huge window of the Great Parlour. He hadn't quite got the effect yet . . . the blossom on the cherry tree down by the drive was the purest white, but its whiteness reflected or absorbed the blueness of the morning sky in a way that was almost impossible to capture.

Gertrude took pity on his obvious wish to get back to the cherry tree and removed herself and her anxiety. There was Lucy, too, to worry about, but William would only remind her that their younger daughter was not yet sixteen, and go back to his painting. Lucy was to go to London to watch the coronation procession of George V with the Trenthams, but it was only a temporary excitement. Gertrude despaired of finding anything else that would keep her mind off the fact that Harry's visits to Providence had abruptly ceased the moment Emily returned to Barham. Her only relief was in Ned, who alone seemed not to hanker after anything he hadn't got.

Even this was not entirely true, because a mulish-looking Ned was at that moment in the estate office being told by George Hoskins that he wanted to run before he could walk.

'But, Gramps, we haven't got *time* to wait for men like old Jim Young and Clarry Briggs to crawl like snails up to each new idea we offer them. By the time they're ready to agree, we probably ought to be thinking of the *next* thing they should do.'

'They've always been given time before, Ned – it's what they're used to.'

'And it's why a bank owns Providence! They're tenants . . . have we the right to *tell* them what to do?'

'We have the right to evict them if the way they farm Wyndham land doesn't bring in enough to pay their rent . . . but that isn't what they've been used to either.'

Ned stared at his grandfather's grave face. 'Of course we wouldn't evict them, but there's no harm in trying to *persuade* them to do things differently, is there? Look, Gramps – wheat prices may never rise, and oats and barley aren't doing much better. But there's an enormous population practically on our doorstep, wanting something better nowadays than the diet of bacon, bread and cabbage that their grandparents were used to. We must still grow wheat, of course, but only where it's economical and large fields can accommodate machinery; otherwise we must switch to dairying, or to the sort of garden produce that we can find a market for in Birmingham. It can't fail to work – not just for us, but for the wretched townspeople who *need* good fresh food if anybody does.'

Ned's face glowed with the energy of his argument and the righteousness of his cause. He *knew* he was right, but even dear Gramps was reluctant to make sweeping changes, and the others (elderly, Ned thought them, though Clarry was scarcely forty-five) were going to be much harder to convince.

'All right, Ned; we'll go and talk to them, as long as your father approves of the idea.'

His grandson suddenly grinned. 'He listened very carefully and, between making up his mind whether a dash of Prussian blue was needed or just a *touch* of Chinese red, decided that we should do whatever we thought best!'

George bowed to the inevitable, and allowed himself to be taken to call first on Jim Young.

By midsummer, with Providence delightfully peaceful for as long as Sybil and Lucy took the sea air with their aunt and Charlotte in a surprise visit to Deauville, Ned could congratulate himself on the fact that some progress had been made. His obvious desire to help *them* as well as Providence had made it hard for Jim and Clarry to turn the scheme down out of hand. They said, reluctantly, that they would give his ideas a try, if only because they couldn't do worse than toil to produce wheat that no-one wanted to buy. Suitable land was earmarked for the autumn planting of fruit, but the rest of their acreage was harrowed and sown with vegetables. It was time for Ned to think of marketing.

He drove the gig in to Birmingham one morning, fearing that his bicycle would do nothing to strengthen the impression he wished to create of a successful man of business. The day was dry and extremely hot, typical of a summer that had been drier and hotter than anyone could remember. He left the gig in the stables of the Old Crown Inn, with the intention of walking around first of all, to inspect the sort of shops he needed for his purpose. The centre of the city was imposing nowadays, with its fine public buildings. One day he'd come back and visit the museum and picture gallery, but this grand municipal area wasn't what he was looking for. He headed towards meaner streets, looking for factories; where they were, there would be people, and people needed feeding.

Away from the open spaces in the centre of the city the

heat seemed even more intense, but he was beginning to be aware that more than the temperature oppressed him. Something he identified as tension lay over the narrow streets. Sullen-looking people, who should have been at work but weren't, clogged the street corners, formed groups that eddied and broke and reformed, and had a frightening air about them that suggested violence being only just held in check.

He'd been in Birmingham before, but it hadn't been like this. He didn't know what was wrong, but it was clear that he couldn't have chosen a worse day to come. Common sense told him to find his way back to the gig and go home. He turned into a street that looked as if it led in the right direction and found himself staring at a number of things – a large building across the front of which were splashed giant letters advertising THORNLEY AND SON, a crowd of men milling around its entrance shouting and jostling to get inside, and a closed door which suddenly opened long enough to allow Frank Thornley to come out and stand on the top step above them. It was the signal for the men to rush towards him in a solid, murderous-looking mass. Ned watched, and despite the infernal heat a cold sweat broke out all over his body. He closed his eyes rather than see the body of Jane Thornley's son trampled underfoot.

A moment later he had to open them again because a voice he would rather not have listened to was saying insistently somewhere inside his head that he would *have* to go and see. Frank Thornley was not a friend, but he was a neighbour; more than that, he was a man who desperately needed help. He was also, to Ned's astonished relief, still on his feet – an ordinary-seeming, unremarkable man looking calmly down on the seething, shouting rabble of humanity swirling just below him. It occurred to Ned also that he looked very lonely, waiting there for . . . what? . . . the chance to speak, to reason with men who seemed far beyond the reach of reason?

Almost without knowing that he did so, Ned joined the crowd, fought his way doggedly round its extremity, and arrived, scarlet-faced, panting, and with a thudding heart, at the step where Frank Thornley stood. Having got there, he had no thought of what he was going to do next, but two of them facing that shouting mob must surely be just a little better than letting Thornley stand there on his own? The sight of someone they didn't know checked the noise for a moment, and it was the chance Frank had been waiting for. He glanced at Ned, finally come to rest on the step beside him, but immediately returned his gaze to the crowd. His stillness held them quiet long enough for him to begin to speak.

'You found the gates locked this morning because half of you refused to complete yesterday's shift. While any single one of you refuses to work properly, this factory will stay closed. What men are doing elsewhere, in other factories in other cities, is of no concern to me. In *this* factory you are fairly paid, fairly worked, and generously looked after. If that is not enough for you, you are free to leave. You are *not* free to tell me how to run Thornley's.'

'We want a say,' a voice shouted from the safety of the crowd. '*We* do the work . . . we should have a say.' It broke the spell that had held the men quiet. Now they were all shouting again, jostling so close that Ned could smell their sweat-soaked clothes and skin, and even the herd fever that gripped them. Without knowing that he did so, he moved nearer to Thornley, tensing his body for the moment when one of them scrambled over the mental hurdle that separated worker from boss. It only needed one to make the vital leap up the steps for the rest of them to follow him.

'You *may* have a say eventually,' Frank said clearly, 'but you won't get it like *this* – I'd rather shut Thornley's down altogether. You think that because other men are striking, you must strike too. *You* have no reason to, and even if their cause is good, you don't help them by doing so. For men you don't know, you're willing to penalize your own families, for nothing.'

'We're willing to help men like ourselves fight injustice – men who, unite us, are allowed the dignity of a union.'

This time the voice was recognizable – Albert Simpkin, disciple of Karl Marx, and dedicated revolutionary.

'There is *no* injustice here; therefore no need of a union. Those of you who share Mr Simpkin's enthusiasm must find yourselves a job elsewhere.'

'We were locked out this morning – *that's* injustice,' cried someone else. 'How can we work if we're locked out?'

'The gates were locked because a half-manned, half-worked factory is a danger to everybody in it. Now, the choice is yours. Either you go back to full working – every single one of you – or the factory stays closed. What do you say?'

Ned waited, feeling sweat running into the palms of his closed fists. The men muttered among themselves, swore, shouted at each other, and wiped their grimy faces . . . stalemate, it seemed, but Frank Thornley's face remained impassive; he had said all he was going to say.

Then a single voice found the courage to make itself heard. 'I say let's work!' Boos and jeers from those nearest to Albert Simpkin, but they were answered, checked, and finally shouted down as more and more of them took up the chant – 'open the gates and we'll work!'

Ned watched Thornley walk down the steps and choose a man from among those nearest to him. 'Unlock the gates, Culley, and then bring the key back to the office. The men are to wash and cool down before they start up the machines.' He waited long enough to see the crowd surge behind Culley, and then swarm through the opened gates, before he turned and stared at Ned.

'I don't know what you thought *you* were doing there . . . you might have got hurt.'

'So might you . . . I thought . . . well, never mind what I thought.' Ned suddenly ducked his head. It was shaming to feel like fainting *now*, but his legs were trembling, as if he'd just run the race of his life and got to the finishing post against all expectation. When he lifted his head he found Thornley smiling at him. 'I was in a terrible funk just now . . . were you?'

'Yes – there are women in the offices behind us . . .' Thornley didn't bother to finish the sentence, but Ned saw why he'd chosen to face the men outside.

'Do you trust the one you gave the key to? Suppose he just clears off with it, and the men with him?'

'Culley's the best of the foremen, and I *have* to trust someone. He was only there with the rest of them because he hadn't quite got the courage to stand out by himself. But he'll be all right now.'

Frank looked at Ned's face, pale still, but not deathly white as it had been a moment ago. 'It was a stupid thing to do, but I'm grateful to you. What brought you here today of all days?'

Ned tried to remember, then struggled with a mad desire to shout with laughter as it came to him. 'Vegetables,' he gasped. 'Oh lord, I was looking for sh . . . shops that might sell our v . . . vegetables!'

He was aware of being propelled inside the door of the building, felt its coolness like a blessing after the sweltering heat and stench outside, and was led to a washroom where he might douse his face and light-headedness in cold water. When he finally emerged, himself again, a pale but pleasant-faced woman waited to conduct him to a room where Thornley sat behind a desk. There was coffee on a tray in front of him, and a plate heaped with biscuits. They made Ned's mouth water, because he found himself suddenly famished. What an extraordinary morning it was being, like no other he'd ever lived through.

Thornley gestured him to a chair. 'Now sit down, and tell me why the future Squire of Providence wants to sell vegetables.'

'He *needs* to,' Ned corrected him. 'We can't get a reasonable price for the product – wheat – we've been used to growing, so it seems to me that our only hope is to grow what people do want to buy.' He was about to add that his host must have more pressing worries on his mind than the financial problems of the Wyndhams, then stopped because the pleasant woman had come into the room with the key the foreman had brought back. 'Tell Culley I'll come over shortly,' Thornley said to her, then turned back to his visitor. 'Now, start again.'

This time Ned told his story, as briefly as he could. '*Is* it a stupid idea?' he asked at the end. 'I have the feeling that everyone else thinks it is, but it seems to make sense to me.'

'It's not stupid, but you haven't thought it out clearly enough. Why waste time running round the entire city, delivering small orders to a dozen shops? Supply one distributor, and let *him* do the running about.'

The suggestion made sense, Ned could see that, but how would he go about finding such a man? Thornley answered the question for him.

'I don't suppose a distributor exists, but I'll set one up in business for you, provided you can undertake to keep him supplied. Can you?'

Ned thought for a moment. 'In a small way, to begin with; we're only just getting started. By next spring we shall be able to do much better.' It went against the grain to ask his next question but it had to be said. 'It's immensely kind of you, but I don't know why you should bother.'

Thornley took off his spectacles, and smiled at Ned. 'Let's say I'm returning a service. Didn't you know that your mother was responsible for finding a market for the products of the Thornley sewing circle? The least I can do is find a market for your vegetables!'

Half an hour later, Ned made his bemused way back to the gig. It was still just as hot, and the city seemed as certainly as before a place he would rather die than choose to live in, but he found himself humming a tune. His idea *hadn't* been stupid, and the new Wyndham enterprise was under way. Jim and Clarry didn't know it yet but they were going to have to grow vegetables for dear life from now on.

CHAPTER TWENTY-TWO

The fierce heat of an extraordinary summer finally burnt itself out, consuming at the same time some, at least, of the tension and violence it had helped to ferment in the crowded industrial cities. There had been almost year-long turmoil in which different groups of working men – seamen, firemen, carmen, and engineers following the example offered by the miners the previous year – fought to establish trades union supremacy over their employers. To William, it seemed to sound the death knell of the once-peaceful, law-abiding England of his youth. The old framework of religion, sobriety, and hard work which had held society together in Victoria's reign was slowly but steadily being dismantled. He had withdrawn from the municipal affairs of the county council, and was by inclination wary of organized societies, but some had come into existence of which he approved. He tried to fire his nearest neighbour's interest in them but Arthur Thornley remained a townsman at heart, convinced that there were more urgent things to worry about than the preservation of common land and age-old footpaths.

'I can see they mean a lot to *you*, Squire,' he said kindly, 'but I reckon, if you don't mind me saying so, that you're living in the past.'

'In a past, what's more, that probably never was,' William agreed ruefully. 'The sort of rustic Arcadia dreamed up only in John Ruskin's imagination, where lords were feudal but fair, and peasants dressed in homespun smocks laboured happily from dawn to dusk with never a machine in sight. Yes, I'm bound to say I should have liked that sort of England!'

'Assuming you were one of the lords, o'course.'

William's smile conceded the point. His friend – for, strangely, by slow degrees that was what Thornley had come to be – was looking careworn and tired. It was scarcely surprising, given the industrial turmoil of the past months.

'You'll be thankful when this year is over. God send an easier 1912.'

Arthur nodded; he agreed with the hope, but didn't propose to say to William Wyndham that he reckoned God had little to do with it. In *his* view the next or any other year was more likely to be as men made it for themselves. 'Your brother-in-law's still busy at Westminster, I dare say?'

'Alec? Yes . . . at the moment very bitter about their lordships in the other House, as all good Liberals must be. One way or another the Commons will have to succeed in limiting the peers' power before long, and the lords will only have themselves to blame when it happens.'

Arthur looked thoughtful. 'I'm not a Liberal m'self, you understand, but I can't help seeing this Government's got plenty of trouble on its hands, apart from die-hard lunatics in the House of Lords trying to stop them running the country and firebrand women shouting to be allowed to have a say in things. I can't see that the Irish question's ever going to be settled to the satisfaction of north and south; that's one ugly problem. Another one is that Germany's building battleships as hard as she can go – not just for the Kaiser to amuse himself saluting to. She won't be satisfied till she's grabbed every colony France owns, even if she stops short of annexing France itself, and from us she'll take command of the seas – that will be the end of a great trading empire.'

Thornley's pugnacious face looked so sombre that William felt the coldness of fear touch his skin. Arthur was saying nothing that he hadn't thought himself, but to hear a shrewd, rational man put the thoughts into words depressed him almost past bearing.

'So, taken all in all, 1912 looks anything but promising,' he suggested despondently.

'That's right, Squire.' Suddenly Arthur's face brightened. 'There's something we've forgotten, though – the Wyndham/Thornley co-operative! *That* looks set to do very nicely.'

'It was good of Frank to get involved in it.'

'Well, as I understand it, he has a high opinion of young Ned, and my lad's good opinions aren't earned easily.'

'Ned's as pleased as a cat with two tails. As a business-man, he's hoping that money is going to come pouring in now that the market gardening is really under way; and as a youthful idealist, he believes that good, reasonably priced food will make the citizens of Birmingham healthier and happier – so joy can be unconfined all round!'

The new year, when it came, justified Arthur Thornley's pessimistic view of it. Ever since Alec Trentham had been concerned in public affairs there had been one foreign crisis after another to strain the fragile mesh of alliances holding European peace together. The Great Powers whose lives depended on foreign trade – England, France and Germany – often collided, some times dangerously, in Africa and the Far East; but a ritual dance of demands and concessions, as elaborate as a minuet, kept hostilities within the bounds of diplomacy. More dangerous, because less predictable, were alignments that controlled the delicate balance of power within Europe itself.

To most Englishmen, the Balkans were a rabble of uncontrollable but trivial states whose preferred way of life was to be at each other's throats. Even their names were outlandish – Serbia, Bosnia, Montenegro, Herzegovina – and their overlords, Ottoman or Austrian, weren't envied for having such a contentious bunch in hand. It wasn't thinkable that anything that happened *there* could threaten the peaceful life of England.

But the first Balkan war of 1912 almost led to total disaster. Turkish oppression and misrule finally provoked the Christian Balkan states into unity for long enough to win a series of brilliant victories against the Turks – victories which, however well-deserved, threatened to involve the Great Powers. Russia inevitably supported its fellow Slavs, and France was in alliance with Russia. The ramshackle Austro-Hungarian Empire feared the example being given to its own Slav subject peoples, and had in its turn to be supported by its ally, Germany.

The fuse of full-scale war was smouldering . . .

But Haywood's End, true to itself, was not interested in the Balkans. It found more to discuss in the fact that Harry Trentham had decided to give up carefree bachelordom at last and settle down. His engagement to Emily Maynard was announced, and received at Providence with a variety of feelings. Sybil was inclined to feel that she was losing both cousin and friend, since it was well known that betrothed couples, being interested only in each other, became useless company to anyone else. Ned didn't express himself quite so bluntly but more or less agreed. Lucy bore up bravely in public, but often wept in the privacy of her bedroom. Surprised in this state by Sybil one day, she waited for her usually unsentimental sister to jeer at her, but the derision she expected didn't come. Sybil's expression was even kind, and invited a confession.

'I kept hoping Harry might wait for me,' Lucy explained miserably. 'I was growing up as fast as I could, and all the time you were away in Switzerland he seemed to still like coming here.' Her eyes fell on the heavy rope of hair lying over her shoulder. 'A pigtail, and dear Amelia Lacey . . . how could anyone take me seriously when I'm saddled with such handicaps?'

Sybil recognized genuine heartache and didn't smile. 'Not for much longer; this time next year you'll be out, with your hair up and the schoolroom forgotten.'

'Too late then. It doesn't matter *now* what happens next year. I kept saying I was going to stay here and keep Ned company but I didn't really believe it. I can see I shall have to start getting used to the idea.'

Sybil offered what comfort she could. 'You've a little time still to find an alternative.'

Lucy shook her head. 'It's not a question of time. I shan't be able to find another Harry.'

Her sister marvelled at this sad and simple statement, believed in with all Lucy's tenacious heart. Everyone liked their cousin – he was a cheerful, competent young man, with pleasant manners and a kind heart. But how did Lucy, and presumably Emily too, manage to see him as the embodiment of every manly virtue? With the thought, Sybil was transported back to the lakeside at Lucerne, where she'd walked breathlessly with Henri Blanchard. Had she been as unreasonably convinced about him? She didn't know the answer to the question; all that was certain was that no other man she'd met since had managed to dislodge him in her memory. The knowledge made her tolerant of her sister's opinion of Harry Trentham.

'Poor Lu . . . I'm sorry,' she said gently. 'It's all the harder when you have to keep on bumping into him. But there *is* a kind of comfort in the end from doing your best not to give in to misery.'

She didn't know what she talked about, but Lucy could see that she was trying to be kind. Sybil felt obliged to make it plain that she *did* know. 'It took me quite a long time to discover it myself, which is why I was so bad-tempered when I first came home from Switzerland!'

It was a revelation, but one Lucy wasn't sure how to accept. Did it help to know that Sybil had been unhappy too, or was it preferable to be the only one who suffered? Perhaps on the whole there was comfort in the idea of shared misfortune.

'You managed better than me,' she said finally. 'Nobody else guessed about *you*.'

'I was a bit older . . . I dare say that helped, and it didn't happen here.'

Lucy stared at her sister's face. 'Anyone I know? No, I suppose not if you were in Lucerne.'

'No-one you know; he doesn't come to England.'

Lucy accepted the brief facts, aware that it had cost her sister something to mention them at all. Her own generosity must be not to ask painful questions. She wiped her eyes and aired a different worry.

'Emily won't expect me to take part in the ceremony, will she, Syb? *That* would be more than I could bear. She'll have to make do with you and Charlotte as bridesmaids, and her fleet of Maynard cousins.'

Sybil made a mental note to deal with this problem when they came to it, then thought she might risk a change of subject. 'Talking of cousins, Papa received a letter from Uncle James this morning. We are to be visited by Patrick and Anita Wyndham. We must hope for the best, I suppose, but they're bound to talk in a strange Yankee drawl and despise us for being so backward.'

'Their mother died when they were small; I think we're supposed to feel sorry for them,' Lucy pointed out. 'Is Uncle James coming too?'

'No, they're travelling with their grandfather – to Dublin first, to see their Irish connections, then here. Mama looked strangely startled at the mention of Mr Maguire's name – I wonder why?'

'I expect it comes of his being Irish,' Lucy said knowledge-ably. Thanks to Miss Lacey's efforts, she had an imperfect hold on the burning question of Home Rule. 'They're being very troublesome at the moment, instead of being content to be ruled by nice King George.'

'I don't *think* Mama was concerned about the Irish in the lump, only with Mr Maguire. I shall have to see what I can winkle out of Grandpa Hoskins about him.'

But for once Sybil was unsuccessful with a man who was normally putty in her hands. He smiled because he could never help smiling when she went to call on him, but she came away realizing that he'd told her nothing more than she knew already.

The travellers reached Birmingham by train from Liverpool in the middle of March. Hodges went to meet them there, and Artie drove the gig, to bring back the luggage. Gertrude had exhausted herself in preparing for their arrival, being so deeply disturbed by the prospect of meeting Daniel Maguire that she could only avoid dwelling on it by organizing an assault on the inside of the house which even threatened the happy disorder of the Great Parlour.

'My love, don't you think a little dust is forgivable in an artist's studio?' William enquired plaintively. 'In any case, they're most unlikely to pay me a visit there at all.'

'You're becoming famous . . . why shouldn't they want to visit you?' She was ashamed of the sharpness in her voice, aware that fear was, as usual, making her attack the wrong person. 'I'm sorry, William. James's children are more than welcome, but I can't even *pretend* that I want Daniel Maguire here.'

He smoothed the fair, silver-speckled beard that in recent years he'd grown instead of an untidy moustache. It gave breadth to his long thin face, making it no less gentle but more dignified. Sybil insisted that when he stroked it reflectively it gave him the philosophical air of the Emperor Marcus Aurelius. She had, he realized, returned from Lucerne notably better informed, but also less inclined to take her dear father seriously. He kissed Gertrude's cheek to tell her that he understood her dislike of the coming visit. 'My dear, Maguire's stay will be very brief, and Ned and I will guarantee to occupy him, and probably bore him to death, with exhaustive tours of the estate. You need only see him at mealtimes and let him talk; he's bound to do that, don't you think?'

She agreed that it was likely in an Irishman, smiled at her husband, and promised to spare the studio in her programme of spring cleaning. A determined effort at self-discipline kept her outwardly calm, but she was very pale when Lucy, stationed by one of the windows in the Great Hall, reported that the carriage was emerging from the drive on to the forecourt. William linked Gertrude's arm in his as they crossed the bridge, and patted her hand when he felt it trembling. Then he heard her murmur at the sight of a white-haired man climbing stiffly down from the carriage.

'William . . . he's *old*! How stupid of me not to have expected that.'

Mr Maguire limped forward, lifting his hat at the sight of them. 'Lady Wyndham . . . William – I think I may be familiar with *you*! We did meet, even though you were only a schoolboy at the time.'

His voice was soft, with still a trace of the lilting intonation of his native land, and his eyes, Gertrude realized with a shock of familiarity, were like her own. He smiled at them both, with the lifelong confidence of a man who couldn't help but charm. She put out her hand, smiled mechanically, and left William to say that he was welcome. With James's children following him out of the carriage at least she could be natural. Anita, three years older than Ned, was an imperfect echo of Kitty Wyndham – with Kitty's black hair and deeply blue eyes, but none of her rounded prettiness. This girl's face was plain, only redeemed by lovely eyes and a look of intelligence. She seemed hesitant until Gertrude kissed her and said warmly, 'Such a long time you've been about coming to Providence, my dear, but we are so happy to see you at last.' She turned to smile at the young man waiting behind his sister. 'And Patrick too, of course. I'm afraid there are rather a lot of cousins for you to meet inside – they all insisted on being here!'

She watched Anita smile at William, and hold out her hands in an expressive little gesture as she looked at the house in front of her. 'Papa tried to draw it for me once, but he said he couldn't make it beautiful enough; he didn't make it *nearly* beautiful enough.'

Gertrude could foresee that William would have little difficulty in getting on with his niece, but in that first moment she was less sure what they would make of Patrick. He was James's son in colouring and build, but his eyes were cool, and she had the impression of someone more reticent and calculating than his father.

Inside, as well as the children of the house, Louise, Harry and Charlotte were also waiting to be introduced. Gertrude felt deeply grateful to her sister-in-law for offering to be there. The social occasion Louise couldn't smooth with practised, cool aplomb had yet to be invented; Gertrude had every intention of letting her deal with Maguire for as long as she was there, and every confidence that she could rely on Sybil to cope with Patrick Wyndham.

In this, as the visit progressed, it seemed that she had over-estimated her daughter for once. Miss Wyndham was accustomed to making an impression, especially when she put herself out to entertain, but her cousin seemed to have no difficulty in resisting her. About this she didn't greatly care, but when he was tactless enough to make it plain that he was unimpressed with what he'd seen of England, she found she *did* care.

'You prefer something larger, no doubt, cousin . . . something bright and new and brash . . . to go with your brash American manners!' she suggested sweetly.

'Something less privileged, less unfairly ordered, let us say. I'm half-Irish, don't forget, and not inclined to regret the fact.'

For the first time in their acquaintance, Patrick's face gave away the fact that she had managed to register with him. She had only succeeded in annoying him, but it was better than making no impression at all. He could have told her that she made a sharper impression than she knew, and he was the more irritated by the fact – she was a dragonfly girl, with slender, vivid body, large eyes, and swift flight . . . he never knew where she would alight next. His only defence against the feelings she aroused in him was to make sure that she didn't know her effect.

One fine morning, with farm papers to be delivered to Bicton for Ned, she offered him her brother's bicycle for the ride there. She was happily sure that a shortened bicycling skirt revealed her ankles, and that Ned's old tweed cap into which she'd crammed her dark hair, lent her an air that was both rakish and enticingly feminine.

'I assume you can manage a bicycle, cousin? Or is it too undignified a mode of progression for you?'

Patrick stared at her, struggling with a strong desire to

pull off the absurd cap and kiss her until she could provoke him no more. 'I believe *I* can manage the machine, but "to pedal the treadles *she* is an effort, an anomaly, a fright"!' He was pleased with this effort, but instead of offending his cousin it made her give an involuntary chuckle.

'You win,' she said handsomely. 'Did *you* just think of that?'

'No, Max Beerbohm said it. I shall agree with him until I've had a chance to watch your performance.'

He was watching intently, waiting for her to be unnerved by his eyes fixed so openly on her body under the skintight jacket and revealing skirt. She must be a little more careful about provoking Patrick Wyndham in the future, it was dangerous – like poking an apparently sleepy lion with a stick. She climbed on her steed and bicycled beside him with a sedateness that gave him no excuse to punish her.

They had left Anita and Lucy being given a painting lesson in the studio, which in turn left Gertrude uncomfortably aware that it would be unreasonable to expect an elderly man to want to play with paints or join a bicycling expedition. The moment had been thrust on her when she was obliged to pay attention to her other guest.

She offered a stilted commonplace about James, which Daniel Maguire totally ignored. His own contribution to the conversation was much more electrifying. 'You don't want me here, Gertrude, and you wish I would go away.' Before she could even register that he'd used her Christian name for the first time, he spoke again. 'There is a faint likeness to my poor Kitty, but strangely enough it's more noticeable that you are kin to Anita.'

She went white under the shock of it, while her heart seemed to stop beating and then catch up with a pounding that he must almost be able to hear.

'I'm not sure I understand you, Mr Maguire.' The deliberate formal use of his name made his long mouth twist wryly.

'I think you do, Gertrude. But if you're wondering how I know, George Hoskins told me.'

'You're lying.' She flung the words at him. 'You've always known . . . *must* have known that you left my mother to struggle with unhappiness and shame, and finally give up life altogether because she could struggle no longer.'

But Maguire's eyes, the same clear grey as her own, told her that she couldn't believe what she wanted to believe because it wasn't the truth.

'I didn't know,' he said simply. 'I wish I had – not because I could have done anything to help Emma . . . George Hoskins had already done everything that a man could do; but I might have been able to help *you*.'

Gertrude ignored this. 'I wouldn't have agreed to your being told,' she said fiercely.

'It's why George Hoskins didn't consult you. Don't blame him, Gertrude . . . he did it out of infinite kindness, believing that I had a right to know I still had a daughter.'

She turned away, unable to go on looking at the sadness in his face. She wanted to go on hating him, but it was unexpectedly hard to hate a Daniel Maguire grown old and frail and lonely.

'I accept your right,' she said quietly after a moment, 'but I shall never be able to think of my father as being anyone but the man who cherished my mother.'

'And I have to accept *that*, but to know the truth is more important to me than I can say.'

It should have been the end of the conversation but, unbidden and unwanted, there arose in her mind the memory of the night she had spent with James. Being married to William hadn't stopped her then, any more than not being free to do so had stopped this man making love to Emma Rastell. Gertrude knew that she had no right at all to judge him, or to punish him; looking now at his face, she didn't even want to.

She moved towards him, not smiling but wanting to close more than the physical distance between them. 'You're right to say I didn't welcome you when you came. If you visit us again I shall be able to do so.'

When she suddenly held out her hand he pulled her closer

to him so that he could kiss her cheek. 'My dear, it won't matter now, whether I come or not,' he said gently.

He set out for London the following day. As a leading member of the Irish community in New York, he was to meet John Redmond, the Irish National leader in the House of Commons. Then he would travel to Southampton to board the White Star liner making her maiden voyage from there to New York.

A week after he left Providence Ned and Patrick shepherded Anita, Sybil and Lucy to London to attend Charlotte Trentham's twenty-first birthday ball. It was the night of 14 April, and the occasion was splendid enough to start a new Season in itself.

Lucy was beautiful in her first long dress, and entranced by her first full-scale ball; Ned waltzed with Anita and stepped almost unknowingly over a different kind of watershed; Patrick tried not to stare at Sybil, dressed in silk the colour of a wild rose, and thought that the ocean tide might just as well have tried to pretend that it was not attracted by the moon.

The music played into the small hours, and Charlotte's guests danced unaware that out in the wastes of the Atlantic another orchestra continued to play as the S.S. *Titanic* listed and sank beneath iceberg-infested waters. The *Carpathia* steamed to her in time to save some seven hundred people, but more than twice that number were drowned.

The news of the disaster was known in London by the following morning. A subdued and anxious little group travelled back to Providence, and the time of waiting began. It was several days before a long, sad telegraph from James gave them the certain news that Daniel Maguire was among those lost. Gertrude had not allowed herself to say so to the children, but she had *known* that this was what the news would be. Another thread in the pattern of her life, random and incomplete until then, had briefly been allowed to reappear. James, Henri, Daniel Maguire – they had all added something precious to the design, and the pain they'd brought was part of its final beauty.

James's long message ended with the plea that Patrick and Anita should do what their grandfather would have wished and go on with their plan to spend the summer in Paris. Patrick, shocked out of normal self-control, finally agreed to continue with a visit which was to provide him with material for an architectural thesis to complete his studies. Anita felt obliged to go with him as arranged, but had no heart for a long visit among foreigners and strangers. Gertrude suggested diffidently that she might prefer to spend the summer with them at Providence until Patrick returned to collect her for the journey home. The transformation in her sad face settled the matter, and Patrick set off alone.

One morning when Ned had driven the girls over to Endlicott and Gertrude and William were alone in the Great Hall drinking coffee together, he suddenly broke the silence that had fallen. 'I keep having to remember that we didn't know Anita a month ago . . . now it seems as if she has always belonged to us here.'

In that moment Gertrude heard Daniel's voice again saying, '. . . it's more noticeable that you're kin to Anita.' She was scarcely aware of the tears that began to trickle down her cheeks, but William came to sit beside her so that he could mop them with his handkerchief, paint-splashed as usual. 'Dearest . . . that was thoughtless of me . . . I didn't mean to remind you of poor Daniel. But now that we're talking of him, I can't help wishing that he had known the truth about you before he died. God knows it's too late now but . . .'

'William, he *did* know.' Her eyes, staring at him, were suddenly luminous with joy. 'My wise dear foster-father told him. I was so angry that I almost refused to accept him, but *something* kept me from making so terrible a mistake. Now, all I have to regret is that we knew each other for such a little time; shared affection might have grown and redeemed old bitterness.'

She smiled unsteadily at her husband – a man she'd twice tried to hate because it hadn't been possible to desert him. Nothing changed the fact that she had fallen in love with

James, or that Henri Blanchard had bewitched her and burdened her with the knowledge of *his* unhappiness; but in a curious way she now loved William *more*, not less, because of those two other men. 'Heaven is sometimes merciful,' she murmured at last, and William supposed that she still spoke of her father. 'There are tragedies we can do nothing about, but it occasionally prevents us making others all by ourselves.'

CHAPTER TWENTY-THREE

It was high summer; a Saturday afternoon in August when the Haywood's End team was doing battle in a meadow at Bicton with eleven stalwarts representing the Thornley factories. Ned, last man in for the village, lay sprawled on the grass, watching the combat and wondering whether it would provoke or appease the gods if he put his pads on *now*. Occasionally he turned to Anita sitting beside him and offered a word of explanation, but she preferred *not* to be taught the mysteries of this strange English ritual. In fact, she was content not to know anything at all; at the moment she simply wanted to be allowed to feel, and absorb into her heart and memory the essence of a summer that would never come again.

Around them flowed the ineffable greenness of the valley and its surrounding hills, ribbed with the deeper green of hedges and stencilled with the soft dark blur of ancient trees. People she knew, and many more she didn't know, sat around the field, intent on the game. The only sounds were the trilling of larks high in the clear air, the crack of ball on bat, and the applause and advice offered by the crowd. New York belonged to a world as remote as the regions of the moon, but she must find her way back to it before long.

She sighed without being aware of it and Ned turned to smile at her.

'Poor girl – are you thinking this is a *very* strange way to spend an afternoon?'

'I shall be truthful and say I can't imagine anything more peaceful or more reassuring. This valley's enchanted, I think; immune to the ugly world outside busily tying itself in knots.'

He rumpled his hair, sure signal she now knew that he felt obliged to disagree.

'Not entirely enchanted, I'm afraid. Thornley's men sitting here so amiably looked a lot less docile when they were demonstrating outside Frank's factory last year. You mustn't think you've found paradise, Anita!'

'We're not supposed to expect *that* here,' she reminded him smilingly. 'But, to be going on with, this will do.'

There was a sudden stir, much clapping, even more groans, and Ned muttered, 'Oh lord, the fool! Anita, I'm afraid you'll have to pray for us now.' He got to his feet and strode off towards the crestfallen man walking towards him. She watched him lift his bat to acknowledge a ripple of applause. Was it to encourage another lamb on his way to the slaughter offered by the Thornley bowlers, or did they simply know and love Ned? This seemed more likely, because she'd never met anyone so easy to love as this cousin she hadn't been aware of a few months ago.

Ned reached the wicket, smiled at Hubert Roberts umpiring at his end, then strolled out for a council of war with his partner.

'Desperate measures now, Artie . . . slog anything you can, as hard as you can, but for the lord's sake don't run me out!'

'Right, Master Ned.' Having no head for finesse, there was nothing Artie loved more than to be told to hit. This he knew he could do. He spat on the end of his bat for luck and smiled joyously as the Thornley bowler thundered up to the crease at the other end. All went well, even brilliantly, for the space of several overs. The score climbed rapidly and the supporters from Haywood's End were roused to fever pitch. Almost certain victory was being snatched from the jaws of defeat.

Drunk with the knowledge that he was indeed slogging not only anything but everything, Artie watched an enticingly slow ball snake towards him, swung round to deliver a swipe that would take it clean into the next field, and promptly fell over, shattering his own wicket. Débâcle! The

Thornley crowd went mad, and Ned realized he'd forgotten to warn Artie that there were more ways than one of bringing the game to a sudden end. Still, it had been fun while it lasted.

The food left over from the enormous tea provided by Jane Thornley in the marquee was considerably disposed of because everyone was now hungry again and, in the lengthening shadows of a golden evening, they finally and reluctantly went home. William drove Gertrude and his daughters while Ned and Anita cycled back through lanes smelling of hedgerow flowers and mown grass. When they reached the track running round the far side of the lake, he pulled up and smiled at her.

'I can never resist stopping here – it's the best view of all.'

She said nothing, simply stared at the picture he pointed to; Providence basked in the evening sunlight, and the moat was stippled with gold. Ned's own gaze lingered on the face of the girl who leaned on her handlebars, looking at it. A summer spent largely out of doors had tanned her skin and made her eyes glow the colour of periwinkles. In his view she was beautiful. In another month she would sail away to New York and he couldn't even be sure of ever seeing her again. He was twenty, to her twenty-three, and it would be years before he could regain Providence and offer her a house that was theirs again, much less one provided with the modern comforts that other people took for granted. For the first time in his life he wanted to rail against a Fate that had been cruelly unkind. She turned unexpectedly and found him still watching her.

'It seems wicked to say so, Ned, but if we hadn't lost Grandfather I'd have gone to Paris scarcely knowing Providence at all.'

'Some people speak highly of Paris,' he muttered.

'So I believe; in fact Patrick does. But why leave heaven when it is laid in front of you?'

He wouldn't even smile at her. 'It's a worrying kind of heaven, I'm afraid. Do you mind hearing the truth?

Farming's been in a bad way here for the past thirty years; the income from Wyndham land has been nowhere near enough to keep everything going, and Providence has been quietly falling to pieces. There's a lifetime's work here to wipe off the bank mortgage and get it on its feet again. That's what I'm going to do, but it's not much of a prospect to . . . to share with anyone else, even if I had the time to think of sharing.'

She hesitated, wondering what might be said that wouldn't hurt his fierce pride. 'Ned . . . Father's a very successful man, but I don't think he's a happy one. Patrick laughs at the idea, but I have the feeling he's never got over missing what's *here*. I know things get arranged differently in England, but might he not share Providence with you, and share as well in the job of saving it?'

'I asked *my* father about it one day, but he seemed to think Uncle James had learned a different point of view in America; people like us had had our day . . . it was time to give in gracefully and bow ourselves off the stage!'

Anita looked at him curiously. 'But you're not ready to do that?'

'Certainly not. My long-dead fighting ancestors would turn in their graves! It's not just that, though. Whatever the revolutionaries and the radicals say, I think we *are* still needed here.'

'Can you possibly succeed?'

'I believe so; prices of the crops we've always grown have steadied at last, and we're beginning to do well with new things. Apart from that, my father's paintings are becoming known and sought after.' He edged his bicycle closer so that his hands could reach out and cover hers lying on the handlebars. 'Dearest Anita, I'd give a lot to be older and richer and less trammelled than I am. Time will age me even if it doesn't make me successful, but it doesn't help me now. I can't bind you, because all I dare think about at the moment is Providence, but I shall pray that you'll want to come back one day.'

His sunburned face under an untidy mop of brown hair

was anxious, and so dear that she wanted to implore him to let her stay, but he hadn't asked for that. Perhaps during the time that was to make him grow a little older he might even change his mind about wanting her at all. She summoned all her strength to speak lightly enough for him not to have to feel concerned about her. 'I'd ask to be taken on as a helper right away if it weren't for my poor lonely father waiting for us at home. Just tell me when you feel old and careworn enough, dear Ned, and I'll be here . . . but please don't wait until you're rich!'

Her eyes were clear and honest and, surely, inviting . . . ? He bent his head and found her mouth, and the knowledge flooded through each separate nerve of his body that he *was* already old enough, and *could* find time enough, for a wife. His love, Anita, must stay, and James must find himself another companion. But the real world was still there when he lifted his head, and in the real world none of these things was yet true or possible.

He said unsteadily, 'How much better Harry would have managed things. Catch *him* being fool enough to kiss a girl when they were both entangled in bicycles!'

She was flushed but smiling. 'I happen to like the way *you* manage things. Ned, I'll come whenever you say.' A promise was given and taken in the look they exchanged, then he sighed and said it was time they went home.

Patrick's return to England at the end of the summer was brought forward a day or two so that he could attend Harry's wedding. He reported that Paris had been interesting, and Sybil was made to understand that he was well-disposed towards the French, if only because they'd never tried to subjugate the Irish.

'They've had more profitable things to do, no doubt,' she pointed out unanswerably. Then her voice suddenly became hesitant. 'Did you find the gallery where Papa's paintings are shown, in the boulevard Haussmann?'

'Of course . . . Blanchard himself was there, and when I explained who I was, he was kind enough to invite me to lunch. A strange sort of man, but his gallery seemed to be full of rich and important-looking people.'

Sybil could see that this had impressed her cousin but it wasn't what she wanted to know. 'Did he ask about . . . us?'

Patrick thought for a moment. 'I don't recall that he mentioned Aunt Gertrude at all, but he wanted to know if your father was working hard. I said I thought he was.'

It was like drawing blood from a stone, but Sybil persevered. 'Is that all he said?'

Patrick's face twitched into a smile. 'He asked if I was enjoying your company at Providence. I replied that enjoying wasn't quite the right word, but the experience was interesting. Does that seem fair?'

'I think so,' she agreed after a moment.

Patrick found himself questioned also by his aunt. Her enquiry was different and he found it harder to answer. 'It's some time since we saw Monsieur Blanchard. I hope he seemed well . . . happy . . . Patrick?'

'Er, yes, I think so. His gallery certainly seemed successful. He took the trouble to show me what he described as the three most beautiful things there – one I'm afraid I've forgotten, another was a picture of a cornfield by someone called Van Gogh, and the third was a painting of Uncle William's – some gypsy children, in rags, dancing in a meadow!' If Patrick's voice sounded dubious, his aunt didn't notice. He saw her face lit by a smile so lovely that it was as if he'd just made her a present of the thing she wanted most in the world. But all she said was, 'I should have trusted Henri to value *that*.'

The Maynard-Trentham wedding was celebrated in a blaze of dress uniforms and swords, drifting chiffon gowns and cartwheel hats, and a dazzling bridal retinue. Emily was a fairy princess dressed in white lace as delicate as hoar frost; a bevy of small bridesmaids tumbled around her in a froth of apricot frills, and Charlotte and Sybil, with dresses and roses in their hair of the same glowing colour, successfully bemused Harry's fellow officers who made up the guard of honour.

Lucy, in the congregation with the rest of her family, hid behind the brim of a blue straw hat weighed down with cream roses. It was a beautiful hat but she was indifferent to it, and to everything else except the struggle not to listen to the words of the marriage service, nor to watch Harry looking at Emily as he repeated them. At Barham afterwards for the enormous wedding reception it seemed easier to avoid them. She could even, since there were so many other people she knew, detach herself from her family, whom she imagined to be watching her – protective but intolerable.

That was how Frank Thornley came to catch sight of her standing alone – a slender, beautiful girl in a blue dress and a beautiful blue hat; a lonely girl with something in her face that spoke of a desolation she could scarcely bear. He didn't know why her family had abandoned her, nor why the fact should make him so angry, but it seemed necessary to work his way across the room at once and hide her from the general view.

She was well-mannered enough to drag her inward gaze from whatever vision distressed her and look at *him* – unfamiliar in grey morning coat and top hat. It was hard to remember a day when she'd both bashed and bathed the head of this stranger, and defended the suffragettes against him.

'The hat is beautiful,' he said gravely, 'but I miss the plait. Has it disappeared for good?'

She nodded, almost smiling at the unexpectedness of finding that she didn't mind talking to Frank Thornley.

'I'm out in the world at *last*. Not to be presented till next spring, but I'm spending this winter in London with Aunt Louise. She is going to be kind enough to polish me up for Polite Society, since I begged not to be sent to Switzerland.'

'What's Switzerland done to deserve your displeasure?'

'Nothing, but either I don't feel adventurous enough to want to go there on my own, or else I love Providence too much to be quite so out of reach of it.'

'Is the polishing-up process pleasurable?' He managed to ask the question, she thought, as if it mattered to him. As if it possibly could; still, it was kind of him to pretend. She gave a little shrug already worthy of her Aunt Louise, and he was aware again of some startling change in her. A charming schoolgirl had, in some way he couldn't understand, become a young woman with all the instinctive ability of her sex to mystify a mere man by concealing whatever she didn't intend him to know.

'I suppose I shall still have to learn things, and only a good report will satisfy my dear Aunt Louise!' Her voice sounded bright, but then Harry Trentham came to talk to a group of guests a few yards away from them and her mouth quivered with sudden pain. Frank now knew *something* she hadn't intended him to learn, but he saw as well the effort she made not to weep. He put her arm through his and steered her competently to where his father, almost restrainedly elegant for once in conventional morning dress, was trying to convince Maud Roberts that she'd got the wrong end of the stick about Free Trade. Jane Thornley was enjoying the contest, but didn't fail to observe Frank making his way towards them with a pale-faced Lucy by his side. Jane smiled with the heartfelt kindness that managed to transform ordinary features into something far more rare.

'Lucy, love . . . what a beautiful hat! It's enough in itself to console Frank for being here. He's not a man who reckons to enjoy weddings normally.'

Lucy kissed Maud as well as Jane and, because Arthur Thornley looked so hopeful in his turn, she was suddenly moved to kiss *his* cheek as if she was in the habit of doing so. She smiled in spite of herself at the blush of pleasure it brought to his face, even while she thought how odd it was that she could bear the day more easily in the company of *this* family than her own.

'I've yet to meet the man who relishes a wedding,' Maud observed. 'I suppose it's the uncomfortable clothes the poor things have to wear, unlike us, whose only obligation is to look beautiful – in which *some* of us succeed better than others,' she added pensively. 'I should like to make that clear before anyone else does!'

Arthur surpassed himself; he bowed, he even kissed her hand. 'The wrapping gets thrown away; it's what's inside you have to think about.'

Watching them, Lucy discovered that she no longer wanted to weep. She had the strange feeling that Frank Thornley had not only guessed she was on the verge of breaking down, but wouldn't permit it to happen. If she looked like doing so again he would wave his wand and conjure up something else to distract her.

Gertrude, watching them across the room, felt thankful to Jane and Maud, thinking it was *they* who'd helped her daughter more than she'd been able to do herself. Then she returned her attention to someone she *might* be able to help. Her sister-in-law, as well as looking suitably elegant as the bridegroom's mother, was noticeably strained beneath the smile she kept pinned to her mouth.

'I'm so thankful not to be a politician's wife,' Gertrude said quietly. 'Do you know something *we* don't know? You look as if you do.'

Louise couldn't help smiling more naturally at this frontal attack. 'You don't change, and it isn't the slightest use, as I well remember, to even *try* to evade you. I hear a little about the problems facing Sir Edward Grey at the Foreign Office; Alec hears much more. I know enough to wish that Harry were not a professional soldier, and that all his father had to worry about was whether to try to improve Somerton when the time comes or have it knocked down and designed into something more manageable.'

Gertrude stared at her. 'There was a time when you thought that inheriting Somerton was much the same thing as getting yourself buried alive.'

'I know . . . it's one of the jokes life constantly enjoys at our expense that Robert Trentham should seem determined to live for ever now that I'd give anything to get Alec away from responsibilities and worries that are shortening his life.'

'Is it as bad as that? William pretends that he's not worried, so as not to frighten me. All the same I know he's been convinced for years that the time will come when we *can't* stand by and watch Germany take over Europe. Meanwhile, there's the problem of Alec. Can't you persuade him to retire?'

'Persuade?' Louise's mouth twisted in a mixture of self-derision and sadness. 'You don't know Alec. He's driven by the simple idea that he's bound to serve; it doesn't occur to him to live in any other way.'

'I see that, and it's all very laudable; but he owes something to his wife as well. He only needs to think a *little* less about England, and a little more about you.'

'Therein lies his *other* simple idea. Our marriage is a convenient social arrangement. I am allowed to do, with discretion, what I like, and he is allowed to do the same. In *his* case that means killing himself with overwork.' She turned to stare out of the window behind them. 'He never once mentioned Henri's name, but I am almost sure he knew. Ever since he's been a kind, courteous and distant partner. He thinks it's all I require him to be, whereas after more than twenty-five years of calm, unemotional marriage I want to go down on my knees and *implore* him to listen to me.' Her eyes shone with tears even while she tried to smile. 'Can you think of anything more richly ironic than that?'

'What I think is that you should give imploring a try,' Gertrude said gravely. 'It's the mistake we all make, to believe that the delusions and follies we begin with are unalterable. Promise me you'll try, Louise?'

There was no time to discover how her sister-in-law intended to reply because they were interrupted by Alec himself, come in polite search of his wife so that she might be reacquainted with someone not seen since their days in India.

Gertrude watched them walk away, and wondered whether it was only what Louise had said that made their separateness so noticeable. Long-married couples usually had an air of intimacy about them that couldn't be missed, especially when they were surrounded by other people. She remembered saying once to William that she found Alec Trentham unknowable; it remained true now. If he *had* learned of Louise's *affaire* with Henri, it might be thought that he'd been generous in ignoring it. Gertrude didn't credit him with generosity; it was the indifference of a man who thought it didn't matter, or the wounded pride of a man who thought it mattered too much. Either way Louise was still being punished.

She shivered suddenly, despite the warmth of the crowded room. Her own life had grown more richly satisfying than she deserved, but it would never have done so if William had known that she'd loved two other men. The marriage institution that held society together had been simpler even a generation earlier when women had been trained to expect nothing but the satisfaction they might find in marriage. If they didn't find it there, they were not permitted to look elsewhere. *She* had looked, suffered, and finally found contentment, but Louise had been less fortunate.

Gertrude was frowning over the thought when Maud Roberts detached herself from the Thornleys and appeared in front of her.

'Elizabeth Maynard is allowed to look sorrowful, my dear, but *you're* not losing a daughter.'

'Sorry, Maud. Weddings disagree with me! I was glumly surveying my children's chances of happiness, and wondering why I can't provide them with what they want just by loving them.'

'You're their mother, not a magician. Like the rest of us they must discover that what they think they want is not the only thing that will make them happy.'

Gertrude couldn't help smiling at her friend's robustly sensible attitude to life, but she gave a little sigh as well. 'Yes, like the rest of us!'

A week after the wedding Patrick and Anita said goodbye to Providence. They sailed the ocean safely, talked and laughed with other passengers as they were required to do, and fell into deep silences when alone together. James was waiting for them on the quayside when the liner docked at New York. In the past six months he had done all that needed to be done in settling Daniel's affairs, had mourned and missed his friend, telling himself that life would seem bearable again when Patrick and Anita came home. Life had changed for all of them because of Daniel's death, but he soon realized that the summer in Europe had changed his children more, in ways they weren't prepared to discuss with him. Patrick talked much more about Paris than Providence, as if his stay in England had been scarcely worth remembering. Anita, usually so candid and companionable, only asked bright questions herself as if all that mattered was what had happened in New York while they'd been away.

James heard himself shout, 'Damn Paris and New York! How did *Gertrude* look? For God's sake talk to me about *her*.' But they didn't answer him and finally he realized why; the shout was loud but only in his own head. Anita didn't know why the expression on her father's face, of polite concern in their affairs, should disappear with the suddenness of cloud blotting out the sun, but its bleakness impelled her to cross the room and kneel down by the side of his chair. When his arms held her close to him, she could feel the weight of a sadness that mirrored her own; she had been right, and Patrick wrong.

'You *do* miss Providence as much as I do . . . don't you . . . after all these years?'

'Years? What have they to do with it?' asked James.

She leaned away from him so as to be able to see his face. 'Couldn't you go back?'

'No, at least not while my brother is still alive.' Then, as if the denial had sounded too sharp, James tried to smile at his daughter. 'Patrick seems not to have liked Providence enough, but I have the feeling you liked it too much.'

'Providence and Ned,' she agreed simply. 'He isn't ready for a wife yet; otherwise I'd go straight back.'

'No need to look so tragic then, my dear one; just be patient for a little while.'

She nodded, but couldn't smile. 'It's our superstitious Irish blood, I suppose, but I have the terrible feeling I shall never go back.'

CHAPTER TWENTY-FOUR

Lucy made no objection to going to London for the winter, just as she made no objection to anything else that was suggested to her. She was nearly eighteen, and growing up to be beautiful in a serene and golden way that had nothing to do with Sybil's vivid, challenging demand on the attention of the opposite sex. Gertrude was often of the opinion that her elder daughter made life more a battle for herself and everyone around her than it need have been, but Lucy went to the other extreme. Sybil had called her meek years ago, but it wasn't the right word for a girl who was prepared to fight when she had to. In her younger days she'd more than once arrived back torn and tearful but triumphant with yet another bedraggled kitten in her arms whose fate otherwise had been to be drowned; and she'd reduced Amelia Lacey to speechless terror in Warwick one morning by flinging herself at a half-drunken carter who was trying to flog his horse to its feet. When she was acquiescent it was only where her own life was concerned, and Gertrude was sadly convinced that Harry was the cause of Lucy's sweet in-difference to what happened to her.

Before the London visit it was necessary to explain the situation to Louise, and Gertrude did her best to be diplomatic. When she reported this to William she was aggrieved to see him begin to rock with laughter.

'I can't see *anything* to laugh about,' she said crossly. 'In fact it's unforgivably callous of you to be amused by your daughter's unhappiness. And if you're about to tell me – as your sister did – that she's like a child with toothache who can be distracted by a new toy, I shall have to resist a strong inclination to throw something at you!'

'Is that what you did . . . throw something at Louise?' William asked with interest.

Gertrude stared at him coldly. 'Nothing of the kind; I was the soul of tact. I didn't even *hint* that if her son had kept his undoubted charm to himself, this would never have happened.'

William fought with himself and managed to look apologetic. 'My dearest, I wasn't laughing at poor, sweet Lucy – only at the picture of *you* giving diplomacy its head and not telling Louise what you thought of her too-charming son!'

'I know that beating about the bush is not considered to be my forte,' his wife said with dignity, 'but I did do my best, William.'

He kissed her cheek to ask forgiveness and then reverted to the real problem. 'At the risk of making you cross again, Lucy isn't very much more than a child . . . aren't we in danger of taking an adolescent heartache too seriously?'

'No, because we have to take it as seriously as she does,' Gertrude answered despondently. 'There has been nothing childish about her feeling for Harry. We can hope that the winter in London will make her forget him – though I'm not sure how when he and Emily now live there on Louise's doorstep – and we can wait for some nice, determined young man to fight his way through the thicket and rescue the enchanted princess, but . . .'

'You aren't very confident?'

'Well, let us say that he will have to be very determined.' She was silent for a moment. 'You see, she's very like Ned. Affection given is given for ever. That's what frightens me for both of them. Ned has given *his* heart to Anita . . . Anita and Providence, and he can't see any way of having both. I hope she realizes that and comes back without waiting to be asked, because Ned might never feel that he *can* ask her to share a future that looks so uncertain.'

William blinked but didn't make the mistake of asking how she knew. His wife always *did* know much more than he, but instead of being irritated by the fact, he found it something to be thankful for.

'Can we, at least, not worry about Sybil, or does she also have problems that I'm too self-absorbed to notice?'

'You're not *self*-absorbed, only given over almost entirely to the business of painting . . . it's not the same thing,' Gertrude said kindly. 'But Sybil has been keyed up about something ever since she came back from Switzerland, and whatever it is prevents her from settling down here. She's offhand to the point of rudeness with the pleasant young men who run after her; she's bored with Haywood's End, but not sure what to do about it. Perhaps it would help if you took her with you to Paris.'

'I'd much rather take you.'

She had anticipated the suggestion and so it was not difficult to smile at him and shake her head. 'Thank you, but I'm not bored and wondering what to do about it. Please ask Sybil . . . she would like to be able to talk French again.' After a moment she returned to another problem that her husband *was* aware of. 'William, I know we're supposed to have made up our minds, but are we right in spending money on Providence instead of saving it for the bank?' The fact that the decision had been taken and work was about to start didn't stop her worrying; it was one of the many differences between men and women, she thought. For them, a decision once taken belonged to the past, it wasn't something still alive, and susceptible to every change of mood that beset a woman.

William rumpled his hair and looked puzzled, as she'd known he would. 'My dear, how can we *not* be right? Providence can't be allowed to crumble indefinitely, mortgage or not; and God knows it's time the running of the house was made easier for you and the staff.'

'I realize that . . . at least I agree about the crumbling, but . . .'

'There are no buts about it,' he said with unusual firmness. 'We haven't money enough to redeem the mortgage, but we can and must repair and modernize the house before it's too late. Putting matters at their worst, your father would tell you that the bank is much more likely to call in its loan on a neglected property than on one kept in good order.'

'I hadn't quite thought of *that*,' Gertrude admitted. 'Very well, I shall be grateful for the new tiles and stonework. Emmie, of course, needs no persuading to enjoy her new cooking-range, and for Ethel and Bess "the electrics" are something magical, like the coming of a new dawn!'

'Hodges refused the offer of electric light in *his* quarters. His excuse was that the horses wouldn't like it! You can't accuse him of resisting change – he's just convinced that it has nothing to do with him, and slightly disappointed that it should have anything to do with *us*. Even if we were suddenly very rich it would be out of the question to acquire a motor-car while he's still here . . . he hasn't yet forgiven the late King for consenting to ride in one.'

'Talking of riches, what did you decide about the sale of the estate cottages?'

William frowned. 'I'm afraid I don't like the idea, and nor does Hubert. Your father is right to agree with Arthur Thornley that financially it would be a sensible thing to do – there are fewer labourers to be housed than there were, and there are people in Birmingham looking for homes outside the city. But I'd far rather see the people who remain at Haywood's End given the vacant space . . . they've been crowded six to a cottage for generations. Apart from that, strangers bringing different habits and different views would weaken village traditions that have survived for centuries. They may be doomed in the end but I don't feel entitled to hasten the process. Ned will have to make his own choice when the time comes, but I believe he will continue to think as I do.'

'My father is torn – he *feels* as you do, but thinks as Arthur does.'

William smiled at the memory of a recent conversation with his neighbour. 'It amused Thornley to suggest that I'm a die-hard feudalist at heart, who wants to go on playing Squire! My dislike of strangers in the village who won't know their place in the scheme of things is much the same, according to Arthur, as Hodges's refusal to accept electricity. I'm afraid there may even be a little truth in the accusation.'

Gertrude thought he sounded more interested in this possibility than in the mortgage – it was another difference between the sexes: the male forever intrigued by ideas, the female obsessed with strictly practical matters. Her dreams were often haunted by visions of money – streams of sovereigns like rivers of gold that unfortunately were always flowing away from them, and showers of coins falling into the moat that became simply yellow leaves again as fast as she tried to trap them in Ned's old butterfly net.

She didn't realize that her face looked wistful until William suddenly put his arms on her shoulders, making her meet his eyes. 'My dear, do you understand? It isn't just the safekeeping of Providence, for ourselves and our children, that is important; it's the preservation of a way of life in which *everyone* is important – Hubert in his church, Matthew in his forge, Biddle and Hodges, Queenie Briggs and mad old Curly Benson, and the village children growing up knowing that they belong at Haywood's End. Destroy that by bringing in strangers and we destroy rural England.'

Gertrude told herself that she would think no more of rivers of gold. She kissed him, knowing that he was right even when cold logic seemed to be on the side of Arthur Thornley.

When William invited Sybil to accompany him to Paris he thought for a moment that she was about to refuse, although refusing would make her even less happy. He hoped he was right in exerting a little unfair pressure. 'Your mother won't leave Providence when there are to be workmen tampering with it, but she also thinks I'm too absent-minded to be allowed in Paris on my own.'

His daughter's pale face broke into a grin. 'Mama is right! I'd better come.'

They set off on a still, cold morning towards the end of

the winter, William excited as a child by the prospect of seeing the work of the new artists who were carrying painting another step forward, or at least another step away from the past. Above all, he wanted to see what the genius of Vincent Van Gogh had made of the violent landscapes of Provence – with cypress trees like black flames against the sun-baked colours of the south that were never seen in the northern light of England. He tried to explain this to Sybil as they braved the cold air on deck to watch the coast of England vaporize into a grey and silver mist. She listened with apparent interest to the story of Van Gogh's brief, tormented life, but the sound of her father's voice was a gentle background noise, scarcely making any impression on inward thought. Her mind was locked on one object, with the concentration of a medieval mystic searching for God. She was making this cold, uncomfortable journey simply in order to see Henri Blanchard again; seeing him, she would know whether or not the handful of memories she'd been carefully tending for the past two years would wither and die in the harsh light of reality.

The steamer seemed to push itself too reluctantly through the water, and the train from Calais chugged towards Paris with a slow deliberation she found hard to bear. 'Hurry, train . . . *please* hurry . . .' the words were a litany in her brain, repeated over and over again as she stared out of the window at the wintry Normandy countryside.

The following morning at breakfast in the hotel William was moved to notice the pallor of her face.

'It was a long cold journey yesterday, my dear. Perhaps I should leave you here to rest this morning?'

She tried to smile at him. 'You forget, Papa . . . I'm here to take care of *you*; in any case Ned would tell you that it requires more than a journey to tire me – he's kind enough to say that I have the stamina of an ox! So there is no reason for me not to come with you.'

They set out for the gallery on foot, William content to be back in a city he found more congenial than London, Sybil convinced that the hat she had finally decided upon had been the worst she could have chosen after all. Should she wrench it off and throw it in the gutter? She might have done so, but before she expected them to have arrived, they were stopping at an elegant door and there was no time to do anything but follow her father into Henri's gallery. She'd been a schoolgirl when she'd last seen him, still trapped in the cocoon of Mlle Lebrun's seminary; she was experienced now, coolly elegant, and confident that with less than Emily's beauty she could make more than Emily's effect. Then Henri, seemingly unchanged, was bowing over her hand, and newly-won coolness and confidence had no chance at all when her heart was beating in her throat and he was staring at her.

His opinion was that she'd grown more self-confidently attractive and therefore less like Gertrude. She had inherited her mother's taste, and a velvet cap pierced by a glowing cock pheasant's feather became her to perfection. It should have charmed him, *would* have done so if the picture that remained stubbornly in his memory hadn't been of something else altogether – a simple white straw hat perched on dark hair.

'Dare I call you *p'tite* now? I think not . . . it must be *chère* mamselle!'

'I see nothing wrong with Sybil myself,' she pointed out as calmly as possible. 'After all, I have every intention of calling you Henri.'

Her intentions didn't stop there, but this wasn't the moment to say so. She watched while he greeted her father, and saw that she'd been wrong to think him unchanged. Silver now shone in his black hair where the light caught it, and the lines that ran from nostrils to jaw were more deeply engraved. It should have been an expressive face, but self-discipline had taught it to be unrevealing. She couldn't be sure that he was glad to have her there with her father, didn't know anything that he was thinking. All she did know was that memory hadn't lied about his power to affect her. His brown hands sketched a gesture in the air and she shivered as if she had felt them on her own body. He turned to smile at her and her heart stumbled in case what *she* had been thinking was known to him.

'*Chère* Sybil, we neglect you in all this talk about painting, but there is much to discuss. You must go with your father this afternoon to an important exhibition, but for now I shall offer you a charming escort, my young colleague Philippe Duclos. He shall have the privilege of introducing you to Paris.'

The charming escort was already coming towards them, obedient to a flick of his employer's black eyebrow. There was nothing to be done; she must smile and hold out her hand to Monsieur Duclos. But before allowing herself to be led towards the door, she turned back to Henri.

'This afternoon seems to be bespoken, but will *you* please give me tea tomorrow? This time we don't have to ask Mlle Lebrun's permission.'

It was an odd and touching mixture of challenge and plea, and a deliberate reminder of a time when she hadn't been quite grown-up, in case he hadn't observed the difference in her now. Henri was aware of all this, and of more besides. She had come with her father not just by chance, or because she passionately desired to see the Tour Eiffel. The coward's way would have been to avoid a situation that would cause him embarrassment and her much pain, but she deserved something more than shabby evasion.

'Tea tomorrow by all means,' he agreed finally, 'but I am also hoping that you and your father will dine with me this evening.'

Her face under the velvet cap flushed with delicate colour at the thought of it. Not for the first time Philippe Duclos wondered why his middle-aged employer should have this extraordinarily beautifying effect on women. He was himself no less ready to perform this service for them, but they remained unaware of the fact.

Sybil allowed herself to be taken to the Île de la Cité and Notre Dame, smiled at an escort who was enslaved without difficulty and had no idea that she thought all the time of nothing but the evening ahead. She spent the afternoon with her father, staring at the exhibited work of artists he called Post-Impressionist. She remembered not a word of what he said to her about Cézanne's sun-drenched landscapes and the primitive strangeness of Paul Gauguin's Tahitian women, but long afterwards she found that she could recall the paintings vividly in her mind's eye. She could recall everything about that visit to Paris.

She dressed for dinner in a gown that Aunt Louise had given her – its topaz-coloured silk threw a warm lustre over her skin, and made a perfect foil for her dark eyes and elaborate coil of shining black hair. Anticipation, longing and fear combined to ignite in her the special radiance that is born of moments on which life's happiness seems to depend. William, waiting in the hotel lobby, watched her descend the staircase and felt humbled by her beauty. He could scarcely believe that this dazzling creature had been the child and schoolgirl whose whims and moods in the past had both puzzled and enchanted him.

'I'm proud to be your escort, mademoiselle,' he said as she reached him. She smiled but unexpectedly found nothing to say, and he was visited by the strange idea that his self-confident daughter was feeling nervous.

Henri's dinner for them was arranged in the private room of an hotel, since his own home was outside Paris. There were three other guests, introduced as Jacques Courbeville and his wife, and Mme Courbeville's sister, the Comtesse de Vilmorin. They spoke the same flawless English as their host, they were elegant and cultivated people, and Sybil took her part in talking to them with a smile on her lips and despair slowly eating its way into her heart.

The comtesse, halfway between Henri's age and her own, she supposed, was sophisticated, feminine perfection, from the silver-gilt hair swirled in a coronet round her head to the paillette-strewn hem of her black evening gown. She was not simply a guest; she was there by right because of her position in Henri's life. Every nuance in her voice when she spoke to him, every glance in his direction, said without concealment or apology that she was there because she was his mistress. Mme Courbeville was puzzled that for once her sister trembled on the edge of overplaying a long-familiar role, but in justice to Héloise de Vilmorin, it was not her fault.

Sybil talked, smiled, ate a little, laughed slightly more than was necessary, and prayed to God above to help her endure pain without disgrace. When at last it was over she said a composed good night to Henri but addressed her thanks, couched in the perfect French that a sudden flare of pride insisted upon, to the woman she recognized as her hostess. It was the moment when he came closest to loving her.

Afterwards, alone with him in her own home, Héloise stared at his set face. 'I think you did not enjoy the evening – let us hope, at least, that it achieved its purpose.'

He took a long time to answer her. 'Oh yes, it did that. You were magnificent, my dear. Between us we murdered hope and innocence quite brilliantly.'

'That *is* what you wanted, isn't it?'

A little shrug answered her. 'Of course!' He smiled, but she thought it was at some unamusing joke he had discovered about himself. 'Shall we now continue our performance in bed, my dear Héloise?'

It didn't surprise him to receive a note from Sybil the following morning, excusing herself from the arrangement to have tea with him. He saw William again to talk at length about his next exhibition in London, but Sybil was unable to accompany her father, being too busy renewing acquaintance with a French friend met at Mlle Lebrun's. When they left the hotel to return to England an astonished chambermaid received as a gift a gown such as she would never have dreamed of possessing – of topaz-coloured silk, it was, and beautiful beyond belief . . . of a certainty, the English were very strange.

Sybil returned to London in a mood of inward-looking despair that seemed to isolate her from the rest of the family. She didn't want help, wouldn't have sympathy; all they could do for her, it seemed, was to leave her alone. She never once mentioned the name of Henri, and it didn't occur to Gertrude that the man who had nearly wrecked her own peace of mind should have had a similar power over her daughter.

When Sybil announced that she was inviting herself to stay with Charlotte in London, it seemed likely that whatever happiness eluded her lay there, and she felt impelled to pursue it.

If pursuit had been all that was required, Sybil would have camped on the doorstep of Henri's gallery. But she had left Paris with the bitterness of rejection in her mouth. Now, she had to find something to do that would fill the endless hours of every day. In London there was at least the excitement of watching – no, of *joining* the suffragette movement. It was time and more that women refused to accept passively what men laid down for them.

Her uncle, like other members of the Government, was a prime target for harassment, and she knew Aunt Louise's opinion of the women who plagued him and his colleagues, but it seemed a cowardly reason not to help the female cause. She was quickly embroiled more than she had meant to be, found herself one morning taking a leading part in a violent disturbance outside the House of Commons, and ended by being arrested with a dozen other women.

When she was released at her uncle's intervention and brought back to Cadogan Square, she was confronted by an icily infuriated Louise Trentham.

'You are feeling proud of yourself, no doubt,' said her aunt contemptuously. 'It's not a *rare* accomplishment nowadays to hurl bricks through windows and set fire to letter-boxes, but not all of us can follow where Mrs Pankhurst and her daughters lead.'

Sybil was aware of having gravely embarrassed her uncle and severely frightened herself; she would have given all she possessed to be at Providence, being teased by Ned for being such a mutt and loved by her mother in spite of being a most troublesome daughter. But she was in Cadogan Square, facing an outraged woman whose hospitality she had abused, and whose overworked husband she had seriously troubled. Even so, she couldn't allow herself to quail.

'Aunt, I'm not proud of getting arrested, but I'm not ashamed, either,' she insisted tremulously. 'These tactics are forced on us by blinkered, self-satisfied men who refuse to accept that our cause is just.'

'Your cause may be just, but what you are pleased to call your tactics are deplorable. Violence has become an end in itself. For many of the women you are consorting with, enfranchisement has become incidental to their protest about other things – their homes, their husbands, their lives . . . anything they want to repudiate.'

'Whatever their reasons, they will succeed in the end,' Sybil said doggedly. 'They'll win the vote on behalf of women who haven't a fraction of their courage.'

'Or a fraction of their stupidity! Can't you see that they have actually delayed getting what they appear to want by disgusting the very men who would otherwise have passed the necessary legislation months, if not years, ago? If you are incapable of understanding that, I am sadly disappointed in your intelligence.'

Her words fell cold as flakes of ice, unanswerable as the voice of doom. Sybil shivered, struggled against a desire to be violently sick, and burst into tears instead. All the sadness and bitter sense of Henri's rejection merged with the strains imposed by pretending herself a militant suffragette, and overwhelmed her in a storm of weeping. She was unaware of her aunt leaving the room, and only conscious at last of being slumped in a chair, exhausted and empty of everything but the knowledge of her own failure.

Louise Trentham's hands gently raised her head. 'The English panacea, my dear . . . a cup of tea!' Her voice had become kind, making belligerence impossible.

'I'm sorry, Aunt . . . I didn't stop to think this morning . . . about you and poor Uncle Alec.' She hesitated but, having started, felt impelled to go on. 'I *am* convinced that we should be allowed the vote, and it seemed cowardly not to help, but I kept thinking all the time that we were going the wrong way about it. I also got involved because I very badly needed something to do.' That was all she need say, all she intended to say, but she heard herself make another confession. 'I expect it will seem absurd to you, but I fell in love with Henri Blanchard, years ago in Lucerne. When I went to Paris with Papa I convinced myself that I could enchant him into loving me, because I wanted it so much. It wasn't just imagination or wishful thinking . . . there *was* a link between us; I felt it every time he visited the school in Lucerne. I thought that all I had to do was grow up a little more, and wait for the moment when he would suddenly *see* me. But in Paris with Papa, he quite r . . . refused to b . . . be enchanted, and I was made to feel a child again.' She tried to smile, remembering that she must have sounded just like Lucy, who hadn't been able to grow up fast enough either. Rather than weep again, she sipped her tea and didn't notice the expression on her aunt's face.

Irony piled on irony till mere mortals couldn't bear the weight of it . . . 'as flies to wanton boys are we to the gods; they kill us for their sport'. Louise closed her eyes against the vision of what was now required of her; surely their sport could do without this final humiliation? But she knew that it wasn't so. If truth would help Sybil to recover, she must be given it.

'There's nothing absurd about having fallen in love with Henri Blanchard,' Louise said deliberately. 'I should have expected you to do it, because I did it myself and, although you might not have noticed it, we are very alike. I had more reason to be sensible than you because I was older and already married at the time, but the heart has its own reasons and they have little to do with common sense or prudence or morality. I was rejected, too, and found it harder to bear than anything I'd ever known, but in the end even the most eager heart accepts the futility of offering itself where it isn't wanted. Eventually it finds that it can attach itself elsewhere and then it loses the dreadful feeling of having been spurned.'

'Why did Henri refuse *you*?'

'Because he was truly in love with another woman here. She was already married, so *he* was left unhappy, too.'

There was a long silence in the room while Sybil pondered the astonishing thing her aunt had said. It *was* very astonishing that a woman she had always imagined to be cool and unemotional could have allowed herself to be swept by passion – and for a man who was the antithesis of Alec Trentham. Unable to think of her aunt in these terms, Sybil's dazed mind considered Henri instead, and the conversation she had once had with Maud Roberts. She was certain now that she knew who it was Henri had loved in England – it explained, as nothing else would, the link she had sensed between herself and him.

He had had to learn to offer *his* eager heart elsewhere, but what of her own mother, tied by affection and duty to her family at Providence? Suppose *she* had wanted something else? Sybil thought nothing was what it seemed, especially in the matter of human relationships; and the most mistaken idea of all was to suppose that her own or anyone else's experience was self-contained; all joy and sadness met and mingled, like underground streams forever running into one another.

Her aunt's voice finally broke the silence between them. 'I said that we were alike, you and I. The hardest thing for both of us to accept is failure; but failure is only a disgrace if we allow it to frighten us off making a new attempt on life.'

Sybil was aware that confessing to her own failure was the most generous thing Louise Trentham could have done, but before she could say so, her aunt spoke in a different tone of voice that said the subject of Henri Blanchard was closed.

'If you want something to do and are anxious to help the suffrage movement, why not join the National Union of Suffrage Societies? Their propaganda activities are law-abiding, moderate, and effective . . . *they* will achieve by persuasion what the militants fail to get by violence.' Her face broke into a charming smile. 'I happen to know they would welcome a new and active member, because I'm involved with them!'

Here was another revelation – Louise Trentham wanted women to have the vote as much as anyone, even if she refused to accept the militants' argument that the end justified *any* means. Sybil nodded, then suddenly got up and kissed her aunt. 'Thank you,' she said simply. The conversation was over, and neither of them ever referred to it again.

She remained in London after that, actively but peacefully working for the suffragist movement, aware in some hidden corner of her heart that it was easier to be with a woman who had also been rejected by Henri; her mother had been the woman he'd wanted, and it was hard to see her now without remembering the fact.

Gertrude accepted with sadness the fact that her elder daughter preferred London to Providence, and did her best to explain to William that they couldn't expect all their children to enjoy country life. Lucy had settled down there again, content to be absorbed in the peaceful procession of days at Haywood's End, and Ned had immersed himself in a single-minded determination to retrieve his inheritance. Gertrude doubted if he ever forgot his other love, but he was a countryman prepared to take one step at a time towards achieving what he wanted.

William's London exhibition the following year finally established his reputation. It might also have established his financial success if it hadn't almost immediately been followed by the assassination in remote Sarajevo of the Archduke Franz Ferdinand. The murder of the heir to the Austro-Hungarian throne by a Serb was the final irreversible move on the board . . . the end of the Continental game of threat and counter-threat, thrust and sudden retreat to safety.

From the end of June to the beginning of August the sequence of events had the relentless rhythm of a Greek tragedy approaching its climactic moment of destruction:

Austria's ultimatum to Serbia, Russia's mobilization in support of her fellow Slavs, Germany's peremptory command that Russia should stop mobilizing and that France shouldn't start . . .

'Can war be averted, even now?' Gertrude asked William anxiously. 'Sir Edward has suggested another London conference, and the miracle worked last year.'

His face answered her before he put denial into words. 'My dear, there isn't the slightest hope this time. What has happened in the Balkans is only the froth on the surface of a cauldron that has been a long time in coming to boiling point. The Kaiser is in the hands of his military men, and the German High Command has been intent on war for years, with or without an excuse.'

'Well, let Austria fight Russia for the Balkans, and let France and Germany destroy each other if they must . . . surely there is no need for *us* to get involved?'

'There is every need,' William said sombrely. 'We were a signatory to the Treaty that guaranteed the sovereignty of Belgium. Germany was another, but she will break that treaty when she overruns Belgium in order to invade France. Even if our national honour were not involved, we cannot allow Germany to control the Channel ports. Our very life depends on keeping the Channel open.'

He was right, and the engines of war were already in motion. Germany declared war on Russia and France, and ignored a final request from the British Government that she would guarantee to respect the neutrality of Belgium. Even before the time limit of the ultimatum had expired at midnight on 4 August, a German army was invading Belgium. Armageddon had arrived.

CHAPTER TWENTY-FIVE

Emily was enjoying married life. Her dear Harry had duties to perform, of course, but in running their small house in Chelsea, so had she. It pleased her more than anything she had ever known to create for him and his friends a charming, comfortable refuge from the rigours of regimental life, and part of her pleasure came from the fact that her success was unexpected. It had always seemed a handicap being such a fool compared with Syb, but Heaven's grace had brought her Harry and allowed her to discover the thing she *could* do, which was to make him happy. Life was unclouded happiness. But the war came, and he was a soldier.

For Harry it was marriage that made a difference, not war. Only a little while ago he'd have welcomed a change from the routine of peacetime military life, which eventually grew boring in England. But now there was sweet red-headed Emily to confront with the news that the regiment was under orders to sail for France. He still hadn't decided how to set about telling her when she spared him the trouble.

'You're going to France, but don't quite like to mention it!'

Harry wrapped his arms about her. 'Not for long, sweetheart. Everyone says the war will be over by Christmas.' He looked over the top of her head while he said it because his own opinion was different, and she had an inconvenient knack of knowing when he was prevaricating. She knew it now, but if he wanted her to believe what everyone else believed, she would do her best.

'When do you leave?'

'Dearest, at the weekend, I'm afraid . . . of all times to have to go.'

Emily would have liked to burst into tears, but she had vowed to herself that she would be no more troublesome than the rest of the regimental wives. It was necessary to smile at him.

'Well, there's no reason why the War Office should know that it happens to be my birthday.'

He kissed her so gratefully that she knew he'd feared a scene that would upset them both. Really, she was doing rather well, but her mother-in-law had been right to warn her that being a soldier's wife was very hard.

'Sir John French has command,' Harry explained – 'one cavalry division and four infantry. It's not a great deal to offer the French, but there won't be anything wrong with the quality of what we send.'

He said goodbye to her three days later and she didn't weep until Louise Trentham called to take her to Cadogan Square for a day that was also her twenty-first birthday.

Harry's unit embarked that afternoon, and it wasn't until late at night in a billet on the outskirts of Dunkirk that he found what Emily had hidden in his pocket – a beautiful miniature Book of Common Prayer, bound in soft leather. On the flyleaf something was inscribed in her own hand: the pre-battle request framed by a much earlier soldier, the Earl of Lindsey, who'd served the King in the Civil War:

'Oh Lord, Thou knowest how busy I must be today.

If I forget Thee, do not Thou forget me.'

Harry favoured this man-to-man approach to God, but the image it conjured up of his wife carefully copying out the lines for him made him feel sick with longing for her. Soldiering was for single men, not for those who went to war leaving their hearts behind them.

His first letters took a long time to reach her; by the time they did she knew what everyone else at home roughly knew. The British Expeditionary Force had advanced into Belgium until, at Mons, it had collided with the German 1st Army sweeping down to encircle the French from the north. The British divisions, hopelessly outnumbered, had fought until the retreat of the French to the south of them had left them isolated and bound to retreat themselves or be wiped out. At Ypres, with the vital Channel ports at their back, they had fought again and held the German advance. The prize was invaluable but the price was the virtual destruction of the small army that had sailed to France. Harry, exhausted and battle-worn, was still alive, but more than half his friends who had enjoyed Emily's little house were dead. As winter closed in the fighting died down, but there was no more talk of the war being over in a month or two.

Emily went to Barham to spend Christmas with her family but she made the most of every excuse to visit the Wyndhams at Providence.

'I shouldn't say so, Syb, but Mama is a sore trial. She spends the time either weeping whenever she thinks of Harry, or complaining because I don't agree to close the house and stay at Barham. I *am* going to close the house, but only so that I can join the VAD. If I were carrying Harry's child, it would be different, but to sit waiting, doing nothing, is more than I can bear. After three months' training I can volunteer to go to France – I shall feel closer to him there.'

She spoke with a sad composure that indicated the extent to which she had changed. Sybil recognized that her dear, featherbrained friend had suddenly grown up.

'We shall either have to wait a bit or lie about our age,' Sybil said calmly. 'I made enquiries – they don't send anyone under the age of twenty-three.'

Emily stared at her. 'You mean you're joining too?'

'Of course. Harry wouldn't like it if I let you go wandering about France on your own.'

'Oh, Syb . . .' Emily's eyes filled with tears, for which she hastily apologized, explaining that her mother's weeping habit must be catching. 'What about things here, though . . . can they manage without you?'

'For all the good I do, they certainly can. Lucy's the useful one . . . I just get in the way when I try to help, not being agriculturally-minded. Ned never stops working but I'm almost sure *he* won't be here much longer. Mama doesn't allow us to mention the enrolment office in Warwick for fear we remind him that it's there. But he'll go before long and then her heart will quietly break in two.'

Emily nodded, but her mind was on other matters. 'Lucy has always been on my conscience, which was terrible because I loved *all* your family. Now perhaps it's even harder for her than it is for me; at least I'm entitled to know what is happening to Harry. I don't have to agonize about him in secret.'

'My mother says Lucy has a tenacious heart, and I think it's true, but I have the feeling she's been learning by herself something that I couldn't manage without help. Maud Roberts taught me that nothing we experience is wasted, even the bits that hurt; but it was Aunt Louise, surprisingly, who made me see that loving one person in one way needn't prevent you loving someone else differently. Lucy will always love Harry because that's the way she's made. But now he's part of *everything* she loves, and, as old Biddle would say, she's a "powerful" lover! Not like me . . . I'm downright miserly when it comes to giving away love or friendship.'

Emily smiled at her. 'If you say so, though I hadn't actually noticed!'

Sybil was right about Ned. A week later he returned from a visit to Warwick and immediately went in search of his mother and put his arms around her.

'I expect you can guess what I've been and gone and done.' He said it lightly, trying to smile at her.

She was silent for a moment, hearing in her memory the voice of a small boy saying 'of course I'm going to stay at Providence, but perhaps I could have some fighting first'. She had thanked Heaven then that the Boer War was nothing to do with them, but the gods had caught up with her at last.

'You've volunteered,' she said bleakly. 'Oh Ned, *why*, when we need you so desperately here?'

'Men are needed in France as well.'

'I know, but anyone can fight. Not everyone can do what you do here, and people must be fed.'

'Grandpa Hoskins and Lucy will help Papa, and so will Moffat.' He saw tears gather in his mother's eyes, but she wasn't aware of them enough to brush them away. He loved her very much and hated to hurt her, but at the same time felt himself to be at peace again after weeks of trying to make up his mind what he should do.

'I *have* to go, Mama. The men in the village are offering themselves. You wouldn't have a Wyndham stay behind, now would you?' His face was grave but looked so young that the very idea of him going off to fight a war ought to have been unthinkable.

'I'd have you stay as far behind as possible.' She knew it wasn't what the mother of such a son as Ned was supposed to say, but the confession was torn out of her. He was kind enough not to look disappointed, and anxious to make her understand.

'It's like this, you see . . . I'm not a great one for reading, as you and Father are, but a chap called Rupert Brooke who was at Rugby a bit before me wrote something that seems to explain how I feel:

"Now, God be thanked who has matched us with His hour,

And caught our youth and wakened us from sleeping . . ." There's more of it, but I can't remember the rest. We *have* been sleeping, Mama, and the world has become a mucky, feverish sort of place. It's time we got it cleaned up a bit.'

She knew what he meant, and couldn't bring herself to damage his shining faith by saying that the slaughter of youth sounded more like a pagan sacrifice to evil gods than a twentieth-century remedy for the world's running sores. She kissed his cheek and tried to smile at him.

'All right, dear Ned. Go and do your bit of cleaning up, but please come back safely to Providence.'

He left as the new year dawned, to join the Warwickshire Regiment, and took with him Gertrude's peace of mind and all the lovely colours that she found in life; everything now looked grey, and she knew it wouldn't change until he was safely returned to them.

His departure seemed to open a gap through which all too many others were remorselessly sucked. Sybil went away with Emily to learn the rudiments of nursing, and village girls who would normally have scattered no further than the big houses in the neighbourhood trickled out of Haywood's End one after another to work in Thornley's munitions factories. Even Sid Moffat's eldest son, barely turned eighteen, insisted that 'if young Squire were goin', he mun go too'. Gertrude felt in some way to blame whenever she caught sight of Sid's drawn face. If she could have persuaded Ned to stay, Norman Moffat might have understood that growing food was at least as important as rushing off to fight.

She tried not to envy the Thornleys a sensible son who refused to be stampeded into volunteering, no matter how many posters with Lord Kitchener's stern face on them stared accusingly at anyone who remained at home. But at Bicton one afternoon she realized that she didn't fully understand the matter when Jane apologized for seeming depressed.

'You must wonder what *I've* got to complain about,' said Jane. 'Of course I'm thankful Frank's still here, but in order to make up for not volunteering he's killing himself in another way – with work. He's so sick at heart that I could weep, just looking at him. I threatened to pin a label on him – "My country needs me *here*!" – but although he knows it's true, it wouldn't stop him leaving if he thought they'd take a man who can't see his hand in front of his face without strong spectacles.'

Gertrude nodded, shamed into remembering that there were more anxieties than those that filled her own waking and sleeping mind. She couldn't bear to talk about Ned, by now already in France, but shared a minor worry with Jane instead.

'Sybil's at a training hospital in London, with Emily Trentham. She writes quite cheerfully at the moment, but I can't help feeling it's the last work in the world that she's suited to doing. Lucy is the one who enjoys performing small, humble services for other people – she's always helping someone in the village. I think the work of a VAD recruit is bound to be humble, and Sybil will either get bored with the drudgery of it or argue with anyone who tries to give her orders.'

Jane smiled but shook her head. 'I know they're *your* daughters, love, but I think the right girl has gone. If there are horrors to be endured, and it stands to reason there will be, Sybil will endure them better. In any case it's Lucy's heart that's in Providence. She'll help William and your father keep it going for Ned. I'm thinking whoever she marries will have to realize that he can't separate her from Haywood's End.'

Gertrude was about to say that she sometimes felt her younger daughter had made up her mind not to marry at all, but an echo chimed in her mind of a young Gertrude Hoskins telling Maud that *she* had come to that conclusion. Girls were not to be trusted in the matter of decisions about marrying. Lucy, if asked, would have said simply that she must help look after Providence for as long as Ned was away. She worked the long hours that Sid Moffat and his two land girls worked, and did her best to stop Grandpa Hoskins and her father wearing themselves out in an effort to take the place of the young men who had gone to war.

By the late spring of 1915 the bloody fighting raging again in France seemed set to go on for ever. The terrible fixed pattern of trench warfare had been set – two wired, mined, and cratered lines stretched from the coast of Belgium as far south as Luxemberg; between the lines, fought for as if it were heaven instead of the nethermost region of hell, was something they called No Man's Land. Young men in their thousands fought and fell to push their own line forward a few futile yards, and lost a week later what inhuman effort had briefly enabled them to call theirs. Those who had gone joyously into battle, like Ned, and still remained alive, now fought and suffered and endured for the sake of each other; not because they believed in any grander reason.

Harry came home on leave a haunted veteran, who asked no more of life than to be allowed to walk through the peaceful English greenness of the valley, holding Emily's hand. He came to Providence and the sight of Lucy expertly steering a tractor even made him smile.

'Let's hope I bump into Ned again,' he said to his uncle. 'He'll have to believe it when I tell him I've actually seen what young Lucy's up to nowadays.'

'She's our rock at the moment,' William said simply. 'Sid Moffat works like three men, and George Hoskins and I do our best, but Lucy keeps things going here.'

'No painting, Uncle?'

William Wyndham shook his head. 'I'll start again when Ned gets home. Young men are making a much greater sacrifice than that, but it's all I can do.' He stared at his nephew, thinking that Harry looked ten years older than his real age. The easy laughter and comfortable certainty that life was bound to be good to him had been wiped from his face, leaving it thin and stern.

'Are things very bad out there, Harry? Ned's letters somehow manage to sound cheerful, but they tell us little more than the fact that he was alive when he wrote them. I should like to know for myself, but I can't ask the question in front of Gertrude. It takes all the strength she possesses to carry on, as it is.'

'Things are sometimes unspeakably terrible, when a push is on; sometimes just unspeakably tense and uncomfortable when we are in the line but both sides are only watching each other and waiting for the next flare-up. The worst thing of all, perhaps, is the feeling that we shall be playing this lunatic, bloody game until both sides run out of players . . .'

William turned his head away to mumble, 'If you *should* see Ned, just say we . . . love him.'

When Harry had gone away again and the normal routine

of work and anxiety had reasserted itself, Lucy took herself over to Warwick one afternoon to visit her former governess. Amelia Lacey's war effort was to replace a teacher who had gone to fight, and there were times when she couldn't help thinking that John Stokes, wherever he was, had the easier cross to bear.

'Those children,' she said tremulously to Lucy, 'so naughty, so wickedly determined not to learn anything that I am able to teach them. It seems sinful to complain when *everything* is so terrible, but sometimes I think they are more than I can bear.'

Her fingers shook among the teacups, and Lucy saw nothing fanciful in the idea that sad Lacey was a victim not only of the war, but of life itself. She was middle-aged, and poor, and gentle; she deserved better than a couple of rented rooms in someone else's house and the daily purgatory of confronting a class of unruly twelve-year-olds who either ridiculed or frightened her.

'Come back to Providence,' Lucy said impulsively. 'There's plenty you could do to help, and Mama would insist if she knew how unhappy you are here.'

Amelia fought the temptation of Satan and managed to put it behind her. 'Oh, Lucy, how kind! But I feel it is my duty to stay here. It may only be the widow's . . . well, in my case, of course, the spinster's – mite, but perhaps even *that* is better than nothing at all.'

'It's not just better than nothing; it's heroic,' Lucy said smilingly. 'Promise you'll come if the little horrors get too much for you, but meanwhile why not try shouting at them . . . you'd have the advantage of surprise!'

Miss Lacey agreed to remember both suggestions, and more cheerfully watched Lucy get ready to leave. Outside, the bicycle that had brought her there had developed an ominously flat tyre, and its only response to energetic pumping was a derisive hiss of escaping air – five miles to push it to Haywood's End unless someone from the village with a horse and cart overtook her on the way home.

She'd gone barely a dozen yards before a voice spoke

behind her. 'I've got the gig at the George, Lucy – leave me your bicycle and I'll follow you there.'

Frank Thornley caught up with her and she turned to smile gratefully at him. 'What luck! I was resigning myself to a long walk; but is there any reason why we can't go to the George together?'

He was making up his mind what to say when Fate, with perfect timing for once, settled the matter for him. A girl not much older than Lucy herself pushed her way between them and thrust something at Frank. It lay in the palm of his hand, delicate but obscene . . . a small white feather that fluttered slightly as if it were ashamed of being there. With his other hand now holding the bicycle upright, Frank was trapped behind it but Lucy was free to move and there was nothing he could do to stop her. She caught up with the other girl and spun her round with a hand clamped to her shoulder.

'How could you do such a wickedly cruel thing? It's monstrous . . . evil.' She was panting, not so much with the exertion of running as with horror of the thing done to a man who had no defence against it.

'Evil, is it? Why shouldn't *he* go and get himself killed? He'll be in good company . . . my husband's already there buried in Flanders mud, if he's buried at all.' She was older than Lucy had thought, or else the mad despair that filled her had taken away not only her youth but almost reason itself. 'Don't tell *me* what's wicked . . . I know! *Men* are wicked.'

'I'm very sorry about your husband, but it *is* cruel to wish everybody else dead as well. If you've got any more of those beastly things with you, please throw them away.'

The woman wrenched herself away from Lucy's hand, and a dreadful, derisive smile touched her pale mouth. 'Thanks for the advice. You look as if you know all about good and evil . . . I don't think!' She turned away and after a moment Lucy walked back to Frank. He was white-faced and furious with *her*, it seemed, not with the girl who'd tried to brand him a coward.

'That was an extremely stupid thing to do, and I'm tired of holding this damned bicycle . . . shall we now walk *together* to the George?'

'You were afraid that might happen,' Lucy said, as if he hadn't spoken. 'Has it happened before?'

'Yes; I'm getting quite accustomed to it in genteel Warwick. The working girls of Birmingham are either less patriotic or less bloodthirsty.'

She winced at the savage irony in his voice, but when she looked at his face, it was quite expressionless.

'Her husband has been killed . . .' She stopped speaking because her voice was suddenly suspended by tears and it was necessary to swallow them before she went on. Frank Thornley glanced down at her as she walked beside him. Her face was very pale beneath the freckles painted on her skin by being so much out-of-doors, and her slender neck seemed to droop under the weight of a heavy golden plait wound like a coronet about her head. Almost of its own volition his free hand fastened on her shoulder, bringing her to a halt, and he felt her trembling.

'Don't weep, please. I'm sorry I made matters worse. Forget the girl, and the feather . . . it's not important.'

She stared at him, aware of the weight of his hand and of a strange sense of familiarity; at Harry's wedding she somehow hadn't minded him knowing about her distress, and now she was with him again at a moment when the ordinary conventions of behaviour had been laid aside. The effect was to make her feel that they knew each other very well.

'Nothing's important except the effect that the war is having on us all,' she said gravely. 'Fear, hatred, despair . . . they're twisting people out of their true shape, distorting them into something unbearably ugly.'

'There *are* other things as well . . . courage, for example; there's plenty of that around, and some of it's being shown by people who would never have thought of making for themselves the claim that they were brave.'

Lucy smiled at him suddenly. 'I know! I'd been visiting

326

my old governess when you found me. Poor Lacey's form of courage is to take on an unruly school class, which for her is about the same thing as confronting a herd of stampeding bulls!'

'There you are, then; a challenge she didn't expect, but if she manages it she'll have learned something about herself she didn't suspect.'

Lucy nodded, then blushed because his hand was still holding her. 'The . . . the poor horse will be wondering where you've got to,' she said hurriedly.

Frank let go of her, but slowly, because a thought startling in its suddenness had just taken possession of his mind.

'Dear Jane Thornley tells Mama that you're working much too hard . . . and Mr Thornley as well,' Lucy offered next, because she felt nervously certain that harmless conversation was needed.

'Like you and Sir William and your grandfather and everybody else, we do what we have to do. That's why I've been in London for two days, instead of in Birmingham. The newly-appointed Minister of Munitions, Mr Lloyd George, sent for me and others like me because there's an acute, in fact a scandalous, shortage of shells and other vital items. Northcliffe and his newspapers are partly right to scream for the blood of elderly generals at the War Office, who have traditionally been responsible for munitions contracts and haven't done the job very efficiently; but in fairness to them, no-one anticipated the way in which this war was going to be fought, with massive bombardments which are theoretically supposed to make infantry advances possible.'

Lucy resolutely turned her mind from the unbearable thought of Ned and Harry at the mercy of such theories, and tried to concentrate intelligently on what Frank had begun by saying.

'So what does Mr Lloyd George want you to do? Work twenty hours a day instead of eighteen?'

A rare smile glimmered on his face, making it look almost youthful again. 'Something like that . . . but he's got the right ideas, and it's time someone had them. Labour, materials, quality controls . . . in fact everything we need, is going to be rationalized and vetted by the Government at last. It's the only way we can beat Germany, by subordinating *everything* to the war effort.'

They found the horse still waiting patiently for them at the George, and Lucy watched Frank install her bicycle carefully in the back of the gig. She thought that, unlike most people, he was considerate with pieces of machinery because he understood them; it occurred to her that he had more than once been similarly considerate with her. Did that mean that he understood *her*? He had a reputation in the neighbourhood for being unsociable by inclination, and morose when trapped by any social function he hadn't managed to avoid, but she had glimpsed now and then shy traces of a matter-of-fact kindness that he must surely have inherited from Jane Thornley. Of his father's rumbustiousness there was no sign at all, but *that*, she thought, she could more easily do without.

They were at Providence and he'd lifted her bicycle down from the back of the gig before she summoned up the courage to say, 'That business of the feather, Mr Thornley . . .' and there she stuck, not sure what she could safely add.

'My name's Frank,' he remarked briefly. 'What about the feather?'

'Don't be hurt by it,' she finished in a rush. 'The poor creature was distraught, and caught up in some dreadful pain of her own. She couldn't know how unfair it was to give it to you, of all people.'

'It was fair in its own way . . . however hard I work, and however many guns and shells our factories make, the fact remains that I stay safely here while others do not.' He answered her coolly, but he'd taken off his spectacles before doing so and she could see his eyes clearly for once; they were so full of wretchedness that she didn't stop to consider what she did, any more than she would have hesitated to comfort anyone else who mattered to her. Her mouth touched his cheek in a gentle kiss before she said, 'Thank you and the horse for bringing me home.'

'The horse and I found it a pleasure,' he murmured with difficulty. She walked away from him into the stable-yard, pushing her bicycle, and after a moment Frank slapped the horse's rump with the reins and the gig jogged back along the drive.

CHAPTER TWENTY-SIX

Sybil came off duty one morning, smelled the reviving sweetness of the air outside the hospital and decided, tired as she was, to walk to her bed in the makeshift dormitory of a local convent. Summer was dying and even within a town in Picardy that was nothing like the valley at home, she could detect scents that spoke of Providence – Biddle sparing her mother his choicest, most sharply sweet chrysanthemums for the house only because he loved her, and heaping up piles of yellowing leaves in the park to burn in fragrant smouldering bonfires. She dwelled nowadays on such memories with the intensity of a miser counting his hoard. There *had* to be a world outside the nightmare in which she now lived; a world that knew nothing of the smell of mud-encrusted uniforms, blood, and infected wounds left unattended for too long.

Her feet echoed on the stone stairs of the convent. They were going to be bitterly cold later on, but she prayed for the winter to come. It would mean a lull in the fighting that had raged all summer; there would be weeks, perhaps even a month or two, without the daily flood of stretchers arriving, among which she always looked for Ned, just as Emily's haunted eyes searched for Harry.

She fell into bed and seemed scarcely to have sunk into the exhausted sleep that blotted out the night's sights and sounds before someone was shaking her awake. It was Celia Stafford, a girl once met in Aunt Louise's drawing-room and remembered for a distinctively clear but husky voice that had sounded as a choirboy's with a cold might sound.

'Syb . . . wake *up*, for pity's sake . . . there's someone asking for you downstairs, and very nice he looks, too!'

She struggled up out of sleep with her heart thudding, scrambled into a dressing-gown, and ran downstairs. A nun sweeping the hall looked at her disapprovingly but Sybil saw only the tall uniformed man who stood waiting. She flung herself at him and his arms opened to catch her.

'Oh, Ned . . . dear Ned . . . I must have conjured you up. I was thinking about Providence on the way back from the hospital. Are you all right . . . how do you come to be here . . . tell me!'

The words poured out in a feverish rush that made him smile; she never *had* waited to hear what anyone else wanted to say. But the smile faded as they stared at one another. She was very thin, but there was something more strangely different about her; in a moment or two he pinned down what it was.

'It's your hair! Whatever happened to it?'

'I had it cut off; we *all* have – it's easier to keep clean like this.'

He considered the short dark cap of hair that swung about her face; it made her seem unfamiliar only until she smiled at him.

'Dear Ned . . . it's *lovely* to see you, but you haven't said how you come to be here.'

'I cadged a lift from Amiens. The regiment is "resting" there, but it's taken me a week to track down someone who was coming this way. He's going back again at noon. I wasted time at the hospital first, but a pleasant woman sent me up here, on a borrowed bicycle!'

Sybil led him to a door that opened on to a tiny cloistered garden. 'Sit out there. If we're in luck and Sister Marthe's on duty in the kitchen, she'll give us some coffee.'

When she returned with it Ned was sitting with his eyes closed on the stone rim of a little pool in the centre of a patch of unmown grass. A bronze cherub stared at its reflection in the water while its fat fingers played a miniature soundless harp. The autumn sunshine fell gently on Ned's face, and he seemed to be listening to the silence. He was recognizable and dear, but changed. A young man had gone away from Providence, not this tired soldier with eyes sunk back in his head, and all the bones of his face almost jutting through the skin that was stretched too tightly over them. With his cap on the ground beside him, she could see a scarcely-healed scar that ran down the side of his face from temple to jawline.

'Coffee, Ned. Marthe even found some sugar for you.' He smiled and became young Ned again.

'Where's Emily?'

'On duty, I'm afraid. We take it turn and turn about – night duty in the wards, day duty on the hospital trains that go up to Calais. They take the cases we can't deal with here that have to be sent back to England.'

Ned put the empty mug on the stone beside him and she saw that his fingers trembled slightly. 'Don't let's talk about what's happening here,' she said suddenly. 'We have to endure it, but I don't think I can manage to talk about it. I had a letter from Lucy yesterday, so I'm probably more up-to-date than you are. Did you know Jane Thornley is turning Bicton into a convalescent home, with the help of my godmother? Maud says *she* is required to revive again, by arguing with them, all the patients that Jane kills with kindness!'

'What about Providence? Father's last letter said they'd had a fine harvest. Everybody left in the village who is more or less sound in wind and limb, including old Curly, was helping to bring it in. Having caught Artie trying to mend the reaper by bashing it with a hammer, Frank Thornley now maintains the farm machinery for them! Good of him to find the time, because Mama says he practically sleeps in his factories.'

'I know . . . Lucy's letter also mentioned him. I get the feeling they've become friends, although it seems very unlikely. Frank's an important man these days, always being sent for to have discussions with a Government minister. Funny to think I once considered Arthur Thornley a dreadfully vulgar townee who had no right to be at Bicton. Now it would be hard to imagine the valley without them. Jane does an immense amount of good, and the Thornley factories employ just about everybody who isn't still working on the land. I dare say Arthur will finish up with a knighthood one of these days . . . for services rendered to the State!'

Ned grinned. 'And *that* will give you your come-uppance! Mama wasn't just snobbish about him . . . she reckoned he'd got his little boot-button eyes on Providence, but Father always maintained that it wasn't simple covetousness; Arthur thought he could take care of it better than we could.'

Sybil hesitated before asking her next question. 'Do you hear from Anita?'

'Yes . . . nothing for weeks, of course, then a whole batch of letters turns up. She does her best to sound cheerful, poor girl, but she longs to come to England.'

Sybil wondered why she didn't just come in that case, but refused to hurt Ned by saying so.

'She'd come like a shot,' he went on to explain, 'if it weren't for leaving Uncle James. Patrick married recently – a girl called Ishbel O'Toole, who is what she sounds, more Irish than American. Having been taught to hate the English so much that she's praying for the Germans to win this war, she's passed on the true faith to Patrick. You can imagine how Uncle James feels about that. They had some blazing rows on the subject before parting company for good. It's a small tragedy by today's standards, but a tragedy nonetheless, and it keeps Anita in New York.'

Sybil nodded. 'Poor Uncle James! I'm disappointed in Patrick, but not very surprised. Even at Providence he half-loved us but half-hated us as well.'

A little silence fell between them and she waited for Ned to break it. But he had closed his eyes again and sat with his face turned up to the sun, as if he craved its warmth and its promise that somewhere life went on normally . . . that there were still places where trees put forth leaves and flowers shed perfume on still air, and men didn't try to annihilate one another.

333

'Things very bad here, Syb?' he asked suddenly. 'You rather look as if they are – a bit haunted, and very tired.'

'So do you! We said we wouldn't talk about it, Ned, but what happens next?'

'Only our generals in their wisdom know. They squander men like confetti at a wedding, and just like confetti the men fall and get trampled on. It's bloody and senseless. The only thing that makes it bearable is the men themselves, but that is also the thing that makes it worse; so many of them are being wasted.' He tried to smile at her. 'Winter will set in early with any luck; then we'll only have the mud and the rats to worry about!'

She saw him glance at his watch and remembered it was almost time for him to leave. While he continued to sit in the garden she went up to the dormitory to dress hurriedly, so that she could walk back to the hospital with him. He seemed content to push the bicycle beside her in silence until they were almost there. Then he said quietly, 'It's a relief to admit what a shambles it all is, but I don't report that to Providence. Mama has enough to bear.'

'I shall say we were able to see each other, that's all.'

The motor-cyclist who had brought Ned was already waiting for him; there was only time for a painful hug before he climbed on the machine, gave her a little salute, and was whirled away. The sudden rush of air shook the leaves of the tree beside her, and she shivered as a handful of them detached themselves and made a fresh pool of crimson on the ground.

By the end of the year it was clear that the ill-fated Dardanelles campaign, intended to clear a route for supplies to Russia and to divert German troops from the Western Front to help their Turkish ally, was an expensive and nightmarish failure. One of the many men who died there, either from injury or disease, was the same poet who had put Ned's dreams into words for him. Gertrude read the notice in *The Times*, but didn't explain why it meant more than any other name in the never-ending lists of casualties.

'He was at Rugby, too,' William said sadly. 'I think he would have made a true poet if he'd been allowed to live long enough to find himself.'

She was silent for a moment, knifed by the pain that memory had the power to evoke when she least expected it . . . a picture gallery in Paris, and Henri's voice saying of William '. . . he'll be judged a true artist, perhaps even a great one.' Now, William never went near the easel in the Great Parlour, and where was Henri . . . gone for ever from their life?

William saw the sadness in her face and came to put his arms round her. 'My dearest, for the moment there's a respite from anxiety; take it, please. And let us take hope from the start of a new year. Douglas Haig is replacing Sir John French, and the Government are bringing in conscription at last. Perhaps we shall now see a final, decisive battle that will put an end to the war.'

She thought he spoke more for her comfort than his own conviction, and turned her mind away from the thought of yet another battle that had apparently still to be fought.

'Ned wouldn't recognize Providence now,' she said, staring out at the ploughed field that had once been parkland.

'No, but he'd agree that we've done what had to be done. Anyway, brown furrowed earth against a winter sky has its own kind of stark beauty.'

Gertrude smiled at him. 'Dear William . . . you're putting me to shame – so determined to be cheerful while I am sunk in gloom!' She spoke lightly with an effort it hurt him to watch. Hard, physical work out of doors which she had insisted on sharing had left her gauntly rather than elegantly thin, but it was the anxiety that kept her company day and night that had aged her face and frosted her hair with silver. He loved her more than words could say, but it was still an effort after twenty-five years to tell her so.

'You keep us and Providence going, dearest heart.' He raised her hand to his mouth and left a kiss in the palm of it. 'For gallantry!'

The tribute brought a tinge of colour to her face, but after a moment she returned to what they'd been talking about.

'As well that we and everyone else grow whatever can be grown. Alec tries to keep worries from Louise, but she knows that one of the worst of them is the German submarine campaign. Food is getting scarcer and more expensive all the time because of the number of merchant ships being sunk by torpedoes.'

'There's a crucial difference of opinion, apparently. The Admiralty persist in believing that the standard of navigation in the merchant fleet doesn't permit of their keeping station in a convoy; men like Lloyd George insist that it's the only hope of keeping sinkings within tolerable limits. The Royal Navy can't hope to shepherd individually every ship coming to a United Kingdom port.'

'It's a strange thing about so-called experts that one notices all the time,' Gertrude said reflectively. 'They know so much about their subject that decisions that require only common-sense completely pass them by.'

'Common-sense or the female flash of intuition! I suspect your argument is a feminist one, because so many of the so-called experts are men!'

Gertrude owned that it might be so, and turned to smile at Lucy who had just walked into the room. 'I think your father is *almost* agreeing that the running of the world would be better left to us women!'

'Not a doubt of it, Mama, though I'm prepared to make one or two exceptions,' Lucy said thoughtfully. 'We'd let dear Grandpa Hoskins have a say in things . . . as Hodges loves to point out, " 'ee sees further than most through a brick wall, that one"!'

She smiled at her parents, then shrugged herself into the thick coat that she'd brought into the room with her. 'I'm off to Bicton with a consignment of vegetables for Jane. Maud says she feeds her convalescent gentlemen as they've never been fed in their lives before; they are so supine with good food that Maud can't get them to take an interest in anything else . . . like basketwork or the study of comparative religions!'

'If Maud herself can summon up any great interest in basketwork, I'm a Dutchman,' William contributed with a smile. 'Tell her, please, my dear, that I shall be there tomorrow to give the poor men a piano recital. They sat uncomplainingly through Bach and Brahms before I discovered that what they really enjoy are sentimental ballads they can sing to!'

Lucy agreed that she would deliver the message and disappeared, leaving her mother looking thoughtful. 'Does it occur to you to stop and think about what the war has done to our lives? I don't mean the men who have been uprooted from northern towns and sleepy villages and flung down in a foreign country in circumstances their worst nightmares couldn't have envisaged. I'm talking about girls like our daughters – now brave and useful and unimaginably independent. Do you suppose they will ever settle down again to the sort of cribbed, cabined and confined life that only one generation before them took for granted?'

'I don't think they will, and it applies not only to girls like our daughters. Women are our equal now in everything but brute strength, and in many areas once thought of as belonging to men they are *more* dexterous, more teachable. Frank has had plenty of opportunity to test the truth of this and has no doubt of it. Even girls whose only alternative to marriage was to go into domestic service now know that they're capable of other things . . . they're out in the world to stay.'

Gertrude nodded but her thoughts had taken another direction. 'Thank goodness for conscription . . . at least it means that people will know there is good reason why men like Frank remain here. He has never told Jane so, but she's convinced that more than one white feather was thrust at him. Pleased as I am with my sex in general, I have to admit that *that* was a peculiarly feminine kind of cruelty.'

'Have you noticed that Lucy seems to get on better with him than most people do? I know that she's very like my mother . . . finds good in anyone who isn't an out-and-out monster. Frank is anything but *that*, but he doesn't make it easy for people to get to know him or like him.'

Gertrude nodded, aware that it would be a relief to talk about a worry that hovered on the fringe of her overriding anxiety about Ned. 'Jane and Arthur love her so much that they can't help but make plain what they feel – their cup of happiness would overflow if they could have Lucy for a daughter-in-law. Frank's feelings aren't so obvious because he takes care that they shouldn't be, but I have the feeling that he regards Lucy as his. You probably haven't seen him glare at any of the charming young men at Bicton who even speak to Lucy. He doesn't begrudge them anything but *that* one thing . . . the opportunity to enlist her sympathy.'

William stared at his wife's troubled face. 'Would it be such a bad thing? I know he's very different, and a good deal older, but after Harry she doesn't seem to notice other young men. Frank would take good care of her.'

'She doesn't need taking care of any longer; she can take care of herself. I think I'm worried for Frank, not Lucy. If he should ask her to marry him, I'm almost sure she would refuse, and *that* would be another unhappiness when the world is full of sadness already.'

As 1916 advanced there was so much else to concern them that the subject of Frank wasn't mentioned again. After almost two years of defensive fighting the Germans launched a spring offensive against the French position in the south. Verdun, the epicentre of a battle that was fought for months, became a legend in French military history, both for its cruel cost and for the valour of its defence. But relief had to be given, and the British to the north of them had to launch an offensive of their own: the battle of the Somme. On 1 July, after an enormous and, as it turned out, almost entirely ineffectual bombardment, the order was given for a mass infantry advance. On that first day almost 60,000 of the men who walked towards the German machine guns were either killed or wounded. Not many weeks afterwards William and Gertrude learnt that their son had been one of them.

There was initial terror, followed by relief. Ned was alive, and he had been brought back to England. They could visit him and, although he had suffered head wounds, there was no suggestion that his life was in danger.

At the hospital in Coventry they were shown first to the medical officer in charge.

'The pieces of shrapnel in your son's head have been removed,' he said deliberately. 'His *physical* condition is now reasonably good.'

Gertrude stared at him, struggling to speak over the fear beginning to clamp itself about her heart.

'You say that as if something else is wrong. Is there?'

He nodded at her, hating his job and despairing of becoming hardened to it. 'There is a condition loosely called shell shock; it covers the effect of being in the proximity of an exploding shell, which the Army regards as an injury, or the collapse which can be caused when a man's nervous system is asked to endure over a period of time more than it can bear. This is regarded not as an injury, but as a neurasthenic disorder.'

'The distinction is very nice,' William pointed out quietly. 'But in Ned's case, the *injury* can scarcely be in doubt.'

'What does it matter?' Gertrude's voice was hoarse with anxiety, but she tried hard not to shout, even though men were at their usual game of concerning themselves with inessentials. 'It's how Ned *is* that matters.'

'It *can* matter,' the doctor said gently. 'In your son's case the medical CO at the special base hospital in France classified him as suffering from nervous exhaustion rather than from more specific damage. In most cases this is genuine, and can be cured by rest, nourishing food and freedom from strain. In some cases it is less genuine and used, perhaps subconsciously, to release a man from what he finds unbearable – the idea of being sent back to the front.'

'You are accusing such men of cowardice?' William's question still seemed to Gertrude an insane waste of time, but something about the way he put it insisted that he asked not about 'men' in general but about her son.

'I'm not in a position to accuse, even if it were my responsibility, which it is not,' the doctor said. 'I'm here to do what I may for those who are sick.'

'And Ned is sick?' Gertrude asked urgently.

'Yes, but perhaps not hopelessly so. The worst cases are so locked inside themselves that they are physically paralysed, unable even to speak. Ned is not that, Lady Wyndham, but he *is* beyond our reach at the moment – withdrawn into some region of his own where we are unable to follow him. It will be very hard for you, but don't allow yourselves to be destroyed by the fact that he will not recognize you. Don't try to force recognition on him – noise, pressure, even someone else's agony . . . these are the things he's trying to escape from.'

William looked at his wife's sheet-white face, and held her hand tightly. 'My dear, let me see Ned on my own . . . perhaps afterwards you can . . .' He stopped speaking because anger with him had brought her face to life again.

'I'm going to see Ned . . . do you *hear* me, William?' Her voice rose, and broke on a sob, but she fought desperately for self-control and said more quietly, 'However dreadful it may be, I *must* see him.'

It was very dreadful. Apart from a stitched scar on his temple, and the shadow of an earlier wound running down the side of his face, he looked much the same as they remembered – darling Ned, their treasure and joy, and the future of Providence. There was nothing to say outwardly that he still lived in some hell beyond their imagining, except his empty blue eyes that stared at them and didn't know them. He wondered why they sat beside him, wanting to hold his hands. But he didn't mind as long as they spoke quietly and didn't demand of him that he should concern himself with them. The lady's eyes were full of tears, it was true, but she talked as if it didn't matter whether he listened or not. He heard a strange word – Providence – that she said several times and it set up a little chime in some outer, unprotected corner of his mind. The chime was painful, and he shook his head fiercely, repudiating its repetition.

'No,' he shouted, 'n . . . not that. D. . . don't like it.'

It was the only thing he said that first afternoon, and it seemed to drive the two of them away from him. They got up to go and he felt glad for a moment that he was to be left alone again. But when they walked away, *that* was suddenly unbearable. The lady must have known, because she turned and ran back to kiss him and whisper, 'We'll be back again soon, dear Ned.'

She came often after that, sometimes alone, sometimes with the man whose gentle smile he was beginning to know. Other times a fair-haired girl came too, and she had the same smile, and a kiss that was like the lady's, full of a kindness that he knew was intended for *him*. There were times when something strained against the barrier in his mind. He was thankful that the barrier held, but unhappy at the same time that it should do so.

He had been at the hospital three months before Gertrude's constant battle with authority, carried on at one level after another, finally brought her in front of a doctor whose authority seemed to extend over all such cases as Ned's. The official was remote and godlike, and convinced that he knew best for everyone; the personification of the male expert once again. *She*, on the other hand, was vulnerable and ignorant and only convinced that she knew what was best for Ned.

'Lady Wyndham, I appreciate that you would like your son to be released, but I really cannot advise it. You are not in a position to understand the fragile nature of the human brain . . . its unpredictability once it has been damaged; the violence it is capable of if equilibrium isn't maintained.'

'I realize something, though not very much, of all these things,' Gertrude said quietly. 'But one thing I *know*! Ned is no better now than when he was first brought here. Left in this . . . this vacuum, he will *never* be any better. I beg of you to let me take him home to Providence.'

The doctor pounced. 'The very word, I understand, that upsets him most. My dear lady, don't you understand? Cases of this kind require peace, stability, the very opposite of anything that disturbs them.'

'Ned is *not* a case . . . he's my *son*!' The word was a cry of pain wrenched out of her and it left a silence in the room until she spoke again. 'Please let me try,' she whispered finally. 'If I have to admit defeat, I promise you that we will bring him back . . . but you have to let me try.'

He had begun the interview determined to refuse, as much for the good of a household that couldn't be expected to cope with the effects of a disordered mind as for Ned Wyndham himself; but Gertrude defeated him. In the thinness and pallor of her face he saw only her eyes, a beautiful clear grey, imploring him to agree with her, imploring him to give her back hope.

'Very well . . . you may try.'

She and William collected Ned the following day. He made no objection to going with them because they had become familiar, and he took their visits now as a matter of course. If they offered him an outing, perhaps it was because they sensed his increasing unhappiness at always being confined within the same four walls. He walked out of the hospital without a backward glance; would have done so even if he'd understood that he was leaving it for good.

There was a carriage waiting outside . . . and horses. These seemed familiar too, and the instinct that still operated beneath the deliberate sealing-off of his conscious mind told him to go to their heads and stroke their noses. An elderly man standing near the horses suddenly hid his face in the neck of one of them. The action troubled Ned for a moment, but he forgot it in the pleasure of climbing into the carriage.

William had chosen the route with care, avoiding the noise and ugliness of towns. Ned looked out of the window and saw only a countryside wrapped in the glowing colours of autumn; there was nothing to disturb him – no barbed wire, no explosion-shrivelled trees, no bodies twisted in the obscene attitudes of violent death. He wished the lovely ride could go on for ever; he didn't want to go back; he liked the little clackety-clacketing noise the horses' hooves were making.

Trees closed in on them and they were driving through a tunnel of green; afternoon sunlight filtered through the leaves, turning the air golden. The carriage slowed, then stopped. 'We're here, Ned,' murmured the lady by his side. 'It's Providence.' The word sounded again in his brain, destroying contentment, setting up echoes that thudded against the barrier that kept him safe. The violence in his head was suddenly terrible, not to be borne. He wrestled with the handle of the door and fell out on to the drive.

Then he began to run – and he thought he ran away from something. But what he ran from lay in front of him – a vision . . . no, a *real* thing, a house that opened its arms to welcome him. He ran until he came to the shining ribbon of water; it should have frightened him because it gleamed like steel but the tumult in his brain had ceased, and the barrier was down. He *knew* . . . Oh God, he knew he was where he belonged.

The lady's voice spoke beside him. 'It's Providence, Ned,' she murmured again.

'I know,' he said clearly.

When he turned to look at her, her face was wet with tears, but she was smiling as well. She was beautiful, he realized.

'I know *you*, too; you're my mother.'

Then she held out her arms, just as the house did.

CHAPTER TWENTY-SEVEN

The *worst* was over. Gertrude repeated the words like a litany whenever she got disheartened. There were still times when Ned fell into a trance-like silence, lost in some private nightmare that had overtaken him, or buried his face in trembling hands because an unexpected noise had sent him headlong into panic; but the in-between times were growing longer. She had anticipated that it would be difficult to coax him out of doors, but he went without any sign of wariness into the gardens and the stable-yard. They held no threat because his friends were there – old men like Grandpa Hoskins and Hodges and John Biddle, ignorant of how to treat mental wounds but guided simply by love in their dealings with him.

Ned knew them now as part of the life he'd lost. Providence and the family were reassembled in his mind, and only Sybil was missing, but he never went to the village, and disappeared if anyone called at the house. Lucy continued to run the market gardens and deliver the Bicton orders. She sometimes took with her there the tears that Gertrude wouldn't permit her to shed at home. It was a relief to talk to Jane; even easier, surprisingly, to share her anxieties with Frank.

'Mama won't even consider the possibility that Ned will get no better than he is now,' she said one day. 'Her own strength is poured out for him, and if sheer love can heal him she will manage it; but I can't help wondering whether it will be enough.'

Frank stared at her tired face, a girl of twenty-one who, but for the war, would have been carried away from him by now into a world he thought of as meaningless – a world of parties and balls and weekend country house visits. She would probably have been married to some eligible young man; but instead of the narrow, pampered existence of a well-to-do young wife, she worked as hard as any man he knew, and contrived to remain in spite of it more beautiful than any other woman he knew. The name of Harry Trentham was never mentioned between them, but he still carried in his mind a picture of her face on the day of Harry's wedding.

'What worries you most?' he asked now. 'Ned himself, the future of Providence, or your chances of escaping to lead a life of your own choosing?'

The question made her smile because it was typical of Frank Thornley – matter-of-factly sensible and concisely analytical. 'Escaping isn't a worry, because I don't want to leave Providence. But the future *is* an anxiety, and I can't discuss it with my parents because they cling to the belief that Ned will recover enough to take charge of Providence again . . . that he'll marry and have children, and the Wyndhams will go marching on for ever! Frank, I'm almost sure he never will. He is perfectly content, helping Biddle or Sid Moffat, and now works very hard again, but some spring of self-reliance has been broken in him. It was going to have been his pride and joy to take care of *us*; now we shall always have to take care of him. *That* is what the war has done to us.'

Tears trickled down her face and she brushed them away impatiently with a scratched, work-worn hand; her fingernails were cut short like a man's because she did a man's work without complaint or self-pity. Her heartbreak was for Ned himself and for her parents, although soon enough the whole burden of keeping Providence going would rest on her. Frank felt a lifetime's reserve and self-concealment melting as a frozen river melts in the warmth of the sun. He must say something that would make her understand she'd been fashioned for gentleness and grace and domesticity, not the hard manual toil of a farm labourer; he must make her understand that his joy in life would be to take care of her.

'Lucy . . . let *me* look after you and Providence. I'm fifteen years older than you, and nothing like the husband you might have dreamed of, but I'd ask nothing better than to remove every problem that destroys your peace of mind.' He had taken off his spectacles, as he always did when heart, not head, was ruling him. She could see the expression in his eyes and it said much more than his tongue was capable of. Demonstrativeness, easy gestures of affection, words of love . . . she knew these were not only outside his experience but things he instinctively distrusted. A woman would look for them in vain; but if he undertook to cherish her, *that* he would do until strength failed him. He was a very admirable man.

She was silent for so long that words were uncharacteristically torn out of him again. 'You can't see me as a husband. I'm an uncouth factory owner, short on social airs and graces and gentility. Being hard as flint, and about as sentient as a lump of sandstone, I can't offer you burning speeches and embraces. In other words, I'm the last man on earth to make you forget Harry Trentham. Is that it, Lucy?'

'No, it's *not*!' She flung the denial at him, angry because he'd dared to mention Harry, and because there was a little truth in what he'd said. Despite the staunchness and reliability she'd come to depend on in him, there had been a lingering trace of condescension in her mind, as if a Wyndham and a Thornley could only meet on Wyndham terms. She was ashamed to recognize the truth of it in herself now, and aware of something in *him* that she hadn't noticed before – in the running of his factories he was supremely confident; in the life of the heart, he had no confidence at all.

'I don't see *anyone* as a husband,' she said eventually, 'and that has little or nothing to do with Harry; he was a charming adolescent dream I finally outgrew. Now I'm quite certain of what I have to do . . . it's to stay here and help Mama take care of Ned and Providence.'

'I offered to help you,' he reminded her quietly.

'I know, and I'm grateful, but it seems to me they're Wyndham responsibilities. I had no right to make you feel sorry for me.' Something about the expression on his face moved her to say more than she had meant to. 'It's nonsense to pretend you're a lump of sandstone; you truly love Jane, and you feel sorry for me.' She might have said more – that he was as sentient as any other man, as capable of passion and as vulnerable to jealousy – but it was hard to say what he hadn't managed to say himself: that though he didn't know how to talk of love, he could feel it for *her* as well as Jane.

A month after Ned's return to Providence he was recalled to the hospital for an examination. Gertrude went with him, vainly trying to convince him for the length of the journey that she wouldn't go away and leave him there. By the time he was summoned to follow an orderly his hands were trembling again and he walked with the staccato jerkiness of a marionette. She sat frozen with terror, oblivious of the people who walked past her in the corridor until the doctor who had treated Ned stopped in front of her and took pity on the tension that held her rigid in her chair.

'They will be a little while with your son, Lady Wyndham. There's time enough for me to offer you a cup of coffee in my room.'

She was grateful for his kindness, and more grateful still for the chance to make *someone* understand about Ned. 'He's better . . . much, much better. Providence heals people, you see, and it's where Ned belongs . . .' she was talking too much, but couldn't stop herself. 'It's only the sight of a military uniform that has upset him again . . . will the Board understand that and not say he must come back here?'

The doctor stirred his coffee, not because it contained any sugar, but merely to give himself time to think what to say.

'The members of the Board are more concerned to decide whether someone like Ned is capable of fighting again,' he said gently.

'Fighting? . . . Ned? Do they *want* to drive him insane?' The words were torn out of her, and she half-rose from her chair as if she would go in search of him and protect him with her own body if she had to.

'They want to be sure, that's all; it's their job. You see, there *are* cases of malingering and cowardice, where the sort of symptoms Ned can't conceal are deliberately counterfeited. From the safety of this hospital, I can't even blame battle-sickened men who try to do it, but the war has to be fought and finished.'

'Ned is incapable of killing anything, ever again,' Gertrude said more calmly. 'What good would he be to them, even if they don't care what they do to *him*?'

'I have given them my opinion of his condition. They also have the report of his commanding officer, which makes any charge of cowardice ridiculous . . . it speaks of him in terms that would make you feel very proud. It also mentions an incident we didn't know about when Ned first arrived here. Before the last big battle began a comrade's nerve broke; he was court-martialled and summarily shot, and he had been Ned's close friend. It was one horror too many.'

'It was inhuman,' Gertrude whispered.

The doctor gave a little shrug. 'By other than military standards, yes.' He glanced at his watch, then stood up. 'You will be more comfortable sitting here while I see if the examination is over.'

She waited alone for another fifteen minutes, trying to concentrate her mind on what the doctor had said. He was wrong . . . the shooting of Ned's friend had been inhuman by *any* standards. 'The world has become a mucky, feverish sort of place,' her son had said; feverishly ugly it seemed to have remained, however much blood had been shed for its redemption. Cruelty bred nothing but more cruelty, and even civilized men like the doctor found themselves required to excuse it. She was approaching near-despair when the door opened and a white-faced Ned stood there.

'M . . . Mama . . . I thought you'd g . . . gone,' he

stammered, and then buried his face in his hands. Behind him she saw the doctor.

'He's not going back,' she said with complete finality. 'I won't let them take him, *whatever* they say.'

The doctor shook his head. 'What they have said is that your son is to be invalided out of the Army.'

The rigidity went out of her body and for a moment he thought she was about to faint, but she lifted her head and smiled, and he was startled to find himself aware that she was beautiful.

'If we owe that to *you*, it's more than I know how to thank you for,' she murmured.

'The decision was not mine, but it is the correct one,' he said gravely.

Five minutes later she and Ned walked out of the hospital, hand in hand. She would have liked to sing for joy, but the morning had left him distressed and unsure; it was necessary to keep up a gentle monologue that required no effort from him, until his hands stopped shaking and he could concentrate enough to hear what she was saying to him.

By the time Christmas brought Sybil home on leave Ned had learned to trust in the knowledge that he would never have to go away from Providence again. He was happy to have the family complete, and only disturbed by the fact that Sybil wouldn't promise not to go back to France.

'It's a bad place . . . *bad*!' he shouted, suddenly infuriated because he couldn't make her understand. She buried her face in his coat rather than have to look at him, wondering how her parents and Lucy had managed not to let their hearts be broken.

She murmured something to reassure him, and didn't say that she felt guilty to be at home at all. Once the initial joy of being there had worn off, she was left feeling exhausted but restless. Only to Maud Roberts could she explain that her life at the hospital was like a drug, both terrible and necessary; it couldn't be talked about because no-one at

Haywood's End would be able to understand, but without talking about it she couldn't release the tensions locked up inside her. She quarrelled unreasonably with Lucy, and had to apologize.

'My fault, Lu . . . I'm sorry to be so unbearable. I've dreamed for months of getting home, but now that I'm here I can only think of getting back to France again. *Folie de grandeur*, of course . . . they can manage perfectly well without one humble VAD!'

Lucy smiled at her. 'Not entirely *your* fault; we're all more quick-tempered than we used to be.'

'It's scarcely surprising. What about the future?'

'You know what Papa used to say . . . Providence had to be kept going for the sake of rural England, just as a keystone was needed to hold an arch together. Now, although he doesn't say so, I think he has lost heart – houses like this one will become a luxury England can't afford, and the communities they used to serve won't exist any more. There are strangers already in Haywood's End, although he still refuses to sell them any of the Wyndham cottages. Ned would have gone on refusing, probably; now, he never goes to the village, and the young man who was going to work a miracle for Providence has become a contented ghost. There won't be another Squire Wyndham, holding Haywood's End together, and perhaps it won't even matter. The village girls who've gone into factories won't come back to domestic service, and if there are any young men left by the time this terrible war is over, they won't want to become farm labourers again.'

'So . . . what about Providence?' Sybil asked again.

'We keep it going, somehow, for darling Ned. He's happy here, untroubled; he wouldn't be anywhere else.'

'Does he ever mention Anita?'

'No – she's become part of a past he remembers, that's all. It has nothing to do with *now*, and since all he asks is that *now* should go on for ever, a future that might have been lived differently doesn't exist for him.'

'Does she know?' Sybil thought her questions must sound

abrupt to the point of indifference, but she couldn't frame them in any other way.

Lucy nodded. 'I wrote to her, after a battle with Mama, who convinces herself day by day that she can see small improvements in Ned. Anita's reply was almost the most heartbreaking thing of all – another life that has to be put together again, thanks to this war.'

Sybil forced herself to ask the most difficult question of all. 'What about you? Are you content to toil here for the rest of your life? I won't ask if you've forgotten Harry, because I don't think you ever will.'

'No, I don't even want to forget him; but I shan't mind toiling here. I wish everything weren't such a worry, but Providence is worth it. Mama, who is only a Wyndham by marriage, feels that as strongly as I do, and it isn't just because of Ned; she is convinced that some healing grace attaches to this place. Perhaps it always *has* been women down the ages who've fought to keep it going.' She hesitated, then added something she hadn't meant to confess to in case Sybil found it laughable. 'Frank Thornley offered to . . . to help. He's become rather important now, as well as having made a fortune out of munitions. I think he feels guilty about that, though there's no reason why he should. I rely on him quite a lot, but not as much as he would like. It's a great pity I can't see him as anything but a true friend; he would solve all our problems if I'd let him.'

Sybil thought of Harry Trentham's carefree charm and ability to be at ease wherever he happened to find himself. If a man existed who was less like Frank Thornley, she couldn't call him to mind. 'If I'm to understand that dear Jane's son brought himself to the point of asking to marry you, I don't wonder you smiled sweetly and declined!'

Lucy nodded and switched the subject of conversation. 'What about you? Do you still remember the man who made you unhappy in Lucerne!'

'He made me unhappier still in Paris. I flung myself at his head when I went there with Papa. He was with another woman, but what made matters worse was my feeling that

351

he was unhappy, even so. I only discovered afterwards why he both loved me and *didn't* love me – I reminded him of Mama!'

Lucy was silent for a moment, thinking how strange it was that children took their parents entirely for granted; their lives were reckoned to be fixed in some predestined pattern, exempt from the emotional storms that played hovoc with their children. 'So *that's* why you stayed in London, to avoid Mama?'

'Yes; it's a difference between us – you accept misfortune more gracefully than I do!'

Sybil said goodbye and embarked again for France and, as always without her, the house felt a little less alive. William drove himself out into the cold winter mornings to work beside Sid Moffat as usual, but despair was beginning to eat its way into his heart. They had a duty to grow food while the war lasted but he could see no future for Providence beyond that. It was in this frame of mind that he received a letter which sent him to the solitude of his studio. He normally avoided the room now in case the longing to take hold of a paintbrush again should make him forget that for as long as the war lasted he was a farmer; but before he could face Gertrude with the contents of the letter in his jacket pocket, he must find some measure of self-control again.

The unused room felt cold and stuffy, but there was comfort in the remembered smell of paint and turpentine that lingered there, and on the easel stood an unfinished portrait of Lucy, which he had abandoned long ago because it didn't satisfy him. He couldn't do it himself, but she deserved that someone who could should paint her . . . in the summertime, when she was wearing a blue dress and a straw hat decorated with cornflowers. He allowed himself to linger on the picture in his mind even while he recognized that he was deliberately postponing the moment when he had to talk to Gertrude.

He found her in the estate office, with her father and Lucy. George Hoskins, seventy-seven now, refused to retire. He still wrote up all the estate account books in a hand as clear and elegant as ever, because he insisted, rightly in William's opinion, that women could see nothing beautiful in a page of properly inscribed figures. They smiled as he went into the room, but despair made him shuffle towards them like an old man, and Gertrude put down the papers she was holding to reach out for him.

'Something's wrong, William . . . my dear, what is it?'

'I received a letter this morning . . .' He'd intended to translate it for them into something less curt and terrifying, but his voice failed him and he simply put the letter on the desk in front of them. The message from the bank was brief, and brutally clear. In view of the continuance of a war that was draining away the country's wealth and leaving more and more landowners impoverished, it had been decided as a matter of policy to call in the loans made to such estates as Sir William's. The bank would be delighted if he could redeem the mortgage within the next three months; if not, regretfully the necessary steps would be taken to foreclose and sell Providence.

There was no sound in the room. No-one protested or wept; except for an immediately stifled murmur from Gertrude, they might have been turned to stone. William heard only the ticking of the clock, an ugly Victorian clock which he'd always hated, but his father-in-law cherished simply for the reason that no-one else seemed inclined to. Then Gertrude broke out of her frozen stillness and walked over to the window. She could see the delicate dark frieze that was Hay Wood against the skyline, and below it the sweep of fields that winter wheat was already painting a brilliant green; nothing that she could see had changed in the past few minutes, but a few lines written on a sheet of paper had destroyed the ground beneath their feet, as effectively as an earthquake would have done.

'Three months . . .' she murmured finally. 'Is there the slightest hope of finding the money in that time?'

William walked across the room and put his arms around her. 'My dearest . . . we must face the truth. There is little hope of finding it within the next three *years*.'

She spun round to face her father, and discovered she'd been wrong. Something else had changed because he had suddenly become an old man, who hid his hands beneath the desk because he was ashamed to see them trembling.

'We were looking at the accounts a moment ago, Papa,' Lucy said for her grandfather. 'There is some money in hand . . . there would be more if we didn't do the things we'd planned. Two cottage roofs must be repaired, but the resurfacing of the back road to the village can wait, and so can the new heating system we were going to install here.'

'Dear child, even if we forgot the cottage roofs as well, it's nothing to what we need to buy back Providence.'

'Then let's *sell* the cottages . . . all of them,' Gertrude insisted. 'We'll sell the land too; as long as we can keep the house itself . . .'

'My dearest, how can we do either? The tenants can't dig money out of the ground to buy their cottages any more than we can; we can't dispose of their homes and their livelihood over their heads, and even if we could, no-one is going to buy an estate without the house that goes with it.'

'Then we must ask James. William, I beg of you to let us ask James, this time.'

It was Lucy who answered her. 'Mama, we *can't*. Think of Anita . . . how could we possibly say to Uncle James that we need his money for Providence and Ned, when we no longer seem to need Anita?'

Gertrude had observed, with pity, mice caught in a trap and unable to find the smallest crack through which they could escape to freedom. She was just such a creature now, scrabbling to and fro, while hope died, minute by minute.

Then her father spoke again. 'I've something saved . . . it isn't anywhere near enough in itself, but it would help, and I meant it for you in any case.'

Gertrude's eyes filled with tears, but she stumbled across the room to kiss him. Hope wasn't entirely dead for as long as they refused to admit that *nothing* could be done. 'There's something else to remember . . . there are men whom the war has made rich, and we have unsold pictures in the Great Parlour to sell to them. Then there's the jewellery your mother left me, William . . . should you mind very much if we disposed of that, as well?'

'Dispose of anything you like,' he said gently. Nothing they could do would save Providence, but he couldn't bear to say so until she had had time to accustom herself to the idea.

'We must ask the bank for more time. Surely *that* is the first thing.'

'We'll do that, never fret,' said George Hoskins. He had sat quietly while his heart recovered from the shock of William's letter. Now he knew what else must be done, but he saw no need to talk about it. Busy with his own thoughts, he wasn't aware of Lucy grappling with the frightening idea that was in *her* mind, but like her grandfather's, it necessitated a visit to Bicton.

On the way there she wasn't even sure that she could find the courage to go through with it, but the memory of her mother's face while she listened to Ned explaining about the flowers he intended to grow when spring came drove her along the road to find Frank Thornley.

If he felt surprised to receive an invitation to walk out with her on a grey Sunday afternoon in February, he didn't say so. He thought he knew what she was steeling herself to say, and apart from being very curious to know how she would set about it, felt only admiration for her. He was right to love Lucy Wyndham; the only pity of it was that, doing so, it was impossible to think of loving anybody else, and for that he might have to suffer.

She talked more or less composedly as they walked across the wind-blown park at Bicton, but now that she was confronted by the next stage of her plan, it seemed down-right impossible to go on with it. Sybil would have known how to entice and challenge a man into losing his self-control, without a single overtly wanton gesture: a small advance, a slight retreat, a teasing smile, and some delicately conveyed signal that she was ready to melt into a man's arms, and the trick would have been done. Lucy wished passionately for such expertise, or for a man whose vanity needed less encouragement than Frank Thornley's seemed to do. It was sheer desperation in the end that made her unusually clumsy in surmounting a stile; she fell over it, landed in his arms, and was very grateful to feel them tighten about her instead of setting her on her feet. The moment she required had come. She closed her eyes, waiting for whatever might happen next.

He stared down at the expression of stoical resignation on her face and might have felt inclined to laugh if the moment hadn't been not only absurd but crucial for them both. He knew what her purpose was: simply to discover whether she could bear to be possessed by a man who wasn't Harry Trentham. The knowledge should have infuriated or sickened him, but all he felt was a vast pity for her, as well as a mixture of aching regret and longing on his own account. Her mouth, close to his own, looked so made for being kissed that it was impossible not to touch it with his own, and feel its softness. Her face was cool against his hands, and he thought that her whole body would be just as cool and silken and gently fragrant. Longing was uppermost now, so hot and urgent that it even drowned the fear that even if she didn't find him repellent, she would at least find him ridiculous. When he finally lifted his head from kissing her, she was flushed and trembling, but surely not repelled, because she tried to smile at him.

Before he could recover his breath enough to speak, she forestalled him.

'Frank . . . listen to me, please. I don't think I set about it very well, but I was *trying* to . . . to arouse you, to see whether we . . . I . . . could manage married life! Then if you still thought of marrying me, I was going to . . . to wait until you asked me again before mentioning our terrible problem – you see, the bank have called in the mortgage on Providence.'

'Why *didn't* you wait before telling me?'

'Because, even for dear Ned, it suddenly seemed an unbearably shabby thing to do. I'm sorry . . . all I've done is upset you and humiliate myself.'

He didn't say that George Hoskins had already told his father about the bank foreclosure. Instead, he stared at a future she had refused to paint in the dishonest colours of love. In return for the gift of herself, *his* gift would be to keep Providence safe for Ned. She didn't pretend to love him, and apparently it didn't occur to her that the salvaging of male vanity might have been worth a little pretence. For most men it would have been, but his own view was that he had nothing to be vain about except material success. *That* didn't make a man lovable, only necessary or useful. It was more important by far for them to be honest with each other if their unusual arrangement was to work, and he would make it work because he didn't deal in failure.

'I'm glad Providence needs help if it persuades you to marry me,' he said finally, 'because *that* is what I want more than anything in life. Your father will remain the Squire, and no-one else need ever know who owns Providence because things will go on just the same.'

'I have to stay there too, because I don't think they could manage without me. Could you put up with becoming part of Providence?'

Frank smiled at her. 'I made up my mind to years ago!'

She thought he was managing this horribly difficult conversation better than she was but, at the risk of being unbearably blunt, there was something left to say. 'Frank, I'm afraid the Wyndhams would be getting the best of the bargain . . . could you put up with *that*?'

His hands held her so that she had to look at him. 'You still don't understand. I can't make you pretty speeches or charm you into loving me, but I *can* take care of everything you *do* love. You shall be my liege lady, and I shall go happily into battle for you, riding full tilt at impertinent bureaucrats and foolish bankers and anyone else who dares to trouble you.'

'I shall never be made a prettier speech than that,' said Lucy gravely.

They walked back to Bicton and Jane kissed them even before they said anything. Arthur kissed Lucy too, stared at his son, and knew he must never give in to the temptation to say, even in fun, that he'd known all along that Providence would finally belong to the Thornleys.

Lucy went home alone, in a strange state of mind that swung continually between relief and the dread of having committed herself to something from which her life would never recover. All she could be certain of was that she was carrying home a gift beyond anything else she could have offered her parents.

Even this turned out not to be the certainty she'd been confident of, because Gertrude, whom she told first, looked more likely to weep than rejoice at the news.

'I thought you'd be pleased, Mama,' Lucy said, hurt but puzzled as well. 'Why aren't you?' Her mother's face looked so infinitely sad that she asked another question. 'Is it because Papa won't like the idea of Frank buying Providence from the bank?'

'My dearest, I can only suppose he would be thankful, but not at *this* cost.'

'I thought what mattered most of all now was Ned.'

'He matters greatly to me and your father, but if I've given the impression that he is *all* that matters, I've been a cruel mother to you. I think I *was* obsessed with the idea that Ned would save Providence; now we need it saved *for* Ned, but if the bank will only agree to give us more time, we must find a way of staying here that doesn't require your marriage to a man you don't love – to a man I'm almost certain you don't love.'

Though not obviously so, it was a question Lucy felt obliged to answer. She took time to choose her words with care. 'I'm not in love with Frank, in the way I fell in love with Harry; I shan't feel like that about anyone else again – so it doesn't matter, not *loving* Frank; I like him and trust him, and that will do, I'm sure.'

'Darling child, you're twenty-two. There's time to find *more* than that still, if you don't throw away the chance by marrying Frank.'

'Perhaps, but there isn't time to save Providence for you and Ned in any other way, and that's what I *most* want to do.'

She kissed Gertrude's thin cheek and gently stroked the wing of white that dappled her dark hair like a magpie's plumage, as if she were the mother and Gertrude her child. 'It will be all right, you'll see.' After a moment or two she spoke again. 'Tell me something, Mama. Were *you* in love when you got married? Was Papa the only man in the world you could have considered sharing your life with, or did love come gradually once you'd accepted that you couldn't have what you thought you really wanted?'

Gertrude was silent for a long time before she replied. 'Love came . . . very gradually. It didn't matter in my case because the man I married was full of humility and sweetness. If you cannot claim as much for Frank, I still must say, my dearest, that you shouldn't marry him.'

Lucy felt again the little stab of fear that had troubled her on the way home from Bicton, but she smiled as confidently as it would allow. 'We shall manage very well because we trust each other, and you and Papa and Ned will stay here. I think it's a beautiful arrangement.'

Gertrude kissed her and said no more.

CHAPTER TWENTY-EIGHT

William accepted the news of Lucy's engagement more calmly than Gertrude had expected, but she had expressly said nothing about the future of Providence.

'I can't say I seriously considered Frank Thornley as a son-in-law, but we did discuss the possibility once before and you were more against it than I was,' he reminded her.

'I'm still against it – not because Frank isn't a good and honourable man, but simply because Lucy is only doing it for us and Ned. She doesn't *love* him, William.'

She found it hard to read the expression on her husband's face. Was he remembering – had he ever realized – that *she* hadn't loved him when she married him? They had coupled without love but good had come of it; it was the only comfort she could cling to for her daughter.

'Are you thinking about Frank as the new owner of Providence?' she asked gently. 'That is Lucy's bargain, you see: herself in exchange for him taking up the mortgage.'

'My dear, I realize that.' William gave a tired little shrug. 'Shall we accept the fact that it doesn't matter now? We have to relinquish the dream of Ned and *his* children keeping the Wyndhams going, and James's pro-Irish son has no interest now in Providence. Why not let Arthur have the pleasure at last of knowing that a Thornley owns it?'

Once upon a time she would have wept over that sad, ironic acceptance, but there had been too much tragedy stalking the world, blunting the edge of feeling.

'Frank will cherish the house, and Ned will be safe. It's not what we dreamed of, my dearest, but isn't it a great deal to be thankful for, provided Lucy is content?'

She asked the question so desperately that William folded

his arms about her, ashamed that the reassurance she needed had had to be dragged out of him.

'Of course it's a great deal, beloved. My feudal instincts die a little hard, that's all; which just goes to show that Arthur was right about them all along!'

He did his best to smile, and when he kissed her she was comforted as he'd intended her to be.

Gertrude tried after that not to watch Lucy too anxiously, and gradually came to the conclusion that her daughter was not unhappy. She was clearly adored by Jane, and even if Arthur Thornley had once coveted Providence, it was obvious that he now reckoned life could offer him no more than Lucy as a wife for Frank; the house had become a secondary achievement.

Gertrude was beginning to feel almost at peace with the idea of the engagement. Then Louise Trentham appeared unexpectedly at Haywood's End one morning, in the motor-car she now drove herself.

Like Charlotte, she worked tirelessly in London for the Red Cross, at the harrowing business of rehabilitating wounded and mutilated soldiers. She always looked drawn with anxiety on Harry's account, but on this particular morning, the tragic sadness in her face as she arrived at Providence convinced Gertrude that the worst had happened. Without daring to tempt Fate by ever saying so, they had come to believe that Harry bore a charmed life. The expression on his mother's face denied that this was so, but her first words frightened Gertrude into different terror.

'Have you heard from Sybil lately?'

'Not for a week or more . . . her letters usually arrive in batches. Have *you* heard something? Tell me, Louise; tell me quickly, please.'

'My dear, *you'd* have been informed about Sybil, not me. I promise you she is all right. She was on the train taking wounded men to Calais when the Germans bombed the hospital, but it is our little Emily who is dead.' For the second time in her life Louise's tears spilled over and streamed uncontrollably down her face, and Gertrude's arms enfolded her. Emily of the bright hair and loving heart buried under a choking pile of rubble . . . what normal mind could accept such horror? Gertrude's thoughts stumbled from one to another of the people who had adored her – the Maynards, Louise and Alec, Sybil, and above all, Harry, grown used by now to the likelihood of violent death for everyone he knew in France except his wife. *This* was the abomination of a war they were engulfed in, seemingly for ever.

It was long after Louise had driven away again that Gertrude remembered one other person who still had to be told about Emily. Lucy took the news so quietly that only the extreme pallor of her face convinced Gertrude that she had heard it at all. She shook her head as if to ward off some intolerable pain, then went away to work beside Sid Moffat until it grew too dark to see out of doors.

Louise and Alec travelled with the Maynards to France, and they returned with Sybil and Harry, both given compassionate leave. Lucy went with the rest of the family to attend a simple memorial service for Emily in the chapel at Barham, but otherwise went on doggedly with the work that needed doing. The spring sowing of the vegetable fields had to be done, with Ned and Clarry Briggs, and she was thankful for any excuse that kept her from watching Harry's face whenever he came to Providence. Sybil scarcely left his side, and Lucy accepted that they were linked by experiences she could never share. The knowledge sent her more often than usual to Bicton, for the comfort of knowing that she *was* needed there, and for the sake of convincing Frank that she didn't regret what she was doing. Within Providence itself she became a silent wraith, and it was Gertrude's consuming fear that she saw her family and her home now only as something for which she had paid a price that seemed intolerable.

Arranging wedding flowers in the church one afternoon with Maud Roberts, anxiety finally overflowed.

'We shall be doing this for Lucy soon,' said Maud, and

was taken by surprise when her fellow-worker suddenly burst into tears.

'Sorry . . . ridiculous at my advanced age,' Gertrude finally managed to mutter, wiping her eyes.

'Nothing is ridiculous, at any age, if it is necessary.' Maud's long face, now much lined and made more severe than ever by the anguish she felt about the war, was suddenly softened by kindness. She knew a good deal about Gertrude Wyndham by now, and interest in an unusual child had warmed over the years into deep affection. 'Safety valve – don't apologize. Our dear Lord knows there's enough to make you weep. Are you worried about Lucy?'

'About her *and* Frank, I suppose. You must have guessed that she's marrying him for the sake of her family. It isn't fair to either of them. I'd begun to think it might be all right, but now . . .'

'My dear, Emily's death doesn't change anything, and Lucy sees that more clearly than you do,' Maud said gently. 'Don't try to stop her doing what she believes to be right.'

'In the world we now live in everything seems to be *wrong* – wrong and cruel and wicked.'

'*Seems*, yes . . . but the truth is double-edged; it's wicked for the Germans to have started the indiscriminate sinking of unarmed merchant ships; but only *that* would have brought America into the war. Hubert looked almost cheerful this morning. He was beginning to be afraid we could never win; now, he says the end isn't in doubt.'

Gertrude had considerable faith in Hubert Roberts, but it was hard to share his confidence in the spring of 1917. Despite the best that the farmers of Haywood's End and everywhere else could do, food got steadily scarcer and dearer as more and more merchant ships were lost. The French surprise offensive on the River Aisne failed either to surprise or overwhelm the German line, and the British supporting campaign in the north was finally extinguished in the blood and mud of Passchendaele. By the time Hubert Roberts joined Lucy and Frank Thornley in matrimony, the war had never looked *less* like being over.

The church was full, because it was unthinkable even now for Haywood's End not to feel personally involved in anything that concerned the Wyndhams; but sadness hung in the air like autumn mist, stifling the usual excited hum of conversation. Everyone quietly agreed that young Lucy looked beautiful in her simple white dress and hat, but 'old' Thornley's son wasn't the sort of bridegroom they'd expected for her . . . he was too old and stiff, and too unfamiliar with the ways of Haywood's End. They told themselves the marriage wouldn't have happened but for the war; but then none of the dreadfulness all round them would have happened but for *that*. Little Norman Moffat wouldn't be lying dead in Flanders, and Queenie Briggs's young son wouldn't have had his legs blown off. Harry Trentham wouldn't have buried his wife in France, and the pride of the village, young Squire, wouldn't be standing beside his parents like a soul who was lost . . . it was all the fault of a bloody, insane war that gave no hope of ending.

Jane had contrived a sort of celebration at Bicton, and everyone did their best to look cheerful. Arthur Thornley, in Maud's opinion, did more than that. His transparently delighted face came near to performing a miracle on the subdued spirits of his guests.

'I can understand that you won't feel much like agreeing,' Maud remarked to the sad-faced woman by her side, 'but we *need* someone like Arthur, who refuses to believe that hope and happiness have vanished from the world.'

Louise Trentham's mouth twisted in a wry smile. 'If that was a veiled rebuke, dear Maud, thank you for reminding me that a wedding guest's first duty is to look cheerful! If Gertrude can manage it, God knows I ought to be able to. And Hubert even conducted the service as if he believed he was consecrating a true marriage.'

Maud put her hand on Louise's arm in a rare gesture of affection. 'My dear, I've no right to remind you of anything or to reproach you for feeling bitter – no children of mine are being sacrificed on the obscene altars of war. But I share my brother's faith: we cannot prevent the evil that stalks the world like the noonday devil; we can only refuse to let it destroy us by transmuting it into good wherever we may. *That* is what Lucy has been doing today, and I think it makes hers a true marriage after all.'

Louise said nothing for a moment or two, then a different smile warmed her face. 'Hubert is right, of course, and so is Lucy, I shouldn't have needed to be told. To make up for it, I shall now go and be charmingly affable to my host!'

Maud was still watching her when Lucy's grave voice spoke by her side. 'Is it all a little better than you feared?'

Miss Roberts leaned forward to kiss her cheek. 'My dear, I *had* no fears.'

It was a trumpet-sound of encouragement, and Lucy was painfully aware of needing it. She had gone through the day in a state of numb, deceptive calm. Even now, as terror began to nibble away composure, her mind clung to the rightness of what she'd done; but her body seemed to be shrinking, nerve by nerve, from the prospect ahead of it. Every time she looked at Frank, disbelief fought with dread that he should now be her husband. Very soon she would have to go with him to what was to be their home – the converted upstairs floor of a servants' wing at Providence, empty since the extravagant days of Edward and Hester Wyndham. For the first time in her life Providence assumed the likeness of a prison.

Dread was the only sensation left by the time they were alone together. She took off her white dress in an unfamiliar room, knowing that if she ever looked at it again it would remind her of this moment – of her own trembling body, of Frank undressing next door, and of the sound of an owl, hooting mournfully in the summer darkness outside.

She went to stand at the window, imagining she could see the bird's darker shadow outlined against a moonlit cloud; fortunate bird, free as the element it moved in, while she was trapped, and terrified. Nausea rose in her throat, and the humiliation of being found in the disgusting throes of being sick on her wedding night became for a moment the worst fear of all. Then, without making any sound on the rugs that covered the wooden floor, Frank had come to stand behind her, because his hands touched her shoulders and she shivered uncontrollably.

'I'm sorry . . . I frightened you.' He turned her round gently so that she had to look at him. 'I *do* frighten you, don't I, Lucy?'

'Not *you* . . . m . . . marriage,' she stammered. 'I thought I'd be able to manage it' was what she had been about to say, but it was a thing that couldn't be said. She *had* to manage it because they'd made a bargain and Frank had already kept his side of it handsomely. 'It takes a little b . . . bit of getting used to,' she said instead.

He turned her to face the window again, and when he wrapped his arms about her she could feel that he trembled as well. 'Will it help if I confess that I'm much more frightened than you are? I could feel every woman in the congregation pitying you this afternoon, and every man wondering how I had the gall to think I could make a husband for a girl as gentle and freshly beautiful as morning dew. It would be a reprieve to put off trying because I'm so very afraid of forcing myself on you. Shall I pretend to be considerate and leave you to sleep alone, knowing that it *isn't* consideration but the cowardice you'd expect of a man who's been let off going to war?'

She wanted, dear God, *how* she wanted to accept the reprieve; but flinching wasn't permissible, nor could she let him believe she thought him a coward. Her mouth felt so stiff that it was an effort to speak, but he heard her murmur, 'I think we must prove the people in the congregation wrong.'

He was an awkward, hesitant lover who needed help she couldn't provide, and their marriage was consummated in the end only because desire finally overrode his fear of hurting her. Her own effort was of a different kind – to renounce the childhood device of escaping what was happening to her by separating her mind from her body. Even so, the moment of fulfilment made her cry out, not for the hurt of what Frank was doing to her but for the pain of what she lacked.

Afterwards, when he slept beside her, cowardice at least disproved, she got stiffly out of bed, wrapped herself in a robe, and went to stand by the open casement window. The owl was silent now, and only stillness and the silver light of a full moon lay over the world.

The soft summer darkness was made for love, but she would never know the thing she lacked – 'a little touch of Harry in the night'. Emily's death had separated them as finally as her own marriage to Frank had done, because she couldn't share Harry's sorrow nor he hers. All she could cling to now was the healing grace of Providence, which was still there for herself and for Ned. It would, must, be enough to make the unnumbered years of life to come bearable; all she had to do was allow it to work.

She wasn't aware of how long she stood there staring out of the window, putting off the moment when she must return to a shared bed, until Frank's voice spoke behind her. When she turned round, he was only a yard away but deliberately not touching her.

'You've been here a long time, Lucy . . . is the reality of being married to me more than you can bear?'

She could detect no trace of anger or resentment in his voice, only the directness of a man who always dealt in the truth, and the humility of one who had no personal vanity. 'If you must steel yourself to endure it when I touch you, I will undertake never to do so again.'

'That w . . . won't do . . . we made a bargain.' The words were torn out of her, not what she'd meant to say at all.

'God and the Devil take the bargain.' It was a cry of pain to equal anything she had suffered, shocking her into the knowledge that she had thought only of what *she* could bear.

'We made a marriage,' she corrected herself steadily. 'If you love me enough to be patient with me, it will be a true marriage in the end.'

'I love you enough for anything in this world.'

'Then it will be all right,' she promised him.

He put out his hand and she let herself be led back to the friendly warmth of the bed.

The daily life of Providence seemed almost unaffected by Frank's presence in the house. He spent six days out of every seven in Birmingham or London, and Lucy continued to work on the farm. If her face was marked by a new and private knowledge, Gertrude told herself that it was the inevitable result of marriage. It had put a small but irrecoverable distance between them and their daughter.

One of her anxieties proved groundless: there was no need to have feared humiliation for William. When Frank was with them he simply never referred to the ownership of Providence. His only single disruption of its peaceful routine was the motor-car in which, to Hodges's manifest disgust, he travelled to Birmingham. If he went out of his quiet way to be tactful to William, he treated Ned with so little special care that fear made Gertrude quarrel with him.

'Frank, we never mention the war in front of Ned . . . *please* don't talk about it again.'

'I won't if you insist, but will you let me say that I think you're wrong?'

The calm statement roused her to anger. 'Allow *us* to know what is best for him. He was a shattered wreck when we brought him home; I refuse to have him disturbed again.'

She knew that she sounded too emotional and much too possessive even before Frank's expression told her so. 'Ned is damaged, but not a child . . . you must let him test for himself the limits of what he can bear.'

Anger couldn't blind her to the truth of what he said, nor to the kindness that sought to teach her as gently as possible. Until then she hadn't credited him with gentleness. He smiled as if following her train of thought, and she hadn't expected that of him either. She didn't know whether marriage to Lucy was changing him, or whether the springs of tenderness had always been invisibly there; but gradually it became difficult to remember a time when he hadn't been at Providence. From then on he continued to talk with William about the progress of the war, and Gertrude finally admitted to herself that she could see in Ned no sign that he found the conversation unbearably agitating.

Towards the end of 1917 the Bolshevik Revolution filled William with mixed feelings: hope for Russia itself, and gloom about its effect on the fighting in France. When he said so, Frank disagreed with him.

'I grant you the Russians must think any régime better than the one they've just got rid of, and revolutionaries here like Albert Simpkin chant Lenin's slogan of "peace, bread and land" with intoxicated fervour; but it remains to be seen whether the peasants have merely exchanged one tyranny for another. I tend to think they have.'

'Time will tell,' said William, 'but at least you must grant my other point: Russia's withdrawal from the war comes at a crucial moment. The Germans have no eastern front to fight on at a time when the French Army seems close to being demoralized, and our own to being exhausted.'

'It's a blow,' Frank agreed calmly, 'but it doesn't alter the fact that it is now beyond human possibility for Germany to win. She has finally lost the submarine war which might have made this country capitulate, her own supplies are being effectively blockaded, and her resources of every kind are almost exhausted. The same might be said of *our* resources, but it no longer matters – because of German stupidity in bringing America into the war, all her wealth of men and materials now weights the scales in our favour.'

They accepted what he said for the comfort of it, and because close Government connections seemed to invest him with a knowledge they didn't have, but by the spring of the following year his confidence seemed dangerously misplaced. A last desperate attempt by the Germans to break the deadlock on the Western Front all but succeeded in carrying them into Paris.

Gertrude watched William's face as he forced himself to scan the daily reports of the fighting in *The Times*, and knew that events nearer home had lost the power to lift his heart. Even the birth of Lucy's son, Charles, in the early summer of 1918 seemed a matter almost of indifference to him.

'It's the best of news,' Gertrude said, when she tracked him down in the solitariness of the Great Parlour. 'Lucy is well, the baby is exercising his lungs very lustily, and dear Frank has gone hotfoot over to Bicton. He was torn between longing to make Jane and Arthur a present of the news, and not being quite sure we should take proper care of his wife and son while he was away!'

William smiled with such an effort that she wrapped her arms about him.

'My dearest, you are supposed to be pleased! Your first grandson should have been a Wyndham – is that what saddens you?'

'What does the child's name matter any longer?' he asked with rare harshness. 'Providence doesn't belong to the Wyndhams, and even if it did, Ned will never give us a grandson.' His hands fastened on hers in a grip that hurt, but he tried to speak more calmly. 'What matters is the price we're paying to preserve for children now being born a world that scarcely seems worth saving. The price *we* have paid is bad enough, but there are millions of people like us, counting their own costs, and we shall be suffering the effects of these tragedies for generations.'

She stared at him, riven by pity for the anguish that consumed him, not only for a shattered world but for his own blank future. He was a landowner without an estate, the Squire in name but not in fact . . . a failure, a superfluity. He had asked of life only that it should be civilized, and in that he had been disappointed most of all.

'I know about the cost, my dear one, but we must go on to the end now.'

He turned to look at her, almost resentful of a spring of courage he seemed to have been denied. 'You're full of hope; is it because of the child . . . a new life beginning?'

'Yes, but mostly because at last I'm certain about Lucy.

I've been so terribly afraid that the price she paid for us and Ned was too high. Now, I know that she's happy – contentment shines out of her, and out of Frank as well.' She kissed her husband's thin cheek, then smiled at him. 'Take heart – the war *is* almost over, Arthur says so, and you know he's never wrong!'

William might have been reluctant to agree except that events in France soon proved Arthur Thornley right. In the very success of the Germans' spring offensive were born the seeds of final disaster. They had exhausted themselves in gaining an extended, vulnerable line that couldn't be held against the combined onslaught of the French, their American allies now fighting in the south, and Haig's brilliant counter-attacks in the north. In the end, his use of a new and insuperable weapon in trench warfare – the tank – overwhelmed the German positions. Ludendorff sued for peace and an armistice was signed on 11 November. More than four years after the bloodiest war in history had started Europe was at peace again.

CHAPTER TWENTY-NINE

Before there was any hope of seeing Sybil home from France, Louise and her husband drove down to Providence. It was a rare event for Alec Trentham to tear himself away from the House of Commons or his Government office, and Gertrude was prepared for the news of some unexpected development even before they arrived. Looking from William to his brother-in-law, she wondered whether the war hadn't been just as hard, in a different way, on the men of their generation who hadn't had to go away to fight. Alec seemed an exhausted ghost of the soldierly, upright man who had come home from India to go into politics. Louise watched over him with a tenderness that was the more touching because it became noticeable in a woman who had always been brisk and competent and un-sentimental. Her face now was radiantly gentle with relief from anxiety, both about her husband and her son.

'I realize that your brother's ill health is the reason for the change,' William observed to his brother-in-law, 'but sleepy Somerton after the excitement of London and the important mysteries of great public affairs . . . shall you both like that, I wonder?'

Alec smiled with such genuine amusement that for a moment his face looked young again. 'Thank you for managing to sound impressed about my humble part in great affairs! The truth is, as any honest politician might tell you, that at close range public life loses all its mystery and most of its importance! I shall leave Westminster with nothing but relief, and Louise assures me that she is ready for country life.'

He looked at her with the shy pleasure of a man who had

discovered late in life that his wife was ready for anything that would allow him to be happy. Gertrude saw the smile Louise offered him before she spoke.

'I don't think I should mind if I never saw Westminster again, though that may be too much to hope for. Harry has already decided to leave the Army, and he appears to be making up his mind to follow Alec into Parliament. It seems an unlikely career for our son, except that he is so changed from the Harry who went to war . . .' Her voice trembled but she recovered herself. 'Alec thinks we shall see great changes now: the young men and women who come back to take up their own lives again won't be content with the old ordering of society. They are going to demand a hand in fashioning the brave new world they've fought for.'

'In which *our* kind, our generation, will be akin to the dodo, I suppose,' said William, with a smile that tried but failed to disguise despair.

The transformed Alec in front of them positively grinned. 'Not *quite* extinct, I hope, my dear William. Louise informs me that I am to take on a new lease of life in the country, and I have great faith in her.'

Gertrude watched them both contentedly. Something good, some small sweet flower of happiness had sprung unexpectedly from the torment of the past four years because these two people had finally found each other. It was an item to add to her little store of faith that life and love and hope had not been extinguished by the war.

'What about Sybil?' Louise asked. 'Surely she will be released soon and sent home?'

'She *has* been released – when she last wrote she was on the point of leaving Étaples, but her letter spoke of a visit to Paris. It gave me the impression that, after all that has happened, she wasn't ready to separate herself immediately from France.'

Gertrude expressed it thus, reluctant in front of William, who longed for his daughter to come home, to confess to the fear that Sybil might never settle down again at Providence.

'Give her time,' Louise said gently. 'There has to be a

bridge between the horrors of that hospital and the peace of this quiet valley.'

Had she been able to overhear that conversation, Sybil would have felt no surprise that her aunt understood, because it was true that they were very much alike. All the same, standing outside a closed door on the boulevard Haussmann, she wondered whether Louise Trentham would have done anything so abysmally stupid as to have made *this* futile pilgrimage. The ground-floor windows of the gallery were shuttered, blankly denying the possibility that anyone would have been there to tell her where Henri was.

A faint, irrational hope had brought her there; now hope was dead, and she leaned against the lintel of the door, aware of an exhaustion that went far beyond the physical tiredness of her body. It was almost more effort than she could make to decide what next small step to take – even in which direction she should walk to find a room in an hotel. She was still trying to make up her mind when the door beside her opened so suddenly that she fell against the man who stood there – Henri himself. He saw a girl whose grey eyes looked huge and haunted in the pallor of her face. She wore a felt uniform hat crammed down over short dark hair, and a dark blue raincoat belted about her thin body.

'Bonjour, *p'tite*,' he said slowly.

She could say nothing at all because her voice found no way past the tears that began to clog her throat. She wanted to weep, to faint, to sing, for the relief of finding him there, the relief that the shuttered windows had lied.

'Come in, my poor little one,' he said in English. 'You look more tired than anyone I have ever seen.'

His voice was unchanged, though he himself was not, and she would have recognized it if fifteen years instead of five had separated their last meeting. He led her up a flight of stairs into a small room furnished as a book-lined study.

'I shall be five minutes bringing you some coffee. Take

off that dreadful hat, but try not to fall asleep before I come back.'

She removed the hat because the past years had taught her obedience and it was, in truth, a dreadful piece of millinery. The chair she sank into was deep and soft, but sleep was now the last thing she craved, because her whole body felt achingly alive, like that of someone who had been saved just in time from the extremity of death by frostbite.

When Henri came back she heard the flick of a switch, and in the soft lamplight that filled the room she was able to look at him – seal's cap of hair more silver than black now, and the sallow skin of his face stretched tight over jutting nose and cheekbones. It occurred to her that she had no idea how old he was – it scarcely mattered now when she had lived through a whole lifetime herself. Cognac as well as coffee was put in front of her; she smiled her thanks, and then managed to speak.

'I was about to walk away.'

'I was at the top of the house and only just heard the bell. You chose the first day I have been here for more than a year. Talk, but drink as well.'

It was hard to begin, easier when she drifted without realizing it into the language which had become almost as much hers now as his. She told him about the terrible, unforgettable years at Étaples, about Ned, and Emily, and Lucy married to Frank Thornley so that Providence might be saved. The early winter dusk closed in outside while she exorcized some of the horrors in her mind by talking about them.

'What happens now?' Henri asked finally. 'I suppose that you are on your way back to England?'

'Yes . . . but not to Providence, beautiful though it is. I don't belong there as the others do, and that richly green valley would stifle me.' She stared at the glass in her hand, then muttered, 'What I'd really like is to stay in Paris . . . find a job of work that I could do.' His face when she glanced at it was expressionless, but she had the feeling that he was as acquainted with grief and loneliness as she was herself. 'You've done nothing but listen to me,' she pointed out. 'What has happened to you . . . has the gallery been closed?'

'Yes, being a linguist, I became an official interpreter, a necessary adjunct to Government ministers and Army generals in their lofty councils of war; I even began to feel that I shared in the responsibility for the dreadful decisions that were made.'

So that, she thought, was why his face looked ravaged, as if memory continually murdered sleep.

'What will you do now . . . open the gallery again?'

'Eventually. I'd almost decided not to, because it had begun to seem such a trivial occupation. Then when I came back here and saw canvases I'd almost forgotten, old friends staring at me from the walls insisting on our desperate need for sanity and beauty, I realized that my occupation wasn't trivial at all. Artists like your father must be persuaded to start work again.'

Sybil thought about her next question and found no way of phrasing it that didn't sound shockingly blunt. 'Is the comtesse still with you?'

'No, she is not. Honesty compels me to say that she rightly tired of a morose, middle-aged lover who didn't sufficiently appreciate her because his glance was always backward at another woman.'

'My mother.' The two words dropped flatly into the silence of the room, unrecoverable now that she had spoken them. 'Aunt Louise gave me a clue,' she murmured after a moment or two, 'and it explained why you always seemed to be looking in me for someone whom I greatly resembled.'

Henri frowned at the spoon his fingers had picked up without him being aware of it. 'It was a long time ago; now, it is a regret that aches a little . . .' His hands sketched a gesture that conveyed emptiness, then put memory aside.

She knew that he would say nothing more about her mother, and retreated to a safer subject.

'My father hasn't painted since the war began; I'm not sure that he will ever be able to start again.'

Henri's face broke into a charming smile. 'Then already I am needed, you see!'

'But I am not,' she said abruptly. 'Will you let me stay with you, if I promise not to be a nuisance?'

Again a well of silence in the room was broken by the echoes of her voice that sank depth through depth of stillness. She had no doubt at all that he was searching for some gentle way of refusing her.

What he finally said was, 'Not here . . . I never live in Paris. You may come to the mill, if you like. It's not beautiful, not another Providence – just an old stone house that sits by a river fringed with poplars and willow trees. There's nothing to do there except pretend to fish while you watch the clouds travelling across the sky. I could always teach you about painting, of course, but what would you teach me?'

'I'd teach you not to be morose, and not to glance backward any longer.'

Beneath ruffled dark hair her face was now tinged with colour, her eyes were alive again, and they met his in a glance strangely compounded of compassion, pleading, and hope. Above all hope, he thought, because she was young and youth couldn't live without optimism.

'Let us make no promises to each other, *p'tite*. I am twenty years older than you, distinctly *usé* as we would say here, and made selfish by living alone. Stay for as long as you like, with no offence taken when you go.'

'I'll stay until you tell me to leave, with no more heartbreak than I can manage when you do so.'

She smiled, and he knew that a different current of emotion was beginning to seep into the room – sweet and exciting and full of a promise he hadn't believed existed any more. The past and present were becoming one. She was Gertrude, and Gertrude's daughter, and someone who was neither of these things but a woman he had yet to discover. When he lifted her hand to his mouth to seal their bargain she wanted to beg him to take her in his arms, but she was wiser than she had been; there was time to spare now, and no thundering guns and groaning men to drive them headlong through the days and nights. She had only to be quiet and patient, and wait for the tree-fringed river and the travelling clouds to work the miracle she needed for them both.

Her first letter to Providence written from the mill at Colombie spent several hours in Gertrude's pocket before she mentioned it to William. At last she went to find him in the studio – not attempting to paint, but standing in front of Lucy's unfinished portrait, apparently lost in thought. He turned when he heard her come into the room – a thin, tired, silver-bearded man who'd lost whatever belief he ever had in the richness of his own contribution to other people's lives.

She hated the thought of bringing him saddening news. 'William, I've heard from Sybil. We shan't see her here for . . . for a little while. She met Henri Blanchard in Paris, and he was kind enough to invite her to stay at his country home because she looked so tired and thin.'

'I know . . . I received a letter from *him*. I didn't seem able to tell you so.'

The expression on his face asked for comfort. 'It may not be a very conventional arrangement, my dear, but she deserves whatever happiness she can find. Her letter *was* happy, and kind and loving in a way that made her seem closer to me than she's been for years. We can't compel her to come back and be contented at Providence.'

'I don't feel entitled to compel anyone to do anything. Nor do I feel compelled to start painting again, as Blanchard seems to think I should. After all that has happened to the world, I can't imagine a more useless occupation.'

'You're wrong, William . . . *wrong*!' She flung the word at him, suddenly angered by an attitude that seemed full of a needless defeat. 'The doing of the good, right thing that any of us is able to do is *not* futile. What *you* can do is

378

paint.' She heard herself shouting at him, and had to make an effort not to go on doing so. 'Come over here, please, and let me show you something.'

He moved reluctantly to stand beside her at the window – the huge mullioned window at which she had once stood with James, trying to engrave on her mind every moment of the night she had just spent with him. The memory was still lodged there, but it now seemed to be the experience of some other woman. Outside, the year was dying into winter but the bare trees made a delicate tracery against a translucent November sky. High above them clouds ran out in bars of purple and gold towards the setting sun. Gertrude pointed to where Ned was talking to her father and old Biddle. Every few moments his arms would sweep the air, and even from where she stood she could see joy blazing in his face.

'Look . . . Ned's explaining the miraculous new flower gardens he's going to create now that we can stop ploughing all the land for food.'

Lucy came out of the house as they watched, ready to share in the discussion, and then Frank, home from Birmingham, walked towards them from the stable-yard. He kissed his wife's upturned face, and stood afterwards with his arm round her shoulders, listening to Ned's vision of Providence bowered in blossom.

Gertrude turned to face her husband. 'Tell me if you dare that the world is no longer beautiful; convince me if you can that we have less obligation than our children to increase the sum of its beauty if we are capable of doing so.'

William had to smile at her. 'My dear, I shall dare no such thing . . . you're much too fierce for me!'

'Then you must do what Henri says. He told me once that you had the intensity of vision of a true artist – of someone who could *make* the rest of us see that the world was beautiful. After four years of destruction and unspeakable ugliness, I can think of no occupation less futile than that. *Now* will you let Henri persuade you to start work again?'

William's face was suddenly filled with its old sweetness. 'How can I not let you persuade me? You could convince a one-legged Chinaman that it was his duty to learn to waltz!'

'I suppose I might if I thought it was good for him,' she agreed cheerfully.

William held her within the circle of his arms as they turned to look out of the window again. In the west the sky was still richly coloured with the afterglow of sunset, and its darkness in the east was fastened with the silver brooch of a crescent moon. Suddenly William's voice spoke just behind her.

'I always had the feeling . . . no, the certainty . . . that Henri wanted to take you away from me. I was never quite sure what you felt about him. Do you mind that Sybil is with him?'

She hadn't anticipated the question from her husband, but thanked God in her heart that she had already been forced to face and answer it herself.

'I told you her letter sounded happy,' she said slowly, 'not only for herself but for Henri as well. That was the best gift she could have given me because for a long time I was burdened with the knowledge that I'd unwittingly destroyed *his* peace of mind. Now I no longer have to feel guilty about him. I can just remember with pride that he found me worth loving, and you must find pride in it, too, because in a way I can't explain we have *both* been enriched by it.'

William was aware that his question hadn't entirely been answered, but he couldn't persist. With the intensity of her own vision of life — that it could only be lived with the courage that refused to accept defeat — she had transmuted loss into gain. It was the sort of alchemy that only women were capable of, and it was so indispensable to the future of mankind that they were careful above all to hand that secret power on to their daughters, down through every age that came.

'I shall take heart as well as pride, my dear one,' he said at last. 'Sybil shall solace Henri, Ned make Providence bloom, and Lucy give us exquisite grandchildren who must be painted. *Your* part must be what it has always been . . . to love us so that all these things are possible.'

'Then there is no problem,' she said confidently.

THE END

A sequel to THE WOMEN OF PROVIDENCE is now in preparation and will be published by Bantam Press in hardcover and Corgi books in paperback. The sequel will be called THE BIRD OF HAPPINESS.

BLACK GOLD
by Iris Gower

'Iris Gower is a novelist who is not afraid to look life, with
its pleasure and pain, in the face'

Marie Joseph

Set against the background of the General Strike, BLACK
GOLD completes the magnificent saga of the men and
women of Sweyn's Eye.

Kate Murphy, betrayed so often before in love, finds herself
caught in the deadly crossfire between her bullying brothers
and Luke Proud, owner of a small mine, and a married man.
As their story unfolds, so the conflict of 1926 begins to rage
about them, affecting rifts and passions in the lives of
ordinary men and women.

'The best saga yet'
South Wales Evening Post

0552 133167

ECHOES IN THE SQUARE
by Sally Stewart

Young Janey Rowland lived in Linden Mews, in the flat over the garage. She was the housekeeper's daughter, the chauffeur's daughter, and even though she was a bright and sensitive child, she had been taught to know her place when it came to going round to the big house – the Marchant house – in Linden Square.

But the two families – on the surface separated by a gulf of birth, wealth, and breeding – were deeply involved and reliant on each other. Old secrets, old emotions, seethed beneath the respectable façade they preserved between them. And then the war came.

As the barriers between the Marchants and the Rowlands began to crumble, so Jane – quiet, beautiful, and with a great capacity for love – began to become more and more the hub of the wealthy Marchant family, the one on whom they all depended, the one who had to unravel and solve the emotional disasters left over from the past.

0553 13467 8

A SELECTED LIST OF FINE TITLES AVAILABLE FROM CORGI BOOKS

THE PRICES SHOWN BELOW WERE CORRECT AT THE TIME OF GOING TO PRESS.
HOWEVER TRANSWORLD PUBLISHERS RESERVE THE RIGHT TO SHOW NEW
RETAIL PRICES ON COVERS WHICH MAY DIFFER FROM THOSE PREVIOUSLY
ADVERTISED IN THE TEXT OR ELSEWHERE.

All Corgi/Bantam Books are available at your bookshop or newsagent, or can be
ordered from the following address:
Corgi/Bantam Books,
Cash Sales Department,
P.O. Box 11, Falmouth, Cornwall TR10 9EN

Please send a cheque or postal order (no currency) and allow 80p for postage and
packing for the first book plus 20p for each additional book ordered up to a
maximum charge of £2.00 in UK.

B.F.P.O. customers please allow 80p for the first book and 20p for each additional
book.

Overseas customers, including Eire, please allow £1.50 for postage and packing for
the first book, £1.00 for the second book, and 30p for each subsequent title ordered.

NAME (Block Letters) ....

ADDRESS ....

....